CHANGING
Stiles

ELAINE L. ALLEN

Changing Stiles

Perfect Perceptions Publishing

www.perfectperceptions.wixsite.com/elainelallen

perfectperceptionspublishing@gmail.com

ISBN- 13:978-0-578-40189-8

ISBN- 10: 0-578-40189-4

LCCN: 2018961520

Published by and for Perfect Perceptions Publishing

Cover Design & Interior Formatting and Design—T.E. Black Designs; www.teblackdesigns.com

Edited by: Patrice Harrison for Little Pear Editing Services www.littlepearediting.com

Inside Photo Credit—Nakita TV (Shutterstock)

Manufactured in the United States of America

*This book is dedicated to my sister, **Crystal Allen** who proved this year, that second chances are possible. She was diagnosed with two types of cancer this year and is still breathing. She is healing and strong and ready to live her best life. Her faith is amazing, and I love her to pieces and am humbled by her strength.*

*And to **Love**…*

*May we all **find** it…*

*May we all **have** it…*

Do you believe in love?
and
second chances

cause …

I wish that we could see …
If we could be …

could be something …

prologue

Alicia

I already told you to stop texting me! My fingers, impatient with fury, slide across the small keys of my phone. I can feel the heat rising. My temperature and attitude are about to erupt, but I have to whooosa this ish out. It's not worth it, and I should continue to ignore him, but the constant texting is about to make me catch a case. I'm at my wits' end with this dating crap.

You refuse to answer my calls. How else are we going to resolve this, so we can get over this?

We don't have anything to get over, Jermaine. You a fuckin' liar and I'm too old and too good for you to explain or break it down. We are over.

Lieas, answer the damn phone. It's your birthday, babe. I have something special planned.

Yup, the big three-three. Nothing to show for it if you ask my mother, except being an author, and an entrepreneur with a big-ass condo, luxury car, health coverage, and a nice nest egg. In this financial climate, you have to have something tucked away for retirement. And until the other day, I had reliable dick. It's like I lost another one and that is all Nicole Stiles-Wright will be concerned with.

The thought of it pissed me off to the astronomical level but I refuse— I mean refuse— to let it show.

Do it with your fake ass cousin. I typed back. My petty attempt to let him know that I remember and there ain't one ounce of nothing that's going to allow me to forget it.

Rolling my eyes, I make quick work of blocking his ass and deleting his contact info. Last time, he was slick and started calling me from his second cell phone. Second cell. Yeah, that should've been my clue. But my ole' trusting, tryna-find-a-man-and-get-married-before-I'm-too-old-to-have-babies-ass was feeling kind of low and I backtracked. Nope, not this time. It didn't get me any closer to the man of my dreams, marriage, or the cute behind babies I think I'm destined to have.

I guess I'm just going to put this out there to let it marinate. I'm going to be single for the rest of my life. Don't have time for the foolishness of these modern-day fuckboys. If you're confused, that includes the jobless, ambitionless dumbasses, lames, cheaters, cheap nuccas, roommates with their baby mommas *"but there's nothing going on ass nuccas"*, live at home with their mommas, and the *"got their shit together but not looking for nothing"* type brothas.

I hate them all.

And I'm done.

Don't want to be done but I am until these nuccas act right. Like damn, how hard is it to be honest, respectful, sane, hard-working, good-looking, and can screw. At the same damn time?

Karma ain't sugar-honey-ice-tea. The thought slipped in there so quickly and slyly I don't know where it came from, but it lives solely to remind me that I could've had it all, and I fucked it up because I wasn't adult enough to articulate my feelings.

I loved hard once and maybe I didn't know how to handle it. And before I had sense enough to realize it for what it was, he was gone. He was not putting up with my stupid behavior. Whatever my excuses were, I'll always say I deserved a second chance; at least a moment to explain and he didn't allow time for any.

No second chance. No happy ending. And no Carter Reed.

And I'm still alone.

I did get a book out of it; so, I guess the experience was cathartic. He was at that point in his life where I am now. He's probably happily married by now.

Some nights, I dream of him and those dreams get shattered by the reality of the next morning when I wake alone, without him and still heartbroken.

I know; it's my fault. With everything that was going on, I put three states- worth of distance between us along with all my other fucked up issues. I ran, and he didn't follow.

So, I guess the love I felt wasn't mutual or as unconditional and forgiving as promised. In the ten years since, I can't really say I've loved, been in love, or felt anything as strong it was with him.

Fuck men.

I'm bad at love… but you can't blame me for trying…

"Whose ass are you are about to kick?" my business partner, Aylonah James, inquires when the creases in my forehead deepen and my eyebrows damn near touch one another. She knows all my faces. Had cataloged them so she could predict when I'd unleash my crazy, so she can talk me down.

My temper and flip lip always require me to have someone around to talk me down. And for the past ten years, she has gladly taken on the task. We knew one another in passing through my cousin Briannah, who also happens to be Lon's closest friend. They used to live up the hill on the other side of Susquehanna Ave. We had never really hung out in our teens. She was always studying and stayed busy. I knew her cousin Chrissy a lil' bit better. She used to date Bri's brother Brian and was around when my cousin and his squad flipped everything in the streets they had to in order to make a come-up. The late nineties was popping for them.

It has always amazed me that they were a family of full-blown Native Americans living in the heart of the hood. There was a period in time when everyone used to claim to have Indian in their family, attributing it to their "good" hair and exotic looks, but Lon and them really did. She's half black, though.

In any case, I happened to run into Lon at a flea market in Friendship Heights and discovered that we were both attending Howard for grad school and had somehow missed one another on campus. I was channeling all this emotional baggage regarding Carter and my father and wanted to get it out in book form. Lon had been writing for years, had an agent, and had already been published. So, she helped me grind to get my five-hundred-page manuscript turned into a real-life, in-your-hand, paperback book.

We've been rocking and rolling ever since, using our collaborative efforts to open J.S. Publishing. With the advancement of the internet and other online services, we were able to maximize the initial rainfall of profits from the skyrocketing e-book market. The rocket is still in flight, and we're still reaping the rewards. We're opening a brick and mortar book-store/coffee shop. Something small that reminds me of The Spot when I used to do spoken word. Even with the changing climate and the dimming future of physical books, people still enjoy coffee and muffins, intimate reading settings, poetry slams, and book clubs. So, it may be crazy, considering so many Barnes and Nobles and Books-A-Millions are closing all across the country. I look at the success of places like Busboys and Poets, and I see the potential for ours. That's our plan but on a smaller scale. We're working tirelessly, building our brand. I have an interactive book reading and signing scheduled at the new Barnes and Noble on Temple's campus for Saturday afternoon and some overdue bonding time with my girls and my mom.

I almost miss real estate and rehabbing properties, the day-to-day checking work sites. The eye-candy. I shake my head. It was definitely another time. A time when I was trying to prove to my father that I could contribute to our family's growing business. That I could be the respectable child that my older brother Grayson had failed to be. Gray is reformed, but me? I'm over it.

Now, I'm like, "fudge it." More so toward my father. Real estate was collateral damage in our relationship.

Myself. I shake my head, tap my cell in the palm on my hand and solemnly say, "No damn body."

Lon frowned, not believing one word. "Your face is defi-nitely saying something else," she read me.

Unfazed, I flagged the pestering thoughts surrounding nut-ass Jermaine and my mom's voice questioning me about grand-children and forgiving my father. "I'm getting the hell old," I laugh.

Lon hit her thigh and laughed a little. Her bronzed cheeks

became rosy beneath the almost copper tone as she added, "You are."

I nudge her slim shoulder with mine as she settled onto the bench seat beside me. "Whatever," I murmur. I look around. My mind is consumed with one thing and one thing only. "Where's the damn cake?"

In honor of my birthday, my office surprises me with lunch and a small party. I'm sure I would appreciate the effort and the thought if I wasn't already on the edge of insanity.

Lon chuckles, "Shhh, you need to stop."

I stretch my arms over my head and yawn at the same time. "I'm leaving in a few. I have to get on the road and make it to my parents' before dinner."

Lon nods "You ready for your mom to be tripping about you still being single?"

Nonchalantly, I flag my hand at the idea. If I allow it, my mother would drive me the fuck crazy from a couple hundred miles away, and I've concluded that I can do that all on my own. "I'm used to her badgering. It'll be the unspoken way that all of my friends will be all crazy happy with their families."

Lon wouldn't understand. I can't remember the last time she was single. And just in the last year, her high school and college boyfriend Jason had shown up in D.C. with the intention of making her forget all their time apart. I would be surprised if she doesn't call me soon to say he popped the question. What the hell are the chances of anyone I loved – really loved— just walking up to me, like, 'Hey'?

I can't imagine Carter popping up out of nowhere like, "What's up?"

My heart races in anticipation of another of my friends tying the knot. I sound like a Debby Downer, but I really do love to see people in love. I'm a romance writer. I love all things love.

I just hate when that nagging ass fear that it'll never be me just plays on repeat.

They dim the lights and begin to sing. A chorus of off-key voices singing two different versions of 'Happy Birthday,' fills the room.

Happiness seeps in with the clashing vocals of my everyday eight. I listen, happily amused, despite my need to wallow in self-pity. "Haaap-py Birthday to ya…" "Happy Biiiiirthday to you…" Finally, the cake makes an appearance. It's a replica of my latest book, 30 Last Dates: A Comedic Tale of Dating in Your 30s. Three long-stemmed sparklers help illuminate the darkness of the room and my mood. I clap my hands in wonder, taking in the fact that these people genuinely appreciate and care for me. The warmth of their laughter and obnoxious singing hypes me into standing up. Lon quickly stands up too, leans in, and nudges my shoulder again.

"Go ahead and make a wish," she whispers for my ears only.

The hairs on the back of my neck stand up; the signing stops for a moment but only in my mind, though. My palms get sweaty and my entire life flashes before my eyes in a three-second blink.

Fuck everything I said. I still want love. Am ready for everything that comes with it.

Closing my eyes, I blow at the sparklers. "I promise I'm ready," I think to myself, praying that God is listening. On one last blow, the sparklers finally extinguish, and I wish for, a second chance.

I CHECKED INTO MY HOTEL AND FOUND MYSELF THOROUGHLY impressed with the accommodations. The bookstore had sent over a beautiful bouquet of seasonal flowers and an edible arrangement with chocolate-covered strawberries. Of course, that was a welcoming surprise. I would love to just fall into the plush-looking king-sized bed with its fluffy, inviting pillows. But I still have to go to my mom's before turning in. Gray, Nesha, and the kids are going to be there. Bri had texted that she'd see me there, so I'm certain my mom cooked dinner and is trying to surprise me with a get-together. I guess I should adjust my attitude to the likely possibility of being up all night with my family. I know I had cake already, but there better be another one involved. My mom makes the best cakes from scratch with thick, buttercream frosting and a handwritten love note that she designates especially for the birthday recipient.

I chuckle. I've shed at least one hundred pounds collectively in my lifetime, but I'm still a fatty at heart.

Not sure how I left my toiletry bag, but it was missing when I unpacked. So, I'm browsing the aisles of Target on City Line Ave, picking up a bunch of shit that I do not need. I swear Target is the devil. Come for a tube of toothpaste and leave with everything except what you went there for in the first place. I head to the mini book section, hoping and praying that I at least see one of our titles on the shelves. Definitely praying that 30 Last Dates is featured. I'm always nervous in a way I can't explain when I'm in the store and I'm wondering if they carry me. I get straight crazy when I see my distribution dollars at work.

The familiar rush of pride settles as I see them there nestled in between other African-American authors. I squat down because, of course, they need to be displayed in a prominent space to get some immediate focal attention. I quickly rearrange them to a corner display and move a couple other titles. Folding my arms, I breathe in deeply and smile. I know as soon as they reshop the floor, they're going to go back to where they belong, drowning in the middle of a sea of other books.

More pride consumes me when I see a woman take a copy. I observe her as she opens it up, reads what's on the page, and then smiles that confident buyer, happy reader smile.

"Yes," she murmurs to herself.

Yup, that's me. And as obnoxious and attention-seeking as I can be, I don't feel like it tonight.

She lets out an embarrassed chuckle when she realizes that I'm watching her. She holds the book up in the air.

"I love her books."

I laugh and from a safe distance, I say, "Me too. Enjoy."

"She's doing a book signing tomorrow," she continues. The smile on her face paying me more joy than any Facepage comment or IG post could.

I can say she fits my targeted demographic. African-American, late twenties/ early thirties, maybe. She dressed down for a Friday night, so it's probably a good book and hot cocoa type of evening for her at home.

"Hold up!" She flips to the back cover and stares at me with more scrutiny as her brows bunch up. Then she tilted her head to the side and the smile widened. "Oh my gosh. You're her!" she laughs.

Authors aren't actually celebrities, so I never expect to be recognized unless I'm at a book related event. But I have a sizeable following on Instagram and Twitter, though. I'm completely flattered. Though, I'm sure my current get-up does not do any justice to my professional cover photo. I'm dressed rather warmly for the biting cold weather in Uggs, jeans, an oversized mule cape, tan baseball style cap, and a Gucci tote slung over my shoulder. I would've worn my shades, but I hate when there's no damn sun and people be sporting sunglasses inside a building.

I kind of smile and shrug my shoulders. "Yes. I'm her." This is usually the part when we smile, take pictures, and I autograph the book. I'm not even going to front. I fucking love knowing that readers enjoy my work. This is why I write.

Well, I'm also crazy. so aside from the joy of love, drama, and mystery, it's the only way to get away with murder without committing an actual crime. And everyone can have a happy ending if I want them to.

"Oh, my gosh. I'm Deidra," she laughs over her introduction. "Can we take a picture?"

"Yea, of course," I reply. I dig my cell phone out my purse, ready to "selfie" us.

"Can you wait one minute?" she inquires, holding up a finger. "Babe!" she calls out, leaving the aisle in search of her companion.

My cell begins to ring, and I answer because if I don't, my mom will call right back. "I'm on my way, Mom," I say idly, looking at Muscle Magazine's man of the month, some mouth-watering creamsicle.

"What are you doing?" she interrogates.

I pray that they don't make an announcement over the loud-speakers as I lie, "I'm leaving the hotel right now. I'll be there soon, Mom," I tell her.

"Ok, be safe. Love you," she happily adds.

"Love you too," I reply, turning back to face the woman.

There aren't enough seconds in the span of the ten years that have passed that would allow me to formulate one coherent thought.

I stare at him unblinking, not moving.

I can't.

Frozen. Eyes wide. My heart stopped momentarily and then sped up, its pace so rapid that I could hear it beating in my eardrums. I breathed in and his scent wafted my nostril. It was a mix of my favorite scented oil, amber white and CK Eternity. It was all him.

I can't even focus as she comes to stand beside me after pushing her phone into his hands. It's like a bad movie playing in slow motion.

The woman sucks her teeth. "Babe, take the picture," she whines, posing, holding the book up in front of us.

He's as motionless as I am.

"Carter?" she huffs.

"Alieas," he murmurs, still staring me directly in my eyes.

"Carter," I return. I know it sounded breathless when it came out, but how else was it supposed to sound? I had once loved the shit out of this man and had lost him.

In fact, the last words he'd spoken to me all those years ago had been, "Fuck outta here, Alieas."

PART
one

Sometimes, we're
destined to learn
the hard way...

CHAPTER

one

Alicia

"SMILE GORGEOUS," A MAN, SITTING in a fold-up chair next to a dinged up rust bucket and who appears old enough to be my damn father, tells me as I walk by him and a group of others who seems too far into the bottle to take notice of the beauty when they see it passing by. I frown instead. I hate it when perverts have the nerve to open their mouths in my direction. The man has to be hitting sixty and has aged very poorly, based on appearance. He has a hole in his dome and all the remaining hair has turned that dull, yellowish gray. He has a small, scrawny, rundown body and a nasty-looking mouth. I can smell his breath and his mouth ain't even open. Makes me want to say, 'Yuck'. Peasants don't speak directly to the royal family; hell, why should drunks speak to me? Niggas of all ages go crazy when they see my ass, though.

Dirty ass, I think to myself but then the good-natured side of me takes over and tries to reason. Maybe he's not trying to hit on me. I contemplate that thought for a good minute while I steal another glance at him and go straight back to my initial thought, *Yeah, he's definitely a pervert.*

I'm cool about it, though. I'm too high to trip, a natural high, of course. I just came from a fashion show rehearsal/preview for my very good friend, Briannah, who's introducing her signature clothing line this fall. My girl got it going on for someone so young. Her hustle game strong. The last year has been amazing, and she is reaping the benefits. And it never hurts to know the right people or have a connect. She has a joint venture in the boutique business with her fiancée, my older and favorite cousin, Tyree, and her grandmother who already owns a boutique. And to top it all off, she's getting married in December. This is the most important year of her life, and I'm really happy for her.

No- I'm fuckin' ecstatic. For her.

"You sure you don't need a ride, cutie?" Another hack driver offers.

I roll my eyes and begin to speed walk as I pass the corner of Broad and Susquehanna, trying to dodge all the invitation for hacks I hear.

I can't wait until I get my Blazer out of the shop. Tired of the bus and train ish. Although, it is a great way to meet people. My mood changes when I notice two fine guys checking me out and of course, I'm loving it. So, I go into flirt mode and lay my feminine charms on both of them. They both respond like flies to honey and the smaller of the two nudges the one I'm eyeing.

This man is FINE, do you hear me? And just my type physically. His good-looking ass should have a sign around his neck that reads 'Just drop the drawers'. Quickly, I scan him from head to toe to make my appraisal. He's brown-skinned, about six feet and a couple inches tall and weighs about two-hundred easily, give or take a couple pounds, but he's as solid as a rock.

All muscle and mouth-watering.

I glance down at his hands first, for they tell you a lot. They look as if they've seen some manual labor, and I'm all about a man who works with his hands. Still, his nails are clean and that says that he takes care of them and himself. He has a square face that is boyishly handsome, amber eyes, the color of Hennessy, and extremely white teeth. I admire a man with white teeth; it is such a turn-on. Anyway, his hair is braided straight back in a simple design, and he has a freshly trimmed goatee. Another turn-on. Do you know how facial hair feels scraping the inner thighs?

Damn good, that's how. I smile one of my seductive grins that display my own pearly white teeth, knowing that'll keep him wanting more.

I continue walking. If he wants me, he can come get me.

"So, it's like that?" I hear a deep voice ask from behind me. I turn and see *Mr. Can I Have Some.* walking to catch up with me.

"Like what?" I ask nonchalantly.

"You gon' flirt and leave a brotha hangin' just like that?"

"So, I'm supposed to approach you? I'm sorry, but that's not how I do things." I smile and decide to continue giving him a preview of my attitude. "And besides, my plan worked well; you did follow me," I say, aware of his amused gaze. He laughs to reveal a set of dimples.

His smile is beautiful. Shit, he is beautiful.

"How far do you have to go?" he inquires.

I look him up and down again, for his benefit, and respond, "Just up the street." Ahhh, maybe it is for my own benefit cause brotha man is *foiine.*

I want him. I'm going to get him.

"Can I walk you to where you have to go?" he asks.

I nod my approval.

Why he doesn't ask me for my name is beyond me, but he better hurry up so I can give him my number.

As we're walking, I ask him for his name because he's taking entirely too long to request mine.

"Carter and yours?"

"Alieas," I inform him.

"That's a very beautiful name."

"So, I've been told." I'm mesmerized already and it's only been a second. It must be the eyes. All dreamy. Not quite hazel. Like a lion's, the same color as mine but they look different on him.

Dayuuuum.

"I can tell now that you're going to be a lot to handle," Carter tells me.

I laugh. "Who says that you're going to get a chance?" I inquire with a little sista attitude.

"Damn." He rubs his heart playfully and teases, "I see you're hard on all the guys."

We arrive at my destination entirely too quickly. I'd like to talk with him some more. "Nawl, just the cute ones." I watch him smile as I stop walking. "You think I could get your number so we can finish our conversation?" Carter looks a little shocked that I'm so forward. I shrug. Can't get what you want if you don't ask for it. "I'm going in here," I point out. He nods.

"Only if I can get yours," he responds as he pulls a pen from his back pocket. I take a piece of paper from my pocket and scribble down my number and give it to him as I wait for him to give me his. After receiving it, I make a note that it is his cell phone number because it starts with 267. To be honest, I'd rather have his home number, so I know that if I call him at two a.m. and he answers, he's probably in the bed and not in the streets.

Oh, well. I shrug. What should have I expected when I gave him my cell number? That's just for precautions, though. Some dudes turn out to be stalkers.

"I almost forgot to ask if you have a man."

"Nawl, I wouldn't call any of them that. Just friends," I let him know. I have a couple guy friends, and I don't need another who's going to be crazy and uneasy about the situation.

"We gon' see about that," Carter replies quietly. "You know Gray?" he asks, indicating the barbershop next to the hair salon I am going into.

I nod and catch the gleam in his eye. He's disappointed. Probably thinks I'm one of Gray's girls. I decide to put him out of his misery and tell him, "He's my brother."

"So, you're the princess of the Stiles family?"

I haven't been called that in such a long time that I smile at the memory and answer, "Yes, I guess I am. You know Gray?"

He nods and says, "Yeah, we went to school together. I kick it with Ty and his boahs sometimes too."

"Oh," I murmur. I don't remember him, so for a minute, I think that maybe they'd been in jail together and that would be a definite no-no on my part. I don't date convicts or guys that hang with Gray. In any case, he would never let me. Tried that a couple years ago and he went the fuck berserk. So now, he kind of fends off all his friends who want me. Just like an older brother should, I imagine.

"So, what do you do for a living?" It's probably a question I shouldn't have asked, seeing how this is the first time I'm talking to him, but I'm twenty-two, and I don't have time to get involved with wannabe thugs. I want a man with a good, secure job and one who can and will provide me with the security and love I need. And if he can't do that then he's wasting his time—and mine. Don't get me wrong, I can and do provide for myself, but I deserve a good man. I have my shit together.

Alieas Zonnai Stiles emits an aurora that shouts *high mainte-*

nance. If I look unattainable to a guy at first glance, then it's probably because I am. I'm a recent graduate of Howard University, have been working for my parents as a real estate agent for the past year, and I am basically the shit. Plus, all of my friends are getting married; I wanna get fuckin married too.

"Construction and contracting."

Good money, I think but don't dare say. Instead, I let out an amazed, "That's dangerous."

He takes hold of both of my hands and for the second time, I get lost in his golden-eyed stare. "A lot of things can be," he seductively replies.

This cannot be real. It's almost like something out of one of my sappy-ass romance novels and so far from the approach I'm used to. The feel of his hands on mine is driving me crazy. I find myself wondering how they would feel against the more intimate parts of my body.

A girl's mind is allowed to wonder.

Shit, I haven't had *IT* in a minute.

"I'ma let you go 'cause I have to get back with my man over there," he tells me, looking down the street.

"Wouldn't want him to leave you," I half-heartedly reply, a little disappointed. "Whenever you want to talk, don't forget that you have my number," I tell him sweetly. "So, don't forget to use it," I add on.

"You can bet that I'll call you. It was really nice meeting you, Alieas."

Of course, I know that he'll call because they all do, call that is. I'm convinced it's a combination of my looks and my smart mouth that catches their attention in a way they just have to "We'll see." And then he turns away from me and starts walking toward towards his friend. I watch and wonder why I'm acting like a dumbass over an initial conversation. It isn't like it was special or anything. But it was a refreshing break from the oldest line ever:"Hey, sis, you are looking too good, and I was wondering if I could be your man." Please. I don't even respond to dickheads like that.

Carter's ass is fine.

While stepping inside of my best friends' hair salon Unique Stiles, I notice that he's coming back toward me. I stand in the doorway, waiting from him.

"Wait; I just thought about it," he announces, once we are face-to-face. "You didn't ask if I had a girl," Carter adds with a grin.

"I assumed since you approached me that you didn't have one. But if you do, it can't matter that much if you trying to get with me." I can tell that he's digging me. He can't take his eyes off mine.

"I think I'ma really like you."

"Oh, you will," I promise. "I do prefer to know if you have somebody, though," I add because I'm trying to secure a man of my own, and I don't share.

"Nawl, I'm single."

Considering how fine he is, I have to ask again, "You sure?"

"Yeah, why?" Carter asks.

Being completely honest, I reply, "'Cause you fine," with a smile. "And where there's a Mr. Fine, there's always a Mrs. Fine."

He chuckles and murmurs, "Thank you. But there's no Mrs. Fine. Dudes probably tell you the same thing all the time."

They do. "I wouldn't mind hearing it from you, though." I love having my ego fed.

"You look good," he compliments, appraising me from head to toe. He licks them sexy-ass lips before he adds, "Damn, for a big girl, you carry yourself really nice and you pretty as hell."

The smile drops from my face and red flags go up. I hate that bullshit. And yes, some niggas are dumb enough to say it.

Damn is all I can think as I mentally cross his ass off my list of potentials.

I just don't get it. Because I'm big, I'm supposed to be sloppy, ugly, and tore the fuck up? It burns me up. *Flames and fury*.

I've seen more skinny girls who look like mud ducks than big girls being tore up, but I guess it's okay to be ugly as long as you have a size zero waist.

Irritated, I look right through him and say, "I thought you didn't want your friend to leave."

"I just had to tell you that I dig your whole package," he tells me as if saying that is a huge compliment.

Considering the fact that I'm angry as hell, I still manage a dismissive "Thanks."

Carter tells me goodbye and starts walking off again.

"Bye," I murmur with a roll of my eyes. A man that damn good-looking would know how to fuck things up with just one word.

Yeah, I'm a big girl and I don't deny it, but damn, do I have to be reminded on a daily basis? One day, I just want to hear a cute guy say, "You cute, ma," even if he's not tryna holla. For once, I want these dudes to forget the "for a big girl" shit.

I'm brown-skinned like those Sugar Baby caramel drops. And at five feet nine inches tall and two hundred thirty-four pounds, I'm a knockout if I do say so myself. My face is the classic heart shape; my brown eyes are symmetrical ovals separated by my small nose; my lips are full in the way only black women are blessed without having them enhanced with chemical fillers. My body is adorned with feminine curves. My thighs are shapely and thick; my booty is fat and all-natural, and I have a sculpted waist and average size breasts. I'm well-toned and not flabby. I work out every day to train my body and keep my ego in shape. But still, in the eyes of others, I'm just a big girl. *Fuck that.* I'm a woman and I look good, no matter what the scale says.

Sorry, I just had to get that off my chest.

Despite his unintentional offense, I still want him but I also know that I'm never going to call him. I'm easily turned off when a guy refers to my being clean and good looking as if he's surprised because I'm not supposed to be. He must be some kind of exception, though, 'cause by the time I get inside the shop I feel a vague sense of disappointment and loss.

It doesn't take a rocket scientist to know that everyone in the shop had been eyeing Carter and me while we were outside talking. I get the usual stares from the skinny girls who can't believe that I can pull a nigga like him. The regulars know the deal. Smart people recognize competition when they see it. And those who don't are in for a rude awakening. Most of them see me often enough and know that I'm just as worthy as most of them.

My two best friends, LyNesha and Tiffany, are business partners and run a hair salon. They both have thirty percent interest in Unique Stiles while my brother, Gray and I share the other forty. As a friend, silent partner, and non-hair stylist, I stay out of the day-to-day operations of the shop and only worry about the bottom line: how much I have to contribute and how often and when I'm getting my cut.

Tiffany comes out of the back office with a huge grin that would put models to shame. Tiff has a slim build and is what my mom likes to refer to as "tall and lanky" like a supermodel. Since getting married, she'd put some healthy weight on filling out more in the hips and booty. Her milk chocolate skin is always glowing. She swears it's because of her daily skin care regiment which she has yet to share but it's been like that since we were kids so, I'm always saying its natural and in her DNA to be friggin' flawless. Her mom is a carbon copy of Naomi

Campbell, and she kind of favors her. So, go figure; her genes are impeccable and she knows how to accessorize the shit out of anything and is hands down one of the best stylists in the city.

"So?" Tiff starts, after waving her left hand that displays her three-carat diamond engagement ring and wedding band. She's so incredibly happy with her high school sweetheart. It makes me sick with envy. Just enough to make me wish that I have what she and Tim have when my time comes. Their relationship is just beautiful.

"Yeah, what happened?" Nesha chimes in. She, on the other hand, is not living the beautiful family life, although she has a beautiful four-year-old son Gray, who just happens to be my nephew.

They both want to know what's going on between my ex-boyfriend, Tony and me. "Some guy trying to talk to me," I respond jokingly, trying to divert the subject.

"We saw that; we're talking about Tony," Tiffany replies, speaking for both of them.

I frown. I'm not telling them my business in their crowded-ass hair salon. My name and my love life will be in everybody's mouth. I really don't have time for the gossiping shit because hoes try you, and I don't want to have to lay these hands-on none of these tricks.

"Nothing."

They're acting as if I hadn't called them last night and explained to them what Tony had the nerve to do. I guess they just wanna hear me say it to their faces. I'm with that, though, because it's always so much better and more dramatic to tell your man drama in person.

Tony and I had been dating off and on for over two years. I've known him since my freshman year at Howard and had been good friends with him before we'd changed the dynamics of our relationship. The shit we were doing was fine for a minute, but I'm at the point in my life where I'm ready for the long haul and Tony isn't. For a minute, I thought that Tony would have been the one to change my fast-paced world by slowing me down enough to be content with his love. Dreams of an adolescent. Woke up real quick and all that naive shit went right out the door.

The past two months have proved to be eye-opening for me. While I professed to be completely ready for the 'long haul', there were a few things that could have used my attention a long time ago. Had I truly loved myself, a lot of the things in that relationship would have been different. Don't get me wrong; the shit seemed cool for us at first. I mean, we were both in our senior year of college and neither knew what we wanted, so we were just chilling. That gave me the option of exploring some curiosities about other guys. (In other words, I was fucking with a bunch of other niggas because the one I wanted didn't want me enough to stop me.) The second year after he broke up with me to explore some of his own curiosities, he wanted me back in an exclusive relationship. Loving him as I had, I broke it off with all of my guy friends. So, for the past year and some, Tony had been my world.

My world. Right. Two months ago, Tony broke up with me and I was a damn wreck. It was only natural that after all that time together I'd want and expect more than him showing up at my place after hours to get some ass. I told him and he didn't seem to agree, so he walked out of my life and left me alone. No one mentioned to him that while he was making exclusive demands of me that the same rules applied to him. Of course, I told him, but some men act like they need their mamas to say it before they'll believe it. Like I said, I was fucked up.

Last night, the farewell party of a mutual friend gave us the opportunity to see one another for the first time in over a month. To say the least, dude was affected by my appearance.

Although it took him all damn night say something. I did admit to the girls that he looked good.

"What he say?"

I don't want to give them the impression that I am at all happy about it. The man didn't even speak until the party was over and when he did, the words that came out of his mouth weren't worth listening to. That muthasucka asked if he could stop by and see me. As if I'd let his dirty dick dip.

"Nothing that I'll dwell on. Where's my brother?" I ask. I can see Nesha's eyes go blank, confirming what I already know.

"Next door," she answers after clearing her throat. I laugh. In all the time she was trying to pump me for my life's info, this hoe neglected to inform Tiff and I that she and my brother Grayson were once again an item. Lil' Gray let it slip that *Daddy* had spent the night enough nights for us to put two and two together. That had been weeks ago, and I'm pretty sure from the look on her face that they're still hooking up.

"I wanna ask him about the guy I just met."

"Oh," she murmurs, somewhat relieved.

"He said that they went to school together," I shrug and bite my bottom lip. "I'm not even going to call him."

"Why?"

"'Cause he said the 'big girl' thing. Y'all know that bullshit gets on my last nerve." Both of them are skinny as hell, but they understand how I feel.

"Stop being so damn sensitive. He was handsome," Tiffany advises.

"You're skinny as hell," I counter. "You don't get the smart-ass remarks," I finish.

"I'm not skinny." Tiff likes to believe that she is thick, so we let her believe it. "And you're not the hell big."

This is one of the reasons I love my friends. They always try to make me feel better by saying I'm not big. Yet, if they saw some other girl in the street the same size as me, they would categorize her as big. I appreciate it, but it's not needed. I know I'm thick, and I accept it. But I've had to work to get it too thick. And in any case, I wouldn't have the confidence I have if I hadn't.

"Riiiiight, Tiff." I turn to Nesha and ask, "Is Gray staying at my parents' tonight or is he staying with his dad?" Amusement lingers in my eye.

Taking a deep breath, she rolls her eyes. "Did he tell you?" There is no question about what she's talking about. The guilt from not telling us is just eating her up.

I shake my head. "No, your son told me."

She looks over at Tiff who smiles and shrugs. "Tim told me." She touches Nesha's shoulder gently and asks in that motherly tone of hers, "Are you sure this time?" There had been a lot of bullshit between Nesha and Gray. After years of being together, they'd broken up because Gray had cheated on her.

He was one of those guys who thought because he had them dollas he could act any way he wanted.

It ain't that much money in the world.

"We're taking it slow," she admits softly. "I'm scared to rush back into it."

I could see why. Gray had Nesha playing the wifey role without the ring. I keep trying to tell my brother my best friend is too damn fly to be cheated on. At a couple inches shorter than me, Nesha is light skin with curly hair. She has big, patient brown eyes and a wide smile. There's always a vulnerable soft- ness to her that I can't explain because her mouth is razor sharp and she doesn't play any games. She straight up reminds me of Vivian Green, an up and coming neo-soul singer we saw sing with Musiq Soulchild. When she's unhappy you know it and she doesn't generally take any bullshit. But she did from my brother.

Evidently, something must have changed if she let him back in her bed.

We talked for a little while longer and joked about nothing. I was able to talk Tiff into twisting my fresh microbraids into a nice style. We made plans to meet each other for the basketball game tonight at Duckery's schoolyard where we could trip and meet new people.

My girl, Catrina said she was gonna slide through as long as she didn't have to worry about possibly bumping into Dave. I don't think he even came to Philly this weekend. I can't wait until they get their messy asses together. The last thing I wanted to do was stress about them when I was stressing about my own ass.

Maybe I'll find somebody new to keep my head in the clouds for a minute. With me trying to lose weight, the Lord knows I could use the distraction.

CARTER

"Shorty gave you her number?" My boah Donte questions when I met him back at the corner.

Stretching my arms overhead, I playfully nod. "Yup. Of course," I reply confidently, although I was definitely feeling less confident than my reply. I witnessed the interested glow in her light brown eyes fizzle out in what I can only describe as a possible annoyance, but I couldn't figure it out. We was vibing and then she almost seemed dismissive. I could see flicks of temper, and I have to admit I like it. She may be a challenge. And I haven't felt up for one in the form of a beautiful sista in a minute.

"I could've pulled her," Donte claims with a laugh. "Plus, light-skinned dudes played out."

I'm brown-skinned, far from being light-skinned, but I guess when it comes to dark-skinned, purple-black dudes, anything lighter than them, you end up being light.

His dark lips formed a smirk. "She looks bougie as hell, and her eyes were all on you, boss man," he admits after a second of consideration.

For the briefest moment, our eyes met. I don't think I can explain it. I felt something awaken inside of me. Shit, maybe I'm a little confused by it. I haven't felt an immediate attraction like this in years. Mentally, I'm tucking her. *She gonna be mine.*

Already. Simple as that.

"Way too much woman for you, yougin'," I let him know, grabbing the water bottle he handed to me.

Honeydrop had to know she was gonna have all these knuckleheaded block boys on her top the moment those denim-clad hips swished passed them, accompanied with that bright-ass smile. I'm a sucka for a big butt and a smile. Add the long legs, thick thighs, wide hips, flat tummy, and a pretty smile, and I'm kind of gawking. She really had me with her smart-ass reply.

Alieas... I run the name over in my mind. It had definitely been a pleasure meeting Princess Stiles in adult form. I laugh, remembering how, as ninth-graders, Gray spoke of her with a mixture of big brother annoyance and genuine love for a little sister. I had met her twice before; I know she ain't remember. Once when Gray and I had done a science project in the ninth and another during the eleventh grade. She couldn't have been more than twelve or thirteen then. The first time, she was a chunky little girl with a cherubim's smile and honey eyes. By the second time I saw her, she'd filled out more, had grown a couple inches taller, her face was more mature, and her eyes were kind of alluring. With the memory of "adult" her engraved in my brain, I decided she had developed into a swan. Not that she'd been an ugly duckling either of those times, but damn, my dick was hard, and I was already spinning fantasies with her as the star.

In those brief meetings, I could tell that their household centered around her, thus the nickname "princess' given by Gray.

Gray. That made me think if he'd be cool with me talking to his little sister. I'm protective as hell when it comes to any of my sisters. Both the older and the younger. None of my friends can holla at them, attempt to hit them up, or just kick it. I guess we'd discuss it if it ever came to that. Until five minutes ago, I wasn't even worried about hooking up with no chicks. Fine and fly or otherwise.

The princess was definitely fine and fly. I'm probably hyping myself up for nothing. She look like the type that likes bad boys, hood niggas. Dudes like Gray. We don't necessarily run in the same circles, but we know the same people. Can't even say we from the same hood because they moved to the county as soon as their pop's real estate business started popping. Gray was still hanging in North Philly like he needed it for his next breath. Some people's paths are different; his led him to dealing drugs and jail. I heard he ran his own block of blocks from 15th to 20th Sts. That's a long reach for someone his age. His dad had put up money for the hair salon and barbershop in hopes of getting him on the straight and narrow. Not sure if that worked out for him. Can't listen to everything you hear on the streets, though. Let some niggas tell it, Gray run a cartel from inside the barbershop. We've always been cool and cordial to one another, ran ball a couple times since childhood. Our ideologies differ because while I'm about making money, I'm also about uplifting the community.

My money clean and so is my conscience. I kick it with his younger cousin Tyree, who is an example of a person who has turned his life around and his homies, but I sum myself up as a good dude. Never had the urge to pollute the earth with any substances. That shit break up black families. I know a handful of men who have no idea who their fathers are or have crack-head mothers, remnants left over from the eighties crack era. And ones who've been raised by their grandmas because neither parent had it together.

Yea, not my style at all. I grew up in a modest, two-parent household. My dad works for the water department while my mom stayed home. I'm the middle of five children— two older sisters and a younger sister and brother, and we're close. Like a gang. We don't play no games when it comes to family. I'm my mom's baby, and my dad's first son, and they damn sure raised a man. When I look at my babygirl, I know I'm doing something to make the world better for her. My mom always nagging that I need to start dating or looking for a woman to be with on a serious level for Mira. I'm good, so she is good. My dad, like, "You still young, son; have fun."

I guess you can say I have trust issues and no patience. None. With good reason. These hoes be scandalous. And my last go around had sidelined me. Princess might be a reason to step back in the game, though.

"Damn, shorty got you staring off into space," Donte jokes.

I throw my head back and chuckle. "Nawl," I deny. Running my hand over my chin, I consider it. "But she fine, though."

"Yea. She definitely cute for a big girl."

I shrug, "I know. That's what I said." I tap him on the arm and then take a swig from the water bottle, before saying, "Text your boy and let him know I'm docking his pay." His cousin hadn't shown up for work. The young boah was on the verge of being fired. I needed reliable workers. I own a small contracting and construction firm. There's so much remodeling, renovating, and building going on right now. I had to get a piece, and I'm not allowing anyone to slice it up. This was the beginning of modern-day gentrification in Philly with the expansion of all the cities' universities and surrounding areas. My father always said they was gonna want their neighborhoods back. The jury still out on that, but I don't mind building it up while holding on to a piece of it because by the time it was over and done, it'd be worth millions. Pulling out the rag I have tucked in my back pocket, I wipe my face. The sun out here burning people to a new color. I poured the rest of the water over my head to cool myself down.

My crew was gutting a house and for the most part, it was summer and humid as hell, and we ain't have no damn air.

CHAPTER

two

Alicas

RING... RING... RING... RING...

WHO THE HELL IS CALLING me?— I look at the digital clock beside my bed, the red numbers blurry as I read them.

Who the hell is calling me at three a.m.? I'm not answering the damn phone. I just got into this bed, and there is no way I'm reaching my hand out to pick it up. It sounds lazy, I know, but I'm just not going to do it.

It stops. *Yes,* I think and then I sink my face deeper into my pillow. I'm tired as shit. All that excitement. Not that I'm a ball fan, but the game was happening. Basically, because I'm a man fan. And the men had it going on. Got me a few numbers so it was eventful.

RING*... I'm going to go crazy.*

RING! *Who the hell?*

RING! *Oohhh why?*

RING...

Before I go straight postal the phone stops ringing, and this time, I do reach my hand out of the warmth of my sheets to take it off the hook. I don't want to talk to anybody; all I want is sleep. And no sooner than I close my eyes to snuggle up, the damn doorbell buzzes. I'm trying to ignore it with all my might, but it just wouldn't stop.

Finally, concerned it could be a family matter, I get out of bed, spare a last glance at my comfortable bed. I put on my robe as I head out my bedroom and make my way through the apartment to answer the door before I even think to look out of the peephole. When I open the door to see that Tony is there, I find myself wishing that I'd stayed in the daggone bed and had better security measures. He shouldn't have been able to get inside the building, to begin with.

"Can I talk to you?" he asks, attempting to come into my apartment, but I block his entrance.

"Do you know what time it is?" I yawn. I can stand my ground with him outside the apartment but up close and personal, I'm liable to be a sucka. I need a moment.

No backtracking, I coach myself silently as I decide to let him in.

"I'm sorry that it's so late but I had to see you. I stopped by earlier but you weren't here," he pitifully explains.

I have to wipe the coal from my eyes, so I could stare at him. I can't believe that he is actually here. From the looks of him, I can tell what this is about, yet this time, I won't be falling for any of his stories, I think I'll find it amusing to listen to what he has to say anyway. I move away from the door and take a seat on the sofa while I wait for him to begin his usual lines of how he needed a break. I can't see his face so I turn on the lamp.

"What is it, Tony? You think you can stop by to get some any time you feel like it?" I inquire, irritated that he thinks that he can just treat me any type of way. I'm more annoyed with myself that I had actually allowed him to treat me any old type of way.

"I was out of line the other night," he replies as a way of apologizing.

"Not accepted," I retort angrily. Tony drags his hands over his face, looking to me as if he's in agony.

"I was drunk," he adds.

I laugh at the fact that he used that as an excuse. "You must be right now too."

He steps forward. "Lieas, I miss you. Last night made me realize that you're the only woman I want to be with."

No, No, and No. I can already see it and there is just no way I'm going to let him drag me back down that emotional road where I'd just been two short months before. Tony wants to think that I haven't moved on and that he can drop in and out of my life as he pleases.

Well, he can't. Not this time; not this girl.

I shake my head at him. "You should have thought about that before you decided that I wasn't enough for you."

"You know I be trippin'. I was scared." He huffs and begins to pace. "You wanna get married and start a family and shit. We're still young. I don't know if I am ready for all that. We should be traveling instead," he adds, looking down at me, hoping that I'll believe him.

I do.

"We could have been scared together, Tony. Now, it's too late."

"It's never too late for us, boo. You my woman, always."

His words still have the power to make me smile. I can remember when he used to say that to me all the time and back then, I'd believed him because I loved him.

But that was another time.

"No, I'm not, Tony."

He stops pacing and stoops down in front of me and takes my hands into his and kisses them.

"Can you honestly tell me that after all we've had, you don't feel anything?"

I snatch my hand away from him quick. I have to get up. I want to be standing when I give him his answer. "I felt a lot of things a month ago, like when I found a bunch of your things in my closet or when I looked at the photos of you and I hugged up." I look up at him because this was something he needed to understand. "I felt some type of way that you didn't want forever with me." I stand still and then I shrug. "Now, I'm over it. I threw your shit in the trash and burnt the pictures, and I also realized that you're not the person I want to spend my forever with."

This is the last thing he wants to hear, and I can see that he's not taking the news well. "So, you don't miss me?" His voice is angry and impatient. Tony lacks the logic to see that this is all his fault. And that's exactly what I want to scream at him.

"Not enough to forgive you and take you back. I'm happy with myself and I haven't been that way in a while. Not even when I was with you."

He completely ignores my answer. "Are you going out with the guy you came to Mike's party with?"

"We're friends, Tony. That's all I'm going to say." He knew what type of friends kept. Well, the type I used to keep. I guess that's why he made this unreasonable trip to my home at three am. This man is jealous and very possessive.

"You fuckin' him?!" he demands.

He's frustrated now because I'm not as easily persuaded as I'd been in the past. Rest assured that it's not going to happen. Tony is the last man I need right now. I'd be damned if I put myself through that again.

Our relationship was toxic. Last year, I fucked his car up;

busted out all his windows, bleached and cut up his clothes, and we were back together in less than a couple of months. I can't get dragged back into anything so destructive just for the sake of saying I have someone. We're not right for one another.

"Anthony, what we had worked while it lasted, but it's over and I've accepted that. I think that you need to do the same."

"I love you but I'ma leave because I wanna give you a little more time to think things through."

As if I need any more time. It's funny that he seems to forget that I've had two months to think. "I'm not going to change my mind, but I do want you to explain to me why you think it's okay for you to try and put my life on hold time after time to pursue whatever it is that you want. It's always been what you wanted. I did every fuckin' thing possible to keep you happy even when I was sufferin' 'cause I knew that you didn't give a shit about me. You made it seem sweet 'bout how you never wanted me to be with anybody else and never once considered that I felt the same."

"Come on now, Lieas, let's be real. You know that I always get what I want," he warned, standing up, his whole six feet three inches of him trying to intimidate me.

I lick my lips. "You don't want me, Tony," I say as I walk over to the door. I open it up and continue, "If you did, you wouldn't have let me go."

CHAPTER

three

JUNE 2002

Alicia

T HE SCALE READ TWO HUNDRED and twenty-four pounds today after my morning workout. So far, I've lost a good thirty pounds since I began my get-healthy workout regimen. I'm proud of myself and kind of happy that when I finally get to my goal of one-eighty-five, I'm going to have to go on a huge shopping spree.

"You should eat something and go get washed," my mother says as she cleans the kitchen counter of the breakfast she, my father, and lil' Gray have just eaten. I'm still dressed in my sweats and sneakers. She hates for me to look non-feminine.

"I ate before I worked out, and I am about to get dressed."

Even though I have my own apartment, I like to spend at least one weekend a month at home with my parents. I'm such a spoiled baby. Anyway, they have a home gym that is absolutely worth the visit.

"Tyree called this morning; he said that Nadia and Pat are

having the initial fittings for bridesmaid gowns. I don't think that you're ready to get fitted for yours."

"Ma! What is that supposed to mean?"

"Lieas, I'm just saying that you still have a good thirty more pounds to go before December gets here. Stop being so sensitive."

Sensitive my ass. "Whatever, Ma, you always got jokes."

"Never. Trina called too; she said to remind you that you need to go with her to pick up something for Mama."

"God, I almost forgot. Nana wants us to go to some antique store to pick up this hairpin that she thinks Bri will love. She wants her to use it as her 'something old'. Any other messages?' I ask, 'cause my mom will give them one-by-one, and we'll end up having a separate conversation for each.

"Bri and Ty are coming over for dinner tomorrow after church. Do you plan on going to church tomorrow?"

I roll my eyes. I'm been making a mental note to look for a new church home. My church pulled a coup on my pastor and he was voted out my freshman year of college. I haven't been feeling them ever since. I loved Pastor Furlow so my allegiances lay with him but he doesn't have a permanent church home. Combine that with the fact that I love sleeping in on Sundays so I'm usually missing her.

I can feel the heat of my mother's stare so I say, "I'll be here."

"Good. There's one more thing; your father and I have a nice young man we'd like for you to meet. We've planned a small dinner party for next week or so and have invited the young man and his family,' my mother tells me as I swallow down half of liter of water.

I don't know who told my parents that I needed help with my love life but every since my breakup with Tony. They've been like a non-stop dating service. Well, my mother at least.

She wants me to find someone so badly. My dad is like, 'focus on building yourself up. "How he look?"

"He's alright."

"That's exactly why I can find my own man." She doesn't seem to think that looks are that important.

"Hmm," she sighs. "What was wrong with Robert?" she asks me. She has that tone that I know means that I am being unreasonably picky. In her eyes, Robert would have made the perfect son-in-law and the perfect father of my children. His being a future black surgeon may have had something to do with it.

"He was stuck up and conceited—"

"Like you're not," she interrupts.

"The whole time during dinner, he talked about himself."

"Alieas, I've heard you do the same exact thing."

"That's when I'm trying to get rid of a guy I don't like." There was no question of if he was trying to do the same.

"He's going to be a surgeon, girl. There are some things that I'm sure can be overlooked," she stresses.

"I overlooked the fact that he wasn't cute."

My mother gasps and holds her breath. "I thought that his looks were acceptable."

"I know. That's the sad thing and the reason you won't be hooking me up anymore."

"Well, you sure act like you don't want to get married anytime soon. You're twenty-two and you'll be an old maid if you don't stop being so nitpicky." Don't you want some of what all your friends are experiencing?"

Old maid? I roll my eyes. My mom can be dramatic at times. She and my father have been married for twenty-seven years. Their relationship is more than half the reason I want to get married. I see what my parents have, and I want it and I'm not going to accept anything less. My maternal grandmother was married at twenty-five and her mother before her was married at fifteen and had nine children. My mother's expectation of me is for me to secure the husband and have the children and then kind of worry about everything else.

"Ma, I just got out of a relationship. I have other things going on in my life. I love my job and I'm losing this weight." I've tried to explain time after time that I like the way things are right now. For a time, I'm just going to focus on me.

"My dream man will come. Who knows; he could be right around the corner," I say to make her happy.

An hour later while sitting on the porch with lil' Gray resting on my lap and my parents nestled together on the swing with my father reading something from a magazine to my mother, I notice a grey Ford Explorer riding by.

Damn, I didn't get a good look at the cutie driving, but I'm wishing I had. I don't need to wish that much because he stops a couple houses up and begins to back up until he was in front of the house. Both of my parents look at each other and then accusingly at me. I shrug; I don't know who it is. At least I didn't think I did.

The guy, Carter, I'd met three weeks before gets out of the Explorer and is now walking toward the house. My mother raises her brow; Carter is very handsome, so naturally, she approves of his outward physical appearance.

"Hi, Mr. and Mrs. Stiles," he addresses my parents, leaving me out.

"Hello, young man," my mother happily replies. My father doesn't say a thing; Lil' Gray smiles and sends a cheerful, 'hi'.

"You probably don't remember me, but I'm Carter Reed and I went to school with Grayson, and I just recently met your daughter," he says to them while looking at me. Nicole is smiling her ass off 'cause she charmed by his fine ass. My father is, as usual, unaffected.

"Your face looks familiar," my mother lies. She can't remember him from like ten years ago.

"Umm, what are you doing around here?" I ask him.

"Checking out a property for a kitchen remodel," he replies.

I feel like I need to explain to him why I hadn't called him. He'd left a couple messages on my cell, but I'd ignored them. I'm up in an instant and putting Gray down so I can talk to him. I don't want to talk to him in front of my parents, so we walk down a little and he takes my hands in his like he had the first day we met.

"Why didn't you ever call back?" he begins.

There is no reason to beat around the bush so I tell him straight out, "I wasn't going to."

"I thought that we agreed that you were," he disagrees.

"No, we agreed that you definitely were going to call me and you did," I tell him, looking up the couple inches to his face.

"This some kind of game you running on people?"

"No, I was actually looking forward to getting to know you better."

"Then why didn't you return any of my calls?" he presses.

"Because I have this thing—"

"What thing?" he inquires, stopping me.

"I thought that it was rude and very stereotypical of you to have said that I looked really pretty and that I carried myself well for a *'big girl'*."

Carter watches me confused. "I offended you?"

"In a way, yes. I thought that maybe you were one of those guys who thinks he's doing a *'big girl'* a favor if he gives her the time of day. And frankly, I'm too good for that."

"It wasn't like that at all. I'm attracted to you and excuse the term, but I love women with some meat on her bones. You look good and I just thought that I was letting you know it."

"By saying, 'You look good for a big girl', it's like big girls don't look good all the time. Do you tell skinny girls that they look good to be thin? I just think that men should watch what they say before they say it." By this time, he'd taken his hands off mine and had put them in his back pocket.

"You could have told me this over the phone or to my face the day we met. Three weeks have gone by, and we could've had something by now. I thought that you were interested."

I smile. "Oh, I was."

"Good, 'cause so was I," he says, inching closer to me.

Okay. I'm so done. Fuck the big girl comment. I've got to have him.

CARTER

DAMN, I REALLY MUCKED THAT UP. I REMEMBER THE CHANGE IN her when I think back on it. That cold splash of water when I thought I was macking. And she had already dismissed my ass.

Damn, the vicious type. Straight cut a brotha off. I rub my ribs. I'm more intrigued.

The way her black capri tight things clung to her thick thighs had my mouth watering. I was digging her style; she had a pair of mid-thigh jeans shorts over the tights and a black and red AC/DC shirt that she'd cut at the neck and shoulder to expose more skin. She'd also cut a triangle out the back. The large earrings dangling from her ears were replicas of Queen Nefertiti on a map of Africa. Her toenails were painted some frilly pink, and she's wearing men's flip-flops. Alieas was colorful and vibrant. I could use some color and a vibrant thang in my life right now.

I wasn't pressed or anything, but I felt a great sense of loss after she never called me back. Truth be told, I was plotting on that ass. The young boahs on the worksite had hyped me up to get on Black Planet, and I did but that shit really ain't for me. Nothing but a bunch of thirsty twenty-somethings looking to hook up for quick dates and fun. I'm cool. Not saying that I'm not down for both.

This shit takes work. You gotta be in the mood. Gotta have incentive.

Taking her in, I just realized that I might be in the mood for more.

The princess is gonna have to work on being more vocal and saying what she means. Men aren't mindreaders, no matter how much women think we are.

I don't waste time. Not by choice so not at all...

Clearing my throat, I extend my hand to her. "Let's start over. I apologize for my inconsiderate comment." There's an interested sparkle in her eye as she accepts my hand. I pull her close to me, causing a feminine giggle to escape her luscious lips. "You think that we could go to a movie tonight?" I invite as the scent of what I believe to be Daisy by Marc Jacobs intoxicates me.

Playfully, Alieas tilts her head up so she can look me in the eyes. "Only if you're paying for it," she jokes.

"I'll pay for this one and you can pay for the one next week."

"Who says that there'll be one next week?" she saucily replies.

Letting go of her hand, I brush my fingertips across her cheek. "If there isn't a movie, I can think of a few other things that we could probably do."

"I bet you could," she snorts with a hesitant giggle.

A car pulls up behind my Explorer and beeps its horn. The street is wide enough for the other car to go around it, but the driver doesn't. Torn between this moment with her and the thought of letting it pass, I linger for a second, just drowning in her golden state.

It was like she'd cast a spell. The car impatiently beeps again, breaking it. "Alieas, I've got to go. I'ma call you, though. You sure you wanna talk to me this time?"

She nods in response.

"Dang, Princess." Surprising myself, I lean down to brush a soft kiss to her blush-stained cheek. "Got soft skin," I murmur close to her ear. "Think about the movie and me—"

BEEP, BEEP, BEEP

"Until later," I promise her before I run off to move the car.

Glancing back, I catch Alieas fanning her cheeks. By the time I get to the corner of the block, I still want to talk to her, so I call her. I'm not a beat around the bush type of guy. I'm pretty straightforward.

Alieas answered quickly, "Hello?"

"Are you thinking about me now?"

Laughter bails out and she doesn't even ask who it is. "Yeah, I have to say that I am," she admits.

"Good, 'cause I'm thinking about you and the last time I saw you."

There was a huff of air. I guess she is blowing out what she assumes is bullshit. "You just now left."

"But I just realized that I didn't want to stop talking to you"

"Well," she jokes, "you really know how to make a girl feel special."

I do and I was becoming increasingly interested in doing so for her. "That's what I want to do."

"Sounds like a plan to me. Tell me a little about yourself," she starts.

If I hit all the basics, I'm pretty sure she'll be able to answer all her mother's questions. "I'm twenty-six— and single," I stop after that. That was the easy part.

"You sure?" she inquires. Her voice is a cross between wonder and skepticism.

The first thing to know about me is that I'm a man of my word. I don't just say shit because it sounds nice. "I told you I'm single. Anything that I say out of this mouth is going be the truth."

"Okay. We'll see," she doubts.

Possibly has trust issues. Something else we could work on. I've definitely had my share. Don't think I've allowed myself to trust in a long time. Trying to settle down is hard, especially when you're a full-time father, which leads me to my next truth.

"There's no a woman, but I do have a three-year-old."

There is a silent pause and then she follows it up by asking, "A three-year-old what?"

"Daughter." My ladybug is everything to me, and she'd have to be as important to anyone I decided to be with. My youngest sister is the same age as Alieas, and none of her friends are into dating guys with kids. She also has a no-children policy. Says she dealt with the baby momma from hell and now, all men with children are off limits. It may be the same with Alieas. I'd have to respect it. But it would be a shame.

"So... where's her mother?" she questions next. I wish we were face-to-face, so I could read her instead of the questioning pauses.

Can't really say I'm ready to discuss my past relationship. I have no emotions toward Latoya. I loved her and then I hated her. The love was wearing off by the time she finally decided that she wasn't going to move back to Philly from Florida. She's probably in a trailer park fucking with some Peety Pablo-looking mofo. I'm not concerned about her. I don't like her because she didn't want to be a mom to my bug. And I can't forgive that.

"Nothing; we were young and she realized the family thing wasn't for her. So, I got Bug and it's just me and her."

"What's her name?"

"Amira. My ladybug." Thinking of how precious she is brings a smile to my lips. I'm lucky to have a village. Between my parents and siblings, she good. We're good.

"Oh. Okay. Fulltime dad. She must be cute." The sound of her voice lightens, indicating that she may be open to it.

Through the phone, I hear Mr. Stiles say, "Children aren't that detrimental to a budding relationship, Nicole." Mrs. Stiles must be having a fit, knowing that her princess is even entertaining a man who already has "excess baggage".

"She has her father's genes." I let it resonate before I approach the next questions. "You think you can handle that I'm a fulltime father and that she has a constant presence in my life?"

"I honestly don't know but I wouldn't mind trying to find out," Alieas breathes out.

She has no idea that if she's open, the possibilities are endless.

"Most women I date aren't trying to be a part of her life because what they really want is me, but they fail to realize that we come as a packaged deal. Amira is the most important person in my life, and she always comes first. I'll always have room in my heart for someone else but right now, this is just the way things are. Can you understand what I'm telling you?"

"Yeah, I understand."

"So, you think you still want to see me later on tonight or what?" I ask.

"Yeah."

"Now, I remember you saying that you had somebody; what's the deal with him?"

I have no time.

No time for side niggas, old niggas, they just my friend ass niggas. I need to know what it is.

"Nothing. Just dating right now. I was in a relationship for over two years with a guy I loved, and now we're not together anymore."

The fine ones always have a story, nursing broken hearts over some nut behind dudes who were never good for them in the first place.

"May I ask why?"

"He didn't want what I wanted. After two years of being together and three years of friendship before that, I think I had a right to want more than what he was offering."

"How long have you and he been broken up?" I question. The same way I want her to know what she's getting into, I have to know what her deal is.

"Like three months," she responds.

"That's not a lot of time."

"I'm over it. I've done a lot of healing and found that I'm content with being alone if I have to be."

You don't have to be alone, Princess. "What do you want?"

"I want to find someone who's going to be there for me when I need him, who will support me through my tough times, who will love me for me and not try to change me. 'Cause changing Stiles ain't easy. I'm crazy as hell." She takes a deep breath and then continues, "I want someone who is honest, responsible, caring, and respectful. Who can calm me down? Basically, I want what my parents have. And I'm not afraid to say it at the risk of scaring you off. I want it now."

"What's wrong with wanting it now?" I dig deeper.

"Nothing. The thing is finding a man who wants those same things. They all say they want it but they be lying."

So, trust is gonna be an issue for her. "Every man ain't your last man, Ma." And because I can see she is quick with the lip, I change the subject. "What would you like to go see tonight?"

"How about we see Enough with J. Lo?" she recommends. "I was gonna catch it on a solo dolo mission, but I'd love some company."

"That sound good. Looks like she gonna be kicking ass in that jawn."

"Yup. I think I want to take a boxing class," she confides.

"Really? I can help you with that," I tell her smoothly.

"Yea, my trainer keeps trying to get me to do a kickboxing class with him. I could kickbox you." The tone of her voice drops, alluding to other possibilities.

I laugh, voice thick and deep. "I noticed that you're a real big flirt. And you have a slick mouth," I say with a smile. I pull over in front of my parents' house and pull into the driveway.

"I definitely have a slick mouth. I'm trying to figure out if you wanna know just how slick it is. You think you're up for that?"

My dick pulsed at the thought of just how slick her mouth could be. "I'm always up for challenges," I let her know. Lust makes my voice deeper and suggestive. I shake my head. I'd be embarrassed if walked inside with my dick all hard and my mom notices.

"What time can I pick you up later? Do you wanna have dinner or anything first?"

"We can do that. So, around seven?"

"Seven's fine with me," I agree. I have to go in here and beg my mom to keep Amira.

"I guess you can pick me up at my apartment," Alieas says, sighing lightly.

My eyebrows crease. She tripping. "You guess?!" My voice is now deep and booming, leaving no doubts that I'm offended.

"Giving your address to people you don't know is danger-ous. Some dudes are crazy," she playfully squeals.

I run my tongue over my white teeth smoothly before letting her know that I am. "Only a lil bit. I passed your test, though?"

"Yeah. You're cool," she affirms. She rattles the address off so quick that I scramble to find a pen in my console and ask her to repeat it.

Alicea

OUR CONVERSATION LASTED SURPRISINGLY LONG. WE SPOKE ON our likes and dislikes. He promised to bring pictures of his little girl, so I could see what, or rather who, she looks like. I don't know how that's going to work, though. I'm thawing to the idea of being with a man who already has a child. And about being around the only female that holds his heart.

A short time after I got off the telephone, my mother came in, holding lil' Gray by the hand. "Go, ahead on to the bath-room, baby. Grandma will be right here if you need anything," she says to him. "So," she let out, sitting down beside me, "he has a child?"

"Yes," I answer easily.

"Where is her mother and how old is this child?"

I shrug. "T'on know. And she's three. Mom, I know that you—"

"Not this time," she interrupts, taking me by the hands. "It's your life and your decision. It's up to you to choose if you want to become involved with a man who already has a child. You're a grown woman. I can't do anything but trust and believe that you know what to do to make you happy."

That's not what I was going to say but I thank my mother anyway.

She pats and then squeezes my leg. "Did you tell him that you're conceited, temperamental, and have selfish tendencies?"

I eye my mother questionably. All of my behavioral traits come directly from her. "Yes and no, but if he sticks around long enough, he'll find out," I tell her in all seriousness.

My mother and I have a close relationship. I can honestly say that she knows me better than anyone. As a child, I could always go to her with any and all of my problems and not be afraid to hold back anything. Of course, things back then were in no way as big and complicated as they are today. She was pissed the hell off when I came home crying again about Tony fuckin' around on me and when he decided to break up with me. My mom told me that Tony hadn't been good enough for me in the first place. SO FUCKIN' TRUE. She's real and that's what I love about her. Of course, she can be dramatic at times because she wants me to be as happy as she is. The search for a mate has become very serious in her eyes, but to be honest, I'm only about five minutes into my bitter 'Fuck dem niggas' stage.

"Then he better start running fast," she replies, hugging me.

"Mom, I am exactly like you." It's something my father always tells me.

The disagreement comes quick. "Nawl, baby. You're just like your damn daddy."

"Riiight," I agree sarcastically. Playfully, she slaps my leg.

"Well," she let out reluctantly, "maybe you get a little of your snootiness from me, but I have no idea where all those other annoying flaws came from."

"You love my annoying flaws," I tease. "And there is nothing wrong with thinking highly of myself or wanting everyone else around me to know that I'm the sh— well, you know." Then she raises her eyebrows at me and smiles. My mom likes when I get carried away enough to think that I'm chatting with one of my friends.

"Yes, I know. Didn't I have to deal with it on a daily basis for over twenty years?"

"Your duty," I return. "I guess it is," she complains playfully.

CHAPTER
four

Alicia

ARTER JUST ARRIVED TO PICK me up and already, I feel that tonight is going to be a night to remember. He's dressed down in jeans, a black Ralph Lauren Polo shirt, and fresh pair of Jordans which means that he hasn't fussed much over the night either. But the jewelry this man is wearing seems to tell a different story. The watch alone is iced out enough to cost as much as a house in the burbs. And now has me wanting to know if he's really a construction worker. They get money but not that damn much.

Frowning slightly, I greet him with a, 'Hello'. Approval is written all over his face as he looks at how my dirty denim boot-cut Lane Bryant jeans fit snuggly over my hips and ass. I'm dressed casually, for the most part, in a cream-colored off-the-shoulder, slit-sleeve peasant blouse Bri made for me, along with my jeans and Timberland wedges.

"You look good," he tells me, leaning down to kiss my cheek.

I want to say, "I know' so badly", but I just reply with a simple, "Thank you" and a smile.

My mom told me that just for tonight, modesty is good in small doses.

Surprisingly, Carter leads me to a black 2002 Chevy Impala instead of the Ford Explorer I' d seen him in earlier.

Two cars? He's into something.

"This your car too?" I ask him, not completely sure. Holding the car door open for me, he nods and closes the door once I sink into the plush leather seats. After he gets in the car, he stares at me for a couple of seconds and without saying anything, he starts up the car and pulls from in front of my apartment building.

I wonder what he's waiting for to start a conversation. His eyes are focused on the streets but damn, I'm sure that he can still talk. I begin looking out my window and after a while, I can feel him staring me. It's like he keeps stealing glances my way.

Did the cat get his tongue all of a sudden? Damn, do I always have to do all the work?

"Why do you keep staring at me? What? You scared to talk now?

"Nawl, I just wanted to enjoy quiet while I take in how good you look."

I laugh. I know cap up when I hear it.

"Oh, is that right?" I question with no doubt that it is.

"You know it is," he replies, reaching for my hand with his free one.

"What's up with you and this hand thing?" I ask as he wraps his hand around mine.

"I wanna make sure they fit," he tells me, intertwining our fingers.

"You have entirely too much game for your own good."

"Nawl, I'm real and soon you'll find out that I'm just what you been looking for."

Okay, so this man is as smooth as greasy forehead skin, without blemishes, lathered down in Vaseline. He has all the right words, but we'll see what his actions are.

"That's what I'm talkin' bout," I confirm as he rubs his calloused thumb over my fingers. I love the way it feels. I love that shit period.

"Females be trippin'. When we say something nice, y'all always wanna twist it around to mean something else. Anything I say to you will be the God's honest truth. A man's word is his bond. If you don't do what you say in relationships, people end up getting hurt."

That quick? We have a relationship now? I roll my eyes because my dad says the 'word is my bond' all the time.

I can't see his eyes, but I know that he's on that sincere ish again. "And they get their dicks cut off." I'm not claiming to be Lorena Bobbitt or nothing but sometimes, you just have to put it out there. Carter looks over at me then with humor in his light brown eyes.

"Yo, you crazy," he laughs.

I agree. "I sure am but if you don't mess with me, you won't have to find out just how crazy."

"I don't plan on it." His head went back just an inch as he erupts in husky laughter.

"Safer that way," I remark, thinking I could fall in love with the sheer maleness of that laugh.

He does that male nod of agreement. "What's the deal with you?" he asks me, turning very serious.

"What do you mean, deal? What deal?"

Amused, he gazes at me briefly and explains, "You asked me all my information. Give me some of yours."

"I told you a lot about me," I object with innocent eyes.

Carter flags his hand, sucks his teeth. "That's surface stuff. I wanna know the things that make you who you are and skip all the stuff about how you graduated at the top of your class."

I frown. I'm proud that I nearly graduated at the top of my class. At the same time, I understand what he means. "Well, I'm terrible to deal with when I'm on my period," I joke. "Seriously, my whole life I've been first in everyone else's. I'm spoiled, stubborn, conceited, temperamental, and very self-absorbed. My ego is huge.I have tendencies bordering on craziness, and I love it when I have people's undivided attention. For the most part, I'm cool as shit but in relationships, I have zero tolerance for bullshit. If you gon' be with me, you gon' come correct. That's the deal."

Girl, you've never been correct with no nigga until now.

"Well," he says with a shrug, "guess we gon' have to see how to deal with that."

"You think you ready to take me on?" I tease as we stop at a red light. Carter turns his head and stares at me again, but he has the nerve to lick those damn 'LL' lips. His eyes are staring straight through me and the thumb that had been massaging my hand ceases.

As the heat between us rises, my cheeks become flushed. I feel it coming and before it happens, I think that I'm prepared for it.

Dead wrong.

He lifts his hand to my face and leans forward. The coolness of his wintery fresh breath tickles my lips. As his lips descend upon mine for the first time, I feel that I'm going to have a meltdown. I can already tell that by the end of the night, I'll more than likely be wringing my panties dry. He gonna have me gushing.

Carter must be an expert at kissing. His tongue is massaging my bottom lip and for one second, I yearn to taste it. My tongue sneaks out of my mouth to meet his. Before I know it, my eyes are closed and my mouth is being ravished by his.

It has to be the most unlikely response for me because I generally don't kiss on the first date, but I'm too enraptured to stop it. Carter pulls away from him me, and I feel crazy 'cause the last thing I want is distance between us.

Heart beating fast, I revel in the aftermath, nowhere near sated. I want more but I pace myself.

I have to act like a lady.

"That was nice," I murmur when the kiss is over and he drives through a light that we hadn't even noticed turned green. His eyes are on the road now, but he's talking to me about something sweet that my mind is too clouded and too hazy with lust to comprehend. I can see his lips moving but all I hear is, *"I want you"*; *"you taste good"*, and anything else I can think of along those lines.

Being this close him is literally making me question all the inspiring quotes to not act like a hoe I told myself prior to him picking me up. Just looking at his triceps, biceps and all those other "ceps" are making me wonder what they'd be like banded around my body. I shift in my seat, squeeze my thighs together tighter and suppress a moan on the verge of escaping.

Damn, I have to calm down. There is no way a small kiss should have me like a dog in heat.

"Where are we going?"

"To grab a bite to eat."

I raise my perfectly arched eyebrows and ask, "I mean where are we getting something to eat from?"

"This place I know in South Philly," he says and after what looks like a moment of consideration on his part, he adds, "It's nothing fancy; in fact, it's a pickup window with an eating area outside."

I guess he's half-wanting me to expect more out of the evening than I should.

"So we gon' grab some food and sit outside to eat?" I question with a slight frown.

"You expected something else?" I could hear the edge in his voice and since I'm not really angry, I laugh.

"No, it's cool. It's only the first date, so I'on expect you to go overboard." Now, if this were any other nigga, I'd be telling him off right about now, thinking he can take me to some cheap ass takeout window.

"So, you're saying that there'll be a next time?"

"If you make sure I have a good time tonight," I respond sassily.

"I really want you to. I know you're used to guys treating you like a queen and all, but how about you try spending a real day outside your palace walls with me?"

More game. He'll have to learn that I don't want an escape. I like being a queen; if he acts right, maybe I'll let him be my king. For a minute anyway.

"You seem to have all the right lines," I tell him.

"I'm not even trying to run lines on you."

"Yeah, that's what you say. Where this place at anyway?"

"Front and Oregon."

I nod. "I know where you're talking about. Some guy I used to mess with a long, long time ago took me down there."

"I been meaning to ask you something," he starts.

"What?"

"Just how many guys were there? Are there?"

"A couple. I've been dating for a minute."

"You still have a couple of friends then, huh?"

If this is his way of asking me if there's anyone else, he could better. We'd talked about my relationship with Tony, but I didn't tell him about anyone else. First, because they're only friends and nothing more and second, because I really didn't have to.

"I'm not even gon' lie. Right now, I'm testing the waters. I've been meeting new people, getting hooked up, and just kicking it with old friends. I'm as single as an inmate in solitary confinement."

"You have a lot of guy friends then?" he rephrases the question.

I shrug. "A couple. A date here and there. I'm not tryna be serious with none of them," I let him know.

I guess that shuts him up because Carter is quiet the rest of the way to Oregon Ave. I sat with my arms folded over my chest, my eyes closed, and with my head resting on the back of my seat for the remainder of the ride. It's not my fault if he gets upset about something that he has no control over. This is only our first date and from the looks of it, it'll be our last. I was honest with him and I don't know what more he wants. If he can't handle it, that's something he'll have to deal with.

I'm through. Sensitive dudes are a trip. They be all in their feelings with the truth.

CARTER

So, the princess is annoyed that I asked about other dudes. She tried to spin me with the friend question. Nawl, no thank you. I like the truth and I'm glad that shorty is honest. Maybe my silence is freaking her out. She is shooting daggers out her brown eyes. And I'm the target.

"Alieas, I'm sorry," I apologize as we come to a complete stop after parking. Amused, I turn to her. The gold of her eyes darkened like a storm was coming. Must be her temper flaring up. I'm intrigued by the attitude. Alieas draws me in as she gives more attitude and adds dramatic sighs.

"What do you want me to say? I was being honest. This is our first date, and you shouldn't be mad to the point where you won't talk to me."

I shake my head, denying her take on it. "I was quiet for like two minutes. Taking what you said in. So, it's not even like that."

"What is it, then?" She folds her arms over her chest.

My smile widens. "I'm really feeling you. You're cute and I haven't been in the dating game for a while. I'ma have to work harder to get what I want," I admit.

The smile is slow to develop and the heat in her eyes simmers. "It ain't worth having if you don't have to work for it."

I nod in agreement. "Can say that again."

Once we got out of the car, we ordered our food, found a table, then sat down. Because she's watching her weight, I had to talk her into ordering some cheese fries and let her share a bite of my chicken cheesesteak. She pulled out hand sanitizer from her purse and gave me a squirt.I laughed when she ordered a bottle of water and then pulled out a packet of Crystal Light from her purse. I watched in amazement as the liquid turned pink. Alieas playfully tilted it toward me and asked if I wanted to taste it.

She don't even know. I don't want no damn water, but I'd damn sure like a taste of her. "Nawl, I'm good. So what do you like to do?"

She shrugs, dipping some fries into the cheese. "I work out a lot. I used to be fatter. Also used to have serious self-esteem issues. Corrected both. So, my main focus is on my weight and my mindset. But I also like movies, I write poetry," she explains. Then she scrunches up her face. "I'm a lil' loud. And my temper is crazy," she admits.

"I have something for that," I let her know. And taking in the woman before me, I can't imagine this outwardly beautiful creature having any esteem issues, but I have something for that too. I guess that is why she went cold when I referenced her as being cute for a big girl.

"Hmmm. I bet. Where are the pictures of Amira?"

Wiping my mouth and hands with a napkin, I reach in my back pocket for my wallet and pull it out and hand it to her.

"She is gorgeous, Carter," she bubbly announces, flipping through the various stages Mira's life. There is a father's pride in my eyes when I show her off. It was reasonable for Alieas to conclude that this little girl has me wrapped around her long, browned-skinned fingers.

"She took these last month," I brag proudly, pointing to the most recent pictures. Aside from the wide smile, Amira is tall for her age; she is shades darker than me but has my eyes. I had twisted her long hair into ponytails. She had on a purple Polo T-shirt and shorts.

"Too cute," she giggles.

"Yeah, she is the best thing to have ever happened to me," I confess. I think I'd go through all the mess with Latoya again if it ended with me getting my daughter. Distracted by the vibrating of my cell phone, I pull it out my pocket and answer.

"Hey, Mom. Wassup?" She sounds a little bit out of breath as she explains that she can't find Mira's inhaler. I clutch my heart and stand up. "Check in the little pockets of her overnight bag," I advise her. "It says Albuterol..."

"I know what it says, boy. I'm going to check her room. I didn't mean to get you all riled up," she responds. "Calm down. It's just a lil' wheezing. The nebulizer is here."

"I'm going to stop by my house and grab an extra one and bring it. Thanks, Mom."

This is another reason why dating hasn't been a priority.

Being a parent doesn't care if you're out on a date; the duty demands your attention. Most women were put off by that. My heart beats quicker, thinking about Mira.

"I'm sorry, Alieas, but I have to go back home..." I quickly explain to her that Mira has a bad case of asthma and that right now, she's suffering from a summer cold and allergies. Horrible combo for a three-year-old.

Surprised by Alieas' decision to go home with me, I offered to reschedule but I was actually glad that she doesn't say she wants to go home. There is no time to take her. I have to get to Mira.Alieas looks out the window; I imagine that she's thinking, "What the fuck am I doing?"

And as a result, this could be our last date.

I'd take that. Sometimes, that's how it went. I almost gave up on a possible second date until she reaches over to touch my forearm and squeezes it in what I can only categorize as support.

Looking over, I smile at her and she smiles back, slowing my heartbeat and calming my nerves.

Alieas

THE MOVIE DOESN'T START UNTIL TEN P.M. AND RIGHT NOW, IT IS only five minutes to eight, so there is still a chance that we'll make the movie. I also realize that there is a chance that we won't. Yet here I am, agreeing to all of it. It would give me an opportunity to analyze his ass in his natural habitat.

Carter turns out to be a wonder with children. Fatherhood must be his niche. I find it appealing when he doesn't just drop off the medicine and try to continue our date. I would have been angry had this been any other man, but if he had, I would question all the things he'd said about his daughter being the most important person in his life. As confused as I am, I find it weird that I'm not mad that we end up staying at his mom's all night because Amira just didn't want him to leave.

A beautiful sight it is; Carter holding her in his arms while she attempts to doze off into sleep. I know that a lot of kids get really irritable when they're sick. They don't want to be moved or touched by certain people. They want what they want when they want it, and I definitely understand that. I'm always like that, no sickness required. I'd hate to be defenseless like that again.

Throughout the night, I observe Carter's facial expressions. I can see the patience in his eyes as he tries to comfort Mira. He rubs her hair, kisses her cheeks, and whispers that she'd be all right and that he'll never let anything bad happen to her. I hear him say, 'If daddy could take the pain away I would.' My heart sinks after those words spilled from his lips. By then, I know that his capacity for love is greater than I'd thought.

We haven't even been on a real date, and here I am, falling in love with him being able to love his child so much. I tend to romanticize everything.I admire this because my father, though he spoils me to death, has never been overly affectionate to me. That is my mother's job.

Mother. That now has me wondering about the woman—no girl— who had brought Amira into this world, only to leave her without a mother's love. Who would give up their rights to such a beautiful child and a beautiful man for something else? For the unknown?

There must be something wrong with me this week. I'm just too damn emotional. My date has just been ruined because of a kid, yet all I can do is smile because father and child look so cute together.

At some point between nine-fifteen and nine-thirty Carter's mom, Sharon, comes into the room to tell us that we'll miss the movie if we don't leave. She playfully scolds him for constantly holding Amira, and she also says something to the effect of him spoiling the child rotten.

Crazy that I spend my first date with his family and kind of enjoy it. Three hours in his company isn't at all bad. I learn that he is a graduate from Florida A&M with a Bachelor of Science in architectural design. That really blows my mind, but it explains the damn house.

The man designed and built his dream house. He'd converted two rowhomes in the East Falls section of Philadelphia into one extremely large single. By our next date, I'll be able to inspect it in more detail. The fact that he's not actively pursuing a career as an architect surprises me, but he told me that he'd worked for a firm in Florida after graduating. Soon after, Carter said he'd found that it wasn't something that he wanted to do for life.

Says that he needed to build something with his hands, and my eyes go right to *those hands*. I look at them, and they are long but strong. His palms are wide; I can see the calloused pads at the base of each finger. I want them on me. But I just listen to him talk. I like the sound of his voice; it's deep and husky. It sends ripples of warmth over my skin but still manages to make my hairs stand on end. It bellows with bass, beckoning my heartstrings to play another love song.

I can't focus. Lust causes me to not listen. And I had to listen. Really listen to his words, not to react or to respond but to internalize who he is.

So, in addition to him not liking the job, Amira had been born and Latoya, Amira's mom, was unwilling to relocate back to Philadelphia from Florida. He developed a passion for working with his hands, and they are part of the reason he now owns a prosperous up-and-coming construction and contracting company.

"I'm sorry about the way things turned out tonight, Alieas," Carter begins as he walks me to my apartment building. We're holding hands and I'm looking up at him. I shake my head and murmur, "Shhh, I enjoyed spending time with you."

"Can I call you when I get home?" he asks.

"Yeah, you should do that. But right now, I think you ought to get Amira home and into her own bed," I reply, glancing over at the car where the child lay sleeping in the back in her car seat. The cuteness of the child has got me tripping.

"In a minute," he says, tipping my face up to his. "I've wanted to do this all night," he adds as his lips descend upon mine.

The kiss is short but sweet. It only lasts a second, but it would last in my memory for a lifetime. Unexpectedly, he kisses me again. This time, his tongue touches mine, and my arms wind themselves around his shoulders. His arms wrapped around me; his fingers begin massaging the small of my back. Gradually, the kiss comes to an end, and we both step apart, dazed.

"Keep it up and you gon' be my woman," he warns me.

Even though the baritone voice is persuasive, I negligently think to myself, *Riiight!!* There is no way I can be so sure. I only smile. We have a lot to get through to determine that. The kid thing is still like a crack in my car windshield.

"We'll see. Call me," I say finally as I begin digging in my purse to find the keys.

CHAPTER
five

Alicia

I'M NOT USED TO BEING catered to. Having all of my whims, flights of fancy, and crazy notions entertained has me soft and agreeable. Soft and/or agreeable has never been me, but I guess I can kind of get used to it. Inhaling the fresh bouquet of mixed flowers, I warm to the idea that it is ok for Carter to make me feel special, even if it is something as simple as a tiny bouquet of mismatched flowers.

The array of vibrant colors easily has me grinning from ear-to-ear. I love flowers and have never received any "just because".

With a foolish grin, I read the card again: *Just because I want to make you smile*, Carter.

"Ooooh, flowers!" my mom squeals as she breezes into my office. My smile is on one hundred. "Niiiiice. They're beautiful, baby," she approves.

Admiring the flowers again before putting them on the corner of my desk, I nod excitedly. "Yes."

I can't wait to call and thank him for his unexpected act of thoughtfulness.

"And who are they from?"

"Carter."

It takes her a moment, but she dims the wattage back on the smile. "Points for the sunflower, but does he know your favorite flowers are Calla Lilies?" she asks. She isn't particularly fond of Carter because he is a fulltime father and a contractor. I have no idea how a girl from North Philadelphia became such a snob. My father moved her out of the county, and now, she acts like she was born with a silver spoon in her mouth. She swears a doctor or lawyer is in my future. I have no idea what's in my future. And because I love her just about as much as she gets on my nerves, I don't want to go down the rabbit hole she's trying to lead me to.

I shrug. No man has ever bought me roses either, so... "Umm. What difference does it make?" I sit down behind my desk and mentally prepare myself when my mom also takes a seat.

"None, I guess. But you have to make sure you set standards for these men. Teach them how to treat you. Let them know what you like. What your expectations are."

"The expectation is to make and keep me smiling and not crying, and these flowers did that today. He's the first man to send me flowers for no special reason, so, you should lighten up. Carter's a nice guy, Mom. And we've only been together a month."

She sighs. "I know but..." She surrenders her current thoughts with an invisible white flag. "Bring him and Mira over for dinner on Sunday," she adds.

"Ok. Thanks, Mom."

"Well, for any man who has the power to make your mean behind smile, I am willing to give a chance. Don't forget the dinner party, though," she reminds me.

Already forgotten. Frowning, I look over at the flowers. I don't want to waste my time fooling around with my parents and their bougie behind friends and their stick-up-the-ass sons. What types of dudes need to be set up by their parents these days anyway? I'm going to be certified insane if she keeps trying to shove all the available suitors she knows my way.

And I've been enjoying spending time with Carter. All my other guy friends have fallen by the wayside. Not saying I'm closed off to meeting new people. It's just that I like him.

A lot.

"Mom, I thought we canceled that."

"I most certainly did not. You promised. If you don't like him, you'll never have to see him again. Now, make sure you wear something dazzling."

I think about protesting, but I agree so I can get back to admiring my flowers. I can't wait to text my girls to let them know I got some "just because" flowers. "After this, no more dates. I am highly capable of attracting my own men. Thank you."

"Of course you are, baby, and that's why you have one now," she says in a voice tinged with polite sarcasm. She gets up and comes over to kiss my head before exiting.

Picking up the telephone, I dial Carter's number. "Heeeey," I say when he answers. "I love the flowers. Thank you."

"Did they make you smile?"

"They were the highlight of my day so far."

"Glad to hear it. Shit— Lieas, I have to take this call. Call you back. Maybe we can go out later," he suggests.

"Call me later," I say. I quickly hang up the receiver. I guess I'm going to have to tell him I already have plans. We haven't discussed being exclusive, and he hasn't questioned how things are going with my other guy friends, so until he makes his intentions crystal clear, the status of our relationship can be left up to interpretation.

COLLECTING NUMBERS IS MY ONE OF MY FAVORITE THINGS ABOUT being single. Although I want something serious with Carter, I consider a month entirely too soon to be calling off all the enamored souls who are lucky enough to come in contact with me.

"So, do you have a man, Ma?" the current soul questions. He has been watching me since we are both in line, paying for gas. He has continued to watch me as I pump mine right across from where he is pumping his. He doesn't offer to pump my gas, so I try to avoid eye contact. There are no gentlemen left in the world.

Carter is a gentleman, though. I shake my head. *Carter isn't here.*

And even though I love being called, 'Ma', I supply my name. "Alieas, and no, I don't," I reply.

He smiles and treats me to a beautiful set of white teeth. "Justin. You just have a lot of 'friends', then?"

I almost laugh but I smile instead. I watch him as he walks over to my car from his. He is sexy as hell. And dark as a Hershey's chocolate bar. His face is handsome enough, I suppose and he has a very nice athletic body. In fact, it looks like he's just come from running ball with his boys. At least I hope that why he's sporting a basketball jersey, shorts, and sneaks in the middle of the day. "Nice to meet you," I tell him as I shake his extended hand. "And why you say that?"

"You look like the type," he answers. "And since you asked me that, I know it's true."

I nodded. "I have friends. But don't you?"

"I guess. You gon' be busy with any of them t'nite?"

Damn, I wish I hadn't agreed to my mom's stupid dinner party. "Why? Do you have something better for me to do?"

"I'm always good company. I'm sure that we can find something that we both would like to do."

Sure, would like to do him. The thought is out before I could check it. This is my muthafuckin' problem. "I'm sure we can."

Sexual attraction always gets me in trouble. I thought I had these types of urges under control.

"So, what's your number?"

"This is an exchange program," I tell him. He laughs and takes his flip chirp phone from his pocket. You have to let some dudes know because sometimes they took your number and don't give you theirs, which could be for a number of reasons, most of them shady. I give him my number and ask, "And yours?" I reach inside my car window to grab my cell.

"You ready?"

I nod then rattle off the number.

"What time is good to call?"

"It's my cell. Basically, anytime you want," I shrug.

He squints his eyes, and I notice that they are chocolate brown.

Damn, Damn. Damn. Why he have to be cho-co-la-te with sexy ass eyes?

"Do you work?"

I chuckle. I guess being available all the time means no job. "Yeah, I work."

Justin licks his lips. "What do you do?"

"Real Estate. Rehabs, Renovations. How 'bout you?" I brace myself for this sexy man to say that he is between jobs, or "self-employed", or worse, a rapper.

"Journalist."

Unable to hide my intrigue, I grin. I usually go for men who have physical jobs, like contracting, construction, or anything that involves strong hands. "Really? You write for a newspaper?"

"A couple; I do freelance work mostly. Magazines, that sort of thing"

"Freelance? Is there any money in that?" I should be embarrassed about asking it, but I'm not.

His chocolate ass looks surprised but he answers, "Yeah. Gotta be good, though. I've been thinking about real estate for a minute now; is there as much money in it as they say it is?"

"Of course, there is, but you gotta be good, though," I shoot back.

"Maybe you can fill me in on it later when we get together."

Such a smooth way to end a conversation. I'm impressed. "Yeah, I can do that. all me."

"And you sure your man not gon' answer your phone, right?"

A smirk spreads across my face. "Please."

CHAPTER

CARTER

I'M IRRITATED THAT THINGS DIDN'T go my way. But I don't make a habit out of sweating over things that are out of my control. In my mind, tonight was going to happen differently. I imagine soaking leisurely in the bath with some Epsom salts and a drink. Today has been a long fuckin' day. Framing the basement and the first floor in ninety-degree weather is no joke. At least the floor at the Albrights' is complete, and I don't have to worry about the smell of turpentine for a couple of days.

I play with the possibility of Lieas coming over and letting whatever happens happen. We've been kicking it on the weekends since our first date. It's been a month and I've been a gentleman, but she could tempt Adam. I wanna be all over her, but it's something that keeps me from taking the kissing and heavy petting further. I wanna put the voodoo down on it, but I'm not sure what she working with and she might have a nigga tripping once I get it. I know my limitations.

So, having my mind clear, focused, and sexual haze-free is how I been playing it. But I'm damn sure interested. I have recently ended plenty of my nights with blue balls. It's real young boah shit to jerk off.In any case, when she called to thank me for the flowers, I extended the invite to go out, only to be told that she already had plans.

Plans with another man, I bet. Under the guise of a dinner party arranged by her parents.

I had to give it a moment to allow what she said to sink in.

Temperature rising, I can feel the heat course through my veins like lava. I had to take the phone from my ear to look at it on some dumbfounded, 'She must think I'm a nut-assed nigga.I only ask if she was sure she wants to do that, and she kicks some story about not wanting to disappoint her parents. Her mom is so into appearances that she doesn't want to embarrass her by canceling at the last moment.

I'm not buying it. At the age she is and knowing Alieas the way I've come to know her, there's no way that she does anything that she doesn't want to. My mom has attempted to set me up on several dates, and I've respectfully declined. I'm past the age where my parents can guilt me into anything.

Considering the fact that we are not exclusive, and that she is not my woman, I have to bring myself down off the ledge. She made her choice and I have to live with it.

Don't like it, not with it at all, and possibly turned off by it. *At least she honest*, I reason. *Maybe too honest.* But I can't really say that there is no such thing as too honest.

Guess a brotha is just salty. Kind of figured I had locked it down without even mentioning it to her, and now, I'm dealing with the results.

Lieas even had the nerve to pretend to be annoyed with me like I should be understanding.

Yea. Hell Nawl. I didn't snap off, but I did terminate that conversation. Cut it short. She can play out in these streets if she want, but she won't be playing me.

My man Rah had hit me up to invite me to the Purple Orchid and the club at 2nd and Cambria on a strip club tour, but it wasn't where my mind was. I'm definitely trying to get some ass to bounce for me, but since I was only in the mood for Lieas', and that wasn't happening— at least not tonight, I declined. Dave had texted me earlier in the week to say that he was coming up for the weekend. I called him to see if they were still going out. They were so, I'm about to be out here.

It would be great to see him and hang out with some dudes that aren't being obnoxious and high. I don't smoke weed, pop pills, or none of that extra shit these dudes out here be doing under the guise feeling good and having a good time.

I have to admit I do need to get my mind off her, though. The next best thing to love and family is money, so I was going to make some money moves. Dave is a financial wiz and is always on 'go' when it came to talking dollars and deals.

There is no need for a sitter since getting with Alieas; my mom has taken it upon herself to keep Mira for the weekend. I guess she figures I could use the private time. She is hype as shit. Thought I would never get into another relationship after Toya. My dad was like, "Enjoy the single life son and get all the pussy you can before you bump into "the one".

I give a quick call to her to check on Mira and to say goodnight.

"Night, Bug. Love you," I tell her, making smoochy, kissy noises into the phone. It elicits a giggle as expected. "Love you too, Daddy."

"Alright, Cart. Ya'll have fun. Tell Lieas I said hi." My mom swears that Alieas is going to be my wife. The jury is still out on if she is even gonna make it to become my girl. Especially after tonight.

"I'm kickin' it with the fellas tonight," I let her know.

"Oh; well, where's Alieas?"

"She out with some otha nigga tonight, Ma." I murmur.

She gasps dramatically, "Carter, no. You ran that poor girl away already? She seems so nice."

What? Ran her away? I shake my head and roll my shoulders to stretch my aching bones. "Mom, please. And don't be all hype. I'm not sure about her," I confess.

"Aww, well; I liked her. So, whatever you did, fix it," she instructs.

I frown. "Ma, I didn't do anything."

"Alright, baby. You're right. If she'd rather be out with some otha fool, let her. She cute but she ain't that cute to be two-timing my baby."

Sharon will ride with me until the wheels fall off. I laugh. "It's cool, Mom. I gotta go, though. And no junk after she brushes her teeth."

"I raised you, didn't I? And you let Ms. Thang know, you don't play that."

"Thanks, Mom. See you tomorrow."

As soon as the call disconnects, Alieas' call comes through. I press the button to decline it.

I will have to decide what to do about her later. I really like her, but if she still playing the field, I have to let her do her. Or I could put up or shut up and force her off the market. That just doesn't sit well wit me.

I take one last glance at myself in the mirror. *A brotha look good.*

Rah texted me on my way down the stairs:

Last chance my nig, There's a wet T-shirt contest.

Once settled in the car, I texted him back.

I'm good, homey. Make sure your ass show up for work on Monday.

LMAO, boss man. Enjoy your QT with the new jawn. You already be actin' like an old weird nigga. You betta have fun before she lock your ass down.

Whatever, man. You betta make sure you wrap before you tap or you gonna be burning like last time.

And without another thought to Alieas, I start up my truck and pull out of my driveway.

Alieas

HIS CREDENTIALS SEEM IMPECCABLE. DEREK TURNER IS BLACK, twenty-five, educated, and he comes from a family that is well-off. Lineage is important to my mom for some reason or another. Wouldn't have mattered to me if the man's father was a second generation bum as long as he knows how to take care of business. Not sex, but the everyday affairs of his life.

The happiness from my day vanishes once my mother informs me that she, my father, and Derek's parents decide that we would benefit from our initial meeting being a one-on-one experience. Here I am a half hour before the damn date and plans have been changed. I contemplate not going to spite my parents, but Nicole would see it as a personal insult and be embarrassed. Still, I don't know enough about this man to save my life. Yet, here I am, waiting for the Maître D to seat me with a man I have absolutely no interest in meeting.

I follow the man to a secluded corner of the very chic and expensive restaurant. As we approach the table, Derek stands up to greet me. I am frozen and amazed at how fate could play such dangerous games with a person's life.

Three years have passed since I'd met him, last saw him, and slept with him. It takes him a moment to recognize me, but there is no mistaking he knows who I am once he does.

"Your name didn't ring any bells," he explains. But then he hadn't asked for anything more than my first one.

I laugh at the irony of the situation. "It would have helped if I'd have given you a real one," I admit as I sit across from him.

Here's the deal; during my sophomore year, homecoming weekend of '98 to be exact, there had been huge parties and mad guys from everywhere. I think back and am ashamed to say that I had a couple in my bed. And Mr. Derek Turner had been one of them.

"This is pointless," I complain, realizing how uncomfortable it was for me to see one of my very own indiscretions studying me throughout dinner.

"Wait. 'Zonnai' is what you told me, right?"

"It's my middle name," I snap. Now, I'm angry and upset.

In college, before Tony and I were together, I was very free with my charms. I had sex with just about anybody who wanted to. There were no ifs, ands, or buts about it. I used sex to self-medicate my depressed mind at the time. Seeing him just made me understand that my shit wasn't as tight then as it was supposed to be.

I'm still up to the same shit, more or less. Less fucking this time around though.

How many guys have there been from the time I lost my

virginity at fourteen? More than I can remember or would care to. When I look back on it, it's something my heart can't take.

"Cool out," he says to me. "I'm only on this date thing as a favor to my parents."

"Same here."

"Look," he reaches for my hand and rubs it, "how about we ditch this place and go get a room?"

Maybe I deserve that for all my past behavior, but I'd be damned if I am going to sit there and let him think I'm just going to him fuck me because he asked nicely.

I snatch my hand from under his and spit, "You fuckin' ignorant fool."

He doesn't answer but just looks at me. His expression leads me to believe that he is actually shocked that I am declining his offer. I get up from my seat and leave him sitting there. This nigga got me all the way fucked up.

Now, I'm standing out in the smoldering August evening, and my eyes begin to water. My pride hurt, I want to shout that I am no longer that easy piece of ass. That I don't impulsively fuck dudes I don't know for fun. That the whore who let him grace her bed no longer exists. That she has considerably matured and treats her body and her mind with kindness and respect. And worst of all that the baby she carried and didn't know who the father was no longer dwelled in her body. That girl wasn't me. An abortion in a lonely clinic was all she needed to snap her out of her reckless ways. The girl had grown into a woman who has become more selective and cautious with her bedmates.

Then, I was still trying to find myself. The current me is the result of much soul-searching and learning from the mistakes of a naïve girl who thought she had all the answers. I yearned to cry and scream. "That's not me." when the first tears fell. I'm saved the embarrassment of breaking down in front of dozens of people when the valet appears with my Blazer. In the privacy of my car is where I unabashedly release all of my tears. Until now, I've never cried over being overly sexual or carefree. Again, for the most part, I'm now more controlled. The past has always been that—the past, and I thought that tears would never change that. But sometimes crying makes you feel better.

During my times of trouble, I found there was only one place I could go to seek solace. The Spot is that place for me. I drive there without a second thought. It is there that I can pour out my heart in lyrical form, in front of a roomful of people, and not worry about being be judged. Since I was seventeen, The Spot has been this poet's sanctuary. I haven't been there in over three months and graced the intimate stage and let my words flow and bless the ears of an audience. I didn't even go when Tony broke up with me because I didn't have the words. I had been a mass of confusion. Within fifteen minutes of leaving The Grille, I am parked and being greeted by the owner. "Hey, Lieas," she says with a huge smile. Then she kisses my cheeks.

"Hey, Empress," I reply with a hug. During my visits here, we developed a friendship.

"You gon' flow?" she inquires as she leads me to my favorite seat that I'm surprised isn't taken. For a Thursday, The Spot is uncommonly crowded. I give a nod of thanks as I sit and begin listening intently to a handsome man speak of the hardships of being a black man in America.

"You need a few minutes?" she questions, anxious to hear what brings me to her.

"Yeah, just sign me up," I reply. Empress leaves me alone with not even a, 'How have you been?'I need the quiet, though, as thoughts race through my mind.

Later, she comes back with a drink in hand and places it in front of me. "You up next," she whispers with a pat on my shoulder. Empress makes her way to the stage, just as a young girl finishes up and is awarded a thunderous applause. She has definite skills; makes me nervous for a minute that I have to go after her. But no young girl is gon' stop me from venting or shinning, for that matter. Not that shining is what this is all about.

"Our next poet is a very special friend of mine and has been gracing us with her presence here at The Spot since she was seventeen. I'd like to introduce to you, The Essence of Words!" Empress exclaims with a cheerful smile.

She holds the mic out to me until I have it secured between my fingers. I mouth a thank you and look out into the audience, which is now hushed with a dead silence.

I greet them, my voice deep with my black mood, with a "How's everybody doin'?" The responses pour in, and I continue. "I'm not hatin' on the men in the crowd, so fellas, don't take offense. This is for all my sistas out there." I lift my eyes to the hovering lights, close them, and then I speak, "Shit is Crazy." I take a deep breath. It's been a long time since I freestyled for an audience.

"The essence of my words lives deep within my soul, yet and still, I had a man in my life that I couldn't hold. I let him lie, cheat, and steal, and a whole bunch of other shit. You niggas out there know the deal. But nawl, that's not what I'm gon' speak on even though I know that's what all you sistas wanna hear." The men in the room begin to clap. For once they have a sista to sympathize with their doggin' asses. Not!

"I woke up this morning happy as shit... had a potential man in my life which also means potential, regular dick... and all of his other attributes... damn, too much... just can't get into it. Peaceful and tranquil, basically floating like a muthafuckin

' cloud... until a crash of thunder came down to earth and fucked up my smile... Some young bitch," I opened my eyes to watch the women in the room, half of them there looking around, the other half waiting for my next words like the air they need to breathe, "And yes, I say bitch because not only is she disrespecting she but the young jawn had the nerve to disrespect me. The girl isn't who y'all think she is but the same one I see every single fuckin' day... And the sad shit about it is that I just can't get the fuck away. We share the same face, voice, the same pussy, the same memories. Memories of a time when I couldn't or just wouldn't say no. Yes, to you all, I'm admitting I used to be a hoe. Yes, the bitch that I referred to is me. I thought I could erase her and chase her the fuck away, but I can't 'cause shit you do in your past will always be there to stay.... Take your time and think about every nigga you done fucked... Can you count them on two hands or is it just too much? We want to blame men for breakin' our hearts and dogging us out when in reality, sometimes, it's our fuckin' fault. Why give them the power to break our asses down? Give them the power to set the definition of what a woman should be? How the hell would he know when the thought of being a real man has got his ass beat? Make wise decisions so you'll never be put in a whore's position... Yo, shit to crazy."

I don't know if I expect people to clap or even respond. I'm on the verge of tears because I still have a lot more things to get out, but I can't find the words. The silent room erupts in applause. I smile and wait for Empress to come to the mic. She put her arm around my shoulder. "You did real good, lil' sister," she whispers in my ear. "Thanks," I murmur in her ear before I leave the stage.

The next few minutes pass as I listen to the melodies of the live jazz band and hushed conversations of others around me. "I thought you had a family thing tonight," the deep, familiar, masculine voice comes from behind me.

I don't have to look around. For the past couple of weeks, I've heard that sexy ass voice over the telephone and in person, smiling, laughing, and joking. Shit, I hear it when his ass is nowhere near me. After taking a deep breath, I finally turn around to focus my eyes on Carter.My eyes have just received a delicious treat. This is the first time I've seen him dressed formally. And— "Well, damn"— is all I can think. This man is Denzel fine, Billy Dee Williams in Lady Sings the Blues fine, from head to toe. He's wearing a black dress shirt with a red silk tie; his black suit pants are perfectly creased down the center of each leg and hits the middle of his expensive Italian shoes that match the designer belt that tapers his waist.

The expression on his face clearly conveys that he's angry. I've talked to him enough to know that lying isn't something that he tolerates. I was even afraid to be as honest as I was with him. I want something with him, so I'm not going to lie about this. "I did," I respond. Without invitation, he removes the chair that is on the other side of my table and pulls it right next to mine. Carter shrugs as he waits for me to explain. "That shit was the worse," I say, rolling my eyes.

"Alieas, I was hot as shit with you earlier."

I already knew he was upset. The first time I called, it went straight to voicemail, and when I called right back it rang twice, and then he cleared the call. I thought about texting him but decided against it. It's only been a month and I am afraid of him. Truth be told. I'm scared of his whole deal. Him, the kid, what he's looking for in a woman, and I'm scared that if he finds out who I used to be, he'll be the one running. They all run.

And since he just witnessed me pouring my heart out, it may be too late for that. When I told him that I wasn't ready to commit to anything serious, he was cool about it. When I told him about the dinner party, I envisioned him laying down the law but he didn't; he was annoyed, hot, from what he's said.

"So, what happened on your "family" date? And what was all that about?" he asks. I knew he would want to know what was up, so I feel that I can tell him.

"Are *you* on a date?" I inquire, just so I can see him smile.

He did and said, "Nawl, I don't have to date around to find who I want."

I flag him. "Whatever, Carter," I reply with a huge smile.

He takes my hand in his and asks, "When are you gon' stop running from me?"

I laugh, loving the feel of his rough hands on mine. I even have butterflies in my damn stomach, but they disappear quickly enough when I think about telling him the truth. "You don't even know me," I laugh, changing the subject.

"I'm trying to know you. You're the one backing away and fuckin' with a bunch of knuckleheads."

"Are you here alone?" I ask because I've wasted enough of both of our time. He is going to find out the deal. I'm going to put most of my cards on the table and see if he wants to fold.

"Dave drove up this weekend. Him and D came through."

Philly is huge but we still managed to kind of know the same people. Dave and Daemon are my cousin Tyree's best friends, and Dave is also Trina's, one of my closest girlfriend's, ex. And Daemon is the man of another girlfriend, Case's dreams.

"Where they at?" I question. In college, Dave used to make trips to see Trina, even when they weren't together. They had enough drama to make my life seem mediocre. And I guess it'll continue at the wedding. Catrina hasn't seen or spoken to him in a little over a year.

Everyone is extra concerned with how'll they'll respond to one another when they do finally see each other. I don't have to worry because since she's planning the wedding; Catrina will be on her best behavior. And Bri will shut Dave down if he tries to start some shit on her big day.

It's been a year since my girlfriend Case had finally worn D down into dating, and I'm sure that their union will soon lead to babies and marriage. They are already head over heels in love.

"Over there in the corner," he replies and points over to a bar seat.

"How about we both go tell them goodnight so we can get out of here," I suggest.

Carter frowns, looks intently at me and asks, "What are you trying to get into?"

"We have the potential to be more. There are a few things that you need to know about me if you're serious about being with me."

He nods. "Come on."

We go over to talk to Dave and D, and I notice that Carter still has my hand in his. The fact that they fit makes me feel safe.

"Look at you, Lieas. Drop that dickhead and start goin' off on bitches," Dave smirks, embracing me. "But you fuckin' with this dude, now?" he laughs, slapping Carter on the back.

I lean down and hug them both. D is the silent type, so he doesn't say much more than "hey". But Dave is the lighthearted jokester out of their man trio.

"He aight," I admit. He is way more than alright, I thought, looking over at Carter.

"Yeah, I'm aight," he mocks.

"Your friend, man," Dave sighs heavily. "She still tripping. You probably gonna be acting all shady with her the next time I see you. Tell her I still love her," Dave confesses. The thought of seeing her must be weighing heavy on his heart. He shakes his head and coughs into his fist. "Anyway, that shit up there was hot. I still got a copy of your poem."

I frown. "What poem?"

"The One Minute Man one. You be hatin'."

I laugh. "They out here in these streets, waiting to disappoint a sista." Laughing, I consider his request. "I'll try to speak to Trina for you. We bout to leave, though," I tell him, giving him another quick hug.

The three of them shake hands, and as we turn to walk away he says, "Cart, you just got yourself a whole lot to handle," D finally speaks.

Carter only laughs and wraps his hand around mine again, only tighter this time.

An hour passes between the time we leave The Spot and I finish telling him about my past and what I want for the future.

"I'm sure that we all have something in our past that we're not exactly proud of. I've slept with plenty of women in my life, and I'm not as nearly harsh on myself as you are," he replies when I call myself a whore.

It's different with women, though. The world views us different. Fucking as many women as you can in a male's world is seen as a big deal. An accomplishment to most. The more women you have, the higher your status. With women, it's the exact opposite. You're viewed as a whore by those same males who do the same exact thing.

"I'm telling you this 'cause I like you." I said that already, I know. But I'm nervous. And I repeat myself when I'm nervous. And obviously, I also overlook shit like demanding to know if we are going to be exclusive. I'm not even sure if I'm ready for exclusivity. I want it, though. I want him to want it enough to ask.

The room seems warm and small. Carter is sitting in front of me on my damn glass coffee table, and I don't even care.

"You seem like you have a lot within yourself that you need to work out...."

Hold up; those sound like let-down words to me. I laugh, shake my head, and shrug it off.

"It's cool if you wanna change yo—"

I stop speaking because he starts laughing.

"I'm not changing my mind, Alieas. I'm saying that I'll give you the time and space you need to do what you gotta do to fix whatever it is that ails you."

Hmmm. I get up. It still sounds like he's saying, 'I can't fuck with you like that,' to me. I begin pacing the room. I do that when I'm wound up, too.

"What the is that supposed to mean?" I ask, thinking that I'm more upset than I should be, considering my omission of Justin.

He stands up. "It means that whenever you're ready, I'll be waiting."

I suck my teeth, eyeing him. "So, you still wanna see me?"

Then he does it. He licks those fuckin' sexy lips and replies, "Yeeeahh."

Carter is close enough to me now to touch me. He takes advantage of the opportunity and grabs my hips with one hand and uses the other to tip my face up to his. He holds my chin as he says, "Listen, I'm not tryna put you off. I'm literally trying to put you on. But I'm gon' be dead straight. I don't think you ready for all the things you told me you want. After what I been through, I'm not trying to be mixed up in all that. But I think you have potential."

My lips form a sneer. How he gon' tell me what I'm ready for? I thought in my Sanaa Lathan voice when Omar was dumping that ass in the third quarter of, Love and Basketball.

"Cut it," he says with a motion of his hand to his neck. "Let's not get into that dramatic shit you be trying to pull." His eyes are daring me to dispute it. "I'm not saying that you don't want it. I'm simply saying that you don't sound as if you're ready for it now."

"How you figure?" I complain, getting a kick out of the fact that he's analyzing me.

"Simply because you are still trying to find yourself. You got it going on." He takes a step back and looks me up and down, nods in approval, and then adds, "Make no mistake about that. You're still young, though. You just said that you're not who you pretend to be. Why do you have to pretend if you know who are?"

I didn't respond, so he took that as I was thinking about it.

"I want to be your friend. I want to get to know you better and the people you love. And since sex has been a huge stumbling block for you in the past, we won't have to worry about it. Friends don't fuck—"

"Hold up," I interrupt. *No sex? No dick?* "What?!" Now this man wants to only be friends?

Carter frowned, creasing his forehead. "How 'bout you listen for a minute?" he demands.

Ohh, I nibble on my bottom lip and consider how that simple request shuts me up. His deep voice when making subtle demands has the power to make me submit to his desires. He could have me right here on my coffee table if he wanted to.

Face down, ass up.

He next says, "Sex is an illusion." The lusty fantasy I envisioned burst like a bubble, the wet droplets landing on my nose to bring me back to reality. "And it crowds all the important things in a relationship. Am I going to talk when we can fuck all the time? Probably not. I want something with you. And before you give yourself to me that way, I want you to know exactly what you're getting into," he explains.

See, this the shit. All his talk be scaring the shit out of me; got me thinking, 'Damn, what am I getting into?'

I don't know but I want to be in it, though.

Carter drops a quick kiss to my lips, moves away, and glances down at his watch. "I'ma gi before I change my mind. I'll call you when I get home. Think about what I said and let me know what's up."

It is clear that he's leaving everything up to me. And for the first time in a very long time, I don't know what the fuck to do. I want him but seriously, I don't know if I can handle him. Damn, there's never been a man in my life where I doubt my ability to reign. Plus, I'm still thinking about him telling me that I don't know myself. I feel a little ache in my heart because half of what he said is true. I've known this man on a personal level for a little over a month, and from one conversation that lasted a little over an hour, he knows that I am lost and confused. A borderline bullshitter ready to reform. But he saw that I was at least worth possibly wading in the deep end of the water for.

CHAPTER
seven

Alieas

I KNOW THAT I'M OPENING myself up for trouble and I can't help it. Justin called me and for the last couple of weeks, we've been talking on the telephone and going out. I'm so into Carter yet here I am with this man.

There's always that one thing about a guy that a girl can't just let get past her. That's the thing with Justin. He has that one thing. And if you ask me what it is, I wouldn't even be able to begin to explain. I know that sounds stupid as hell— young as hell—but trust that I am neither.

There's about to be some trouble in these waters, and I know I'm going to need a lifeboat. This man is educated, employed, doesn't mind spending money, is funny as hell, and child-free.

"Come on now, Lieas," he announces as he starts up his car, "you really don't want to know."

I'm laughing hard as hell. "You're a clown. Yes, I do."

Justin holds up his hands and shakes his head. "No, you don't."

"Yes, I do," I argue.

"The last time a chick asked me about another chick and I told her, she stopped messing with me. And I liked her. I learned my lesson."

"Oh, please. I ain't about to stop talkin' to you over no other girl."

"That's because you a pimp and you think I'on know."

"Justin, please. You're the pimp."

"Alright. I got a old head; she thirty-two with a couple kids, a good job, good credit, and fine as hell."

It always intrigues me to listen to men describe other women. "So, what's wrong with her?"

"Nothing really. I can't just call her up and say let's do this; she has responsibilities."

I understand that. My exact yet unspoken issue with Carter. "So, who else?"

"My young buck. Now, she a ryder. Don't ask too many questions, always got my back, cool as shit. No kids, but she live at home with her parents when she not away at school, and they're always in her business."

I could see from his expression that she was the girl that he was really into. "So, you really like her."

"She cool."

Just like a nigga. "How long y'all been talking?"

"Met her on New Year's Eve. You done?"

"I'm just tryna see where I fit in."

He chuckles. "Game and so much of it. I'm still waitin' for your man to roll up on us."

I adjust my seat so that it leans all the way back and put my feet up on the dashboard. "You know me better than that."

"You must have dude in check. Wouldn't happen over here." He gives me a long look and taps my calf so I would put my feet down. When I ignore him, Justin shakes his head and sighs. "Be real with me though; do I have a chance?"

Honesty is always the best policy. "There is somebody."

"Tell me about him."

"We been dating for two months. He has a three-year-old daughter, works real hard, is fine as hell, and is really into me. He also has an extremely intense personality; he knows what he wants and goes after it. I admire that in men."

"If he's all that what are you doin' out with me?"

I shrug. It was that one thing plus I wasn't 'bout to pass up an invitation to The Cheesecake Factory. "You wanted to take me out. And I like you."

"Two months? That's like a month before I met you. I could still get you."

It is the way he says it that has me eyeing him cautiously without him knowing it. "You're just tryna sleep with me."

He tilts his head and licks his lips then sighs. "You know I wanna hit that."

I chuckle. It has definitely crossed my mind. "Yes, I know. You ain't gettin' it, though."

"That's cool. 'Cause if I hit that, you gon' be looking for me. Like, Justin, why you'n wan come over? And all that... I'ma have to back you down if I break you off with this."

"I told you you're a clown."

"Nah, I'm playin'."

"No, you are not."

"You're right. So if you gon' be dating both of us, how you divvy up your time between us?"

"On the real, if I hadn't told you about Carter you would never know about him. You gotta make everybody feel like they're the only one."

"You cain't do that. Someone is gonna feel left out. You gon' enjoy one person's company more than you do the other. There is no equality when it comes to bein' in multiple relationships. I hate to think that if I'm gettin' in that that someone else is too."

I nod because I agree. "Everything does not boil down to sex. Plus, all men think that way. But you having sex with your old head and your young buck. Me, I'm not having sex with anyone."

"Ohh, come on. You ain't let boah hit?"

I shake my head. "We on a different vibe. I want what my parents have, and he seems like he wants to give it to me."

"Yo, you sound like boah your man and all. I'm really not tryna step on his toes. And you definitely can't get what your parents have with him if you out on a date with me."

Oh, God; he is right. "Justin, it is not that serious," I lie just a little.

"I'on want no nigga tryna wild out on me over they girl. And a nigga would definitely wild out over you."

"Now, who got game?"

There is a glint in his eyes when he says, "Just let me know when you don't wanna play no more."

CHAPTER
eight

CARTER

"I CAN'T BELIEVE YOU CAN'T skate," I tease Alieas. Leaning back to catch her eyes, I squint and add, "And how is it that you never been here? You sure you from North?" I playfully push her leg off of mine.

Carmen's Skating Rink used to be a staple in the community, and hearing her say she's never been here has me dumbfounded. All the churches in the neighborhood had parties here. People had selling parties and fundraisers galore here in my youth. I have plenty of great memories at the rink. My aunt throws a skate party every three months, so I bring Bug when I can. She straps on her Fisher Price 1-2-3s and tries her best to think she at a roller derby. Mira was extra excited when Alieas said she was coming. Over the last few months we've been dating, we've been on play dates with Alieas and her nephew, so Bug is familiar with her and enjoys Lieas' company.

Laughingly, Alieas holds a finger up in the air while

rolling her neck. "Don't let the color of the street signs fool you, son," she sassily replies in reference to the street sign colors that distinguish the county you live in. "And I didn't say, I can't skate. I said I haven't been skating in forever. Like, since I was ten maybe." Alieas shrugs and then makes a production out of putting her leg across my knees. "These heavy ass skates. I'm just gonna sit over here and watch you skate with Bug."

Running my hands over her calf, I squeeze. "Aww. You want me to get you a pair of the Fisher-Price jawns she has on?"

I follow her gaze over to where Bug is skating and stepping with Nesha and lil' Gray. "Aahhhh... no."

"You scared of busting your ass in front all these people?" I taunt, reaching out to tug on to a loose tendril of hair.

Lieas smiles and quickly nips my finger. "I ain't never scared," she asserts, shaking the hair of her side bang out of her eyes.

The wicked gleam in her eyes quickly turns me on. "You wish. And if my behind did fall on the floor, you gonna have to carry me up out this piece."

Damn if she doesn't just hit the nail on its head. I'd love to see her ass all bent in the air. And I'd throw her over my shoulder like a caveman and take her ass back to my cave. Tonight, it's beautifully clad in some rust pink-colored jeans. The tight Express t-shirt got her titties popping; they even look a little bit larger than I remember. My dick instantly comes awake and aware. And even though I want to think with that head, I think better of it and let out a long sigh of regret instead. "You ain't getting out of skating that easy. Now, come on."

Standing up, I pull Lieas with me. She wobbles and then places a steadying hand on my forearm. "If I fall—"

I lightly grip her elbow. "Trust me. I got you," I pledge and then add, "I promise" when she gives me an unsure glance.

Linking our fingers, I slowly skate backward toward the rink with Lieas taking precautionary strides.

We're still approaching the sexual aspect of our relationship in baby steps, much like the ones she is taking now. I figure the reason is as much for her as it is for me. There are things I want to explore with her that goes beyond the physical. The jury is still out on determining if she's ready emotionally.

It seems as if so many niggas have left their mark on her that she doesn't know how to be intimate without it involving the sex. Since I had suggested it, I gotta stand by it. With every passing day, I want to peel away the armor she's protecting her heart with. Demand that she let me in, so she can realize I'm not interested in being one of the dudes that require her to armor up.

"Ms. Thang scared to skate, baby?" my mom cheerfully cackles as she swirls on by us.

"I got her, Mom. She gonna learn today," I laugh back.

"Your mom gon' clown me too, though?" Lieas jokes as she nervously follows my lead onto the skate floor.

"Skating is like riding a bike." *Like riding dick.* "You can't forget. It'll come back to you." I catch her off guard by quickly pulling her close, tucking her along the side of me. "Right... left... right." She follows my guidance, laughing as she stumbles around the rink.

After two laps around the rink, Lieas is more comfortable, her strides confident. So confident that when I loosen my hold on her she doesn't scream but just skates on her own. Excited, she calls out for Nesha who is skating rings around the kids, making them giggle as they attempt to copy her moves.

My heart shifts when I see Bug reach out for her hand and swells even more when Lieas captures it. I laugh to myself when Lieas leads her closer to the edge of the rink so she can hold on to the wall for support.

My little sister, Autumn, slides up alongside of me. "Mommy said you was bringing a date. I figured I had to show up just to see this with my own eyes," she chats. Autumn circles me with quick footwork.

It's funny that my entire family finds dating life as 'major family news'. Even knowing that, I'm surprised that Autumn would spend her Friday night with us. "You here with somebody?"

She signals over to a group of people that include her two best friends and three other guys. "Riah, Maya, and some guys."

"How cute," I tease. "Y'all on a triple date."

"Of course. I go nowhere without my hittas. Where is your nut behind brother?"

Shrugging, I turn my attention to Alieas for a moment. "Dunno. Think he ducking Mommy 'cause he stuck her with them fish fry tickets."

Autumn shakes her head. "Vince be tripping. I'ma battle you when the electric slide come on. So, be ready," she challenges me.

"Sis, you and your girl squad ain't no match for me."

The DJ announces that's it time for couples skate. I wave Autumn off and find myself skating over to where Lieas is exiting the floor. "Hold up, princess." I capture her hand in mine as the first chords of Next's *Butta Love* fills the room.

"Check this out." I spin around her. *"You're like my homey... My shorty..."* Skating backward, I lead her into a competent and consistent rhythm. *"... And you're so special to me. We been kicking it for a while..."* Pulling her close, I'm intoxicated by her scent.

Face–to–face, I stare down at her, singing the words to "Butta Love". As I hold her back for support, we sway through a verse. Then I make a show of my sensual skate skills. Totally into it, Lieas chuckles and surprisingly does not lose pace.

Her smile, brilliant and beautiful, spreads as she points over to my parents. They are hugged up, slow-skating the rink.

"They're so cute," she coos.

In a quick motion, I maneuver our bodies so that we mimic theirs. "We're cute too," I let her know, whispering her ear. "Just trust me. I'll never hurt you."

The look she gives has my lips devouring her in two easy gulps. The heat consumes me as our tongues twist and duel for supremacy. There's a hint of frustration on my part because I wanted to do this all evening. So, I hold on to her as I take it depths deeper until we're both drowning. When we finally break apart, needing air, we eye one another. A knowing smile graces those luscious lips, and I take one more kiss. And as if on cue, I pick the song right back up at "…And I liiiiiike it aaalllll."

Alieas giggles as I serenade her. Our relationship is headed in the right direction. And that makes me happy.

Maybe love does still exist.

CHAPTER
nine

Alieas

NEEDLESS TO SAY, I'M IN over my head. I have been dating both Carter and Justin. I'm always wondering if it's possible to feel just as strongly for two different people. I would have always testified that it wasn't. I'm not saying that I'm in love with either one of them, but I feel for both of them. They couldn't be more opposite. And yet the differences in them are what attracts me to them. Carter is fiercely dedicated to his daughter, and I love that about him. But Justin doesn't have any kids and is free of the responsibility. Justin used to be a block hugger and to my distaste does think he can rap. His flow is tight. If your girl wasn't on lock, he could've rapped these panties off. Carter, on the other hand, is a straight-laced, working man and may have never hugged a block in his life. Carter represents the future that I want to have, and Justin represents the freedom I wish to hold onto.

When did the lines in my life get so crossed? Two months ago, I was focused. I knew what I wanted: a man... some goooood dick... marriage... maybe some babies. And them fuckin' dollars.

I know karma is a bitch, so I'm trying to stay balanced and by balanced I mean continuing to date them both without getting caught. This shit is trifling. Justin knows about Carter, but I haven't uttered one fuckin' sideways ass word to Carter about Justin.

The thought of having to fess up makes me sick. I know that he wouldn't go for it— at all.

I already know what I need to do.

"Yo, Lieas," Tyree calls out to me, and my head pops up from the book I'm reading. "Aunt Nic told me that you're dating two guys now," he adds as he sits on the arm of the recliner I'm relaxing in. I swear Tyree stays on some protective big brother shit when it comes to me and men.

"So?"

"You vicious. You know we all cool with Carter, right?"

"*We all*" meant his circle of friends with whom I share friendships with as well. "I am friends with your female friends."

"Ooookay. I thought you liked dude?" he asked.

"I do. Don't tell me that you're concerned with whether or not I'm dogging out your friend?"

"You too grown," he chides me. "So, who is the other dude?"

"Why? You'n know him." I roll my eyes. "He ain't from around here."

Tyree shakes his head. "When you bringing him over for dinner? We want to meet boah.". His dark eyes are serious. He plays no games when it comes to me, his sister, or his future wife and baby girl.

As if she knows that I was thinking of them, Bri comes over with their bright-eyed one-year-old perched on her hip. Smiling wide and showing those tiny white chiclets for teeth, Nia reaches her chubby arms my way.

I love her, and my heart melts with longing every time I am within ten feet of her.She reminds me of a black cherub, all chocolaty, covered in rolls. Her cap of black curls is always adorned with a flashy or flowered headband. She has the cutest lil' gold bracelet circling her wrist, and the sparkle of her diamond stud earnings matches the twinkle in her beautiful eyes.

I take her in my arms and nuzzle the side of her neck. The light fragrance of baby lotion and Dreft sink in. I hug and tickle her until she erupts into a bale of laughter.

Bri is eyeing me suspiciously. "Someone has the baby touch," she teases, nudging Tyree's shoulder.

"Moo ain't thinking about no babies. She out here running the streets," Tyree blurts out before I could object.

I narrow my eyes at his ass. "She's single," Bri butts in. She must have caught his meaning too. "She can do whatever she want."

Tyree rubs his chiseled jawline. "Cart got a kid. He a good dude. You can't be—"

I roll my eyes. "I can't what?" *Be a hoe? Be fucking them both?*

Tyree sighs and shakes his head. "I shouldn't have to say it. You should already know."

He's right but I'm not about to admit it to him. I look at Bri instead. "Get your man."

Bri is giving him the, 'Now, you know you should keep your mouth shut' look with a slight tilt of her head and narrowing of her eyes.

My dad must have heard him; he chimes in, "Leave that girl alone, boy. She's too young to be serious with either one of them." He and my mother are on different vibes when it comes to marriage, children, and having a family. My dad has been kind of distant since I decided not to go to grad school last year after graduation. A college degree and a real estate license aren't good enough for him. "She just got out of all that messy shit with Tony." His voice is dripping with disgust and disdain. I think some of the sparkle in my princess tiara dimmed in his eyes. Could be the knowledge of me burning Tony's shit or being accused of vandalizing his car that had him pissed.

"Darien, watch your mouth!" my mom exclaims with a disapproving grimace.

For the first time in my life, I witness my father's irritation with my mom's preoccupation of seeing me married off and settled down with kids. "Nicole, please stop filling the damn girl head up with fantasies of marital bliss. There's time for all that later!" he snaps out, his words harsh. Then he looks at me. "Moo, there is still time to register for spring semester."

My mom's hand flies her mouth quick and dramatic as if my father has slapped her or something.

"Oh shucks," Bri mouths, reaching out for Nia. Once she has the baby, she slips away.

Tyree watches silently, nodding his head in agreement with my dad.

"Daddy, we agreed I'd take a break for a year," I stubbornly remind him, even though that year was technically up in May.

"It has been a damn year. The longer you wait, the less likely you'll actually go back," he declares.

Now, my mom is mad, standing here giving my dad the wounded bird look. I throw my hand up at both of them and get up. I walk off in the direction Bri went with the baby.

"What?!" my mom yells.

"Nic, baby, you gotta stop this shit. You're gonna drive the girl crazy. And these young niggas out here cutting up ain't 'bout shit!"

I walk back to where my parents are now debating my

future and announce, "Mom, I'm not getting married no time soon, and Dad, I'll keep my end of the bargain and register for classes like I said I would. I did well on my GMAT, so I won't have to worry about retesting. Will that make you happy?"

"Don't act like you got no damn attitude wit' me, girl." My dad's tone is firm and unwavering. He looks me dead in my eyes. "Your word is your bond, baby. If you don't keep your word, no one will trust or respect you. In business or in your personal life," he adds. To even out his harshness, he kisses my cheek.

I suck my teeth but don't say anything in response. Your word is your bond. That's what he'd taught us. There is no refuting the truth. Though we try. People twist and turn it to bend it to their will. They wrap lies up in pretty lines with colorful language to disguise the truth. I was becoming good at that.

Annoyed, I stomp off to the kitchen. My dad is right. I've been putting it off long enough. I could've been halfway done with my master's by now. I needed a break, though. I wanted a taste of the real world. I had lived in Baltimore last year working at a realty management company there while finishing up my last couple of credits. Because I only had class on Tuesdays and Thursday I had also volunteered at a homeless and women against abuse shelter. I was trying to immerse myself in the culture and make a difference there after seeing the miniseries, The Corner on HBO. That wasn't enough freedom from school but that was enough of Baltimore.I had enough of D.C. at that point too so grad school got put in the back burner. Plus, Tony had lucked up big time by securing a full-time position at a tech firm, a hookup from one of his line brother's uncle back here in Philly. I was so insecure; I couldn't fathom letting him come home and me staying at Howard for another two years while he was here fucking any and everything.

Hell to the nawl. Not the brightest idea.

In retrospect, it was an idiotic and immature decision, considering that we're no longer a couple. Now, that the thought of freedom has me wide open, I want more. While I want to further my education, at this point I really don't see the need. I already have a solid career.

My dad wants the MBA to add to the company's credentials. We went back and forth about it. One of the stipulations for the "free" year was that I had to get my realtor's license and be willing to either go back to Howard or to Temple for my master's. My parents are helping to pay my rent because I wheedled my way out of living in one of their properties. And they're also paying my car note, so, maybe, I will chill on the rebelling shit and check out Temple's program.

I lean against the counter and I dial Carter's number. Even though my dad is right, I'm still annoyed. The line just rings, but I disconnect before his voicemail picks up.

I thought maybe we could hang out. Shoot the breeze. I should've taken him up on his offer for dinner with his family, and it is apparently a big deal with aunts, uncles, and all his siblings and some cousins. I was a lil' bit afraid. I'm not even sure why I enjoyed their company the last time I went. His older sister Savonn was extra about my intentions with her brother. I had laughed but big sister was serious. She was giving me the ice all that night. The guilt over also being with Justin ate at me for a moment and I was uncomfortable. The other sister Savannah is extra bubbly, very pregnant, and newly married to one of the cutest regular white guys I've ever seen. Me and his little sister Autumn had hit it off immediately and swapped numbers. She writes and goes to poetry slams and readings, too, and invited me to one she was hosting. Now, she has two best friends with her, and one best friend has a crush on Carter's brother Vince. The other friend is sending dove eyes at Cart. I give her the evil eye and am like, Nah, not him sis. That's me. I'm gon have to keep my eyes on that heffa.

I try him again but there's still no answer.

"You good?" Tyree questions from behind. He leans on the counter beside me with an apologetic glance my way. "I'm sorry," he apologizes.

I shrug my shoulders. "It's cool. I'm about to leave anyway," I tell him.

"Lieas, don't leave. You know Unc only concerned with your future. And Aunt Nic gon' always gon' be Aunt Nic."

"You the one who started it," I pout, poking my bottom lip out.

He holds up his hands. "Don't want no parts in that." Like the annoying older cousin, he tugs my braids. "But ain't nothing wrong with going back to school. If you don't wanna go back to DC, don't go. But you do need to do something 'cause Cpt. Stiles is on that ass," he declares with a laugh.

"Yea. How did you go through six years of school straight?"

Tyree sighs, putting both of his hands on top of his head. "When I got out of the Mills, your dad was like, you can be like Gray out here doing any and every illegal thing in the book or like my mom— dead before she even had a chance to live. Or I could be honest and do right. I could go to school, get a good job, or make a job. Walk the straight and narrow, you know? The street shit was dying. D and Dave were both getting accepted to colleges and shit. So, I was like fuck it; why not? Tommy was straight wildin'. It was a lot; writing essay after essay, getting recommendations after CCP to get transferred to Temple. After Tommy got killed, I knew that I was making the right decision. It was school and money moves for me 'cause it wasn't nothing else out here. And I'm sure if I was just some hood nigga, Bri would have neva talked to me."

My phone rings; hoping it was Carter, I hold up a finger to Tyree and answer.

"Hey, beautiful." The deep voice that greets me belongs to Justin. I can't lie; I'm a little disappointed that it's not Carter because seeing him would have made me feel better, but Justin will have to do.

"What you up to?"

"Nothing. I'm at my parents'. Sunday dinner. They gettin' on my nerves so, I'm 'bout to bounce."

"Think about what I said, bighead," Tyree jokes as he exits the kitchen, leaving me to chop it up with Justin.

"Who was that?"

"My cousin. Wassup? What are you doing on this good Sunday night?"

"I was hoping to kick it with you, Ma. You wanna catch a movie, go skating, bowling, my crib to chill?"

I glance down at my watch. It's only six; I have a couple hours to burn. I don't want to be around other people, though, so, his house is fine. Maybe a walk on the pier down Delaware Ave would be cool. The way I'm feeling, we'll be fucking if I go home with him.

"We can walk the pier and talk."

He laughs. "You want me to come scoop you?"

I know he tryna fuck just for the simple fact that I haven't let him hit yet. That bothers the ish out of him. He slick as shit and screwing him gon' cause the drama he claims that won't. And he ain't even tryna be in love with me.

Carter is, a nagging voice reminds me. *I do want love and have it love me back, right? Just don't go.* The sensible part of me warns.

"I drove but you can come get me if you want. My parents live in Cheltenham. Right off Old York Rd."

"You gon' let me meet your peeps?" he suggests.

I shrug my shoulders. My parents would be cool with it.

"Sure. Why not?" I give him the address and wait for him to come get me.

Within thirty minutes, I hear his music before he even calls to say he is outside. I peek out the window. "Aight, I'm out. Bri, I'll see you this week. Bye, bighead." I mug the back of Ty's head.

My mom jumps up, coming to where I am at the window. "You're leaving without eating dinner, Lieas?"

"You can at least tell the nigga to turn the music down, park, and come in," my dad advises, his eyes never leaving the football game. The Eagles were winning for a change.

"Tell him to come in and have dinner," she offers.

My cell phone rings and instead of answering, I open the front door and wave for him to come up.

"So, you gonna be the type of girl who run when they beep the horn and hit you on the cell phone? Huh?" The disdain drips from my dad's words like overflowing water.

I sometimes am that type of girl, which annoys me more. The disappointment is so clear in his eyes. He shakes his head. "Loud ass music. No respect," he adds, just as the music stops.

It is loud as hell; you could hear the bass dumping.

I shake my head. My dad is gonna be ramming, so I grab my jacket from the closest and punch my arms into the sleeves. Just as Justin walks up to the door, I step out into the late September air. His eyes widen in surprise as I grab his hand and pull him back in the direction of his car.

"I'll call you, Ma." I flag my hand towards my mom in a negligent wave.

"I guess meeting them is out," Justin surmises.

"Let's go," I order, the cool air caressing my cheeks.

He's eyeing me to see if he can read me. The heat of my annoyance burns him. There're always casualties in war. My sanity is currently one.

I slip into the leather passenger seat of his cranberry Nissan Maxima after Justin opens the door for me. He frowns. "Are you cool?"

"I'm fine," I respond. He goes around to get into the car and smiles at me. "What are you tryna get into?"

"You," he laughs with a nod. He turns the volume back up in the car stereo, and it picks up on the chorus of one of my favorite songs.

...from the center to state property.

Uh. Young Chris in full effect and all I need is one reason just to pull this burner cause y'all told me to go next and I'ma be goddamn if I'ma give my turn up.

Young Chris in full effect and all I need is one...

"Hot, right?" he smiles.

Yes. Philly rappers are on the map. Freeway, The Young Gunz, and State Property had all been signed to Roc-a-Fella records. Proud of them just because they're from my city, and they had skills. I was really hype, waiting for the Young Gunz to drop their upcoming album. The neo-soul movement was popping too. Musiq Soulchild and, not to mention, Jill Scott are all getting crazy airplay. But I wasn't trying to take no long walks with him.

"You rhyme, right? We can hit the studio and fuck around for an hour if you want?"

It was a great idea, but I wasn't in the mood for none of that. When I'm all revved up, my blood starts boiling; as embarrassed as I am to admit it, sex has the power to calm me down.

"Nawl, let's go to your place."

CARTER

SUNDAYS ARE FOR FAMILY. GROWING UP, WE WOULD ALTERNATE between my grandma's, my aunts', and my parents' crib, or a restaurant. So, Sundays pretty much mean church, family, food, and football since I was a kid. I generally swoop in somewhere after church but before the food. They're grilling in the backyard, taking advantage of the last days of nice weather. And today for some reason, every one of my siblings manages to make it, along with two of my aunts and one of my uncles on my dad's side. My family is huge and is always in each other's pockets and business.

Vincent even brought a date with him. I think it is to make Mariah jealous. Autumn is still pissed that he's acting shitty to her best friend. This is the reason friends and family don't always mix.

Poor little Riah, I thought. Can't figure his angle, though. He has been halfway in love with her since she was like sixteen. Whatever it is, I hope it gets worked out. Sometimes, Vince could be such an asshole.

The sun starts to go down, making its descent into the distant sky. The moon would be full and massive. Amazed by the beauty of nature, I watch mesmerized. My mom turns the stereo on and the smooth grooves of old-school R&B filled the yard.

From my spot in the doorway, I watch my brother-in-law Jackson pull my very pregnant sister Vanna up for a dance. She giggles as she swirls to the sounds of Keith Sweat's *Make It Last Forever*. He is singing and joking with her. Ole' boy got pipes and rhythm.

I love seeing her happy. Family means everything to me. And before I met Alieas, I wouldn't have even been all extra sentimental, but seeing my sister and her husband so in love stirs something inside and makes me immediately think of her.

I turn at the sound behind me and am surprised by

Autumn's other best friend, Amaya. I let her by and I don't think much her nudging my shoulder with a secretive smile.

It's only when she turns back and looks up at me. She tilts her oval face to the side and grins. "Are you still seeing the girl you brought to the skating rink?"

Cautiously, I stare at her. "Why? Wassup?"

She shakes her bangs out if her eyes and starts, "Well," leaning closer to me so she could whisper, "I thought since you were dating again, maybe we could go out?" she offers.

I guess I missed whatever signs had come before this. "Umm," I chuckle, unsettled. I glance down at her and have to remind myself that I watched her grow up. "Lil' Maya, Vonn and Vanna used to babysit you. How would I look going out with my *baby* sister's best friend?"

Her chocolate eyes roll as she quietly sucks her brace-covered teeth. "I'm a grown woman, Carter," Maya confidently asserts with a sultry smile.

Admittedly, her body has developed in a way an older brother figure shouldn't notice. She's Onyx-stripper built, but the bubblegum pink of the rubber bands on her braces shouted *BABY*, not to mention, the girl is damn near family. I'm content with Lieas and don't need anything or anyone extra. Sparing her feelings, I simply reply, "Yeah, I am."

Maya shrugs her slender shoulders. "Well, let me know when that's over. I've been crushing a long time," she confesses and walks off. Completely thrown off, I just stare after her. She is thinner than I like my women, but she does have a fat ass. Guilt has me looking around the yard to see if anyone witnessed our exchange. I catch Vince's eye, and his dumbass is giving me the thumbs-up and a cheesy-ass grin.

Shaking my head, I laugh.

"Don't be tryna put your voodoo dick on my friends,"

Autumn warns me from behind and mugs the back of my head as she walks by.

I stare down into my cup to rid myself of the memory of Maya's bubble walking away in her Apple Bottom capri pants. "Hey, she came at me." Holding up my hands in surrender, I tell her to relax and that I'm not interested. Rubbing the back of my neck, I lightheartedly admit, "Lil' Maya grew up, though." I quickly sip some of my mom's homemade lemon iced tea.

Autumn playfully slaps my arm and shrugs. "She swears it's open season. In her defense, she has had a crush on you since we were twelve."

All of this is news to me. Then she dramatically grips my forearm. "Please don't fuck my friend."

I almost choke as I spit out some of the iced tea. "Wrong brother. You should have warned Vince not to mess with Mariah. What's up with that?"

We both glance over to where Mariah is standing. She is giving Vince the death stare, alternating with sad doe eyes.

"I don't know. Your diva ass brother is too needy. So… yea. It's a damn mess," she spills the details.

"Where is 'new girl'?" my oldest sister Vonn asks as she comes over to us. My sisters are like the police.

"Her name is Alieas, and she kicking it with her family tonight," I explain.

"Oooh. I thought I was going to get to see your eyes sparkle as you moon all over her." She lights up like a tree and grins widely.

"Whatever, girl."They all extra hype that I'm dating again.

"So, I saw Malika the other day, and she said that Toya is pregnant again and that she supposedly moving back up here. That bitch try to contact you?"

Before I can even respond, Autumn frowns and butts in, "Don't talk about that trifling hoe."

I shake my head. "Nawl. She don't have my number. And I ain't interested in anything she has to say."

"I just wanted you to know that she might pop up. I still owe that bitch a ass-whoopin'. So, just know that if we ever cross paths, I'm kicking her ass."

Agitated, I shrug. I need room to move. "Vonn, I don't give a fuck about that girl."

My mood all messed up. My eyes roam the yard ,searching for Mira. I spot her tucked under my mom's arm, sitting on her lap. She spots me and my heart melts.

Determined to get to me, she wiggles out of my mom's grasp and comes barreling towards me. I am amazed. My heart, in human form, is gunning in my direction. "Daddy!" she giggles on unsteady legs as she covers the distance between us. "Daddy!" she gushes again as she gets closer.

Autumn and Vonn both clap and cheer her on. "Come on, Mira. Come get him."

I step off the porch just in time catch her as she lunges into my arms. "Hey, Bug. What were you doing?"

"Sitting with Granma." She points to where my mom is sitting with a couple of my aunts and uncle. "An' Pop-Pop."

"Let her show up," Autumn grits out. "It's the fuck on," she finishes, punching her one hand into the other fist.

"Oooooh!" Mira places her hand over her mouth, knowing her auntie just said a bad word.

Autumn diffuses the situation and starts kissing all over her face, making noise and tickles her out of my arms. She dances away with her, "bad word" now forgotten.

Vonn softens up and hugs me. "Watch out for her, bro."

Of course, I will. I will protect and lay down my life to keep my child safe, even from her own mother.

The hug is not successful, though, at comforting any of my shattered nerves. My mind is racing as I run about ten different scenarios through my brain. None of them ended with Latoya being happy.

"Fuck outta here," I murmur absentmindedly into the breeze, wishing I had a cigarette. It was a bad habit I'd quit when Mira was born.

I need something to calm my nerves. I pick grab my phone to call Alieas and I see that I missed two of her calls. I dial her number but there's no answer. I text and wait a while and still no response.

I guess I'll eat some cake and go sit with my parents who are surely reminiscing about the "good old days".

CHAPTER

ten

Alicia

C ARTER CALLED AGAIN LAST NIGHT for the third time as I was climbing into bed. I ended up turning my phone off so I could get my story straight.

I had to get my mind right. I debated answering and just telling him the truth. Hadn't I spent my entire life spouting, '*Honesty is the best policy*'?

Fuck that; if I tell him that I'm involved with another man to the extent that it has me ignoring his calls, he'll fall back. Fall off the face of the earth, and I won't be able to find his ass with a flashlight in the daytime.

I want him. I enjoy his and Mira's company, but sometimes, I'm emotional and impulsive. And just plain stupid. I do impulsive shit all the time like shopping and spending money I don't have. Eating shit that's not on my meal plan or conducive to my new healthy lifestyle. Or Being intimate with one person while I'm trying to build something with another person.

Shit. I need a list of pros and cons for each man. What the

hell am I even talking about? Justin's ass is Disney World. While amazing and fun, Disney is a vacation. You ride the rides and see a few attractions then you take that ass home. It is a fucking visit; it's impossible to fuckin' bring Magic Kingdom to Philly. Carter is the house in the gated community; home. The place you want to be at the end of every day. The place when you get tired of the vacation and you want to lie in your own bed.

Yes, bitch; home.

I had to stop playing young girl games if I want a home. If I want him to be my home. And honestly, he is both. I love his mind. He makes my juices flow. The timbre of his voice leaves me entranced, and I love it. His voice is like the tips of his fingers trailing slowly over my skin, making goosebumps appear and the tiny hairs stand on end. I can't wait to hear it while he's inside me. I'm ready now, so I'm just not sure why he hasn't attempted to get all up in me yet.

It has been months, so maybe something is wrong. I don't know anyone who has ever waited this long to have sex with me. Just 'cause I'm a hot ass doesn't mean that he's supposed to be too. And just because he isn't trying to jump my bones don't mean shit.

We flirt with each other constantly, but still, nothing has happened. He hasn't even peeked at the pussy. I haven't had a glimpse of the dick, other than the sweatpants dickprint. And yes, he is packing!

Wait; he can't possibly be home if the dick is whack. And at this point, I have absolutely no idea if its whack or not. I highly doubt it, but what if it is?

There's only one way to find out.

The thought of him fucking me thoroughly as he has done in my dreams has me biting my bottom lip. Appreciatively, I hum aloud.

"Dick must be good," Nesha jokes.

The comment stops me midstride on the elliptical. Forgetting I'm at the gym, I open my eyes to see her grinning over at me. I should be working these stank ass pounds off instead of worrying about anything. This last twenty is trying me.

"Wait… What?"

"You moaned. Out loud. And your eyes were closed," she supplies easily, "And… I am working out here," I disagree.

Nesha laughs as she swishes quickly on the elliptical. I want to tell her to increase the resistance, but I don't get a chance to before she continues, "Sounds more like you getting worked out."

"I wish,".

Her mouth opens and she raises her eyebrows at me in question. "You mean you haven't done it yet with either one of them?!" she exclaimed with a look of utter disbelief on her face.

I frown slightly; I should be offended; she says it like I just give it up all the time. But then again, based on my past experiences, she should have reasonable doubt. I'm not offended, though.

"Nothing with Carter. I let Justin eat me out, though."

"But you like Carter more, though, right?"

I halfway love Carter. "Yea. I'm fucking up. And I don't need you to go all lovey-dovey on me or be extra virtuous or preachy."

"Me?" she inquires with a dramatic hand to her chest.

"Yes, you, heffa." She always has that way of voicing exactly what she's thinking, regardless of whether or not you want to hear it.

"I wasn't going to say nuffin'. So, what's wrong with him?"

"Nothing is wrong with him," I defend, wiping my sweaty face with my hand towel.

"You like him but you haven't had sex?" I'm sure this has to be a crime in her book. "But you let the other boah taste it? You trapping backwards. I've listened to you go on and on about wanting marriage and babies, best friend. But I've also seen you do things that suggest otherwise."

Here she goes. I knew there was going to be a well-intentioned speech lined up somewhere. I tilt my head as I wait for her to deliver it.

"I'm just saying that you should see where it goes with Carter if you want Carter. Now, if you want Justin, you should see where that goes. The only place you will end up seeing where it goes with both is trouble."

"It's not that serious," I lie. I don't feel like hearing shit I already know.

"Riiight," she laughs.

"I'm saying Justin is fun. I don't know if you would under-stand. He's free and can just pick up and go. Whenever he wants," I shrug. "And as far as Carter goes, he has Mira and on top of that, we're both looking for something special, and sex would probably mess it up." Then I get cocky and add, "If I give him some ass, I may never be able to get rid of him." It is hardly like I want to. And it probably the other way around.

Nesha laughs. "I forget that your shit is good like that," she jokes, out of breath.

"It is. You remember when I used to mess with Kevin. Before we started having sex, he used to try and play the shit out of me. As soon as I started giving him the good— good, I couldn't get rid of his ass," I laugh. It was the truth. Is still the truth; I still can't get rid of him. I drink some water from my water bottle to prevent from choking.

"You crazy as shit. I guess that's why Tony won't leave your ass alone too then, huh?"

What can I say? I gave him time to think about his stupid actions and now, he can't get me off his mind.

"He still think he can get me back if he wants to. I saw him yesterday and he was all like, 'Hmmm, Lieas, you look good. And I was wondering if I could stop by your place to see you'. The nigga will not take no for an answer."

"Must be all that good— good."

"It is." And I think that it's past time that I share it with Carter. "Nesh, I don't want to mess it up with Carter. I think he's what I've been looking for. You've seen him with Amira and—"

"It's only been like a month."

"Three and a half months," I correct. When I'm dreamy about relationships, they all want to dismiss it like it's nothing. I can't win. "It's not that serious. He's a loving father and a patient and caring friend. But I like Justin too. Hence the dilemma."

Nesha clucks her tongue. "Look, we're getting too old for games. It's like I said. Decide what you want to do and stop messing around. Nobody wants to be toyed with, left in the shadows, tucked to the side, or any of that shit," she adds as her machine beeped its completion.

I can tell that she's annoyed but she smiles at me despite it. As her skinny ass comes to a complete halt, she takes a sip of her bottled water and hops the hell off, happily. That's skinny girl shit for you. I have ten more minutes left, and you can bet that I won't be jumping my ass anywhere when I'm done. I still have a half hour to do on the treadmill when I'm done here.

HOURS LATER, I GIVE IN AND CALL CARTER BACK. I'M PREPARED for him to be distant and a little standoffish. When he answers, his voice is dry. None of the emotion that I've become accustomed to can be felt. I could be reading way into things because I'm riddled with guilt.

"Wassup, Lieas?"

"Nothing. What are you doing?"

"Finishing up some paperwork. I called you last night," he grumbles then adds, "four times on your cell phone and once our your house phone. And I texted you."

I can imagine the scowl plastered all over his face. And it's there because of me.

Fuck… Fuck… shit… Fuck.

Biting down on my lip, I start lying. "I know. I was at my parents and I missed your call. I was kind of annoyed with them, so I didn't feel like talking. I went home and just went to bed." This is my damn problem. Ain't no way I'm saying I ignored your calls because I was coming all over my other dude's face.

There was a heavy sigh on the other end. "The last time I called, it went straight to voicemail. Look, I don't know what you're used to doing in a relationship, but I want to let you know that I'm not that dude. I'm not going for it."

Damn. "I'm sorry, Carter."

"Nawl. Don't apologize; be real. Be upfront and always honest. If we gonna have anything, you're gon' need to get your communication skills together."

His voice, though rough, is somehow tinged with sincerity. The guilt spreads; I can feel it seeping in. I feel like a ten-year-old being admonished by my father.

Blended with the sincerity, I tell him I detect some type of condescendence in his tone to balance my rising irrational need to check him.

And, yeah, that won't do. No matter how accurate his assessment is, I'm not the take it lying down type. "I apologize for the miscommunication. I was pissed at my parents, so I turned my phone off."

"I figured you were out with one of your niggas. I thought I was going to be cool with that, but I'm not. So if you still wanna kick it with otha dudes, let me know. I'm trying to be here, with you, so I need you to be here too."

CHAPTER
eleven

Alicas

"Then I stood
… and laid me down
To sleep…
After loving you…"

I FINISH NIKKI'S WORDS WITH emphasis on the words 'loving you' as I zero in on Carter. The small club is filled to capacity with people of all shapes, sizes, colors, and backgrounds, all joined together for their love of words.

The dim lighting almost illuminates this stingy little stage I'm standing on. My nerves tingle, and my blood spikes at the thrill of the applause. But beyond the glow of the lights and the cheers, my eyes are locked onto Carter's.Across the distance of our heated stare, I feel him pulling at me. Not physically but mentally, telepathically calling my name. His gaze, both laughing and sinister, intrigues me. Admittedly, I'm getting inebriated off of the sheer intensity of his presence as I drink him up with my eyes.

Those sexy lips part into a huge smile as he claps proudly, his eyes never leaving mine. For a brief moment, the entire club is silent. On mute. And I only see him. I can feel him as easily as if his hands were actually on me.

My heart beats excitedly as my feelings for him starts to spread through me. And it is in that moment that I realize that I love him. There are no illusions, no embellishments; there's just love. Automatically, I press my hand to my chest to make sure my heart is still there. Its beat, strong as ever, convinces me that it is.

The smile slips from my lips as I contemplate what it all means. What it means to love him. More importantly, I'm trying to figure out if he loves me. I'm so distracted and caught up in my feelings that I don't hear the host all but dismiss me from the stage.

I don't hear him but I burst into confused laughter as Carter steps forward, reaches over, and grabs me from the stage, pulling me close so that our bodies touch.

Cautiously leaning back, Carter searches my face. "You cool?"

Unable to form any words, I nod stupidly until I can, and then I say, "I'm great."

I'm in love. Does he feel the earth move beneath his feet too?

Carter shifts so that we are an arm's length apart. He cautiously studies my face. "You sure?"

Shaking off the fog that's clouded my brain, I assure him. "Of course." My smile widens just in case he requires more than my words. "Did you like it?"

Sheepishly, Carter nods. "That was dope, ma. You wrote that?"

My face twists up a little. "Ahh, no. All the credit goes to Nikki Giovanni," I school him.

Processing my words, Carter scratches his goatee. "I thought poets had to write their own material at these jawns." Carter links our hands and tugs me toward the back of the club. He easily creates a path for us to walk, and we find a small uninhabited roundtable. He kisses our joined hands. "I thought you were inspired," he confesses huskily against my ear as I take my seat. My mouth waters at his implication.

"You want something to drink?" he offers, looking back toward the bar.

Fanning myself, I realize how thirsty I am. And not just for no damn drinks. How hot it is in this tiny place with all these glaring spotlights everywhere. With his eyes everywhere. All over me. "Just some water. Thank you."

Carter presses a soft kiss to my lips. "Be right back," he promises when our lips part.

I blow out a long breath watching him walk over to the bar. Absently, I place my hand over my heart to steady it.

Damn, I'm in love, I think to myself. *With Carter.*

Well, that is the plan, right?

Absolutely! I was getting in my own way messing around with Justin. Only took a week or so after Carter let me know that he wasn't going for my having casual male friends, and it was over.

I broke it off. No hard feelings. The fact that one of his girls found out made it easier. I'm over the entire situation. Now that hoe playing on my phone and shit.

Definite no… no… Justin is texting and claiming that they aren't exclusive so he don't understand why she tripping. I'm not for none of that back and forth with chicks.

So, it is what it is. Making a sound decision like that cleared the path for me to focus my attention solely on Carter, and I'm glad that I did because now, I'm in love with a good man.

Not that it matters, but I can't pinpoint the when. It could've been since the first time he kissed me. Or sometime between one of our early morning— midday or evening phone calls. I love them.Have grown accustomed to hearing his voice multiple times throughout the day. I'm an irritable baby if we don't get a chance to talk. The flowers and random text messages just to let me know he's thinking of me goes a long way.

Being in love feels refreshing. Not how I felt with Tony. Everything there felt— forced. It was like me begging for Tony to make me a part of his life. Like, *I'on have no invite, but I'm showing up anyway.* And I didn't mind just showing up. Turning shit out. But I always ended up leaving alone.

Loving Carter is like having a special invitation to an exclusive party and always winning the door prize.

Shit, maybe I'm close to needing him.

I guess you really don't know until you do, I surmise. We're still abiding by some unspoken rule that I'm not ready for intimacy. He jokingly mentioned *dickmatizing me,* and that he didn't know if he was ready for that. Or if I was ready for that.

Ready my ass. I'm in love. I could click my heels together and dance a jig. Instead, I'm going to make my next move.

CHAPTER
twelve

Alieas

I WOULD SAY THAT TODAY was such a drain, but I can't. Not when I'm completely filled to the brim with contentment. Nothing that happened today seems to matter at this moment. The contractor at my very first rehab was testing me. I've known Eric since we were children and he was seriously giving me grief over the last few details.

Wasn't in the mood. Justin's ryder still blowing up my text messages since last month. I'm like, *Chill bitch. We ain't even fuck. And you right; he your man. As far as I'm concerned, you can have him, sis. I choose Carter.* I love him and I'll be damned if I let some dumb shit happens and ruin it.

Carter never asked me again about any of the other guys. He was like I'm not doing it. I heard him loud and clear and cleaned up my act. I texted Justin for him to tell his jawn to chill. He called back and I ignored him.

Right now, all I muster up enough strength to care about is the man who is sitting beside me.

My cell phone vibrates in my back pocket. I pull it out to see

Justin's name flash across it. I decline the call quickly and just in time before Carter takes it out of my hand. Quickly, I sit up and laugh as I make a grab for it out of his hands.

Carter presses his hand to my chest and pushes me back. Then he tosses my phone on the recliner next to our chair. I could shit in my pants right now, but he doesn't even look at it. Instead, he leans down and murmurs against my lips, "Nawl, not on my time."

I giggle, but my heart is beating hella fast in my chest. Even though I didn't do anything wrong, I still feel guilty as shit. I've been ignoring all of Justin's calls since his lil' girlfriend called me trying to check me about what her man doing with me.

I half expected him to be all over me tonight, trying to get some, but he is romantic and holding back his desire as usual. Well, I'm going to fix that. Carter doesn't know it yet, but I'm not leaving here tonight until I know what it feels like to have him inside me.

Momentarily, my thoughts are consumed with a seduction plan that will make this man drop to his knees with need for me and only me.

Now that the decision has been made, all I have to figure out is how I'm going to make my move. Since all of today's worries are behind us and Amira is sleeping, Carter and I are quietly wildin' out like a bunch of teenagers at Bobby Dances. Bubba Sparxxx's *"Ugly"* is bumping out of the huge stereo speakers, loud enough to have fun but not loud enough to wake up Mira. She's upstairs in her bedroom and we drew the doors to the living room closed so the music wouldn't travel throughout the house.

"Oh, oh, look!" I speak excitedly as I break away from him.

"What?" he asks with a surprised smile. I started doing the heel-toe, a dance that is about a hundred years old. It took me forever to learn how to do it, but I finally got it down pat.

My willingness to share it with Carter seems corny but..."I just learned how to do it," I confide as I demonstrate the moves.

"You hype," he observes.

I stop, look over my shoulder at him, and tell him to shut up. "You just mad 'cause you can't do it."

Carter grins foolishly and jumps up off the sofa to prove me wrong. To my amazement, he does the heel-toe, plus all the extra steps that had been added to it over time.

"So what?" I tease with my hips cocked.

Carter chuckles and without warning, grabs me by the waist. "Now, it looks like you're mad," he taunts while holding my hips in his strong hands.

Yeah, he's going to get it tonight. The feeling of his enormously erect dick pressed into my back is all the proof I need to deduce that he is just as aroused by me as I am by him.

"Dance with me," he whispers in my ear.

Considering that R Kelly's *"Feelin' on Your Booty"* is coming on, I suspect that feelin' on my booty is what he wants to do. I'm down for that, and his ass is in for a treat 'cause I'm a straight up hoe on the dance floor. Once in college, I made a guy bust just by bambin' my ass on his dick at a party while dancing to "Back That Ass Up". Shit… and back it up I did.

Carter holds me as I began to sway my hips slowly to the music. I close my eyes and let my head rest on his shoulder as he wraps his arms around my waist and sways with me. After a minute, he bends his head to my ear and whispers huskily, "Yo, if you get any smaller, I ain't gon' have nothing to hold on to."

I crack a huge cheesy smile. I've lost forty-nine pounds since the day I met him and knowing me as well as he does, Carter feeds my ego. "I still look good, though, and you know you like it."

"Ain't that the truth," he agrees, rubbing his calloused fingers over my belly under my shirt. I get lost in the sensation as we continue to sway to Kells. The song fades and then my current favorite dance song comes on. I go straight freak on his ass to the thumping beats of *"Oochie Wally"*.

I started grinding my ass in his crotch, bending over, swatting down, and just plain ole pushing the ass on him. It doesn't take him long to join me in the mutual dance floor fuck. Most guys dance the same exact way, so the girl usually does all the work.

By the time the song is over, I am tired as hell, and Carter is pulling me by the belt loops in front of him as he takes a seat on one of the bar stools. I smirk and turn to face him. I don't lead on that I'm, but come on now; I'm still a big girl. "I'm not gonna give you a lap dance," I inform him. The whole time I'm eyeing his fat dick beneath the fabric of his jeans and thinking that I really wouldn't mind dancing on his lap just as long as I'm dancing on that dick. "Unless you're willing to pay me for my services," I offer.

Carter grins from ear-to-ear and counters with an offer of his own. The wicked gleam in his eyes vanishes and is now replaced by the romantic haze that I'm accustomed to. Carter pulls me closer to him, wrap his arms around my waist, and buries his face in the hollow of my neck before saying, "Tell me something I can give you that you've never received from the legion of men you had. Or something that you've always wanted to do but haven't done yet."

Damn, more sweet shit. He's turning my heart inside out.

This is my opportunity to finally get what I've been obsessed with since Nesh mentioned it last month. Carter is offering me the dick and doesn't even realize it. But I understand, that in his heart, he is offering me something much more. He is offering the chance to make me happy. I know that there are no more doubts.

Tonight, I'm going to make love to the man I love.

Love... Love...

As if on cue, Mya's voice sings out, and I blend my vocals with hers.

Take the stars out of the sky for you

There's nothing in this world that I wouldn't do

If I could be your giiirl... If I could be your giiirl

"*Zagga zow. Zagga zow zow,*" he croons the way Beenie Man does, lowering his mouth a breath away from mine before he kisses me, lips meshing starting the slow burn.

I chuckle, twining my arms around his neck. I quietly but clearly state, "I want to wake up in your arms tomorrow morning after having made love to you all night."

I hold my breath as he positions me so he could look into my eyes. He's too quiet, though, which makes me nervous. So, I continue, "I know we talked about waitin' until we were ready, but I'm tired of waitin'. I want your ass now."

Carter laughs at my confession-turned-demand and at the way my eyebrows crease over my eyes. Quietly, without a word, he smoothes the creases away with his fingertips. My heart flutters with girlish joy and almost stops when they begin caressing my lips. My prayers are finally being answered. It seems crazy that I just realize that I'm completely in love with him. With this man; this beautiful, perfect man. Silently, I send up a prayer of thanks.

When Carter begins to kiss me, all my heavenly thoughts cease. Gently, his soft lips play with mine as his fingers massage the small of my back. Hungrily, I take the kiss deeper. I run my fingers through his unbraided but freshly greased hair, making sure to hold him close to me as I attack his mouth. We kiss for what feels like an eternity as the CD changes, something that goes unnoticed as I lose all my senses when he takes over the reins.

"You sure?" he finally questions, against my lips, between breaths.

Carter is so sincere I want to laugh, but instead, I lift my head up, take his face between my hands, place a small peck on his lips, let go of my heart, and nod, almost too emotional to speak.

"You act like this is my first time," I tease, looking directly into those baby brown eyes.

Carter chuckles softly and replies with a small kiss. "It is—with me." "Our first time together is going to be just as memorable as either of our first times," he promises, taking my hand in his.

Already, I know what he's saying is true. I've never felt this way about anyone before. I had lost my virginity at fourteen, and trust me, there had been nothing special about thinking, "What the fuck am I doing?" running through your mind when your hymen is being pierced by some inexperienced minute-boy.

Carter doesn't speak when he links his fingers through mine but stands up and begins walking towards the stairs with me in tow. There are no words coming from my mouth now, only the heavy breathing escaping my lungs as I follow him up the stairs. They seem endless as we make the climb, my nerves rattling with each step.

It never makes a difference how many times I enter his room; the sight of the massive sleigh bed still astonishes me. He told me that his mattress had to be specially made. There's enough room for about four people to sleep in it comfortably and they would never even touch. The rest of the room boasts the same "bigness". From the entertainment system to the television to the black art pictures that decorate his walls. When I first saw it, I linked it to his ego, which is just as big as mine.

"You still think you ready for me?" he inquires with a sleek grin.

I lick my lips as my hands reach the hem of his shirt. "You think you ready for me?" I return, inching his shirt up toward his stomach.

"It's been months, Alieas," he complains after I get the shirt off.

In my mind, it has been forever. I suck my teeth. "You're the one who suggested we wait, remember?"

"Well, the waiting ends here."

Blood spikes through my veins. I've anticipated this moment since the night he suggested that friends don't fuck. The friendship is over then because I'm making this man my property. Excitement tingles up my spine because I'm ready for him to knock the bottom out. Carter has been celibate longer than I have. Yet he still actin' like the wait doesn't matter. It is taking him an eternity to get my shirt off. I shouldn't get so wrapped up in the expectancy of the act but rather be content with the beauty of this momentous occasion. I'm trying to savor the moment, but the realization that in a few minutes, this perfect man is going to be inside me is body shattering.

"I want you," I declare, touching my lips to his. "I need you." That comes out a little breathlessly as my fingers go to work on his belt and jeans. Carter put his hands over mine to still them. Then he backs away. He goes over to the black leather chaise and takes a seat. He licks his lips and smiles at me before he begins to unlace his Timbs.

Carter kicks the boots off but stays where he is. "Come 'ere," he orders lightly. I slink over sexily to stand in front of him. He grasps me from the waist, those magnificent working man's hands possessively digging into my flesh. Breathless, I stand as he pulls me closer. He lets his head rest on my stomach and then starts to kiss a short trail from one end to the other and flicks his tongue in my navel. My fingers roam aimlessly over his head before I tilt his head back to stare at him.

Now that he's looking up at me, I'm fixated. No, enraptured would be a better word to describe the desired effect his baby browns have on me. Carter's gaze is so penetrating that I feel exposed to him in a way I've never be with any other man. The look we share is so intimate and for one second, I think he is going to tell me he loves me. I don't know why he hasn't said it yet, but he needs to get with it.

I'm in love, so his ass better be in love.

Carter breaks our connection and reaches around my back until his fingers are able to complete their magic on my bra snaps. I close my eyes as he stands and gently pushes the straps off my shoulders. When my arms are free, Carter bends his head to the hollow of my neck, where he kisses me and slowly descends to my erect chocolate nipple. I want to let my head roll back when his calloused fingertips caress the other breast instead. I dig my fingers into his wild mass of hair to hold him still as if he were my child. His other hand holds my back as he feasts to both of our delights.

Minutes pass before he pulls me down beside him. He kisses me until my back becomes trapped between him and the arm of the chaise.Carter takes his time kissing a straight line from my swollen lips to the top button of my jeans. He unfastens them, and unhook the latch on my chain belt, which falls to the floor with a clinking thud. Carter covers my wanting body with his as I opened my legs to willingly accept him.

His kisses grow hungrier and more forceful now, devouring me like his favorite meal, and I arch up to meet him. My hands caress his strong shoulders and the taut muscles of his back where they traveled into his jeans and find his boxers to grab those ass cheeks that are like stone. I move my hips against him in invitation. In a minute, he's going to have me begging. He already knows how badly I want him.

Shit, "I need you, Carter. Oh, God," I plead as I hook one of my legs around his hips.

He chuckles then looks me directly in my eyes. "You love me?"

Whatever happened to just saying how you felt? I wasn't going to answer him, but then he kissed the breath out of me. "Yes," I huff. "You?" I tease with a roll of my hips.

"Oh, yeah," he finally admits. His body moves away from me but his hands never leave my body. They travel down my legs as he starts to peel my jeans from my body. To assist him, I lift my hips and raise my knees to help him get them off. "Say it then," I demand when the jeans are thrown on the floor.

I want the damn words. I want to hear him tell me he loves me and know without a shadow of a doubt that what he says is real. I want my heart to skip a beat as it trips over his words. I want his love and I want him to give it to me.

"In a minute," he responds, spreading my now closed thighs. "You got something that belongs to me," he purrs seductively, dropping light kisses on the inside of one thigh. I move my hips involuntarily. My pussy knows what that means, and she is so ready for it that she's sending out an open invitation. Carter positions himself so that he can remove my panties and just fall face-first all up in it.

My eyes begin to roll in the back of my head when the calloused pad of his finger touches my wet clit. I just know that I'm going to die. A man hasn't had his face down there since the night I let Justin taste my goods.

No thinking about other men.

I push at the unwelcome thoughts of sharing myself with other men while I giving myself to Carter. I haven't busted a nut since that night. I promised myself that I wouldn't come again until I had his dick in me. I haven't even given in and masturbated. All I want is him.

"You taste good," he mumbles as he ran his tongue up and down my slit, tonguing my silken folds. I attempt to close my legs, but he holds them firmly apart with both hands. My juices are flowing like ocean currents. The suckling noise is erotic music to my ears. I want to beg him to never stop as he spanks my clit with his thick ass tongue.

"Ahh, Awww. Yes… yeeeeesssss," I moan, unable to say much more after his whole mouth begins to manipulate my temple. I start clenching my fingers into a fist for lack of anything else to do with them. If I put them in his hair I'm going ride his face like a mechanical bull. And if I do that, I know I'm going to come too quickly.

This is the first time I've had someone eat me so thoroughly. I want to savor this feeling of complete relaxation forever. But the latest swirl of the tongue has my back tensing, so I put my fingers in his hair and begin to gyrate my hips.

"Caarteeer," I moan helplessly when he places my left leg over his shoulder and exerts pressure on the right one to keep me within his control. I'm almost at the point where I'm about to go buck wild. My orgasm is brewing and from the mounting buildup, it's going to one hell of an ecstasy storm. It is over when he lightly bites down on my clit. I think I break into a thousand quivering pieces as I hold his mouth to me. The sensations have me ready to break down in tears.

I can't even speak. Fuck, I can barely breathe. My man has a serious tongue game. Whew, goddamn, I'm still shaking.

Carter lays his head on my belly as my body began to calm. I remove my hands from his hair and flex them so they release the death grip I'd been holding. I lie here for minutes, just melting into the leather of the chaise and rubbing his head.

I lick my lips as I relish in the most explosive orgasm I've had in my entire damn life. Carter inches his way up my body and kisses me with those same lips that just devoured my pussy.

He presses his forehead to mine and quietly utters "I love you" for the first time. Gently, he smoothes away the stray hair tendrils that lay across my face from thrashing my head around.

I capture his face in my hands,"I love you." And I mean it. Not in some young girl insecure type of way. Saying it lightens the pressure I've been carrying around since I realized it. Hearing him say it overjoys me. I laugh as he kisses me.

"I love you so much," I repeat, hugging him to me.

"I told you that you was gon' be my woman," he laughs arrogantly.

"You ain't finish the job yet," I tease. The orgasm being as unraveling as it was still can't make me forget my original objective.

"Oh, I'm 'bout to," he comments with a nod. Carter makes a motion to get up and pulled me along with him. Naked, I follow him to the bed, where he pulls back the black down comforter and sheets.

While he takes his time stepping out his jeans, I get comfortable on the huge bed. I try to avoid staring at his dick as it is being revealed to me but I couldn't. My eyes are glued to the magic stick I've dreamed about for the last four months. When the boxers finally slip down his legs, I see my prize. I have to close my eyes quick before I gape with my mouth wide open. The dick is beautiful. I knew my baby was carrying that work, but it's nice to have direct confirmation.

Smiling, I hum in appreciation and trace my lips with the tip of my tongue. I think he is standing there just so I can gawk at him. His ass knows that he's fine as hell and that his equipment is about to fix my problem. I crook my finger and motion for him to come to me. And he wastes no time bringing me what I decide to claim as mine.

Just when he is beside the bed, he opens the drawer. I watch him grab a handful of condoms, dropping all except one beside the lamp. I suddenly realize that protection has been the last thing on my mind. As a secondary thought, I wonder just who in the hell is going to use more than five condoms in one session? While my mind wonders, Carter sheaths himself in a condom and climbs on top of the bed with me.

On top of me.

Doing my part, I spread my thighs to accept him comfortably. At first, he just rubs the head of his dick on my pussy, teasing me until I whimper in protest. Then he kisses me into silence as his hands slip under my butt to bring me closer for swift penetration. Arching my back, I cry out as we make initial contact.

"Shh, you gon' wake Mira up," he whispers, gathering me up and holding me tighter. I didn't realize that I was that loud. I don't realize any activity going on around me. Only inside me.

"Come on, open up, baby," he coaxes quietly, lifting my hips higher so he can dig deeper. "Let me in." The seductive tone of his voice drugs me into submission. I'm high, getting addicted with each slow, practiced stroke and hushed comment.

Carter lets both of his hands roam along my thighs as he pushes my knees back. In so deep, I draw short breaths as he pulls out, almost to the tip and slams back in. The repeat motions have me reaching for things that aren't there. Closing my eyes and biting down on my bottom lip, I wrap my legs around his waist and cross them at the ankles. My body moves rhythmically with his as he dances inside me. I arch my hips, moving them in circles, trying, yearning, reaching for a deeper sense of intimacy when he provides me with one.

He searches for my hands and takes them in his, intertwining our fingers. Those amber eyes are staring into me as if he can see clear through me. "I love looking into your eyes," he admits pumping furiously into me.

"I love having you inside me," I moan. "Deeeeeper, Carter. I want you deeper," I beg.

That is all the confirmation Carter needs to start fuckin' my ass rough like a porn star. I mean, he really started putting in work. Deeper? Did I say deeper? I want to take my words back when I feel his dick all up in my stomach like it was going to come out through my mouth on the next stroke.

One of his hands holds my ankle while the other holds my shoulder; this is to secure me because he realizes that I can't handle this shit. My moans turn into screams of pleasure. He quickly covers my mouth with his to smother my screams that would surely awaken Amira. How am I supposed to remember there is a child in the house while he's fuckin' me like he's been in jail for the past twenty years?

Just as I think I am going to die, the hand that's held my ankle finds its way between our bodies and begins to massage my clit.

The dick is steadily slamming in and out of me. His skilled fingers are going round and round, manipulating my shit. I am starting to go buck on his ass. I want him to go deeper, and I strain upward towards his hand. I take hold of his head and hold it tightly to my body as I fight to cum. I ride that wave for a minute.

"Damn, baby," he breathes, slowing his pace but increasing the pressure of the hand rubbing my clit.

"Make me cum!" I plead. "Carter, baby, please make me cuuuum," I beg, on the verge of unleashing another powerful orgasm. My eyes shut on their own accord while I bite down on my bottom lip to keep from screaming.

"This my pussy?" he demands.

Yes, it is his. Any man who can take ownership of it like this definitely has exclusive rights to the pussy. Now that I think about it, I'm kind of surprised he asks me he never seemed to be the type of man who needs macho affirmations in the bedroom. He's always been respectful about intimacy, never demanding to know whose pussy he's in. But then again, up until tonight, I had never made love to him before.

"Yesssssssss, it's yours."

The tremors begin at the soles of my feet, rushing up through my thighs, which has him clenched tightly at the waist, into my stomach, down in my buttocks, and inside the walls of my pussy. This odd feeling of euphoria fills my chest as I struggled to breathe. I don't care if I die from busting a nut this huge. Alieas Zonnai Stiles is going to die a happy ass camper then 'cause my orgasm isn't going to wait. My heart is pounding in my ears, begging for a moment of relaxation.

He put it on me so good, I'm still chanting "It's yours" when I come. I shake like crazy but that doesn't stop Carter from achieving his ultimate goal. His ass continues to work that huge dick in and out of me until he finally comes.

Spent and out of breath, he lays his head on my chest and asserts, "Now, you're my queen."

CHAPTER

thirteen

Alicia

I'M HAPPY. I MAY JUST have all the things I've ever dreamed about. I don't want to jinx it. So, I'm just going to enjoy. My mom is always throwing huge ass parties for some reason or another, I hope that I'm getting some cake out of this shindig. Aside from that, she is testing my limits, though. At first, she didn't approve of Carter, now she's supposedly giving me tips on how to keep him happy. She should be concerned with my happiness. And she should've been more selective with her guest list.

My cousin Janelle is walking around with her nose in the air. I'm like, "Bitch, please sit your attention-seeking-ass down somewhere." And they know that I can't stand her. Shit, hardly anybody can stand her. The only reason I'm going to ignore her is because it would upset dinner. That and my mom would have a heart attack.

Janelle makes me sick. Flipping her long hair and smiling

like she fuckin' sweet. *She is a horrible person.* Growing up, I was the biggest, weight-wise of all the grandchildren, and that bitch never let me forget it. Janelle always had jokes and little smart remarks about my being fat. I don't know how many fights we had over it. I beat her ass every time, though.

As we got older, her bitter attitude towards me turned into envy. Knowing I'm the shit placed me on her can't touch list. Plus, I've always been everybody's favorite, and she can't stand it. We haven't spoken a nice word to one another since her boyfriend decided that he would have rather been my man instead of hers.

I didn't want him for the simple fact that she was my cousin. But of course, "Ms. Cutie" couldn't fathom the thought that he would want me over her in the first place. She had handled it with the grace and elegance of a fifteen-year-old and called me a fat bitch, a couple of 'fat bitches' over the years. I shrugged off the irritation. It's cool. Not my fault her nigga loved fat bitches. Was begging to bury his face between the apex of these fat ass thighs.

Janelle had to learn just like all of these other girls who think that they can punk and play me 'cause I'm big. Fuck that big shit. It's not even an issue for me. I can get who I want when I want, and I dare any hoe to try and stop me. Ain't no sleepin' in this spot, so this hoe better step off.

"You finally lost all that weight," Janelle comments back-handedly. The nerve of this bitch, who looks as if she needs to do a couple of sit-ups herself. I want to wipe that self-serving smile clean off her ugly ass face, but I just smile. My parents would have a damn fit if I acted a fool.

"And?" I retaliate. If this girl thinks she can back me into a corner, she's dead wrong. I'm a good two inches taller than her, so I stand up. Janelle looks me up and down and then smiles. "You look nice," she compliments, surprising me into silence.

"Thank you," I sputter, shocked that she actually said something nice to me for a change.

"Lions; Lions." I smile at the little voice that's calling me. I think it's cute. I bend down to pick her up. Then she tells me, "Daddy told me to come find you."

"Well, you found me," I reply, smiling at the chocolate drop in my arms.

"Well, what's your name, pretty?" Janelle asks Amira.

"Amira," she answers.

"That's a beautiful name, sweetie."

"Thank you." Then she turns her head and looks at me with her big, bright eyes. "Lions, will you fix me a snack."

"You hungry?"

She nods. "Excuse us, Janelle." Without another word, I walk away from my cousin with lil' mama clinging to my neck.

"Alieas, Alieas." My mother comes up behind me.

I suck my teeth and turn to her. "Yes."

"What is your problem?" she asks me.

"Nothing," I reply, confused at her question and ask why.

"I asked you to be nice to Janelle."

How nice am I supposed to be? I haven't been nasty to her, so my mother shouldn't be hounding me. I roll my eyes and suck my teeth again. "Gosh, I was civilized to her." What? Does she want me to play with the bitch?

Sighing heavily with concern for her incredulous child, my mom takes Amira from my arms. She loves children and is completely taken with Amira. I think she fell in love with her the day she met her. I know the feeling.

"Mom, I'm about to get her something to eat," I protest.

"I'll get it. Now, I want you to be nice to your cousin. And make sure Carter is ok." She leans in closer to me and whispers, "You gotta feed your man to keep him. Now, go ahead."

I frown. "Yes, I know, and she was never nice to me."

"That's when you were children," she hisses.

"Yeah, I guess that makes it all better," I say bitterly. My mom walks away with Amira, leaving me to think about my actions.

I'm not being nice. Ain't no such lie being told, so we can definitely cross that off my list. I'm not the forgiving type.

Forget her. I'm one of those people that will forever remember things done to me, good and bad.

"Why you frownin', 'lil sister?" Gray asks, slinging his arm over my shoulder.

I shake my head and look up at him. Then I smile and shrug. "Your mom be trippin'. As usual," I confide.

He laughs and tugs my hair. "You know how she wants her dinner parties to be perfect."

"She shouldn't have invited Janelle then."

"It's so unlike Nicole Stiles to be deliberately ignorant. So unlike her daughter."

"She knows how I feel about her," I pout.

"Times change, boop, and people grow up."

Hmmm. Is he tryna say I'm being petty? He's right. "Oh, shut up."

Nesha comes up to us and fits her body tightly against Gray's. He, in turn, kisses her forehead. "You aight? he asks.

"I'm fine. Just a little tired," she mumbles in a tone that I suppose is for his ears only.

"Maybe you should sit down," he suggests. There is definitely something going on. Something I know nothing about.

"I'm fine, Gray. I just came over to tell Lieas to watch out for her man."

Watch out for my man? I think, even as my eyes scan the room looking for him. What I see isn't a huge shock to my system, but it does get me steaming mad. That hoe has her hands on his shoulders. Things, and people, that belong to me are, without a doubt, off-limits to her ass. I excuse myself from both Gray and Nesha. I have business to take care of.

"Hey," Carter speaks, upon noticing me. He must not know that the temptress Eve is standing before him. Carter reaches out his hand to me. Smiling, I take it and am pulled down onto his lap.

"What are y'all talkin' about?" I inquire.

"Catching up, actually," Janelle answers with a smirk. How the hell does she know him? I'm pretty sure that she's not his type. She's skinny, for one thing.

"You know each other?" I question. Carter tightens his hold on me.

"Yeah, we went out on a date once."

"Really?"

"It was a blind date," he clarifies. "And we didn't hit it off at all," he adds when I look at him.

"Good," I retort, wrapping my arms around his neck. Let me put a stamp on the man 'cause she'd try to take him just to spite me. "Now, you're mine," I finish. From the corner of my eye, I can see Janelle roll her eyes.

"I guess I'm going to go over there," she finally says and before she walks away, she has the nerve to tell him goodbye in a flirtatious tone.

"Hmfp." Carter kind of makes a half frown and then shakes his head. I guess he's decided not to ask me whatever was on his mind.

"Excuse me. Everyone?" I turn to the direction of my brother's voice. Gray is standing in the middle of the family-filled room with Nesh at his side. Her eyes are glassy, and she has the biggest smile on her face.

Aww, he asked her; he actually asked her, is all I could think.

"I'd like to inform everyone that I asked Lynesha to marry me and she said yes!"

There is only a second of complete silence but that is quickly followed by loud, thunderous clapping. Has me wondering just how many people are actually in the room.

My mother is the first person I could see giving both Gray and Nesha a hug. Of course, Nicole had been crying, even though I'm sure she knew that Gray was going to ask Nesha. In my family, you don't just do things; you talk it over with the parents first.

Carter and I make our way over to the happy couple. I give Nesha a hug and then give into my own tears. They are both very special to me. And the proof that Gray is finally going to do right by her touches me in a way I can't explain. Carter is shaking Gray's hand and making idle conversation with him when I grab my brother for a hug. "Don't fuck this up," I whisper.

Aww. My best friend gonna make my brother an honest man.

CHAPTER

fourteen

CARTER

I HAD CLOWNED AUTUMN ABOUT being in a group date, and here I am, kicking back, reflecting on my first one. Alieas had somehow successfully managed to plan a six couple date for the theatrical release of Brown Sugar without anyone dropping out or canceling. We ended up going weeks after the release, but it had worked out. It had been a close call; I heard her going back and forth with Trina who doubted if her date would feel out of place amongst a group of men he didn't know, a group of men who were all cool with her ex.

Truth be told, dudes usually feel out of place when they are all but forced together in one place and they don't have any type of relationship with the other guys. Most of us knew each other in one way or another, so that wasn't the case for me. Dates are usually intimate, but this was like a full-blown get-together. In my experience, men will do just about anything to please their women...

Which brings me to how I got here. It wasn't as cumbersome as I thought group dates to be. In fact, we all had a great time. We ended up taking up a corner at Little Johnson's Diner up on Ogontz Ave and discussing the movie.

We all agreed that we loved the music and had even liked the film, but it elicited some thought-provoking discussion on fidelity, friendship, and love. There was a little tension between Gray and Nesha as she detailed catching him with another girl in his car much the way Taye Diggs's character Dre had with Nicole Ari Parker's character Reese at the restaurant with Richard Lawson.

And because they have reconciled, I saw a softer side of Gray, attempting to keep it that way. We debated over each other's hypothetical response to the same situation. Gray and dude that Trina brought said they were straight wildin' on the spot. Tyree and Tim both copped out by saying they couldn't fathom the possibility of either Bri or Tiff in that situation. Which is funny 'cause both Bri and Tiff said they were kicking ass if situations had been flipped. Daemon said he'd walk away, and I'm inclined to think at this point in my life, so am I. I had done all that arguing and back and forth shit with dudes before. When Toya first start fucking with her dude, I was ready to hurt a nigga rolling up in what's mine. But at the end I'd the day, it was her choice. I can intimidate a dude all day, but I ain't making a spectacle of myself for no one. So, yea. I'm clinking my spoon against the wine glass in celebration of "*my divorce*". I'm walking away.

At some point during the conversation, I observed Alieas smile at the whimsical thought of friends becoming lovers and the possibility of being in love forever. Over, the months she has softened and is not as cynical about love as she used to be. I feel my heart roll over, rumble in my chest, restless at the thought of catching her with another nigga.

Let me take back my earlier statement. I would probably lose my shit and act crazy as a mf.

Alieas is mine and I love her.

"It was nice, right?" Alieas asks through her yawn.

We're stretched out on the couch in her living room, comfortably clad in our nightclothes, recapping the movie again. We're listening to an R&B mix of this year's hottest songs that I burned for her earlier today. We both love music, so this is kind of our wind-down routine. She was extra hype that I also made her a CD with all the commercial pop music she loves. Was ecstatic that I'd included "03 Bonnie and Clyde" by HOV and Beyonce. She was hype as shit about their collaboration and swore that they were getting together.

The song is a hit. Don't care nothing about celebrities and their relationships, though. I'm only concerned with mine.

Y'all know how I meet her.
We broke up
Got back together.
To get her back, I had to sweat her.
Now she roll with bad boys...

I rap along with Common, right on time enough to elicit a laugh from her.

When the song is over, Lieas yawns again, covers her mouth, and stretches out, all over the top of my lap, like I'm some damn pillow. When I look down at her, she yawns again, more dramatic this time, and swipes at the meaningless tears it produces. It's well after midnight, so fatigue is looming. If I didn't have other plans, I'd be tired too. Propping my hand on her knee, I search her eyes. "You tired?"

The melody to Nelly and Kelly's latest song *Dilemma* begins to stream from the stereo speakers. "Not if you have something else in mind," she sleepily returns, shaking her head. A knowing smile crosses her lips before she catches the bottom one with her teeth. After giving it a quick nibble, she playfully puckers her lips and blows me a kiss.

"We can read and act something out," I offer. We've been playing out the fantasies in Zane's book, The Sex Chronicles. Don't get me wrong; my girl is a straight freak and is seemingly down for whatever and I'm extremely in love with the na-na, but I was surprised at her limited sex game after she had boasted about her expertise and how hooked niggas were. She had some skills, but I had to teach her what I like, though.

Now, she open. Shit, I can't lie. I'm open.

The look she's giving me has me wanting to rip this flimsy ass tank top nightgown off. The plump, caramel globes and taut nipples are straining against the purple cotton fabric, beckoning to be licked.

"Nawl, we don't need the book. We can make a video, though," she purrs.

"You gon let me tape this ass," I playing slap the back of her thigh. "taking this dick? Lieaaass?" I can't hide my excitement.I've been trying to talk her into it for two weeks now. I guess she's a little apprehensive because she think she's fat. She been dropping weight all crazy, and she still has curves for days. My manhood rises to the occasion.

The smile she gives is wide and inviting, and even though she offers it, something in her eyes days she might still be unsure.

Joking, I lean down to nibble on a nipple then I give a conciliatory kiss to her nose. "It's cool, babe. I left the camcorder at home. You get points for being game, though."

My hand travels lower, brushing over the inside of a bare thigh. Bringing her other knee up and allowing it to gape to the side, Lieas lifts her head to meet my descending lips. I tease her with a light press of my lips to hers. My fingers remain busy, leaving a burning trail of across the span of her soft skin.

I can feel her urgency in the way her body strains upward to meet both my mouth and my roaming fingers. "I got the remedy for this," I whisper obligingly in her ear, only a hair's breath away. Slowly, I slip my finger beneath the waistline of her frilly, lace panties.

"Carteeer!" my name pours out in a long sigh as I begin to delve my fingers into the heart of her passion. Soaking wet, she gyrates her hips upward to meet my stroking fingers.

Thick thighs and heat envelop my hand as she encloses them in the cradle of her warmth. Probing fingers manipulate her temple until she can't take it. The pleased sighs and moans drive me. I want more.

Leaning over, I pry her thighs open so I can see how pretty and pert her clit is. Alieas attempts to close her thighs again.

Swiftly and lightly, I smack her thigh. "Hold them open. I wanna see how much you want me," I gruffly instruct, inspecting her overflowing juices.

"Any— Anything, babe. It's whatever you say," she deliciously obeys, arching up, spreading her apart further.

Torn between everything I could indulge in at the moment, I listen to her wanton pleas for me not to stop. As I lean down, Alieas arches up and in a quick maneuver, I bury my face in between her thighs, piercing her core with my talented tongue. After licking every quaking inch of her, I French kiss her lady lips and top it off with a lingering, smacking kiss.

Alieas mildly protests when I make a motion to move away to shed my clothes. It only takes a moment, but impatient as she is, Alieas sits up and pokes her lip out in a pout that has me sliding down to kiss her.

Our lips mingle, our tongues mate as we descend into the plush sofa. A month ago, she was afraid to taste her own juices; today, she frantically binds me to her, tangling her long arms around my neck. And we kiss, just loving the feel of our warm bodies pressed together as one.

Turn your lights down low...
Never—never try to resist...
Oh no...
...Oh let your love come shining in...

Lieas begins to sign along with Lauryn Hill. The CD disc charger must have switched the player after the last song ended on the mixed CD. She winds her hips to the reggae tune, breathing the lyrics into my ear.

"...I love ya... I love ya. And I want you to know right now...
...That IIIIII... That I ahahahahah. I wanna give you some love.
I wanna give you some good—good loving...
Oh, I—Oh I.

I wind my hips against her as Lieas clamps her legs around my waist. I press into her waiting softness. She sings, not missing a note as the moist flesh yields to me. Her heat envelops me, pulls me in deeper. I press my forehead to hers and she opens her eyes. Our eyes lock and those sexy lips of her curve into a seductive smirk that matches the daring gaze. Alieas' breath catches as I press deeply into her. Moaning, she picks right back up on Lauryn's rap.

This potion might...
This ocean might...
Carry me in a wave of emotion
To ask you to marry me..

That line reaches inside me and tightens its hold on my heart.

I never knew love like this. I get lost in the feel of her beneath me, wrapped around me. Impatiently, I reach out to link our fingers. Pushing our joined hands into the space above her head, I pound into her. The need to sate this all consuming desire that I have for her has me stroking Lieas into a quick and fenzied orgasm.

Lieas giggles a little as she comes. And her recovery doesn't take long. When she is ready, we stroke our way through Dru Hill, Silk, and R. Kelly before I finally collapse on top of her.

CHAPTER

fifteen

CARTER

"WHATEVER, CARTER," ALIEAS LAUGHS. "HANDS down, the best show ever. Not taking opinions."

I can imagine her smile as her voice cheerfully declines my thoughts on her favorite TV shows. So, basically, her favorite shows are, in this order:

1. A Different World. Says Whitley reminds her of her mom, and that kind of cracks me up 'cause Mrs. Stiles damn sure does. And Dwayne and Whitley's wedding is her all time favorite episode in T.V. history.

2. Sex and the City. She has Carrie and Big fever and loves NYC.

3. The Jeffersons 'cause Florence's mouth is slick as shit, and she ain't never get fired.

4. Is a three-way tie between Buffy the Vampire Slayer, Charmed, and

Dawson's Creek. For some odd reason, she couldn't choose between any of these whack-ass shows.

And 5. Amen, 'cause she loves Thelma's struggles to get Ruben to notice and fall in love with her.

I entertained her by watching Buffy and Charmed a couple times, but there's no way in hell as a black man that I'm watching some teen soap opera ass drama like Dawson's Creek.

"Please. And how you not taking opinions when this topic is especially about our personal favorites? I'm entitled to my own thoughts. And I don't see how you don't like The Sopranos but Godfather II is one of your favorite movies," I shoot back.

"It's not the same. And Tony got eer' nigga out here thinking they a part of the mob," she asserts.

"True that. I guess it's the same for women and Lifetime," I breathe. And speaking of Lifetime, we both love cooking shows. So much so that we're exploring international cuisines by trying out recipes in cookbooks from different cultures. "I grabbed a new cookbook while I was at the library with Bug. Now, are you cooking dinner t'night or am I?"

We've fallen into a rhythm. She stays at my house a couple nights a week, and I stay at her place when Mira is with my parents. It feels natural. Like she belongs there with us.

"I thought *we* were making Italian. Every day, I'm closer to thinking you love your women barefoot and pregnant."

Barefoot and pregnant... I've never been a male chauvinist, so that is not true. If being a provider and a protector who is respectful and demands the same is perpetuating this conclusion, I might be doing something wrong. And pregnant— well, we haven't discussed having children together. We both know we eventually want a larger family, but for right now, Lieas is on birth control. "I love my woman. That much is true. I prefer you in heels, though. And if you wanna cook naked, you won't hear me complaining." In fact, I'm weaving together a fantasy of her in heels and an apron, and it has me hot, instantly aroused.

"Maybe I can whip up some dessert once Mira goes to sleep." The offer comes out in a seductive whisper.

"Think we can meet at lunch for a quickie?" I'm already calculating how long it's going to take to get to our spot in the park.

There's a sultry and throaty laugh at my proposal. "I gotta check on a project near Temple around two. When that's done, you in there," she sang the last couple of words.

That's what I'm talking about. Shit, if I suggested that she shut her door and play with herself, Lieas would. The webcam on her laptop is broken, so it's cool. I can wait. "All up in there."

I don't know how I survived without having someone to satisfy all my appetites. I am sexually, emotionally, and intellectually fulfilled by her. And she loves Bug. Before Alieas, I was closed off to relationships and had never allowed anyone to get close to me, and they damn sure couldn't be nowhere near Bug. But she came through and made herself at home in our hearts.

Alieas could be 'the one'. I think. Who am I fooling? Every day, I'm becoming increasingly more aware that maybe she is. Now, I'm compelled to spill my heart out to her.

"I wasn't looking for love. Ain't want nothing to do with it, but you managed to change my mind. I love you, Lieas."

"Awww, Carter," she sighs. "I love you, too, babe,"she finishes.

"Aight, I'ma call you later," I tell her.

"Oook." And just as I click the line off, I hear her say, "Tony, what are you doing here?"

Alieas

I FUMBLE, REPLACING THE PHONE BACK ONTO ITS CRADLE. "What the hell are you doing here?" I demand, getting up from my desk to stop him at the door.

Tony steps inside my office door and reaches out to grab my hand once he's close enough to me. "Listen up," he starts. He's dressed for work in gray slacks and a white oxford button-up that's opened at the collar. I haven't seen him in a couple months, and I'm not pressed.

Snatching my hand away from his, my immediate thought is who the hell let him in here? And who the fuck does he think he's talkin' to?

"No! You listen. You have no right coming to my place of business! God! Why would you just show up here unannounced and uninvited?"

"If you would have fuckin' answered my calls, I wouldn't have had to show up here. You've been dodging my calls all day."

Tony hasn't called in over a month and then out of the blue, he texts that his cousin saw me out with Carter and Bug and that I looked happy. Just like a nigga to show up and wreck any chance at your happiness. Flagging him, I turn to walk away. I don't want to sit on the couch; it would make him feel welcome. And the last thing I want for him to feel is welcome.

My desk phone rings, but I ignore it. I want this muthasucka to be uncomfortable. Before I can even get three steps away from him, he puts his damn hands on me. It is just a light hold, but still, I don't want his damn hands on me.

"Alieas, don't walk away from me."

I stop and look down to where he is holding me. I can feel the storm within my heart brewing. There are things that I've been keeping to myself that just have to be vocalized. Things that the muthafucka needs to know.

"No, Anthony, walking away is what you're good at. And frankly, I was tired of being the one who got walked out on. And get your damn hands off me. I let you walk in and out of my life too many times, and I can't do it any longer. I don't love you anymore."

Tony's eyes widen in utter shock at my bold declaration. We've been broken up for almost a year. What the hell is there to be surprised about?

"In fact, I'm in a relationship."

"With boah with the kid? You might as well break that shit up then," he snidely remarks.

Because his eyes and voice leave no doubt that he's serious, I assume it to be an order. Instead of being a computer programmer, he should have been a comedian. I want to laugh in his face but refrain. I know he isn't that funny.

"Lieas, I'm serious."

The fact that he believes what he'd come here to say only makes the situation funnier. I have only thought of one question. Am I supposed to care?

"I'm ready to get married. I'm ready to marry you."

For the two years we had been together, I don't think a moment went by that I didn't want to hear those words from his lips. I'm not even trippin', though. But I do come to the conclusion that he is. To the dumbness that came from his mouth, I reply, "You must be the fuck out of your mind."

"Isn't that what you want? For me to marry you?"

Months ago. I can see the anger rising and can't wait for it to erupt in 5, 4, 3, 2…

And like clockwork, Tony explodes. "I'M FUCKIN' ASKIN' YOU!"

This fool is actually yelling at me at inside of my parents'

place of business. I can't believe the sheer arrogance. Then, I
see him reach into his pocket. Lately, I've been watching entirely
too many Lifetime movies because for a split second, I swear
that Tony is pulling a gun out to shoot my ass down with.

I scream.

Dramatic? Yes, I know, but I scream anyway. It helped with
the full effect of things. That's when I see the ring box.

I'm speechless. He isn't just talking out of his ass after all.

A group of realtors and my mom rush to the door to see if
I'm okay. My mom steps into the room. "Is everything okay?"
Her expression reads no real concern, though. There's more
annoyance than anything as she gives us the death stare.

I'm not. Of course, I'm not, to say the least, but not for the
reasons she seems to have thought. Finally, I was brought out of
my reverie when I hear Tony mutter something I consider
completely ignorant.

"I'm sorry," I apologize to my mom. "He's leaving; Mom,
give us a moment, please?" I ask. I know that she is pissed and
embarrassed. She walks out and dismisses the rest of the staff.
This nigga lucky my dad isn't here.

My cell begins to ring before Tony could start talking to me
again. I glance at the caller ID and answer by giving a
polite, "Hey."

"I just called your desk phone," Carter's deep voice greets
me. "You didn't answer. I swear I heard you say, Tony," he
states.

Taking a deep breath, I admit that I did. "He just stopped
by out of the blue. I'm not sure why," I let out, hopeful that he'll
believe the actual truth. I'm not trying to argue with him over
something that is beyond my control. The minute my desk
phone started ringing, I knew he'd heard me say Tony's name.

He cuts me off and asks, "As in your old boyfriend Tony?"

I huff at hearing the edge in his voice. Any female could

predict what he is thinking. So, I have to clear it up. "Yes, babe, listen…" I use 'babe' purposely to let Carter know that I have made his presence known to the other man. "It's not like that at all. Let me deal with him, and I'll call you right back."

"Aight, I trust you, Alieas, but make sure you call me back."

The fact that he lets me know that he's placed his trust in me is kind of a warning. He may as well have said, *Don't break my trust.* But it's also a reminder of the faith he has in me. And I realize that I would never do anything to jeopardize what I have with him.

"You know I will, Carter," I agree and put the phone away.

"You need to leave." I turn on Tony. "And you must be outta of your damn mind if you thinkin' that I'd marry you."

Tony sighs heavily. "What the fuck do you want from me?!" he shouts.

Oh, I forgot that this whole conversation revolves around what I want.

Riiiight.

"I want you to leave me alone. There is nothing between us. Even when there was, you were never around. And you didn't want me."

That's what bothers me the most. I'm mad that I let it out that I still care that he wasn't there for me when he needed to be.

"I'm sorry, Lieas, for not being there when I should've been. I didn't know how much you meant to me until I didn't have you anymore. Being without you is driving me crazy. There is no doubt that I fucked up. I know."

It's so sad but true that you don't know a good thing until it's gone. And that's just where I am, just like that boy band N'Sync's song, *Gone.* He is still talking when I tune back in somewhere around, "I've changed. I'm different now."

I bet. "I can't take you back, Tony, because I'm different. These past months have changed me too."

"So, you lost a lot of weight, Lieas, but that doesn't make you different."

So? I think that is where I get stuck. This man has the nerve to say, 'so' about something I consider a monumental moment in my life. Along with the excess pounds went the lost, lovesick puppy that used to be me. I'm burning up. *So?*

"Understand this: I don't need you in my life. I don't want you in my life. It is over," I stress.

"We can't even be friends?" he mutters as a last resort. Friendship. And I wasn't even going to give him that.

I decline. He sucks his teeth and hisses, "Come on, Lieas, you'on even want to be friends?"

I shake my head. "No. I'm in love with my boyfriend, for one, and secondly, I just don't want to have anything else to do with you."

That reaches him. I don't love him anymore but am admitting to being in love with someone else. The news isn't sitting well with him. It has to hurt. But I know with him, it is more about his arrogance than anything he feels for me.

Without another word, Tony takes a few steps away from me after a moment of just staring at me then he turns and walks away.

The only thing I could think is how happy I am he hadn't done what he did today six months ago when he came to my apartment to "see" me. I'm pretty sure that I would have taken him back with all the preliminaries. But now, at this moment, I'm sure that there isn't a better thing he could've done than walk away.

Taking a moment, I sit down on my couch and inhale a deep breath. "Whew."

After exhaling that breath, I place a call to my man. "Hey, babe. He's gone."

"What did he want?"

"To proclaim his undying love," I summarize.

"And how did that work out for him?"

"He'll live." I wanted to let him know that there's nothing to be up in arms about. "Thank you," I say.

"For what?"

"For not spazzing out." I laugh it off as I say it, but I'm more grateful that this hasn't turned into a shouting match. "For trusting me to begin with."

"Alieas, I love you and I'm not worried about no nigga who didn't know what he had when he had it so long as you know what you have in me."

Disaster averted, I smile. "Oh, I know what I have."

CHAPTER
sixteen

Alicia

TODAY I'M A BRIDESMAID. WHO knows? Tomorrow, I could be a bride. As usual, Trina has outdone herself with the planning of this wedding. Ever since last year's hugely successful wedding, she's blown up in the event planning business. This is truly one of those not-to-be-missed events of the winter season. I can almost predict tomorrow's headline of the Black Street: 'Up-and-coming Fashion Phenom to the African American Elite Weds Ex-thug Turned Bonafide Businessman in an extravagant ceremony.'

This nineteen-person wedding party is striking, all of us in varying shades of silver. There are the bride and groom, the maid of honor and best man, the flower girl and the ring bearer, six bridesmaids and groomsmen and of course, the baby. The sheer elegance and simplicity of the event has enraptured all the guests and promises to leave them breathless. Me, Case, Trina, and Lon are looking beyond beautiful. Even my little cousin

Zah has emerged as a beauty queen. The more time she spends with Bri, the softer she becomes. The wedding plans have gotten her all excited that she now wants to be a wedding planner.

To start off they are marrying in Bri's church, The Temple of Divine Love Church in North Philadelphia. Upon their arrival, guests are led into the sanctuary and down the side aisles to their seats by the ushers. The side aisles are used so that the middle aisle is left untouched by anyone who isn't in the wedding party.

Pink roses cover the floor of the middle aisle. The entire bridal party, with the exception of the bride, is wearing floor-length, strapless gowns with sweetheart necklines in a universally flattering shade of sparkling silver.

I feel like a fairytale princess, and all I need is a tiara. I didn't wear one today because well, it's not my wedding. I sway from side-to-side, pretending my dress is a giant bell. Yes, I am still a kid at heart. I can't wait to dance. I can't wait to see their first kiss. I can't wait until Carter peels me out of this dress. The black lace undergarments gonna have him wanting to pull out the handcuffs, whips, and chains tonight. Hard work and determination really pays off, I consider, as I run my hands over the curve of my hip.

I look spectacular. I've never been this fit in my life. Never felt more beautiful than I do right now.

"Yeah, you look fabulous." The comment startles me from behind. Rich, confident, sensual, and forbidden. I take a deep breath and turn to the man who matches the voice.

"Don't I always?" I flippantly reply. Justin nods and reaches for my hand.

Nervously, I stare at him. "What are you doing here?"

"I told you I was covering a fancy behind wedding for a magazine," he reminded me. "This is that wedding."

I recall him asking me to be his date for a wedding he had to do a story on. I had laughed it off because bringing a date while you're on the clock would have been akin to crashing it. My mouth drops open in sheer terror. Immediately, my eyes scan the area for Carter.

"I miss you, talking to you, hanging. When we gonna get that back, Lieas?"

He steps closer to me, and I stumble back a step to keep him from touching me. "I can't do this. This is my family's wedding, Justin and I'm… I'm here with Carter."

He throws his head back and snickers. Then he says, "Oh, right! Your dude. Are you going to introduce us?"

I look at him like he's lost his damn mind. "Negro, please."

"I would love to meet the boah you dropped me for."

"Why you drawling? And your ryder has definitely called my phone, getting all fly. Playing on my stuff. You and your half lying behind self." What did I expect? He told me what it was, and in all honesty, I felt no type of way that he was dating someone. I knew that we were just passing time til I got my shit together. I had no problem and had let it go.

I'm not into arguing with broads over their dude. Ever.

Damn it; Carter spots me and his facial expression changes as he takes in Justin's proximity to my personal space. The look on his face reads everything except understanding as he approaches us.

"Not at all. I took care of that. Have lunch with me?"

I shake my head. "I can't."

"You know what I want," he whispers.

Me grinding my pussy on his lips. And the flood waters break. Why I'm prone to trips down memory lane I will never understand, but I snap out of it quick enough when I see Carter approaching us. I shake my head and start to walk away before Carter can reach us.

Unaware that Carter is who he is, Justin says, "Save a dance for me." Just as Carter reaches us.

"Her dance card is full," Carter informs him, slipping his arm around my waist possessively.

Carter reaches his hand out, waiting for an introduction.

"Carter, this is Justin. He's writing an article about the wedding."

Justin takes his outstretched hand and shakes it. "Nice to meet you."

Carter is giving him the death stare. "Y'all know one another?"

That was quick and before I had the chance to get my story straight, Justin shakes his head and answers, "No. I simply saw a pretty lady in a beautiful dress, and I couldn't resist." He holds up his hands in mock surrender. "No harm, no foul." And with that, Justin walks away.

I hate that he lied. I was contemplating kind-of-sorta telling the truth. He did save my ass 'cause Carter would want details and now is not the time or place. I seriously doubt that he'll be able to handle being in the same room with guys who've seen me naked, let alone confess to Carter that Justin is the other guy I was dating before we became exclusive. Colliding thoughts and emotions quickly wreaked havoc on my ability to finesse the situation, and the only thing I could do is go along with the lie.

"Trina asked me to come find you for pics," Carter announces.

He's talking to me yet his eyes are watching Justin, who elicits a sneer from Carter when he looks back at me and smiles.

My eyebrows lift at his audacity, but I am just going to act like I ain't see him. My heartbeat accelerates when Carter leans closer to my ear. "Stay away from that boah. He definitely look like he wan' fuck that dress off you. That's my job."

Surprised at his bold declaration, not sure if I can breathe, I laugh nervously instead, lightly hitting his shoulder. I have to be regular and make sure that Justin isn't gonna be extra. "Watch your mouth," I chastise him, walking towards where Trina is.

"Make sure yours don't spend too much time talking to that boah," he warns.

"Really, Carter?" I'm irritated now. I don't like being told what to do.

"Yes, really, babe," he laughs. Carter kisses my cheek, and I just shake my head, grateful he doesn't suspect anything more between Justin and me. All I want to find Trina, so we can take the wedding photos and then dance the night away.

LATER, I REVEL IN THE FACT THAT TWO OF MY FAVORITE PEOPLE are married to one another. I had butterflies in my stomach as I watched them exchange their wedding vows. This has to be the single most important moment in their lives next to the birth of their children. Their sacred bond represents the union of four lives and their extended family and friends.

It's one thing to watch people get married and hope that their relationship is able to withstand the constant trials and tribulations that they are up against and another to know that no matter what, they'll always work out. I have that gut feeling about Bri and Tyree. Shit, I think everyone who knows them would agree. They have truly been blessed.

Mmmmmm, must be wonderful. I can't imagine what I would feel like after having said, 'I Do' to the man I'm destined to spend my entire life with, to the man who is my spiritual partner as well as my soul mate. I got that from Bri, who just said it as part of her vows. It's something that will stick with me until it happens.

I remember looking over at Carter; he was watching them

intently as they shared their first kiss as husband and wife. His expression showed traces of pride when his fellow brother decided to commit to his family. Tyree is the first in his circle of men friends to take the step. All the rest of them are suited to follow.

I'm watching him now. As if he can feel my eyes on him, he looks up and catches me in the act. The way the smile spreads across his face turns my heart to mush. Carter whispers something to Amira, who is happily sitting beside him as she takes in the all the pretty ladies in their princess gowns and the endless flower arrangements adorning the chapel.She looks at me and waves energetically.

My heart flutters; I love her so much. I realized that before I even realized that I was in love with Carter. I guess that is different, though. She's a child with no faults or flaws and I love her with a fierce possession that I can't quite explain, which is astonishing in itself considering I didn't want to be in a relationship with a man who already had kids. Love truly does conquer all.

"Who invited him?" I whisper to Trina when I spot Tony on the crowded dance floor.

"Now, you know he cool with Tyree.He was on the list for the save the dates initially," she confides. Trina is no joke. She dislikes Tony because of how he treated me and finds it funny that he's now the one doing the chasing. I'm not saying that's why he's here today, but come on; it is my cousin's wedding. He knew I'd be here.

Okay, enough ego food for today. I just hope that he saves tryna get with me for another time. Carter would whup his ass and more than likely, dump me in the process. They've never met and I'd like to keep it that way.

"You would think he'd have the good mind to not have come. If he tries to talk to you, ignore him," she suggests.

She's such a pro at it. Dave has been giving her the 'I'm

helplessly in love with you' look for three days now, and she still refuses to even entertain it or him.

I don't think that'll be possible. Tony has never been one to be ignored. Plus, he just caught me watching him and that'll give him a reason to come over here.

"Too late," I mumble into my glass as I roll my eyes.

"Hello, Catrina. You look beautiful as always," Tony compliments, prompting her to suck her teeth in response.

I look up at the sound of his voice and smile as if I am happy to see him. "How are you, Anthony?" He isn't fooled by the smile 'cause I'm sure he can feel the frost in my words. His ass has been crickets since showing up at my job. I was certain that the realization of my unavailability had sunk in.

"Great, now that I've spoken to you". "You looked beautiful up there—"

"Oh, please," Trina laughs, cutting him off. I look at her and then I laugh too.

Tony doesn't respond to Trina's jab, only shaking his head instead. "You wanna dance?" he inquires hopefully.

I shake my head. "No, not with you."

"That's fair enough. Can I at least talk to you for a minute?"

"For what reason?"

"Just wanna spend a couple minutes wit' you. We talk; I leave you alone. Please?"

I look at Trina but she looks away. She must have a feeling that I'm about to do something stupid like agree.

"Okay," I sigh. I'm only agreeing so that he'll leave me alone for the rest of the evening.

"You sure you don't want to dance?"

I nod. "I'm sure," I say, getting up from my seat at the head table. I scan the room for Carter but I don't see him. He must be taking Mira to the restroom, so let me hurry up and talk to this jackass before he comes back.

Tony attempts to hug me when we find ourselves a quiet spot to talk, but I put my hands up to shield him from me. "Come on now, Tony, don't touch me."

He steps back and puts his hands into the pockets of his slacks. "I've been watching you all afternoon. I had to talk myself into coming over to talk to you, but when I saw you staring at me, I thought, 'What the hell?'."

I knew that's why he came over. "I wasn't staring at you. I was just surprised that you would show up, is all. I thought we had settled everything the last time we saw one another."

"I've thought about it, and you were right. And I'm sorry," he says sincerely. "I had no right doing that to you. I just wanted you to know that I wanted you back. I wasn't thinking clearly at the time, so I just did what popped into my mind."

"Just forget about it, Tony. I have. I don't want to give you the wrong impression about why I chose to talk to you. I just want you to leave me alone. I'm happy—"

He nods and interrupts me, "Yeah, I saw you with your boyfriend and his daughter. Never thought I'd see the day you'd be happy with someone else." He appears sad, glancing down at me. "You look happy, Lieas." He put his hand over his heart and adds, "It hurts that I'm not the one making you happy when I've made so many promises to you that I would."

This man is apologizing to me, and it appears to be from the heart. Does all my anger towards him vanish? *Fuuuck no.* But if I hadn't been trying to hold onto nothing for long, it wouldn't have been so bad. He was only treating me that way 'cause I allowed him to. I expected him to change his cheating ways 'cause I had changed mine. It doesn't always work that way, and this was one of those times it didn't.

For the first time, I accept my part in this. "I blamed you 'cause it was safer— no easier to blame you than accepting my own stupidity. I'm far from being some nut-ass broad; I just acted like one."

He shrugs in agreement. "I really did love you, though, Lieas."

I nod in acknowledgment and reply with a smile, "I loved you too. More than your man-whore ass deserved." I don't feel like I did when we first began this conversation.

Tony smiles. I can see it in his eyes that he'd rather choke my ass than swallow what I am dishing out. "Maybe. I want you to be happy even though it's not with me," he offers, pulling his hands from his pockets. "Just make sure that your dude is going to treat you right."

CARTER

"I AM," I REPLY THROUGH RIGHT LIPS AT THE EXACT SAME TIME as Alieas says, "He is."

Dude turns to the sound of my voice, and Lieas' mouth hangs in shock because I don't think she saw me coming over here. It surprised me, walking into the ballroom, to see them talking. From the way she was standing, she seemed annoyed. When I saw Trina, I calmly asked who she was talking to. I didn't expect her to say it was Lieas' ex. Weddings addle your brain, soften your heart, and make you fantasize. Have you wanting more, expecting more. I wasn't sure if I was the one who was doing all that or if I'm pissed that she's not.

"Carter," I put my hand out for him to shake it. He shakes it and introduces himself, "Tony."

Alieas bites her bottom lip but wisely informs him that I'm

her man. I've met only a couple of exes in my lifetime, none of whom mattered.

She matters.

We make awkward small talk and after a moment, Tony leaves us alone. Relieved that I didn't have to go apeshit on him, I remain eyeing her.

I wasn't aware that I possessed the gift of polite conversation when it comes to other men poaching what's mine. Assuming that the crash collision is adverted, Alieas reaches for my hand before noticing the glare in my eyes. "So how many more guys at this wedding have you talked to? Messed with?" *Fucked* is unspoken but that's what I'm thinking. I don't grab on to the outstretched hand.

Now, she's annoyed, her eye sparking fire. "Excuse me? Did you just ask me what I think you did?" she demands.

"Yeah, I did," I angrily admit. "Every time I turn around, some boah in your face and you in his. What? You think I'on see you?"

Holding up her hand, Lieas shakes her head. "Cart, I don't know what you gettin' at, but I'm not in the mood," she spits through clenched teeth.

Curious as to where I'm going with it and why I'm all bent out of shape, Alieas just stares. "I'm sayin', keep these men out of your face." My voice is firmer than I ever remember it being. My brown eyes are straight and direct, and everything in me feels a little dark as I step closer towards her.

Instantly, she steps back in retreat. "Are you drunk?" she asks suspiciously, even though she knows damn well that I'm not.

"No, I'm not drunk.". Maybe I'm being irrational. I'm confident with my place, but I'm admittedly jealous and territorial when it comes to mine. She is mine. Alieas knows it. But other men don't.

"Well, what the hell is your problem then?"

"My problem? I walk up on you twice talking to other guys, and I heard another dude said he used to fuck witchu." A headache the size of Mount Rushmore begins settling over my left temple.

"Well, what do you want me to do?" Holding her hand out to me again, I look at it before I take hold of it. "Carter, you can't get mad over me guys I messed with before you."

Checking myself, I pull her closer to me. If she was in my shoes, I know she already would've been wildin' out and showing her ass right here too.

"Babe, they don't mean anything," she all but purrs as she twines her long arms around my neck. "You're my man," she declares.

Taking a deep breath, I drop my forehead to hers. "Babe, I'm goin' crazy thinkin' that all these dudes have touched you." *And I know for a fact that a fair amount have.*

I get caught up in her golden gaze. "I can't change the past," she kisses me, "not even for you. And I can't help it if everybody still want me," she jokes and provocatively swings her hips into me.

I grunt from the torture of her rubbing her ass close to my dick. She kisses my lips lightly. "They all still want you but they ain't getting you—"

"'Cause, I'm in love with you," she replies seriously.

"You better be," I inform her.

CHAPTER
seventeen

JANUARY 2003

New Year... New You...

Alieas

I'VE BEEN ABLE TO KEEP my nookie reserved only for Carter. I have to confess that I do randomly answer Justin's messages on BlackPlanet and AOL messenger. They aren't nothing explicit or out of line. I was talking to him about his hookup at the studio he uses to record an album of spoken word. Then I thought better of it so no sense in setting myself up for an L.

And I'm happy that this man has been completely mine, and I love every minute of it. Before, I found myself envious of all my friends, especially Bri with her extravagant wedding. Their happiness is sickening. Ughh! I want to be sick in love like that. It's cute. I'm starting to think that Carter has me sick in love like that.

So, I don't need a ring— at least not this precise moment.

Carter has made an occupation out of making me happy. As

a present, he surprised me with a trip to Atlantis, an all-inclusive resort in the Bahamas. We've already been here for the past three nights, and we only have one more to go. I'll be sad to get back to reality and cold weather.

But right now, I'm so excited about being here, with him that is.

Since the wedding, Carter has been acting jealous if a man even looks in my direction. It's cool in small does, though. This afternoon, we were chilling on the beach with me in a revealing black one-piece with a plunging neckline. And for the first time in my life, I didn't feel like Shamu in danger of being harpooned.

The weight thing is under control. I've reached my goal weight of one-eighty-five and of course, I'm loving it, reaping the fucking benefits of better clothing options and male appreciation, although at times, unwanted.

People thought I was conceited before, *Shiiiiiid*, they better watch out 'cause they haven't seen anything yet. I'm lying here, soaking up all the warm rays of the sun, body all oiled down, and guys are checking me out. None of them say anything 'cause the look in my man's eyes let them know that he wasn't having any of that, especially after my boob popped out while I was playing a game of volleyball with a couple of horny college guys on winter break. There were no words for the embarrassment I felt so I laughed until my sides hurt and didn't stop until after Carter came to save me— well, cover me up, to be exact.

We go to this local spot that did karaoke. I sing Lisa Loeb's song, *Stay* and jam to *Margaritaville and Hotel California* for happy hour with a mix of tourists and locals. It's all fun. This is the first time I've been on a real vacation with a man. Carter promised that in the summer, we'd take Mira to Florida to go to Disney World.

There is even more grownup fun after we get back to our

suite. He murders my kitty kat, right up against the door. It has taken him like two seconds to get my piece of suit off and to get all up in me. So, in the last few months, I've discovered so much about myself sexually that I didn't know. Multiple orgasms have become something that I'm familiar with. I used to have to fake it and now there's no such thing. We've role played, used toys, handcuffs, screwed in the front seat of his truck— I've always thought I was too big to have sex in a car. In his workshop at home. I don't know. I can't explain but with him, I feel liberated, free to explore all the things that might have made me afraid. Like choking, the thought of those calloused hands wrapped lightly around my throat is— Whew... I realized that I love it rough and that I also enjoy it slow.I must have been out of my mind to have ever thought that the dick was whack. I must have been out of my mind to think I knew anything about sex.

Eyes rolling back, I'm in heaven. God, I may bust a nut just thinking about how he keeps me coming. My eagerness to make Carter happy extends far beyond the bedroom. I want to make Bug happy and be happy too. He has actively taught me what love is. With him, I believe that I can have it all— my attitudes, my moods, my mouth, and him. We match in a way that we balance each other out type of thing. Carter is moody but measured, crazy but really rational. I'm impulsive and flighty, but he anchors that. He is so fuckin' manly. And he's mine.

Me and my dad had a heart-to-heart, and he continues to push the narrative that while being in love is great and wonderful, there were more things to be concerned about in life.And of course, returning to school was one of them. I'm working it out. We agreed that no matter what, I'd be in a program by fall. He likes Carter and respects him but seems indifferent to my declarations that he's the one. I'm basically just going to chalk it up to his concern for me as a parent wanting what they think is best.

At this point, I'd like to say, I know what is best for me. And that is Carter and Mira.

"Why are you smiling?" Carter questions, squeezing my left hand as we get onto the elevator.

Shaking my head, I reply, "Nothing." Then he looks at me in that way when I know he has something on his mind but never says one word.

There are multiple thoughts parading through my mind, all of them about him and so easily summed up in three simple words: "I love you."

"Really?" he inquires, pulling me to him. "What's that for?" Carter is usually the one who has sporadic testaments of our unwavering love and more often than not, he says it first.

"Yes, and for no reason but to simply make you smile," I inform him.

He laughs and nods. "You do, boop. Every day," Carter confirms. "Who would have guessed that Miss Conceited would turn out to be my Mrs. Right?"

I know that he is not talking. This man can be my ego twin. My hotheaded twin. "What's wrong with being conceited?"

"Nothing. You know I love that confident shit," he assures me.

"You better," I play. I cock my head and show my arrogance. "You know what the deal is."

He nods in agreement, licks them sexy lips, and sends me a knowing grin. "You gon' find out what the deal is," he warns.

Trust me. I want to. "When?" I inquire impatiently, glancing up at the floor indicator. The quicker I can get his stiff one in me, the quicker I can quench the ever-growing lust I have for him.

All I wanna is party and bullshit and fuck… Fuck… Fuckk.

"As soon as we get back to the room."

I feel like jumping his ass right here. Instead, I wrap my

arms around his neck to soothe my growing need to touch. I then kiss him softly on the lips, bestowing a promise of sweet love when we get back to the suite.

"Nothing can affect how perfect right now is," I whisper as the elevator finally beeps as it reaches our floor. I close my eyes, relishing in this moment of absolute peace.

Of absolute love.

I find myself opening my eyes just as the door of the elevator slide open. Just in time to see my father's lips rise from the lips of a woman who is not my mother.

Tears come to my eyes instantly as we stare at one another in complete shock, on his part 'cause he's just been caught cheating by his daughter and on my part 'cause this is my fuckin' father, the man who shares the other half of the perfect relationship I've always wanted as my own.

I blink to try and rid the image before me, but that's just not happening. The elevator alarm goes off because I'm stuck and blocking the ray so the door won't close. Carter pulls me from the elevator, but I'm unresponsive, motionless but full of emotion—anger; hurt; disgust.

"Lieas, sweetie, let me explain."

I finally can hear the words coming from his cheating mouth. I also know that he's reaching for me, but I'm backing away.

"Come on, baby," Carter interrupts so casually that it's almost as if this isn't happening

I shake my head. I have a bunch of things to say. Just have to get my stride back.

"Darrien, who is she?" the woman has the nerve to ask. I almost break my damn neck snapping my eyes to meet hers for the first time.

"I'm his fuckin' daughter!" I shout, "Who the hell are you?"

"I'm his girlfriend—"

"WHAT BITCH?!" I turn to my father, who is now looking at the female like she's crazy.

"Tonya, I need to speak with my daughter," he tells her.

"I DON'T HAVE SHIT TO SAY TO YOU!" I yell. There are other hotel guest staring at us now, but I don't give a fuck. Let them look. I'on care.

Bile is bubbling in my stomach making its acidic way up. I swallow to rid the watery taste in my mouth from my mouth. I don't have time to reach a trash can, so I double over and begin to throw up all over the other woman's shoes.

My stomach isn't feeling any better and minutes have passed. I guess it's because I'm staring at the sight that made it sick in the first place. I feel like standing up and throwing up all over his ass. We're in the bathroom of our suite. My father is here, minus the mistress this time.

Carter helpingly hands me a full glass of water and says, "I'll leave the two of you alone," and leaves but not before giving my father a disgusted stare. He shuts the door behind him.

My hands are shaking, and I have tears in my eyes when I finally muster enough nerve to stare at my father. I don't even want an explanation because it'll just be an excuse. All I want to know is how he could do this to my mother.

My loving mother. This nigga is supposed to be at a fraternity convention.

Fuckin' liar.

"It just happened, Lieas."

I ball up my fist, flex my fingers, and shift my weight from one foot to the other.

This muthafucka. I hate liars. I seriously feel like taking a swing at him.

"SHIT LIKE THIS DOES NOT JUST HAPPEN!!" I'm waiting for him to say more buts he's silent. "You don't bring some bitch that is young enough to be your daughter to the fuckin' Bahamas while your wife of twenty-something years is sitting at home, loving you."

"Alieas, stop yelling and listen. Please?"

Listen? Listen to him justify why he's cheating on my mom?

"What do you have to say, Darrien?"

"It's wrong, I know. I love your mother. I really do."

"Love? You don't love anything but your dick apparently!!"

What does he know about love?

"Alieas!" he exclaims.

I can't believe that this is my father. I don't see him. I only see all the niggas in the past who have done me wrong.

"This girl doesn't mean anything to me."

"Just get out."

"Sweetheart, you don't understand what's going on. I need to ask you that you let me tell your mother," he fruitlessly pleads.

I suck my teeth and even that hurts. "Are you crazy? No. I'ma tell her as soon as I get home. NOW GET OUT!!!"

"Baby, don't—" He can see that I'm not going for this act of his. This has probably been going on for years. To think I wanted my future husband to be like him. Tears roll done my cheeks so rapidly that I don't even attempt to wipe them away. "Baby, don't be like that."

"CARTER !!" I holler at the top of my lungs for my boyfriend. "GET HIM OUT OF HERE!"

Carter opens the door just when my father is reaching to take me in his arms. "Babe, calm down," he advises because I'm wheezing. Then he looks at my father. "Mr. Stiles, I think that you should leave."

"Listen, son—"

"Now, please," Carter requests.

As soon as he exits, I fall into Carter's arms. There are no words to describe what I'm feeling right now. Trembling, I cry uncontrollably as my tears become racket sobs and Carter takes me into his arms.

I AWAKEN A COUPLE OF HOURS LATER, BARELY COHERENT. A headache is pounding like drums on my temples. "Carter," I whisper, slowly opening my eyes. He's right beside me.

"I'm here," he quietly says, supportively squeezing my hand.

"I need some Motrin. Please."

He leaves me on the bed for a second to go into the bathroom. When he comes out, he has a glass of water and two pills for my headache.

"Thank you," I say, swallowing the coated tablets and then drinking down the water. "How could he do this to my mom, Carter?"

I can see that he wants to be supportive, but he doesn't know how to respond without hurting me any more than I already am.

"I don't know, but I packed up our things while you were sleeping. I called the airlines to see if we could catch an earlier flight."

I roll onto my back, "I'm sorry, Carter". This is his gift to me, and my family is ruining it. Damn my father.

"That's your family. You gotta take care of your business. I ain't goin' nowhere."

CHAPTER

eighteen

Alicia

For some unknown reason, my mom decided to let my dad come over to lunch to talk about their separation. Of course, I think that it is a bad idea, but she knows what she's doing. He hasn't slept a night in their house from the moment I told her. At first, I suspected that my mom wasn't as blindsided as I was. She took the news way better than I expected. After my intuition told me to dig deeper, I discovered that this isn't his first indiscretion. There was a trail of many women and years of tears beneath the façade of their "perfect" marriage. Most of that façade was built up by me. My idea of their relationship without actually seeing their relationship. Growing up, I was mesmerized by their attraction to one another. Both are attractive, still, to be almost fifty. They were always touchy-feely, full of love. My mom's eyes light up with pride when she watches my dad, unaware that she'd been watched by me. I can't recall ever seeing them overly upset with one another or in horrible fights or anything like that, growing up. Yet it seems everything I thought I knew about love and life proves that I don't know shit.I've based my dreams of lasting love on my parent's marriage, and it's all been a fucking lie.

My mom confessed with teary embarrassed eyes that they'd been through marriage counseling my freshman year of college, and my dad had even moved out for a couple months during my junior year. How did I not fucking know this? Gray knew and ain't say shit to me about it. Must be hereditary. Him and my dad been at odds forever over Gray's choices and lifestyle. Now, I'm thinking that contempt could go both ways. He still on my damn list for not saying anything to me.

Tyree is pissed. He'd modeled himself after my father— a good man, strong family values. He's not speaking to him either since my Gram let it slip that my dad had dated his mother, my aunt, my mother's older sister, before he dated my mom. Family rumors go that my Aunt Layla was as loud and rowdy as she was beautiful. Like all the men who paths she crossed, my dad had wanted her, had loved her. She was too free and reckless for him, though. She wasn't the marrying type, so he settled for the calmer, sweeter sister. I guess that's why my mom clung to him, always, like he was a prize. She'd won him, so I guess he was.

And my dad; Mr. 'My Word is my Bond' is a liar and a fuckin' cheater. Still hard to swallow. Even harder when I'm pretty sure my mom wants to reconcile with him. I'm beyond pissed at this point. Pissed the fuck off that she doesn't realize how fuckin' decent she is.How beautiful. How wonderful she is as a mother— and as a person. Anyway, I told her that I'd come over after breakfast to be the buffer and give my dad the death look.

"Carter, I know that I promised to go, but my mother needs me today," I explain, disappointing him. Today is the Universal Negro Improvement Association's day of celebration for the traditional African family. And before all this shit happened with my family, I had agreed to go with him.

Carter sighs and looks away from me. "We need you too," he says so lightly that he might as well have breathed it. "For the last month, you've been running to the aide of your mom—". He stops as he catches the death stare in my eyes and begins again. "Babe, don't get me wrong. You're supposed to be there for her, but you're not supposed to forget that you also have obligations to others."

I shake my head. I don't want to argue about it.This is not the first time that he's mentioned that he thinks I'm neglecting our relationship, and I'm not in the mood for it. "My family is falling apart and you want me to go to some damn celebration. What do I have to celebrate?" I've been spending most of my nights at his place as it just seemed natural because he has Mira and his place is so much larger. I don't think I've slept in my own bed for more than a handful of days since week arrived back home. I figure I can use some space. Maybe he can too.

Feeling closed in and overwhelmed, I go over to my designated dresser drawer and pull out the jeans I'd just brought over and put them back in my overnight bag.

"It's not about the celebration, Alieas. You been ducking out on plans with us all month." He motions with his arm to my overnight bag. "You packing up your overnight bag and ain't even tell me you weren't staying."

I can't figure out why I'm so angry with him but I am as I put my toiletry bag inside the bag with the clothes. "I wasn't aware that I had to let you know my plans," I snap.

"Alieas, your parents are going to be fine. If you would just stay out of their business and allow them to work out whatever they need to discuss between them."

Now, I know why I'm upset. We are in total disagreement about what my parents should do. I think that they should get a divorce. But for some reason, Carter thinks that my father's indiscretions should be overlooked because of the years they have invested in their relationship.

The memory of catching him cheating is still fresh in my mind. He wasn't wearing his wedding ring. So, not only did he pretend that he wasn't married, he forgot that the ring represented the family he and my mother made together. Therefore, he disregarded his children. That is one thing I will never forgive.

"We've discussed this, Carter. It's not alright that he cheated on her!" I yell.

He steps toward me; I step away, farther from him and my rational emotions.

"I never said that it was, only that you need to back out of it and let them work things out for themselves," he clarifies.

I roll my eyes. "I have to go," I tell him, zipping up my bag in angry jerks. I walk around the bed towards the door.

Carter grabs my arm. "Alieas, I'm not done talking to you," he grits out.

Jerking my arm from his grasp, I return with equal annoyance, "I'm done talkin' to you."

He steps in my path. "This is bullshit. You need to take some time out for your own relationship," he warns.

I step back and look up, my eyes shooting daggers at him. "What the fuck is that supposed to mean?" I question angrily.

"It means that while you been so busy consoling your mother and her broken relationship, you basically forgot that you have one of your own," he replies smugly. The darkening of his eyes signals that he is beyond upset.

So, that makes two of us. How he gonna say that our relationship is in trouble? I can't believe that this man has the nerve to stand in my face and question my feelings for him.

But if he feels that way, he may need a couple days to think about it.

I'm leaving.

Carter steps aside when I reach for the door handle. He follows me down the stairs and through the first floor of the house to the front door. Trying like hell to shield the hurt in my eyes, I force a blank stare before I turn back to face him.

"If this isn't working out for you all you have to do is say so!" I shout, grabbing my coat and angrily putting it on.

"You know that's not what I'm trying to say. Is that what you want? To leave? You'n wanna be with me no more?"

My mind goes blank and now, I can't even think clearly. I don't have the heart to contemplate if breaking up with him is even an option.

"That's not what I'm sayin', Carter. It is important to her that I be there today," I stress, hoping that he can take that and leave all this breakup talk alone.

"It's important that you be with Amira and me today. Like you promised," he reminds sternly without touching me. I want to say that promises are made to be broken so bad, but I think of Amira.

I understand that he's giving me an ultimatum. "Don't make me do this right now," I plead, not caring if I sound half as whiny as I feel.

He stands firmly with his arms now folded over his chest. "Is there a better time to do it, Alieas? Either you gon' be here or you aren't. The choice is up to you."

I hate ultimatums. They make me defensive and resentful, but my mother needs me, and that's my only thought as I continue for the front door.

"So, you're just gon' leave?" he asks when I reach past him for the handle to the door.

"I have to," I reply sadly with my head still held high.

Carter nods and shrugs the answer off as if it doesn't even

affect him. "I guess you have to do what you have to do."

That just pushes me over. Even knowing that this could be the biggest mistake of my life, I turn the handle and let myself out. I lean against the door for a moment, expelling the breath I'd been holding. I want him to follow me because now, I want to be talked out of leaving. Carter has never been one to placate me, so I know that he's not.

His pride won't let him.

And mine won't let me go back in and admit that I'm wrong. That I want nothing more than to spend my life with him and Amira.

A champagne-colored Mercedes Benz is parking in front of the house. I take note that the driver is a heavyset, light-skinned female, and since the neighbor's house is about twenty yards away, I assume that she is here for Carter.

I pause as she steps out of the car. Casual clothes mean casual visits. She's bundled up in a black Baby Phat bubble jacket, pulled down to her hips, jeans, and Timberland boots.

Who the fuck is she? I wonder as she begins to approach the house. Without a second thought, I make my way over to her.

"Yes, can I help you?" I ask, even though I know I have no right. The first thing this woman does is look down at my hand. She must be checking for a ring.

She smiles and asks, "Is Carter home?"

"And who might you be?" I question, tapering down my anger that this— "stranger" was just checking for a ring.

"I don't think that that's any of your business," she retorts angrily as she eyes the shit out of me.

I roll my eyes just as she lets out an agitated sigh. "You must be the girlfriend," she wonders nastily.

"That's right," I confirm, staring her down and prepping for a beatdown.

"No need to be so defensive, girl."

I'm frowning now. *Did she just call me girl'?*

"I'm not interested in your man, rather something he has that belongs to me—" We both turn our heads toward the house when we hear the front door open.

"Well, hello, Carter," the mystery woman purrs. She has a slick grin on her face that I want to slap off with my freshly manicured acrylics.

"What the fuck are you doing here, Latoya?" Carter growls.

Latoya?

She starts walking toward the house. "Is that any way to greet the mother of your child?"

"Mother of his child?!" I repeat loud enough to have them both turn to me.

That's who this bitch is? And she has the nerve to be giving me a hard time? Fuuuuuck that. "I know you don't think that you're just going to walk up here and be able to spend time with Amira," I interject before I give Carter an opportunity to respond to her question.

"She's my daughter!" she shoots back.

I'm close enough to reach out and bust her lip if I want to, but I won't. "You didn't think so when you left her, now, did you?"

Carter gives me a dismissive stare. I know that her arrival is a complete surprise for him. Bitch just showing up here to fuck up my family.

Latoya and I are so busy taking pot shots at one another that neither of us notices just how pissed Carter really is. "Alieas, don't you have somewhere to go?" he finally interrupts the arguing.

What? I stop talking and eye him for a minute, assessing his cool demeanor and the firm set of his lips.

"It can wait," I tell him just as firmly.

"You do what you have to do, remember? I have this under

control."

He says it so easily that my feelings are hurt instantly. The ball of hurt lunged right into my chest. I rub my hand over my heart. "You cannot be the fuck serious," I respond.

I admit that after all that's gone on today that he is entitled to his anger. But petty, selfish, and stupid? I guess he will need a couple of days.

"Yeah, I am," he says clearly enough to create a couple of ripples in my heart. It seems like he's staring straight through me.

That's Fine. "You take care of your business, 'cause I'm damn sure about to take care of mine."

CARTER

UNHINGED WITH RAW EMOTIONS, I GRIMACE AT TOYA. HER coloring had returned; she didn't have the dead, uncaring eyes she'd been sporting the last time I'd seen her. She was plumper than she had been when we'd been together. Remembering that Vonn had mentioned she'd been pregnant, I figure that she must've still been holding on to some stubborn baby weight.

I ain't care about any of that, though. I'm trying to figure out how she got my damn address. "Like I said, just what in the hell do you think you're doing here?"

The nervous smile inches up over her lips uncomfortably. Nerves also have her clasping her hands together before she lets them go. None of the attitude she gave Lieas was present. She finally speaks, "Carter, I'm sorry."

This bitch, I think to myself but don't say aloud. I had loved her once, and she did give me Mira. I generally don't make a habit out of disrespecting women, even women I despise. The calm, reserved brotha in me is fighting to let the fuckin' Hulk out. Rational and calm thoughts aside, I don't give a fuck about no apology.

I raise my hand to cut off any potential words liable to fall from those lying, traitorous lips. "Just stop. You're not seeing her. So, you might as well take your ass back to whatever hole you crawled out of."

Defiantly, she lifts her gaze to mine, but then she bites her thumbnail. It's the telltale sign that she is nervous. And bracing herself for my anger. "I was sick. I was so sick, Carter," her voice begins in a low whisper. But her tone is elevated and clear when she next asserts, "I want to see her."

No damn way...

Closing my eyes, I gather my strength and patience. My jaw clenching, blood boiling, and nerves ticking, I ball my fist and let go. "Are you fuckin' retarded? Hell nawl. Never gonna happened. You abandoned her once. I'm not giving you a second opportunity."

Silent tears stream down her face. "I was sick, Carter! I couldn't feel anything. Do you know how that feels? Knowing that I should love something and not feel anything? Can I please come in?"

Toya is out of her mind if she thinks she's getting anywhere near Bug. There is murderous rage flowing through my veins, demons commanding actions that I could never carry out. I stand my ground. "I don't give two fucks about how you feel, what you feel. My daughter is never going to know you. That's on you. You have to live with that. Not me."

I can see the humility leave as the anger emerges. As bold as it was for her to show up, she has to know that she wouldn't be welcomed with open, least of all, forgiving arms.

"If you don't let me see her, I'm going to file for custody. If you think I'm going to allow some otha bitch to raise my daughter, you outta your fuckin mind!" she rants. She's careful not to move any closer. My fingers tingle, itching and burning to wrap my hands around her damn throat.

"What, bitch?" This time I do call her out of her name. I step off the landing to move closer to her. "You do that. Last order, you didn't even ask for visitation. You think some judge gonna just give my daughter to you now because you all of a sudden wanna be a mother? Fuck outta here."

As reality sets in, Toya changes her strategy as she let's put frustrated sigh. "I was a very sick person. I was having horrible thoughts and visions. Post-partum depression. I know you don't want to hear it, but I'm better now. I'm ready to be her mom. If I could just see her," she pleads, taking a step closer to me. Toward my house. Toward my daughter.

Whatever heartstrings she was trying to pull didn't exist. Not for her. "Don't worry about her. She good." And for the second time today, I told someone to "do whatever it is you have to do".

Without another word, I turn and go back into the house, leaving her out front.

I peek in on Bug and just the sight of her four-year-old body sprawled out over the couch settles my racing heart. Overwhelmed, I lean into the doorway. I suppose for support. Toya's sudden reappearance knocks the wind out of me, kicks my legs from beneath me. I've always put the thought of her reappearing in the back of my mind, daring her to fuckin' try. I just always knew I would be ready...

But I wasn't. Not when it came to my little girl. I had to stand my ground; she needed me now more than anything. More than some spoiled-ass princess. More than some reappearing mother.

When I glanced out the window, Toya was still standing there. She could stand there until hell froze over, for all I care.

CHAPTER
nineteen

CARTER

W ELL, THE NEW YEAR IS already off to a shitty start. It's only February and it seems, and it seems like every-thing in my life that could've gone wrong has. Don't know why I'm at the damn mall. I hate crowds, especially when I'm in a mood, but I thought seeing a movie would distract me and get my mind off the fact that I allowed my child to be in the same room with the woman who had abandoned her. The movie did not help clear my head.

Toya showing up blew shit up. I don't even have time to run after Lieas, who is acting crazily stubborn. Generally, I love that about her but after two weeks, I'm still pissed. I need her, though, and she is decidedly absent.

I've been trying to figure out Latoya's angle. To just reap-pear, unannounced and uncharacteristically unfazed by my feel-ings of distrust and anger toward her, makes me highly suspicious.

God bless my mom because she has entirely more patience for bullshit than I do. To her credit, she helped hell thaw out and me calm down by just insisting that I get over my own personal animosity for Toya and see what would be more beneficial for Bug. Initially, I didn't care what Toya's excuses were. That woman left her baby. I knew that men did that shit all the time but not women. Not a woman I'd hand-picked and had loved with everything in me.

I mean, I thought I loved her. I've been adding this shit up in my head for two weeks. Piecing together things I'd forgotten about, I came to the conclusion that I only thought that she had loved me and she'd never loved Bug. In the hospital, she had only held her a few times. If I wasn't there, the baby was in the nursery. I couldn't figure it out. We'd been happily waiting on her arrival for the entire pregnancy.

I don't know where the sparkle of the expectant mother went, but by the time we'd arrived home with Bug in tow, there were no more stars. The quirky, funny girl that I'd fallen in love with as a teen had transformed into a shell of her former self. Bug couldn't latch on after numerous attempts to nurse her, so she couldn't breastfeed as planned. It had disappointed Toya; she was heartbroken. I'm not sure if that disappointment and frustration festered and turned into postpartum depression. She is now saying that it had escalated into a full-blown psychosis and that she was too afraid to admit that something was wrong. I missed the signs. In hindsight, I could see that something was wrong but I didn't understand. I was too young. Too stubborn.

Vanna was like, it's real, 'cause I was on some shit that it was fake. She showed me a case where a mother had killed all five of her children due to severe post-partum depression. I can't imagine Toya being murderous. But I also find it hard to believe something that I have absolutely no knowledge of. She claims that she'd been afraid to discuss it, so it was easier to push us away.

As my rage settles and calms, I process the information

that she gave me. I prayed about it and He answered with mercy for her. So at my family's urging, I allowed Toya to visit Bug, supervised, at my parents' house, and she couldn't tell her that she was her mom. Toya didn't get those privileges until I could trust her with my lovebug's heart. She was talking shit about introducing her to her boyfriend and her new baby and still threatening to file for custody and them being one, big family.

Nah. Not at all. She has a family. I felt like I was gonna choke that hoe with my bare hands.

I needed distance. I needed— I looked up into the large ceiling of the mall, closed my eyes, and instantly thought, *my girl.* Fuckin' stubborn ass woman. I shake my head at how unyielding pride fucks up good situations.

"Cart," I hear my name being called. I look around and spot Tyree and Bri with their baby girl. We kind of meet in the center near a cart selling high-thread count sheet sets.

"Hey, Ty, wassup? Bri." Briannah smiles and squints her eyes and then wags her finger at me. "What you do to my friend?"

Tyree looks down at his wife. "Babe, mind your business."

I laugh, shake my head. "Your friend. Man."

"She crying her eyes out because you haven't come by," she informs me.

"I have a lot going on. She has a lot going on. All that drama with her parents kind of took precedence over our relationship. So, she is where she is," I explain with a shrug.

"Babe, I'll meet you up there," Tyree says, pointing in the direction they were initially heading.

Bri frowns as she looks to where he is pointing. "There are more subtle ways to say you wanna talk to him alone," Bri tells him. "Bye, Carter."

Tyree runs his hand over his head then shakes it. "Women."

Next to the cart is a group of seats. We both sit. "Is this the part where you ask what my intentions are?" I joke.

He tips his head back and chuckles. "Nawl. You a good dude, Cart. Good for my cousin. She loves you. I know Lieas inside out, and I've never seen her happier. So what happened, man?"

"We disagree about her parents. About what's between them is between them. I need her here; she busy being over there. Then my BM popped up out of nowhere. I'm pretty straightforward about my needs."

Tyree nodded. "Yea. I really looked up to my Unc. Taught me everything I know. I can't wrap my head around him cheating on my aunt for any reason," he shrugs his broad shoulders. "But beyond that, Lieas has idolized their relationship her entire life. Had to put a crack in her heart. I was hoping that you was gonna help her mend it."

"You have a family, so you'll understand this. Everything I do is to make sure that Mira is safe and loved. Promises made to her are important to me. I'm not a whiny dude, but I need one hundred percent and for you to be present. Miss me with all that in-between BS. I love her but I'm having a hard go at it right now and need her to have my back."

"Damn, bro, what happened?"

I explained what was going on with Latoya's return as he listened intently. We've busted it up for years, so I felt comfortable sharing with him. He has a baby mama from a previous relationship and he understands.

"It was big of you to let her see Mira. I think my initial feeling would be like, bitch, kick rocks. But then again, I don't know my dad. I wouldn't be able to pick this nigga out of a lineup. My mom was out there, so it's possible he doesn't even know I exist. I think if he would have just showed up sometime after my mom died, my Gram would've been like hell to the nawl. My aunt Nic would've been cool with it because she's proper and polite." Tyree stops and clears his throat. "Not sure how my uncle would've felt because he's always had that job. Looking back, I think I would've liked to have known him. Family is important to me. Knowing where you come from is important so at the end of the day if Mira's mother wants to participate, let her."

Damn, I didn't know that about him. I just thought his pops was absent. Tyree smiles but it doesn't quite reach his eyes. *Alieas makes the same face.* "Thanks, man," I tell him reaching out to shake his hand.

"Lieas loves hard. She stubborn as hell, though, so sometimes you gotta pull at her and just show up. She ain't that mad; all your shit still intact. Let me go before Briannah come back to grill you." He stands up and stretches.

We both laugh, knowing that Bri would do just that.

CHAPTER
twenty

Alicia

I'M NOT EVEN GOING TO dwell on the fact that it has been fourteen days, three hours, twenty-nine minutes, and three, no, four seconds since I was last happy. But as always, I'm dealing with it. Not gon' let a nigga get me down.

"Girl, are you the hell crazy?" Tiff demands to know as I prepare for my first official outing since the man I'm supposed to spend eternity with is stupid enough to let me go without even so much as a call.

"Tiff, please. He's the one who told me to leave." That's what hurts the most. "So, fuck him!" "Your ass was just crying over him yesterday," she reminds me sarcastically. As if I need her to.

"Well, I'm not now. I'm going out tonight to have a good time and the last man I'ma be worried about is Carter."

"Riiight. Just like last night, huh?"

Tiffany would bring last night up. That was a slip and slide back. I'm not used to hangin' out with my friends on weeknights. I'm usually hugged up in the bed with my man—. Oh well, I guess that's over. Anyway, those hoes decided to get a hotel room at the Palace so we could have a girl's night out. I got pissy drunk and made the biggest, most childish mistake of my life.

I played on Carters' phone, his cell, not the house phone, because even in my drunken haze, I understood that would be off limits. Mira was at home sleeping by that time, and I'd be damned if I would disrupt my baby. I miss her like crazy, and the thought of her real mother coming back into her life is making me insane. Driving me out of my fuckin' mind, actually.

She has no rights.

But then again, neither do I. Still, I've never felt the parental bond that I'm feeling for her. This is why I should've stayed away from his ass when he told me he had a child. Now, two things that I love are out of my reach. My heart is aching at the thought of never having her fall asleep while sitting on my lap or when she's scared and she wants to sleep with Carter and me.

"Hey? Are you listenin' to me? You better call that man!" she orders.

To hell with that man. It's time for me to start looking for something else with someone else.

"I'm not calling him. He knows my damn number and where I live. He has a fuckin' key. He's the one who dismissed me as if I were a gnat gettin' on his last nerve. I don't play that shit. He must not know how many niggas want me." Matter of fact, Justin had hit me up on BlackPlanet. I told him I'd meet him for drinks.

Tiff shakes her head. "Alieas, you're upset because he told you he could take care of a situation by himself."

Not just any situation. "That is not a situation he can handle without talking it over with me. It's a family discussion. I'm a part of Amira's life—"

"Oh, shut the hell up and get over. He had a right to be

angry and you know it. Everything is not about you and your world. Other people do live here!" she exclaims hurriedly before I can interrupt her.

Tiff is on point, as usual, when it comes to making me feel like a piece of shit. I never said everything was about me. I may think it from time to time, but I've never said it. I've learned to be less self-centered since Mira has come into my life. A lot of things are now about her. The majority of things actually revolve around her father.

I'm pissed. Shit, Carter needs to get himself together. I need to get myself together. I'm angry 'cause all I can think about is him, my empty ass heart, him... him... and him. I must be going the fuck crazy. I let a man get me irked.

Damn, he's not just any man.

He's the right man.

I broke my damn cell phone on day three throwing it against the damn wall when I realized he hadn't called. Like all men, he's supposed to come around and try to get back at me. No such luck with him, though.

It's cool. I won't be waiting by the telephone anymore. My ass is going out.

"When are you going to grow up and become that woman you want to be?" Tiff demands, throwing me completely off guard.

"What?!" I flip. "Where the fuck did that come from? You my best friend; your ass is supposed to be supportive—"

"And your ass is supposed to be reasonable," she argues. "I've seen you fucking around with so many guys since we've been friends and—"

Jumping up, I burst through what she is trying to say. "I can't believe you gon' bring that shit in here." I know she not about pull that past shit up. Nobody ever lets you forget that you made irresponsible decisions at one point in your life, especially when you're susceptible to make many more.

She takes a deep breath. "Alieas, calm the fuck down. You know damn well I'm not throwing anything in your face. I'm just pointing out shit that you're too blind to see. Carter is everything you say you want. You let something that happened to your parents, something that you have no power over whatsoever, affect what's between you and the man you love. I'm your best fuckin' friend. I love you and when you hurt, I hurt. No outside shit that has nothing to do directly with us is coming in between me and Tim. Not my parents, not no baby mom. I'm cutting a bitch for me and mine." She reaches out across space and touches my hand. I look her in the eyes. "Call your man or just show up at his house. But fix it before it's too late."

Because I know this to be true, I sit back down and look negligently out the window. "Lousy bitch," I mumble. "What the hell am I supposed to do? He may not want to talk to me. He hasn't called and I'm not the one for that apologizi—"

"Sometimes you need to be the one to suck up your pride," she says, reminding me of my mother, who told me the same exact thing. To avoid Tiff and her steely stare, I glance away from her. She's waiting for me to fall into a fit of tears. I can feel myself getting ready to when I notice the blinking light on my machine.

"Hit the button on the machine for me," I say to her because the phone is right next to her.

"What?"

"The answering machine."

As the machine drones in its robotic voice, 'You have two new messages', my heart flips in my chest. I close my eyes and my fingers grip the arms of the loveseat as Carter's deep voice flows from the machine and directly into my heart. "Alieas, if you're home, pick up the damn phone. I'm tired of this bullshit.

Yo, where the fuck are you? And what happened to your cell phone?" He takes a deep breath. "We need to talk. You need to call me when you get this message. If you don't, I'll be there exactly at nine pm."

I must have been in the daze 'cause it isn't until I hear Tiff gasp, laugh, and applaud that I open my eyes and just stare at the machine as if I'm looking at him.

"Oh shut up." My heart is trembling in my chest; my pulse is ready to jump right out of my neck.

"Umm, isn't your date supposed to be here at nine?" she laughs.

Oh, my god. What am I going to do? "You think that this is funny?!" I spit, eyeing her suspiciously.

Smiling, she replies, "Hell yeah, that shit funny" and then looks down at her wristwatch. "You have a good hour and a half to make your decision."

There are no decisions, no choices to be made. The man has come to his senses. My baby called.

Confident that all would be reconciled, I canceled my meet-up with Justin. I told him I didn't feel good. He was nonchalant, told me to hit him up whenever, and hoped that I felt better. Showered, lotioned down, hair on point, and makeup, flawless, I am ready for my man. I look at the clock, and it's almost nine. Where is he?

THE TIME ON MY DVD PLAYER STARES BACK AT ME. 1:10 A.M.

Yes, one in the goddamn morning, and I haven't seen or heard from Mr. Reed.

I called him and his phone went straight to voicemail at ten and again at eleven. I messaged him on AOL.

No response.

Frantic, I dial his cell again. It rings, like magic. It stops ringing when a woman answers.

My heart sinks. A sense of dread flows through it like ink dissolving into clean water.

I pull the phone away from my ear to check if I'd dialed the correct number. It was his number. So, immediately, I'm thinking why the hell is a female answering?

"Carter? Babe—

"I'm sorry. This is Latoya. Carter is busy. I'll have him call you back tomorrow," she says and quickly disconnects the call.

I'm up like a bullet. Spaced out, I stare at the phone and dial his number back-to-back as it rings and the calls are sent to voicemail one after the other.

What the fuck?! I start to pace my bedroom; I scream because there's nothing else for me to do with my frustration. I knock over a small vase with fresh flowers in it onto the floor.

By two a.m., there's no return call. No Nothing.

That's exactly what I feel right now as the last tears I'll ever shed for Carter fall down my cheeks.

CHAPTER
twenty-one

Aliens

I T'S CRAZY HOW TIMING WORKS. What's even crazier is how impulsive humans are. I'm burning. I want to speak to Carter, and I think of driving to his house at two a.m. and making a spectacle of myself. But I'd done that shit with Tony and just knew that this time was going to be different, that Carter wouldn't put me **in** this position. Here go life teaching me that I obviously don't know shit about love.

And that maybe love is just not for me.

My phone rings. It has to be Carter. I turn in a circle quickly, trying to remember where I had tossed the cordless phone as it continuously rings. By the time I found it under the couch, it stopped ringing. Then it begins ringing again in my hand.

"You feel better?" Justin asks.

"Nawl." *Fuck love.* "But I know what would help me."

Justin laughs. "Oh, I got some feel good," he murmurs roughly.

"Can I get a couple doses?"

"Be there in like ten minutes. Call you when I get out front," he announces eagerly.

I go to the bathroom and look in the mirror. I'm a damn mess. My eyes are all puffy and red. My damn nose has a little bit of snot around the nostril. I can't let Justin see me like this. I turn the water on in the shower, quickly take off my clothes, and jump in.

Fuck love. Fuck love. Fuck love… My mind chants as I wash up. The heat dulling my senses and any ounces of love I had in my heart. Remnants of my tears mingle with the stream of shower water and get washed away.I wet my hair beneath the spray and get lost in the rush of the water. More tears escaped but I shrug them off. I could hear the phone ringing but I don't budge. Justin could wait. He'd waited this long; two more minutes wouldn't kill him.

I get out of the shower, dry off, towel dry my hair for a moment, and quickly brush it into a ponytail. I walk into my bedroom to put some lotion on. I admire my naked body in the mirror over my dresser. It was finally shaped in a way that I had dreamed about my entire life. But when I lift my gaze to my reflection, I only see the pudgy, tall girl with all the self-esteem issues staring back at me.

I rub some, of my favorite scented oil; lick me all over, on my hands and rub them together then over my shoulders and arms. I roll the vile of oil between my breasts, rub some on my hands to then again rub down my entire body.

The phone rings and then the buzzer sounds.

"Buzz me up," Justin practically begs into the intercom.

I press the button on my phone that's linked to the buzzer, wrap the towel back around my body, and walk out of the living room. I unlock the door, crack it a little, and just stand there, leaning up against the wall.

When he opens the door and discovers me standing in what

I like to think is an alluring pose, Justin smiles, that one damn dimple winking at me.

Fuck. I'd almost forgotten how down right sexy he is. Justin rubs his hands together and blows on them to heat them up.

"Damn, baby," Justin breathes out as he shuts and locks the door.

I plaster a smile on my face and let out a playful laugh. Justin kicks off his shoes, shrugs out of his blazer, and lets it fall to the floor. Then he just grabs me by the front of the towel.

Next, he kisses me as we unleash eight months of pent-up desire in a feverish frenzy of twisting tongues. My heart is racing because my body readily betrays it. My girl starts speaking in her favorite language. I'm soaked; the familiar pulsing, beating between the folds of my womanhood has me dragging him further into the kiss.

"Boah must've really fucked up," he slurs into my mouth.

Don't mention him. All I want to do is forget about "boah"

Just fuck and forget. I used to be so good at it. Here I was thinking I could finally have real love and have it love me back.

Just fuck and forget, I tell myself as Justin pulls the towel from my body.

Holding my waist, he guides me backward, into the living area. Justin hisses through his teeth as he takes in the sight of my naked body.

He kisses my hand. His eyes are glued to mine as he places his hand on my chest to feel the thumping of my heart. "It's beating fast. I'd never hurt you," he reassures me as he leans in to kiss me again.

Just fuck and forget… The pain… The promises...

Him.

Justin cups my left breast in his hand and bounces it, testing its weight. He gently toys with my nipple, rolling it between his finger before taking it into his mouth. He laves it greedily with his tongue.

Closing my eyes as the warring sensations build, I feel the slight force of energy igniting the familiar tingle. I hold his head to me as he feeds. His free hand drifts along my skin, traveling the curves of my body before resting it at the small of my back and begins to feast on both breasts. One to the other. He clasps me tight, fingers digging in.

A moan escapes my lips, and I run my tongue lazily over my bottom lip. I bite down on it to trap the next one before it oozes out.

"You smell good enough eat," he huskily whispers in my ear. He licks the inside shell then travels to nibble on my earlobe. Tongue, slick and wet, trails a thin line down my neck, burrowing in the delicate and sensitive hollow as he playfully takes a bite.

Fuck and Forget... There's no turning back now. I'm drowning.

In a misty vision, I see the "me" that I was claiming to be, sitting on the edges of the shore. She stands up and lifts her hands up to shield her eyes from the sun to get a better look, attempting to spot an iota of her in me. Off in the distance, past the safety line, I'm waving, arms flaying in the air. After a moment, she puts her hands down. The search is over; she can't see me. She turns and walks off in the distance.

Away from me.

An appreciative moan escapes as the tension of the inner war I'm waging dissipates.

I broke our kiss, faintly tasting the sweetness of Grand Marnier and swallowed. I push him back a step, just enough that I could reach down to unbuckle his belt. I unzip his jeans as he quickly does away with the buttons on his crisp white shirt.

Seconds pass as I admire the results of his daily trips to

the gym. Ripples of muscles jump beneath my roaming fingers. I push the shirt from his broad shoulders, letting my hands travel over his well-toned arms. He grasps my hips again, fusing our bare chests to one another. He wraps his arms around me and in one fell swoop, lifts me off my damn feet.

Justin walks across the room and presses my back up against the wall. He kisses and playfully grinds himself into me. I laugh, still a little amazed that he was capable of lifting me, even with my significant weight loss. Greedily, he sucks the bare skin along my collarbone, which I'm sure will leave a mark.

"What's up, ma? You too quiet," he murmurs.

He's talking too much. I close my eyes and Carter's smiling face forms perfectly in my mind.

I can't do this…

I don't realize that I'd said it aloud until Justin lifts his hands to frame my face and ask me to open my eyes.

"Alieas?" His forehead dips to touch mine. He sighs heavily to get his lust in check before he leans back and looks me in my eyes and says my name again. "Alieas?"

My heart trips. It's not too late.

"I'm soooo sorry, Justin," I nervously let out.

He steps back and lets me go.

Embarrassed, I lift my hands to my mouth. "I'm so sorry," I mumble again. I slide from between him and the wall and race across the room and into my bedroom.

I frantically dig through my drawers for something to cover up in and I grab Carter's ball shorts, a sports bra, and one of my sorority t-shirts.

I know I still have to face Justin because he doesn't leave. He isn't the type to just leave. I suppose he's sober enough to want to discuss it, but I am completely mortified. I palm my forehead and just stand there for a moment.

Suck it up, heffa. This could've gone way left. This man could have raped you. Gather your composure and go handle your business.

I take in a deep breath, effectively sucking it up and heading out to the living room. Justin's shirt and pants are back on and he's sitting on the couch, rolling up a blunt.

He clears his throat when I sit beside him. "You mind if I blow?"

I shake my head. And before I can stop or control it, a shameful tear escapes. I quickly rub my bottom eyelid, praying that the familiar cloudiness in my head doesn't mean that I'm gonna start balling all over him.

And of course, I do...

Justin takes a toke, holds the smoke in his mouth, and then blows it out. "So, you definitely love dude."

I nod and mumble, "Yes."

He is quiet as he tokes it two more times. "Damn, Lieas," he blows out the words in a puff of smoke.

"I'm sorry. I'm so embarrassed."

"You?" he laughed a little. "I was hype as shit," he drawls. "You look good as fuck, but I ain't no nut ass dude."

"I know." I can't apologize anymore because this was so fucked up of me to have done this to him.

He flicks the ashes in the blunt wrapper then taps the blunt out on the paper. He let his head fall back to rest on the back of the couch.

"Damn, ma. You cool as shit. What happened with boah?"

My emotions wild, I ignore that I'd just had my tongue down his throat and tell him. I can't believe that he is listening. This is why I feel connected to him. While not in love, I care for him. I had even kind of missed him. Now, I feel even shitter.

Hurt people hurt other people. The thought bounced around in the hollows of my heart.

"Thank you, Justin," I say, grateful that he hasn't flipped out on me.

The marijuana must have started taking effect because his eyes were lowered and he had a drowsy twist to his lips. "Can I chill here til the morning?" he stammered as he dragged his hand down his face, hoping it would bring down his high. "C'mere," he slurs.

I nod and lean back into his arms. I quickly fall asleep.

Hours later, this is exactly how Carter finds me— asleep. In another man's arms...

PART

two

Time. So precious,
it waits for no
man...

CHAPTER

twenty-two

Friday

Alieas

REUNITED AND IT FEELS SO *good...*

Yeah-the-fuck-right. The amber eyes that assess me are skeptical, harsh and reflect shades of downright distrust. Still, I search them for a fleck of forgiveness, understanding, and possible warmth.

I'm coming up empty.

I built up the courage to glance down at his ring finger and was relieved to see it free of bands and any tan lines. My gaze peruses the rest of him, devouring every inch from head to toe. Digesting him with my soul, I revel in the visual delight that is unadulterated, raw, uniquely him.

Masculine as fuck! Still handsome as ever and confidently owning that shit.

The hair that I once braided in straight backs is now

tapered down to a sea of black waves infiltrated with a few noticeable grays. The goatee had grown into a full beard, leaving my mouth dry. I'm officially on the beard gang train.

Yes, Lawd!

The damn-near uncontrollable need to take him in my arms and plead my case is stomped out as the once-happy-fan clears her throat. Our eyes meet again after my daring exploration of him, and then I turn my attention to her.

"So, y'all know one another?" she thoughtfully inquires as the prolonged silence and unspoken tension continues.

"Yeah. In passing," he explains, diminishing our months of love to a fleeting moment in time.

My heart expands painfully in my chest at the unfeeling characterization of what I'd professed to be the love of my life. And even though we have many mutual friends, today is the first time I've seen him since our breakup. "Come on if y'all taking this pic," he states, his words tinged with annoyance.

I put on the show face, and she poses, once again, as he snaps the picture and then hands the phone back to her.

There's clear confusion marked in the woman's pretty face, but she accepts his word and reaches her hand out to mine.

"It was nice meeting you." The slender outstretched fingers are also ring-free. "I guess I'll see you tomorrow," she says softly, almost afraid to now speak.

"Of course. I'll look for you, Deidra."

Carter doesn't utter another word before he walks off. Deidra follows him with one glance back at me.

Yes, if in passing means in-fucking-love, I think to myself.

CARTER

In passing? Maybe that was a little harsh, I consider as I made my way through the exit doors. She looked fucking amazing. Extra tall, kinda thick, and fine.

I can't even figure out why I'm annoyed. I had wanted to stay in tonight. Mira has a couple friends over, but Deidra insisted that we make a Target and pizza run.

I hate being thrown off.

Alieas' appearance did more than just throw me off; it knocked the wind out of me. There was a moment of complete shock on both our parts. Alieas just stood there, mouth hanging to her chin. If I didn't know any better, I could swear her golden eyes were pleading, wounded, and seeking at least one ounce of feeling from me.

But I wasn't ready for her. To give in to that demand of emotions was something I was still working out. She was still bold as ever, her eyes examining every inch of me. My dick grew hard as if he could sense her eyes on him. And when our eyes collided, I swear there was a faint smirk on her lips.

Impatiently, I shifted my weight from one leg to the other. *None of my brain cells are going to work after this.*

Sometimes, you think about dipping your toe in the pool and fate comes alongside and pushes you all the way in. I was going to contact her.

"So… exactly what was that?" Deidra finally asks once we were settled into the car.

I walked off, had needed some air after taking their picture. So, I told her that I'd meet her at the car instead of waiting for her at the register.

"What was what?" I reply, feigning ignorance and pulling out of the parking spot.

"You never said you knew her," she starts.

I'm so not in the mood to have this conversation. The way I'm feeling, it's going to lead to a place I'm not sure she wants to go. We are already going through the motions, halfway togeth-er/halfway broken up. She wants things that I'm not ready for with her. That I don't want with her. I guess it was as simple as that. "I didn't know that I had to tell you about every woman I've been with."

Deidra glares at me, twists her lips, and rolls her neck. The brown eyes that are usually patient and trusting now bear a hole through me with a hint of anger. "Carter?"

More annoyed with her than I should be, I sigh and shrug. "Why the hell you mad that we bumped into someone I used to talk to?"

"I saw how y'all were looking at one another."

And? "Stop making stuff up where there is nothing. I haven't seen her in over ten years—"

A hand went up to stop me from continuing my now rant. "I know when you're lying. And your dick got hard when she was staring at you because I know that dick print well. And to make matters worse, you didn't even introduce me."

I'm flabbergasted at her keen observation. It doesn't surprise me that she noticed; women notice every damn thing, and there was no use denying it, so I kept it neutral. "I'm going to take you home now."

She expels an angry puff of air then she points accusingly at me. "Are you fucking her, Carter?"

There was the reason for her anger. Right off, she is defen-sive. She has no idea how I know Alieas, and she the hell mad already. And it's not like anything I say will make it any better, but damn.

"What did I just say?. I haven't seen her in over ten years and, I am *not* fucking her."

She sucks her teeth and impatiently stares at me. I take it the folded arms and angry eyes mean that she is pissed. "You damn sure looked like you wanted to. So, are you going to tell me what's going on or not?" she demands.

"I used to love her," I admit while assessing and planning my next move.

"And?" she inquires, waiting for more.

Throughout our eight-month relationship, I've shared pieces of myself with Deidra but have kept the innermost aches to myself. Not sure if I'd ever admitted aloud that Alieas had hurt me to anyone. Fuck, that she'd broken into pieces what was left of my heart. Nawl, I couldn't admit that to anyone, so I left out the specifics. The most she knew about my romantic past was there was someone I loved and we hadn't worked out because the woman wasn't willing to give me what I needed.

That was then and this is now. My heart has since healed. Many, many relationships and "situationships" later, it is still intact.

Now, after knowing what I know about that last night, I'm not entirely sure that if anything was as it seemed.

"Is she the one?" she presses after an awkward silence.

Be honest. Why the hell not? "Yes. She is."

"Hmmm," she murmurs thoughtfully then settles back into her seat.

Deidra remained quiet on the ride back to my house. Once I reached Ford Rd., I realized that she had driven to my house and that I had to turn around so she could get her car. When we pulled up to my house, the silence continued.

"Deidra," I started but had no idea what I was going to finish with.

She shook her head. "Don't, Carter. Just don't." Her eyes were shielded, but I could tell my revelation had an effect on her. The last thing I wanted to do was hurt her.

And I imagine the last thing she wanted to do was be hurt. I didn't say a word or make a move to stop her as she quietly got out of the truck. I sat still for a moment, watching as she briskly walked to her car and got in.

When she pulled off, I parked in the driveway, climbed out for the truck and slowly walked to the front door of my house.

The sound of loud music booming from inside the house greeted me at the door. Shaking my head, I let myself in. Bug had set up a stage in front of the fireplace, and she and her two girlfriends were belting out Katy Perry's *Roar* into karaoke microphones. She had turned the family room into a campground, fully furnished with tents and a projector that would display stars on the ceiling.

Leaning against the wall, I watched them then applauded obnoxiously when they were done. "Great job, ladies!"

She squinted her eyes at me. She'd taken her glasses off and had put on lip gloss and some sparkling glitter on her cheeks. Deidra had actually made them up before we left.

Time sure passes quickly. Soon, my babygirl won't be content with nights in with her girlfriends and karaoke. She'll have some asshole sending her home in tears. And my glock will be cocked and ready.

"Hey, Dad," she greeted me as she comes over.

"Hey Mr. Reed," her two friends spoke.

"D has the pizza?" she asked.

Shit, I had forgotten all about it. I wince, trying to figure out how I am going to explain that Deidra had gone home.

"You know what, Bug? I forgot the pizza. Something came up and Deidra had to go home. She said to tell you goodnight and that she was sorry."

"Oh, is everything okay?" she asked, her concern for Deidra apparent.

When she asked those type of questions, I realized that she's also maturing. "She's fine."

At my reassurance, concern was quickly replaced with interrogation. "Did she end up getting the book she wanted? She said that the author was dope. Do you think I can read it?!" she excitedly questions.

"You're getting big, Bug. But not that big."

She shrugged and laughed, dancing back over to her friends. She's fourteen now, and I know she's been exposed to shit far beyond my control. In the last couple of months, I've read a couple of Lieas' books, and there wasn't anything for my baby girl in between those pages.

Shaking my head, I cut that notion real quick. "That would be a no," young lady.

"Oh," she replied and went back to whatever decision-making process they went through to select the next song.

I went into the kitchen ordered their food then made a tropical green smoothie for myself before I grabbed a bottle of water and headed out. I figured I'd put in some time in the shop; I had to draw up plans for a full remodel of a restaurant in Lower Merion.But my mind kept going back to Alieas and how good she looked and how I wanted nothing more than to take out ten years worth of frustration out on her, long dick style.

There was something nagging at me, reminding me that I had once loved the fuck out of this woman. Then reality set in and reminded me that I had been hesitant to act on my love due to our lengthy time apart and the fear that it had been entirely too long ago to do anything about it.

The look in her eyes said something else altogether. It said that love never dies... My heart felt it.

I peeked my head into the family room and called out to Mira, "I ordered the pizza and wings for delivery. Make sure you're up by nine. Your mom said she is going to take you to dance class." I dug out money to pay the delivery guy and put it on the mail table.

The years had been good, and the village had expanded to include Latoya and her entire family. It had taken some spiritual counseling to forgive her, but I'm fine knowing that however it had begun, she was here for her child now. Learning how to share Mira had initially been a struggle. Our parenting styles are different and sometimes, she and her ratchet ass family drive me crazy. Toya is more lenient than I am, I believe she thinks being her friend makes up for the time they were separated. For the most part, with time and patience, we had gotten through the years successfully. The most important thing was that Mira had benefited from it and finally discovered a mother's love.

"Don't stay up too late," I told her. "Night. Ladies."

Mira ran up to me and grabbed the money from the table and gave me a kiss on the cheek. "Night, Dad. Love you."

Looking at my watch and seeing the date, I latently remember that today is Lieas' Birthday.

CHAPTER
twenty-three

Alieas

ALL OF THESE WOMEN ARE married. I was a bridesmaid in all of their weddings. I was even present for the births of some of their children. I was a shoulder to cry on. While men were frequent but few stuck around, I was always there for these women—they were mine. My friends, my sisters, my mirrors.

About a half hour ago, Bri, Nesha, Trina, Tiff, and Case surrounded me in a circle of prayer for continued success, blessings for another year of life, and a hope for love. Words can't explain the power of prayer. I can't begin to explain how important it is to have your people praying to whoever they worship, for you and never against you. Their best intentions, hearts full of hope, requesting what's best for you in the purest form of submission to the most high.

All I want is love, feel it deep down in my soul… love.

I laugh as they all whine about the latest antics of their children, husbands, and employees. The men are upstairs with all the kids, watching Sports Center recaps while my mom is probably already in the kitchen putting everything away.

In their presence, I find myself at home. At certain moments, we're all eighteen or nineteen again, sprawled on the floor of my parents' basement, dreaming of our future. Funny shit, all of them were dreaming about the men they are currently married to. Meanwhile, my ass sitting on the sideline dreaming about the past.

What the fuck was I doing wrong?

Being a hoe. Steve said you gotta make they ass wait ninety days.

Not all of their roads to everlasting love had been easy, but once they reached their destination, they had settled in.

I suck my teeth. "I love/hate y'all heffas," I blurt out, pointing my fork at them accusingly. So instead of baking one herself, my mom had ordered a cake. It's this massively round, three-layer chocolate cake with raspberry filling, covered with cream cheese frosting and chocolate chips all around the sides. She orders them from this baker lady in Jersey and it is to die for. For the life of me, I never remember her name, but the cake is always so damn good. I'm going to have to get her number. Maybe I can order me something the next time I come up. I dug my fork into the cake for another taste.

Bri smiles, laughs and ruffles my hair. "Don't hate, honey. And in any case, why would you?"

My face says it all, but she continues. "I'm telling you His timing is perfection."

Of course, it is, I mentally agree. "Says the happily married with children squad."

She kisses my cheek.

"What if he is still being worked on in preparation of receiving you. Or," her eyes sparkle and she clears her throat, "if you need work. What you call it? Changing Stiles on 'em?" Trina offers.

I guess I could use her as my example of God's timing. Less than three years ago, she'd been stressed out and out of sorts, waiting for love to take root and grow. Now, she is married to Dave with two babies. My heart melts as she nurses her infant daughter Niayla. She so darn happy now. Ugh.

Okay, I have to let go of this self-pity.

"You are a lot to handle, Lieas," Tiff chimes in. "And Mr. Right is going to have to come correct."

"Yes, child," Nesha laughs. "Subhanahu Wa Ta'ala is working it for you, baby."

"Yes, Jesus is!" Bri adds.

"I know. I saw Carter at Target right before I got here. How did I ever fuck that up?" I confess.

"Aah-he," one of them coughs.

"How did that go?" Tiff inquires.

I shrug. "He still the fuck mad. Still sexy as all hell. He was there with his girlfriend…"

I then explain to them how it all went down.

"Damn."

"We invited him to our anniversary party." Bri confessed. "He still kick it with the guys sometimes. Maybe…"

Shaking, my head, I decline. There's no point. He's with someone. I'm not trying to involve myself in any mess. I'm too old for that shit. And I won't find my Mr. Right poaching someone else's. "I doubt if he comes. He ain't come to Case's or Trina's weddings."

"He also hasn't seen you in over ten years. You look great, boo," Trina reminds me.

I looked fucking fabulous the last time he saw me. Since then, I gained about fifteen pounds but the way I'm toned, no one would know. Not that it would matter; he used to love thick women.

Bri disagrees. "He can't be that mad after all these years because he did ask Ty about you a while back. I remember him saying something about him having a girl and it being complicated, though," she adds.

I sat up, mind at full attention. "He asked about me and you ain't tell me?"

I can hear their laughter, but I curb my tongue as my mom calls, me making her way down the back steps.

"Yes?"

"Come up here, please?"

We haven't had any real moments alone since I arrived. It'll be just my luck that she wants to grill me on why Jermaine isn't with me. Reluctantly, I go up to meet her, and she resumes washing the dishes. I shake my head and almost laugh at her because she has on a full apron that reads, "*Smile, I'm the best at what I do.*"

"How was the drive up?" she inquires.

"It was cool. Traffic wasn't that bad," I shrug, leaning up against the counter. "Cute apron," I tease.

As expected, she turns her nose up. "Mitchell bought it for me." Her new husband is wonderful to her. " And I thought you were bringing company," she eased in slyly.

I huffed out, "It's late, Mom," as I jump on the counter.

She rolls her eyes and turns to face me, "Girl, I'm not worried about your warnings and get your ass off my counter."

I laugh but I do as she commands. "I love you, Mom. I truly missed you." Wrapping my arms around her and holding on, I breathe her in. She smells like peaches and cinnamon.

"Well, of course. I miss you too, baby," she coos.

My heart swells. I can't say I've ever grown accustomed to not seeing her regularly. As much as she nags all my nerves, I love her with everything in me.

The sharp brown eyes that, in my youth, scared me straight was replaced by a softer side that soothed my hurts.

"You have that look. What's wrong?"

"I need for you to call your father."

The request is unexpected even though she is an advocate

for our relationship and has begun a forgiveness campaign in his honor.

I clear my throat. "Why?"

"Because it's time to. Past time to," she amends.

I let go of the breath I'm holding. "Not from where I'm sitting," I stubbornly reply.

"Still perched atop your pedestal, huh?" She pulls out a chair from the table. "Sit with me."

As she sits, I observe her and prepare myself for what feels like the end of the year heart-to-heart. Quietly, I sit beside her.

"Baby, you've allowed what happened between your father and me to turn you off from love," she begins.

This assessment couldn't be farther from the truth so naturally. I object, "I didn't."

She shakes her head, dismissing the notion before I can even speak it. "But you did. Look at you. You're so beautiful yet you're running from love."

Running from love? *Neeegative*. That shit is running from me, but I don't interrupt what she's saying to correct her.

"You're carrying around the weight of our mistake on your shoulders—"

"Ma, please," I interrupt.

She's still shaking her head. "Your father, he was far from perfect. But he was so handsome and strong. I felt so lucky that he chose me, especially after having been with Layla."

"Mom, you really don't have to—"

But I could feel that she needed to say what has been in her heart for a while. This issue was serious in her eyes and at the mention of my aunt, I understand that she has some things to get off her chest.

"I do. I do, sweetie. I had made up this beautiful façade of what our relationship was. How could anyone think different? I had loved him like a young girl with a crush when he dated

Layla. It was only for a moment, but he *loooooved* her. He couldn't make her leave the streets alone, so he lost her. And then he loved me. And we were happy. So happy until we weren't. I'm not sure of the "when" or the "who's", but there had been many women over our twenty-something years of marriage. There was a part of him, deep down inside that I couldn't reach. He cut it off and reserved it only for her. He'd even slept with her while we were married. Don't know exactly when. It came out later. She was so out of her mind, off her meds, on them drugs, and a piece of him always loved her. He thought that his love could save her. And blamed himself when he couldn't. I knew all of this, and I stayed anyway."

Tears were pouring from her eyes now. She wiped at them with the strap of her apron. She leaned back and crossed her long legs. If she still smoked, I could imagine her taking a long drag of her cigarette before continuing her testimony. "And we were happy for many years. But all the unspoken issues between us festered and spread. I tried to hold us together. When you were gone away to school, it was easier for him to cheat. We did the counseling thing, and it worked briefly. But I was tired of not being enough. Of not being able to fill the hole that a dead woman had left in him."

It sounded so sad that she'd even been trying. But who wouldn't try, for love?

"How could you marry him knowing he still loved Aunt Layla?" It is a question I'd never allowed myself to ask. It goes against every girl code I'd ever established with any of my squad. I can't even remember my aunt. I was four when she died. She was so beautiful and full of life until the schizophrenia and drugs gotten the best of her. Tyree missed her but couldn't really remember her either.

She stretched long limbs. "I was so young. Barely eighteen. I loved him and he slept with me. Started a relationship with me, but he didn't love me. He married me because I was pregnant, and it was the right thing to do. He *ended up* loving me." She laughed a pitiful chuckle.

I'd never heard this side of things. My gram had let pieces out over the years but never told the entire tale. It's crazy, the secrets that are kept amongst family members.

"We all make mistakes, Lieas. Mine was allowing you to think that our relationship was perfect. That we were perfect. Having you think that you had to live up to that and have it all fall apart. I'm so sorry, baby."

"How did you forgive him?"

"I let go. I took responsibility for my part in all of it, and I let it go." The words were almost a whisper. The shrug made the statement seem indifferent, but the streaming tears made it sincere.

Instantly, I'm disagreeing with everything she's just revealed. "You can't be blaming yourself for him! Excusing his behavior!"

"No. I'm saying I knew about the many affairs. Turned a blind eye to the indiscretions. Kept secrets. But after so many indiscretions, you're no longer the victim of, 'How could he do this to you?'. People start to look at you like, 'Why do you allow this?' That's the look you were giving me when you found out. And I knew I deserved better but only if I was willing to take a step towards getting it."

I guess I've never looked at it that way.

"I felt insane, willing to do the exact same thing for the umpteenth time, actually expecting a different result."

I laugh. It was a personalized definition of insanity.

"In any case, that was between us, your father and me. I wouldn't have wanted him to lose you and Gray over our problems, and that is exactly what happened. He's tried to make amends, but you're so stubborn."

"He lied to us, Ma." I have no place for it in my life. Lies had cost me everything.

She shrugged again. "Don't we all? A little white lie here, a bigger omission there?"

It made sense. In some cases, lies were essential. But our tolerance for them is always based on who's doing the lying and who's on the receiving end.

"Heal what you have with your father. It may heal your own heart a lil' bit. I think it's holding up my grandbabies and your happiness."

She takes my face between her hands, makes me stare her in the eyes. "Everyone deserves a second chance, Alieas."

Wasn't I secretly begging for the very same thing from Carter?

I shrug and she kisses me on the nose then goes back to washing the dishes.

CHAPTER
twenty-four

Alicia

THOUGHTS OF MY CONVERSATION WITH my mom and her words lingered well into my book event. It stayed in the back of mind, lingering and nagging at my conscience. I figured I would call my dad once I wrapped this up and was back at my hotel room. We could meet up for lunch or breakfast before I drive back to D.C. tomorrow. I miss my family, so I may even stay an extra day.

Right now, I have to smash this interactive skit. I am kind of relieved when I don't see Deidra in the crowd. She must have changed her mind when she found out that one of my books is about her man

"So, I need a volunteer." I look out in the small crowd of about twenty women, in addition to my girls. No one raises their hand. I get off the stool. "Don't be shy. It'll be fun," I persuade as I walk through their chairs. Trina raises her hand at the same time as another reader.

Excitedly I point to the reader and playfully roll my eyes at Trina. "Have you read the book yet?" I ask the reluctant volunteer.

"I just bought it today," she admits.

"That's ok. Pick a number between one and thirty."

"Twenty-four!" she excitedly supplies.

The last date, twenty-four was a disastrous enough pick. It honestly left me feeling like there was no hope left in the world and then shockingly twenty-five came through and showed that I was indeed shit out of luck.

I tap Trina on the shoulder. "Come on up here. You ladies are going to do a replay of date twenty-four." I led them to the platform I'd been sitting on. It would be our stage.

Introductions were quick. I gave them both books and instructions to read over what they'd be acting out. While they did that, Lon helped me set up a small table for the scene. This was always the fun part. It was my innovative way of engaging the readers. They seemed to love it, so I'm going to continue doing it until they get tired of it.

"So, who is gonna be me and who is going to be him?" I inquire, eyeing them both.

"She can be you," Giselle answers, tipping her book to Trina and then finishes up with, "I'll be the guy."

Rubbing my hands together in anticipation, I ask, "So y'all ready?"

"Yup," Trina responds, taking the single chair. I watched as Lon leads Giselle to the back of the crowd.

As Trina begins reading, my mind is already taking me back to that day.

"At this stage in my life, I like to think that two attractive people can meet and arrange to link up at a coffee shop and chat a little. So, here I am, just waiting for this man to show up. I checked my watch," She looked down at her watch and sucked her teeth, "he's already five minutes late. I check myself out using the camera on my phone. I look fabulous and there's not one hair out of place. I take a couple quick selfies."

Trina lifts her phone and does just that, take several selfies. She elicits some giggles from the crowd. Her portrayal of me is spot on. She has my stance and mannerisms down pat. This comes from years of knowing one another and just straight old school busting.

When the replay of the date was complete Trina and Giselle take their seats and I think about to it and laugh. I pick up reading where they left off to provide an idea of the after.

He texted ten minutes later, but I didn't answer; in fact, I ignored all his calls and text messages for about two weeks that followed.

A hand popped up, followed by this comment, "So, you just left him there?"

I laughed. "I wasn't even about to set myself up, so, yes, I did."

I thanked Giselle and Trina for participating. I caught sight of a slight movement in my peripheral, causing me to glance in its direction.

Surprised, my eyes widened as they met Carter's. My imagination, vivid and full of expression, had my pupils dilating and me wanting to pass and sprawl out on the floor. There's a bright, shining light behind him, almost ethereal, and only for me to see. A confident smile spreads across my glossy lips, quietly contradicting the butterfly wings of uncertainty fluttering in my stomach.

Next, latent mortification sinks in as I observe that he's cradled a copy of my book in his hands. And then he speaks.

"Did you experience all these dates in the book?"

I tear my eyes from his for a moment to glance over at Trina, Bri, and Lon. They are all sporting stupid ass grins.

I close my eyes to regain my senses and center myself. My

insides have me feeling like Tweety Bird with those obnoxious hearts in his eyes as he's floating in the air, feet barely touching the ground.

"Yes, I did," I confess. "Which brings me to some quick statistics regarding the African-American dating and marriage rates in the U.S.," I return my attention to my group.

I couldn't let his presence distract me from the goal at hand. I still had to handle my business and finish up the signing.

I can feel his eyes on me. I want to pass out from the heat of his steely gaze as we discuss the statistics I had referenced and a few ladies shared some of their worse dates.

Carter raises his hand again when I ask if the crowd has any more questions. "So, is the character's thirtieth last date her last date because she gets a happy ending or just because she's through with men?"

Bri coughs, and a few women turn their attention to Carter. Years of practice make me shine a bright smile his way. I shrug. "I guess you'll just have to read to find out."

My girl begins to pulsate when he throws his head back to laugh. The sound is rough and rich, sending my senses into overdrive. I vividly recall this man wrapping his hands around my neck as he dicked me down with that same sexy, maniacal laughter. "I'm interested. I missed the beginning; can I get you to sign mine?"

Interested? In me? What the heck is he even doing here? And where is Deidra?

Lon comes up behind me and gives me a nudge and that look that said, "Get that, gurl!"

"Well, I would definitely like to thank everyone for coming…"

Carter plays the background as the crowd thins out and I sign a couple books. Lon and Bri decide to straighten up as I make my way over to Carter. Trina called out to him from

where she stood to speak. He nods and waves in acknowledgment.

I have no idea what to say to him. For the first time in a long
time, I'm speechless and worried foolishly about how I look. For
years, I've dreamed of seeing him and entertained just sparking
up a regular conversation with him.

"Hey," I mutter. "I didn't expect to see you here." My nerves
are all rattled. There is no way to decipher his thoughts. I'm still
stuck on the fact that he's actually here, standing before me,
looking all perfect.

Ten plus years and he still has the power to make my insides
quiver like I was still that twenty-two-year-old girl.

Carter clears his throat. "I was surprised to see you yesterday. You look wonderful. Beautiful, in fact. Happy Belated
Birthday."

My heart quickens at the fact that he remembered my birthday."Thank you. But what are you doing here and where is
Deidra?" I get it out smoothly enough that I don't sound like a
bumbling fool.

"Deidra?" He shrugs his shoulders, laughs, and then fixes
his eyes on mine. "I have no idea, but I'm here to see you."

I start flicking the retractable pen with my thumb to calm
my nerves. "Why?"

He steps closer to me and leans down to whisper in my ear.
"Because you ran and never came back." His breath tickles my
neck and the hairs on my body all stand at alert. "Because we
were unresolved. Because it's ten years later, and when I saw
you yesterday, I felt the same way I had the first time I ever
saw you."

Cautiously, I give him the once-over. Well... the "twice-
over". No amount of well-put-together words is going to have
my head in the clouds. I am a queen of well-put-together words.

My word game is strong. "Is that what you explained to Deidra when she asked about us?" I counter.

I step away from him because we could both benefit from the distance. It would help us to think clearly. Well, for me, anyway. Smelling him, being in this close proximity has me wanting to just drag him to my car and take out years of loneliness and frustration on him. The dull ache of unrequited love expands, and I want to fix it the way I have fixed it my entire life.

With great sex.

"Well, it actually— that is exactly what I told her."

I blink. "Wait. What? She is your girlfriend— I mean, you're with her, right?" Hadn't she called him babe?

"Would you like to go to dinner or something?" he offers, not answering my question.

My heart stops. Then it races. "Are you single? Or you plan on bringing Deidra with you?"

He reaches out to catch my hand before placing them in his. The calloused pads let me know that he still works in construction.

"Are you single? That's all I'm concerned with."

Oh, Lawd. The temperature in the room soared, thanks to the imaginary flames in my mind, and only Carter's hose could extinguish it.

"Dinner would work," I all but purred as memories of simple caresses and hand-holding have me feeling extra nostalgic.

"Tonight."

"To— tonight?" I stutter, my words tripping over one another. "No— I can't. I have— I have— something."

"A date?" he sneers, amber eyes, peering, laughing, judging perhaps. "Your dance card stays full, huh?"

I squint my eyes suspiciously. I'm not completely sure if he's doing a call back to my hoe days or not. "No. I'm only in town for the weekend, so I sort of already have plans."

"We can link up whenever you have time. I know you're a busy woman, so I'll take breakfast, brunch, lunch, tea time, dinner, dessert, or anything and everything in between. I am at your will," he nearly pleads.

I shake my head. And just like that, the past is the past? "Carter, I don't understand."

He kisses my hands. "You're a smart woman, so, of course, you do."

My brows lift in confusion, which pales in comparison to my overactive imagination. It already has my face down and ass up in the restroom at his welcoming advances and overtures. "I— I — we haven't seen one another in a very long time. And frankly, we didn't part on very good terms."

He acknowledges the complicated truth with a nod. "Pride is a mutha. But I'm hoping we can rectify that."

Grab the olive branch so we can build a damn vineyard…

Vineyard? Not likely. But he could be fun…

Fuck fun. This is the type of impulsive shit that keeps me single.

Or I can just see where it goes and have fun until we reach the destination.

I lean into him. "Is this some type of game? Are you just tryna screw with my head to get back at me?"

Instantly offended, Carter drops my hands. He steps back and gives me the most serious of looks. I remember baring my soul beneath that gaze, and I am as naked and vulnerable as I've ever been, this second and every second that follows.

"Games?" He shakes his head. "Nawl, ma. I'm far too old for games. I figured you would be too."

"Exactly. Too old for games and any and everything in between that."

"So, what's it going to be? Dinner, breakfast, or both?"

My smile spreads; my cheeks warm and display a blush beneath my caramel skin. He thinks I'm still loose with my vagina. "Carter."

"Lieas, I have some things to say. Let's go to dinner to talk about it. Let me get your number." He pulls out his phone from the pocket of his vest.

There is no doubt that I want to give him my number. But watching all these modern-day Lifetime movies and ID channel shows has me questioning his true intentions. I'm leery as fuck of men swallowing the big pill of forgiveness. If he hadn't been able to digest it over the last ten years, how had seeing me face-to-face done that?

"Wassup? Trina and Bri look like they bout to come here and plead my case," he coaxes.

I rattle off my number and he enters it into his phone, simultaneously placing the call. "Now you have my number," he adds as my phone vibrates loudly in my back pocket. "Lock it in," he commands, still bossy as ever.

"How is Mira?"

At the mention of his daughter, Carter's chest swells with pride. The seductive eyes brighten. His smile widens, displaying those perfect teeth. "She's wonderful. Beautiful. A teenager now," he laughs.

"Damn. That's insane. Do you have any other children?" I inquire, hopeful that his answer is, no.

"Not yet," he quickly responds. "Take care of what you need to and hit me when you get settled for the night."

"I darn sure will. I'm going to go see my dad."

"That's what's up. Tell him that I hope he's feeling better." He leans in and kisses my cheek.

He turns away before I could ask what he meant, but I go to Bri and ask her instead.

"Lieas, you should call Gray or Tyree or your mom," she answers hesitantly before looking at Trina.

CARTER

THERE WAS SURPRISE IN HER EYES WHEN SHE NOTICED ME standing amongst her most loyal fans. I noticed this morning, on my way to the gym that Deidra had left a copy of the book on the front seat of the Benz when she'd gotten out last night.

I contemplated taking it to Deidra and apologizing for last night, but instead, I opened it and flipped through the pages. Read the dedication page, and it simply stated, To Love… I wish I never let you go… Those words pulled at my heart. And for a moment, I wish that I had never let her go. It made me hopeful that she was still yearning for me. The way I was for her. Deep down beneath all that I had said, all the anger, all the indifference, the thought of her was always there. Always present, reminding me how perfect I felt having her. How complete I could feel again if I had her back.

I ran it by my homies King and Aaron at the gym during our workout session. Both of them were newly married and in love with their wives who happen to be sisters.

"So, you think your old girl is sending you subliminal messages through her writing?" King surmises from what I'd explained to them.

The way he said it made me feel like I was grasping straws. It wasn't that. "I don't think they're for me to see but more about how she feels about me." I highly doubt that she even suspects that I've read any of her work.

Aaron shrugged as he settled on the shoulder press machine.

King adjusted the weight and starts counting reps as he extends his arms out then pulls them back. "But you think they're about you?" he grunted but continued to push out his reps. "What shorty do again?"

"Yea, why did y'all break up?" King also asks.

"She had some nigga in her crib. When I got there, they was all hugged up asleep," I explain. The image is still burned into my mind.

"You caught a nigga in your bed and you ain't in jail? And you still thinking about getting at her?" King asks in disbelief like I'm not in my right mind or something.

I shook my head as I finished my weighted shoulder hunches. I set the forty pound dumbbells on the floor and rolled my shoulders.I already did the rundown in my head about how I'm sure I would have hurt someone if I'd actually caught them in bed. When the anger wore off, all that remained was hurt. "Nawl, they was out on the couch. They had on clothes and shit. I seen this boah at her cousin's wedding, so I figured that she got his number and invited him over."

Aaron and I switch places. "What did she say when she saw you?"

I shrug because the memories started to collide as I replayed it in my mind. It all happened so fast. We were loud, that's for sure. I was ready to ball dude up, and I wasn't trying to listen to no explanations or excuses. "That I misunderstood what was going on. Dude ended up getting ghost after he made sure that she was cool with staying alone with me. Told me ain't shit happen."

"But you didn't believe her?"

I think of the answer as I count to twenty. I push through the last five reps of my set before I replied. "At the time, I didn't. I just cut her off. I wasn't going for it. Recently, I read something that has me thinking that maybe I should've listened, but you know what they say about hindsight."

"Sounds like you already made up your mind about giving her a second chance. You saw her and she still look good?" King laughed.

Even though I normally am not as forthcoming about my feelings, I'm a grown-ass man. "I think my heart stopped. I can remember still loving her like it was yesterday, and I haven't felt that way since her."

"Damn," Aaron grins. "I know the feeling." His smile grew larger; I assume that he thought of his wife.

I switch with King at the lat machine. "Are you thinking about trying to reconnect on a love-type level, or are you just tryna hit that?"

I want her. It's been about eight months of waiting, wanting. I just don't have the time for the messy bullshit that may come with her, but nothing quelled the ache I felt for her, though.

"Talking ain't never hurt nobody. Ask her out and see what she says," King had suggested.

And that is how I had ended up attending the Barnes and Nobel event. Deidra had texted me to "F off". She is beyond pissed, and text after text after text continued to pour in. I had to end it. She deserves someone who isn't in love with another woman. She is worthy of someone who would be emotionally available to her because she is a good woman. And that is what I had told her when I finally spoke to her after I got tired of texting. After our exchange, I knew it was safe and that Deidra wouldn't be there, so I made the decision that I would be.

I had asked Alieas if she wanted to go out, and she let me know that she was busy. There was a rumble of jealousy in my stomach halfway ready to erupt, but when she explained her plans were with her dad, I felt better. The honey in her eyes sweetened the pot for me, even though she declined my offer. I saw them light up with curiosity and that had me wanting to kiss her until she turned to mush. The faint smell of Good Girl danced around my nostrils when I hugged her, and the intoxicating scent lingered on my clothes as I walked to my car.

Since it was a no go with Alieas, I settle for my family as company. Mira and my mom were over at Vince and Mariah's, helping them settle into life as brand new parents. My mom was rocking the baby in the same dusty ass chair she'd rocked Vince in when he was a baby.

"Ms. Thang back in the city now, huh? Got your nose all open. What about cutie pie?" my Mom laughs.

Vince slaps his leg. "Damn. D is a nice girl, though," he snickers.

My mom flags her hand at Mariah as she tries to collect the baby. "Let me hold her now. You been holding her the last nine months." No one states the obvious fact that it was inside her body. "Now, Sister Sadie from Mt. Vernon has a beautiful daughter. Think she said she's a anesthesiologist ova dere at University of Penn."

In the background, behind my momma, Vince and Mariah are both shaking their heads no. "Stop that," she says to them. "She is such a lovely girl," she adds.

Coughing because she got caught, Mariah picks up the cordless house phone. "Just in time," she said into the phone. "Cart is here and guess who he saw... Hold on I'ma put it on speaker."

I hear Autumn's laughter on the other end. My sister did always like Alieas and was furious when I cut her off. In the aftermath of our breakup, Autumn tried to be a voice for her but ultimately, I demanded her loyalty . Told her that she had to pick a side. I was under the impression that had been it.

Or so I had thought. "When was the last time you saw her?" I ask, suddenly suspicious.

"Book signing for her last book. She asked about you but said not to mention it to you. I kind of got the feeling that she still loves you."

The eye-rolling and frown on mom's face is hilarious, but I ignore her.

Then Riah speaks up. "Maybe it wasn't the right time. She was really young, and if it wasn't for what happened between you, both your lives could've been different."

I am a firm believer in God's timing. Its perfection, even when we doubt the fallout. "She was young and some issues."

"Take me and your brother. He is such an a-hole, but I loved him. It took us like six years to get it right."

I glance over at Vince, and he's just waiting so he can jump in on her story.

"I didn't know if we were ever going to get down the aisle without tripping over this girl and that girl, so I let go. I let go, went on with my life, and he came back around, ready. He needed time to grow into who he is today so he could be the man that me and Skye needed him to be." Riah went over and sat across his lap. She wound her arms around his neck and kissed his head.

"She was messing with some lawyer dude. I felt it getting serious, and there was no way some otha man was gonna end up with my woman," Vince recalls, kissing her full on the lips.

"Ain't Mommy in the room?" Autumn's voice came through the speakerphone. Her hearing was on point.

"Ain't nothing that I haven't seen or done," my mom laughs.

"Eww. Get your mom. I gotta go, though. Miles is ready for..."

I can imagine her making faces and pumping the air as she laughs and hangs up. I'm glad she didn't finish her sentence. She and her husband were trying to conceive a baby of their own, and sex is the only thing on her mind. Now, it's stuck in mine.

As a matter of fact, my mind time travels back to a time when me and Lieas was fucking every chance we got. Any and everywhere. I haven't had that spontaneity of anything goes... well, almost anything goes since her.

My mom teased that she has me open. Yup. Open WIDE and soon, Alieas will be too.

CHAPTER
twenty-five

Alieas

I CONTEMPLATE SEEING MY FATHER for the first time in a really long time. And I can't even go in. Physically, there feels like a magnetic force is keeping me glued to my seat. But I know that it is more mental than anything, I suspect.

"Just go in. He's waiting for you," Gray urges.

I listen to his voice as I eye the South Philly brownstone. "Maybe, I'll just call him instead," I offer.

"Alieas, get out of the car and go in and see Dad."

They'd made up years ago. But their relationship has always been a contentious one. Gray is now so far from the wild man of the streets he'd been ten years ago. It still surprises the fuck out of me that my brother is a law-abiding, taxpaying, hardworking citizen.

Well, I guess being almost forty, having a wife and an ever-growing family has something to do with it. That and Allah commanding that he stay on the straight path and that he treat his parents and family well.

"Don't call him. Go inside, baby girl. I'm not sure what

Mommy or Ty has told you, but it's not good, Lieas," he says solemnly.

Silence ensues. A vision of the huge floating clock comes to mind, seconds of life always ticking away. *Precious time. How much did we have left?*

What would I say? That my mom got me in the divorce even though I was an adult woman capable of making my own decisions? But I had made my own decision to cut him from my life. Maybe that was too drastic, given the circumstances. But here I am, afraid for the first time that I was wrong. That I'd wasted time. Years of missing hugs, kisses, stern looks, advice, love. That once I reach him, the ground is going to be ripped from beneath my feet and there will be no gravity to keep me from falling and he won't be there to catch me.

"How bad is it?" I ask. No one had prepared me for this.

"He refuses to have any treatment."

"What it is? Cancer?"

"Nawl. Diabetes, congestive heart failure, possible renal failure, and some other stuff, but he won't go on dialysis. He doesn't want to stop working, but he can't work like this anyway."

I let go of the breath I was holding. Diabetes? They had me thinking this negro was about to kick the bucket. "Okay, I'll call you after I'm done."

"A'rd, sis."

With a tap to my screen, I disconnect the call and I grab my bag and collect my courage before exiting my vehicle. Taking a deep breath, I run over to his house. I knock nervously, waiting to set my eyes on his handsome face to put to rest the building anxiety.

"Good evening," a pretty woman in purple scrubs answers the door. I place her in her forties. A nurse? Maybe a home health aide? Knowing my father, it could be his girlfriend or something.

"I'm Alieas. Is my father home?"

She smiles. At the mention of my name, her face brightens. This must be the girlfriend.

"He's gonna be very happy to see you. Happy Belated Birthday," she says, pulling me into the foyer. "I'm Shelia," she introduces herself. "It's so wonderful to meet you. I've heard so many things about you," she continues.

Definitely the girlfriend.

I'm not entirely sure how I feel about it, so I simply nod. "Thank you very much, Shelia," I respond respectfully as she takes my coat.

She takes my hands in her so quickly that I don't even have time to react. I just stand, looking down at her. I see the sparkle of tears in her eyes. "Darien really misses you, and you have no idea what this means to him."

I remain quiet but I nod.

"I'll show you to the den. Your brother is here with *him.*"

Ummm. Gray is here and ain't even say shit. Coaching me to come in. I follow her through the lower level of the house until we reach the den.

Tyree, not Gray, is standing beside my father, who is kneeling in a high back chair and leaning over the top of it. "Look who's here," Shelia announces, causing Tyree to look up.

My father turns his head. His eyes brighten when he focuses on my face. The smile widens and then he winces in pain as he attempts to get off the chair and turn around.

"Be careful," Tyree hisses as he steps back to assist him. When he turns around, I can see that his stomach is extended. "Hey, Lieas," Tyree steps over and kisses my cheek.

"Daddy," I whisper placing my hand over my mouth to stifle my cry.

"Moo. My Moo," he wheezes out in a struggled breath. "Come over here and let me look at you."

The man before me is not the man I remember. He is but a mere shadow of the tall, dashing, charismatic man who hand-charmed and won my mother's heart. In sickness, he was small and feeble, a former shell of himself. His back and once broad shoulders were hunched in defeat as if he'd surrendered his life force to whatever was staking its claim. "How? Gray said you had diabetes."

My father gathers enough strength to take hold of me, and I break as his arms surround me. The raging waters break the dam and I am a mess of tears. His weak arms grasp me tighter in a final show of strength. "I'm sorry, Moo. I'm sorry that I lost you," he chokes out.

I stand there, holding him, realizing that I never should have let go. "I'm here now, Dad."

"I'm so happy. Your mom told me you were going to come. Happy Birthday, baby." He kisses my forehead.

I need a moment to get myself together and back out of the room. Tyree follows me. Angrily, I push at his chest. "Why the fuck didn't y'all tell me?" I ask. I wipe my face and push him again.

"He asked me not to. He's wanted to see you for a while now. I did tell you that."

"Why the fuck didn't you tell me this?!" I demand again.

Tyree wraps his arms around me and holds me while I rock out my anger, frustration, and despair.

"What's wrong with him?" I ask, breaking from his embrace.

Tyree drags his hands over his head and then leans against the wall, folding his arms over his chest. "His body isn't naturally getting rid of the waste or fluids. From what Ms. Shelia saying, he's looking at renal failure. He won't go to the hospital.

We've all tried to talk him into it. He needs a kidney. I was gonna get tested to see if I was a match, but he refuses."

Men are so damn hardheaded. And for some reason, black men are the worse when it comes to regular doctor visits and taking care of themselves.

He can barely move. How did they allow him to get like this? My mind starts racing. Mentally, I'm all over Google and MSN looking shit up. "I'm not leaving until he agrees to go," I tell him. "And Ms. Shelia; is she his girlfriend? His caretaker?"

"Both."

"Moo. Alieas?" I hear my father's voice call out from the den.

I shake my head in disgust as I make my way back into the den. "Hey, Dad. You gotta go to the hospital," I tell him point blank.

He's sitting in the same chair, this time facing front and on his bottom. "Come sit with me."

I comply and take a seat on the couch next to his chair. "My daughter. I told you she was beautiful, didn't I, Shelia?"

"Daddy, you have to go to the hospital. This isn't right."

"Tired of being sick, baby."

Denial sets in quickly; shaking my head is my way of denouncing his thoughts. "You're only sick because you aren't getting treated. What is your doctor saying?"

"That I should go on dialysis. That I shouldn't put my loved ones through this. Until, I got sick, I didn't have any loved ones," he coughs.

The pain ripples on his face. "Well, you do have loved ones. Ms. Shelia, Gray and Tyree, and me."

"Baby, a man reaches a point in his life where he wishes that he'd done things differently. If I'd been different, this would've ended differently. I fucked up on so many fronts," he shakes his head, quickly glancing at Ty and adding, "I prayed that I lived long enough to make them right. Whatever I was to your mama, I loved you. I only wanted the best for you."

Tears flowed freely; the feeling I get is that he's resigned to his fate. Liked, he can tell he's dying. And the more troubling issue is that he seems patiently ready for death.

Perhaps, he was ready for death but what if death wasn't ready for him? What if I wasn't ready to let him go in such a permanent, forever type of way? What if God wasn't through with him.

Ready? No, not when I wanted to make amends. Ready to make up for lost time.

A kidney. He needs a kidney.

I have one. Well, we all have two... He can have one.

Just like Mama said; everyone deserves a second chance.

And for the third time in three days, I prayed that God was feeling generous enough to hand out more second chances.

CHAPTER
twenty-six

Alicia

So, miracles do happen. My father was admitted to the Jefferson University Hospital and received an emergency dialysis treatment this morning. The triage nurse had looked at us with disgust as she questioned the exact words I'd asked: "How'd you let him get this way?"

I gave Tyree a weary look. The rest of the night passed in a blur. Doctors rushing in, checking this level and that level. They'd given him some Bumex to help release the fluids, and then they'd given him the dialysis treatment.

I cried and cried. I can't remember the last time I cried so much. I haven't lost anyone since my grandmom on my father's side, and she had died when I was like ten. All I remember is the fear of seeing her in her casket. I look down at my wrist watch, and it read fifteen minutes after noon.

Exhausted, I flop down onto my hotel bed. All I can think is that the bed is so comfy as I melt into the mattress. I replay the last eighteen hours and find myself grateful to have been strong enough to endure them.

I need to have tests run to confirm if I am a kidney match. Tyree and Gray are also going to get tested to see if they are compatible, just in case.

I can't think straight and probably won't until I get some sleep. I wish I was one of those people who could turn their brains off and rest. Even with my impulsiveness, I still overanalyze and have what I like to call "afterward anxiety". I close my eyes and just hope that everything is alright.

THREE HOURS OF SLEEP WOULD HAVE TO DO BECAUSE I'M UP AND that's all I'm functioning on. I was able to stop past my mom's and talk to her about my dad and discuss the testing I would have to go through. The process can take several months. You have to do psychological testing along with multiple blood tests, genetic markers, speak to social workers, and whatever else it takes.

"Whatever else" it takes, I'm ready for it. My mom told me to slow down and that I had been running on all cylinders since I arrived home. She sent me packing back to my hotel to get some rest.

I usually play my playlist from iTunes but occasionally, I listen to top forty radio to find a couple of new tunes. I'm pleasantly surprised at the joy I get from rapping this.

It's a guarantee… They say I think I'm the shit— well apparently.

I laugh at the fact that this is playing on the damn radio. I haven't heard it in years. But even with all my female empowerment mottos, I still fall short. And am subject to be ratchet and hood and freaky ass shit all at once.

I get head in the strangest places…

...taste it savory it...,
vanilla ice cream...
oooh, my favorite..."

The phone rings and I answer automatically while Lil Wayne wraps up his verse on *Suck it or Not.* "Hello?" I hum with 'Lil Wayne.

"So, you're not into backtracking brothas, huh?" a mocking tone flows through the cellular waves, causing me to laugh. And before I could answer, he adds, "What are you listening to?"

Perversely amused, I turn it up so he can hear it and rap along with it.

A nigga wanna know, baby girl, you gonna suck it or not?

I can't believe this shit is on the radio. "You don't allow Mira to listen to this type of music, do you?" I was wilding out by the age of fourteen. My favorite "outrageous" song back then was Akinyele's *Put It In Your Mouth.*

"No, and you ask me that even as you hum the tunes. Interesting. Were you gonna call me or not?"

"I was." With everything going on with my father, I haven't even had an opportunity to think of anything else.

Carter clears his throat. "I'm going to be forward. If you're not interested, you can let me know. I won't hold it against you."

"It's not that. I saw my father yesterday, and I wasn't aware that he was seriously ill. I was tied up at the hospital all night, and I only got three hours of sleep."

I hear him sigh. "I knew he was sick. Is everything alright with him?"

"Right this moment? Yes. It may not stay that way."

"Why didn't you know your father was sick?"

"We haven't been close since that shit that went down in the Bahamas."

"Damn. That's fucked up. That was more than a decade ago, though." His voice sounded doubtful.

I shrug. "What can I say? I hold grudges. That's something we can both understand," I flip out.

He chuckles. "Grudges? That's what you call it? Where are you now?"

"Driving."

"Driving where? We need to talk. Today." Carter was so good at giving orders that he didn't question anyone's abilities to follow them.

"I was on my way back to my hotel. You want to grab dinner to have this talk?"

"I'm wrapping a project up in Ardmore. I can meet you at your hotel's restaurant in like forty-five minutes if that's good for you?"

"I don't think you're giving me a choice," I muse.

"It's simple. Are you interested or not?"

Simple. Cut. And dry. It seems. "We can talk. I'm staying at the Hilton behind Target. I'll see you in forty-five."

I check my watch when I hang up with him. There's just enough time to get primed and pampered. Or maybe I should just stay low key...

I text Nesha and Tiff. **Meeting Carter in my hotel for dinner. He wants to talk.**

Inside the restaurant, right? Nesha responds quickly.

I roll my eyes and text back. **Yes! Inside the restaurant. I wasn't saying my room.**

Well, I say go for it, Tiff texts back.

I'm not sleeping with him. I'm saying dinner... We're having dinner to talk.

Well, don't end up being his dessert LOL, Nesha responds.

Get your friend. My hoeing days been over, I type.

Hahahahahahahaha. Is that right? Nesha mocks.

Have fun. Call us when you're done, Tiff texts.

Yea, kisses. Isha bout to come in, Nesha adds.

I am so hyped that I let the valet park my car. I rush to get ready only to wind up spending fifteen minutes agonizing over what to wear. Being the queen of petty has me tempted to walk into the lobby wearing sweatpants and comfy Uggs just to prove that I'm not beat over his sudden interest or eagerness to have dinner. But the devastating diva that I'd spent my life becoming wants his mouth to water when he sees me. To pay him back for all the moments I've dreamt of him and woken up alone, in heat. And heartbroken.

So, I ultimately decide on a pair of faux black leather pants that hugs all my curves, a black sequined tank, four-inch stilettos, and a duster to complete this lethal ensemble.

The restaurant is almost full, but I spy a couple of empty tables scattered throughout. The Maître D informs me that there will an available table in about five minutes, so I turn to find a seat in the waiting area, and just as I'm about to sit down, Carter approaches.

He reaches me and plants a kiss on my cheek. "You look amazing," he observes. Carter rubs his hands together and blows into them. "It's cold out," he explains."Damn," he adds when I take a step back from him.

"Thank you." I smile appreciatively, seeing his desire for me expressed in his gaze.

Yeah. His mouth is watering.

Score. For me. He's possibly thinking the same thing, considering my body language has to be giving off the "please-dick-me-down" vibe. The sequins are hiding my perky, erect nipples when he grasped my arms to kiss my cheek.

When he said he was finishing up a job, I'd assumed that he'd be dressed down in work boots and jeans, but he is casually dressed in a pair of black wingtips, tailored slacks, and a custom-fit blazer.

Yesssss. He knows how to set a thirst trap with his fine ass. I will give him that.

Shallow women would trip on the view alone. They would be bonafide goners once he opened up, I know.

The hostess finally leads us back to of table. I bite my bottom lip as Carter rests his hand on my lower back and guides me through the restaurant. He pulls out my chair and waits as I adjust my seat before sitting in his own. The hostess informs us that I'll server will be right with us, and while we wait for the waitress, he grabs my hand and rubs the inside on my palm.

"What's up with you, beautiful?"

"Curious about the change of heart. And you?"

"I guess it's new to you. I've been thinking of you a lot. And then there you were, and now we're here."

It sounded simple. Our parting was not, however. Not from my side of things. He had cut me out of his life. Out of Mira's life. He had listened for a moment but ultimately dismissed what I had said as lies.

And that was it. And that was all.

"You didn't believe me then, so now you do or are you just over it?"

Carter shrugs his shoulders. "That was a decade ago. You know what they say about time healing old wounds."

Deflated and disappointed, I pull my hand free. "I wasn't lying, Carter. It never should have happened. But I didn't lie—"

He sighs heavily and tilts his head. "It was the same dude you were talking to at the wedding."

I nod my head. I knew that omission was gonna come back bite me in the ass. I clench my teeth, trying not to sound like an asshole. "So, are we going to go through the long version or the short one?"

"I loved you," he said. It wasn't flattery or pity. It was the truth.

The waitress came and took our drink orders.

Squaring my shoulders, I look him directly in his eyes. "I'm sorry. I should have been honest from the jump when you asked if I knew Justin. But he spoke up before I did, so I didn't say anything. I should have said that I knew him and that I'd been seeing him socially."

Carter takes another deep breath. "You mean fucking him."

Frowning, I shake my head in denial. "I didn't. I was going to but I couldn't. He was only there because your baby mom answered your phone at one o'clock in the morning."

"That's not an excuse," he shoots back.

"After all these years, there are no excuses. I was young and I didn't know how to deal with her coming back into your lives. How was I supposed to know that you were in the hospital with Mira?"

"You were supposed to trust me."

Taking a deep breath, I wince, attempting to recreate the same headspace of my twenty-three-year-old self. "I wasn't thinking rationally. We hadn't really talked in two weeks, and I assumed you were with her. I wanted to stop feeling jealous and abandoned, so I tried to make that happen the best way I knew how."

The waitress reappeared and set our drinks down on the table and asked if we were ready to order. I haven't even glanced at the menu.

"I can give y'all more time," she smiles then walks away when we agree.

"I didn't have sex with Justin. There's not a day that goes by that I don't regret that I allowed him to come over," I explain.

This is a moment I've replayed repeatedly in my mind. I had told myself if I'd ever get the opportunity, I wouldn't leave it until he understood that I was sorry and that I'd never meant to hurt him.

"But you did, Lieas," he responded. "How would you have felt? You tripping cause she answered my phone. You knew me. I wasn't some scheming ass, stupid nigga fucking around on you. You lied. Bug asked about you for weeks."

That hits home. I missed Mira beyond what I thought capable. Now, I can only nod. It's possible that Carter is fooling himself into thinking that he is ready and open to forgiveness or whatever he thinks is going on here. "Are you truly still interested in me or are you simply seeking closure?"

"I'm looking to close one door so I can walk through another one," he clarifies.

I am salty... It's grainy... Cut and crystallized like sea salt. I can brush it off my shoulder, but I can't swallow it and my mouth is full of it. And it's my damn fault.

Taking his feelings into consideration, I don't flinch, but I feel like he just tore a bullet into my chest and it splintered into several pieces, shattering my heart.

This fresh heartbreak feels no different than it had the last time. "Ooh. Well—" I clear my throat and take the time to figure out my next thought— "I guess that's fair."

"Deidra is a huge fan."

"Aaaah, Deidra. Is that the door you tryna walk through?"

He lets his head fall back an inch and chuckles. "Nawl. I've been walking out that door for a while now."

I chew on the inside of my bottom lip. "So, you wanted closure? Did this give it to you?"

The waitress comes back, and I still haven't even looked at the menu. Because I didn't want her to have to come back, I order the grilled chicken salad.

Carter glances at the menu and orders Chicken Alfredo and quickly returns his attention to me.

"So, what's up with y'all? Seemed really cozy in Target," I blurt out, barely able to contain my cynicism.

Carter laughs as if I'm making some damn joke.

My new shit is that I'm too old. *Too old for this... and too old for that. Too old to be fuckin someone else's dude. Too old to make foolish decisions. Too old to entertain the road to nowhere. Too old to think with my pussy.* It is not the fuck reliable.

"I read your book, thanks to her," he admits and takes a sip of his water. He's eyeing me over the rim of his glass. "My first time over her crib, she had your book on the table." He blew out a stream of air. "Messed up my fuck game that night. Was it true?"

The book was fairly autobiographical, a detailed, yet "fictional" account of that very brief and life-changing experience that was our love. "You read my book?"

"My First Love," he recites the name. "Was it true?"

I look down into my water and aimlessly swirl it with the straw before meeting his stare.

If he's read it, he already knows what happened, knows that I was seeing both him and Justin. But that I'm sincerely apologetic. I had dedicated the book to my lost love. But yet, here I am, sitting here with him putting me on the spot. "For the most part, yes."

Across the small distance, he stared. Silent but his gaze is arrogant, demanding, boastful. With nothing more than an assured grin and invading eyes, he was pulling every ounce of everything I had for him out of me.

Although his stern gaze assesses me, I felt the warmth of his touch without him even laying one finger on me.

Breaking our connection, I close my eyes to gather my thoughts.

Don't be a hoe.

Don't be a hoe.

"Let's go," he says, abruptly standing up. He reaches for my hand.

Surprised, I just glare at him, confused yet intrigued.

"Your food will be ready in a few. Can I freshen your drinks?" the perky waitress asked. I haven't even touched my Coke Zero.

Appraising him up and down, her appreciation of his good looks is obvious and sends a knowing smile my way.

He shakes his head and takes out his wallet. "No, we're fine. Can you wrap our food up to go?"

A mischievous smile spreads across her face as she takes the credit card he gives to her.

"Go where?" I ask once the waitress walks off.

"Somewhere dates one through thirty couldn't take you."

CHAPTER
twenty-seven

Alieas

O KAY, ONE MORE TIME. *YOU can be a hoe one more time,* I convince myself as I swallow his kisses, reveling in the sensation that his touch brings to me.

Yes, one more time.

No…

Heat. Lust… Love… all tangled up. I'm too emotional for this to be just meaningless sex.

"Carter," I whisper as I try to break the kiss. "Carter," I breathe as his lips masterfully manipulate my mine. "Wait," I pant, putting my hand on his chest. His heart is racing. "Maybe we should take it slow."

He braces himself by placing both his hands on either side of my head.

"We took it slow last time. Clearly, I gave you entirely too much room to breathe." His breath is warm as it tickles my nose.

My breath stops short. I'm afraid to look into his eyes. Every step from the moment he grabbed my hand and led me out of the dining room of the restaurant was building up to this.

My heart palpitates erratically as he fights to reign in his desire.

I close my eyes for the briefest of seconds to bank my own fevered urges. Tangles of wanting rope themselves around my heart, ready for the taking, and I fear that if I act impulsively, I'm gonna lose him. Again.

Carter drops his head and leans in closer, so close that his beard tickles my cheek. "Ten years wasted," he murmurs, causing a moan to involuntarily escape from my swollen lips.

Open and unbounded by pride, he kisses my neck and buries his face in my hair. "Alieas, I don't want to waste another second without you," he adds, switching sides and placing soft kisses across my exposed shoulder.

As my panties begin to soak at the thought of being thoroughly loved by this man, my heart almost bursts with overwhelming joy and relief. Over the years, I had foolishly prayed that Carter would make his way back to me. That all I needed was one small twist of fate or amazing act of God and he would be mine. And in all that time, deep down in the hallows of my heart, I couldn't fathom that I'd end up here, back up against the door, with him about to lay it on me.

Carter caresses my cheek and tilts my face up to his. "Look, I know you're hesitant and unsure. I respect that. I need you to know that I'm the same intense brotha I was years ago. I already had it made up in my mind that I was coming for you."

The bravado seeping out in the timbre of his voice pulls me to him like a magnetic force. I turn my face and kiss his palm.

"All or nothing?" I inquire, allowing my lips to drift back to his.

"All… Everything…" he whispers and takes my lips again.

Silence ensues we feast on sweet offerings of one another.

My arms twine around his neck. Without breaking the kiss, Carter, pulls off my duster, lifts me off my feet, and carries me the short distance to the bed.

Carter lays me down and settles atop me, between my thighs, and he continues to kiss all of my fears and apprehension away.

My mind is racing and overanalyzing things, though. He kisses my brow then he rains kisses over my face and then gyrates his hips in direct alignment with my womanhood. He's speaking her language and she starts to speak back. *Get that... Get that...* I arch up to meet his winding hips.

Urgent hands race over my body, pulling, stretching, assisting, and removing the unyielding fabric in their wake. Some of his clothes... Some of mine...

Removing my heels one after the other and letting them fall to the floor, he kisses the instep of my feet, one at a time sending ripples of unexplainable desire coursing through me.

I grin as his gaze devours my body with lust-filled intentions. I lift my hips off the bed as his skilled hands grip the waistband of my pants and begin to pull them down my legs until they are completely off.

"Fuck!" he hisses and leans down to grip one of my thick thighs in his hands. He kisses it then the other.

Those magical lips trail a path of kisses up my thigh, across my pelvic bone, and dips to the space between my thighs before inhaling the cloth that separates him from paradise.

I giggle, arch my back, and capture his head between my hands. Carter makes his way back up to my lips and drops a single kiss. He gets off the bed to take off his unbuttoned slacks.

Damn, he's filled out more. Packed on some muscle. Everything felt bigger, better, and more improved. Like wine, his body has gotten finer with age. I admire the huskiness of his back and the width of shoulders and can imagine holding on to them as my body yields to his.

I love watching a grown and sexy Carter undress in the dusky room. I can make out the faintest of smiles as he reaches into the pocket of his blazer and pulls out a couple of condoms along with his phone. He turns back toward me and gifts me with a full view of the dick that had put me to sleep plenty of nights in my younger days.

I bite my bottom lip to suppress an appreciative moan, certain he still knows how to work it. It is as impressive as I remembered, hard and standing at attention. Waiting for my attention. That moan finally escapes and he glances at me with the cocky smile. He plays with his cell phone until the music starts.

As Shopaholic raps , *I need you back*, Carter messages the length of his shaft repeatedly in a slow, methodical motion, and I lick my lips at the sight, mesmerized as it grows even larger. Carter rips a condom open and makes a show of slipping it on.

Instinctively, one of my hands cups my breast as the other slides down into my panties. I gyrate my hips as my fingers slip into my silken folds.

"Carter. We're waiting," I purr licking the top of my breast.

He is quick to join the show, not content with being an observer. In less than three strides, he is beside me, grabbing my hips and nearly ripping my panties off.

We both chuckle at his impatience when he finally drops them on the floor.

Leaning down, Carter traces a nipple with his tongue. He sucks it into his mouth while he plays with the other on between his fingertips. The nipple pops out his mouth, and he stares intensely into my eyes. The weight of his stare pierces my soul. "Do you promise to respect me in the morning?" he jokingly asks as he covers my awaiting body with his.

Nodding, I laughingly assure him, "I promise."

He nudges my legs apart and slams inside of me, stroking, coaxing me to open wider with a husky murmur.

"Mmmm hmmm," I moan, meeting him stroke for stroke and tracing his back with my fingers, memorizing every inch of him, and archiving it with all my other memories.

"Pussy all warm," he sighs appreciatively against my ear as he gathers me closer, burying his full length inside of me. "I want it all. Or nothing at all," he chants, in tune with the person singing the chorus.

He gives a deep stroke. Then two more short ones followed by a long one met by a swing of my hips. He rocks; I roll. My eyes roll back as I shift with the ebb and flow our sensual mating.

Tingles of pleasure start to overtake me. "Ooh... Yesss!" I scream. "Yes. Still the best diiiick eeeeever!" I praise as he increases the intensity of his strokes.

I could hear Rihanna off in the distance.

Looooove. Love and affection.

"*Give it to me on the daily...*" I utter the lyrics, mind high, feeling like I could float on cloud nine and stay there with him forever.

Carter's lips seek mine, kissing as he breathes out, "Still the best na-na I've ever had."

My vaginal muscles clench around him, pulling him deeper, holding him in place. *With me. Inside of me.*

I wrap my arms around his back and lock my legs around his hips as he grips my bottom and starts to drill into me. My body meets every downward stroke with a thrust or circle of my hips.

"Ummmmm. Right there, Carter. Right there."

"You bout to cum for me?" the husky voice demands. With every stroke, he's tapping my g-spot lightly then banging it as you would a gong. The intense vibration sets off my orgasmic release.

"Right nooooow!" I let out a satisfied cry. After I come, I always feel deliciously free. My limbs relax and my mind fills with dreams of traveling to a distant galaxy on a blinding star.

But Carter doesn't stop. In and out, he's drilling into me, butt clenched tight as he strokes. His mind is focused on one goal, and I surrounded him with my warmth. It's gushy and tight, soliciting a second orgasm, and moments later, Carter explodes on a harsh curse.

Carter pulls out, takes the condom off, and collapses on top of me as I accept him like I'm memory foam.

We fit, sealed tight to one another. We lay like this until I fall asleep, the past colliding with the present mingled in lust, love, decidedly afraid of what tomorrow could bring.

CARTER

A CONFIDENT SMILE SPLAYS ACROSS HER LIPS. ALIEAS LOOKS deliciously tired from being ravaged all night, into the wee early morning hours. I might be too old to be dishing out this much dick.

Shiiiiid, of course, I'm not.

I imagine one of those whimsical images of sunlight beaming through white sheets and her smiling and rolling all around trying to free herself. I could kiss her awake. My heart tightens as I realize that I've missed this. Watching her sleep. Arousing her into consciousness with my subtle touches.

Stretching her arms wide, she let out an enormous yawn then instinctively rolls into me, still rousing herself from sleep.

Long lashes flicker slowly as she blinks, honey eyes sleepily focusing on my face. A slow smile spreads across her lips.

"Good Morning," I drawl, reaching out to gather her close. She still sleeps wild as hell, arms and legs everywhere.

She covers her mouth and mumbles the same. I figure she must be nervous about her morning breath. It's funny that I've had my tongue over every inch off her caramel skin and she's concerned about morning breath.

She always wakes up looking flawless. I recall watching an episode of A Different World when Whitley got all primed and pampered before Dwayne had woken up, and Lieas revealed that she made a practice of doing the same thing. Thought it was funny as shit. It was a long night, and I wasn't letting her out of my sight.

Her body is all warm and soft; I could just melt into her, and the last thing I want to do is let go. If I get out of this bed, the moment is over. But I gotta get up to take Mira to school and then get on with the rest of my day. My mind runs through everything on my agenda, yet all I wanna do is lay here with her. I love the feel of her in my arms as I tighten my hold on her, caressing her back with long, sensuous strokes.

"I gotta go, Lieas," I whisper into her hair. "I don't want to, though." I squeeze her again, hoping to share this sudden need I have for her inside of me.

Alieas rubs my chest before burying her face into it. "I know."

But neither of us make a single motion to untangle ourselves. She kisses my chest and sighs like she's resigned to our inevitable parting.

"But first things first. What are we gonna be to each other?" I inquire, lifting her face to mine.

"I guess we kinda skipped over that part of the discussion," she responds absently.

Pillow talk between the hours of lovemaking helped us piece together our decade apart. I'm impressed with the woman she has become. There is no surprise that she owns a business or that she writes. She has always loved words. I was surprised that she'd given up on real estate altogether, she used to enjoy it. We had even talked about doing some projects together back then. She's a mentor to high students and runs a literacy project to get the adults of Baltimore and D.C. reading.Knowledge of her endeavors only serves to drive my desire to new heights. I want her. Have wanted her since I read My First Love.

"Alieas," I breathe her name, hoping to pierce her heart, just wide enough to allow me in. I take a deep breath and then—and then, I lay all my cards on the table.

I have no time. "I meant what I said. I want it all."

I need to slow down, put on the breaks. There is so much to work out. So much to discuss before there can be an "us". And yet, right this moment, all I want is for there to be an "us".

"Carter. I don't know how it's gonna work, but I want you too."

Feeling the uncertainty, I kiss her forehead and sigh.My muscles relax beneath her touch."We can start with that. Come to dinner tonight so you can see Mira. Have dinner... Stay."

Always...

"Okay," she agrees, her smile ridiculously wide.

She leans in to kiss me. Our mouths and tongues tangle, the mounting heat fuses and transfer from her body and into mine.

"You better go," she reminds me as more than the heat rises and my dick comes to stand at attention. Alieas makes a suggestive smirk, and her hands begin to message him.

Closing my eyes, I roll over onto my back and let out a jagged breath. "Aaah. Yes. Babe, yes," I breathe as she shifts her weight and her mouth joins her hands.

Full, pouty lips caress and tease the tip before drawing my entire shaft into her mouth.

Damn. Her mouth is all heated up, dripping wet like I remember her pussy being when I hit it raw. She glances up, allowing my rod to slip from between the warmth of her lips. "Shit, babe," I hiss as the air turns my dick cold. She grins and nibbles on her bottom up. I rock my hips in invitation. Quick to oblige, she takes my throbbing member back into her mouth. A patient hand cups my balls and lightly squeezes. My mind soars as she licks and flicks her tongue from the base to the tip, making love to it, mouth sliding sloppily up and down slowly and then faster. Pushing my knee aside, her tongue traces a line from my balls to the tip, taking it lower and lightly licking the space between my balls and my ass. I clench my ass cheeks when she blows air on my hole, unsure if she was going to lick it. Alieas chuckles and then returns to the original task at hand.

My hands grip her hair as she masterfully deep throats my dick like no one else has ever. "Fuuuuuuck," I curse as the beginnings of my orgasm build.

I want to be deep inside of her when I do, so I pull her up and push her into the mattress. I silence her with a kiss when she protests. I know she wants to continue giving oral until I bust but I want to be inside of her. "After this," I let her know, climbing between her thighs. A pleasured moan escapes as I bury myself inside her. Heat surrounds me, pulling me in. Running her hands over the bulging muscles from my shoulders to my back as I turn her inside out, stroke after long delicious stroke.

Alieas comes, screaming my name at six -forty-three a.m.

CHAPTER
twenty-eight

MONDAY

Alicia

I SLEPT FOR ABOUT ANOTHER four hours after Carter left and awakened to my phone being completely dead. I had never gotten around to charging it. I plugged it in then went to the bathroom to take a shower.

Brain cells fried, body sore, limbs limp, I survey myself in the mirror. It's all over my face that I had been thoroughly loved, masterfully manhandled, and left to my own devices until we could have a repeat performance. The remnants of our fiery reunion are still evident in my eyes, traces of lust still lingering in my gaze. The heat of our passion displayed in faint rosy cheeks and pouty full lips. My hair is completely sweated out and all curly at the roots.

And I don't give a damn.

I bite my lip in satisfaction and begin brushing my teeth. Dreamily, hop into the shower and I wash up. I spend like fifteen minutes under the steaming water recapping the night and dreaming up the future.

Like a lovesick fool, I'm already writing a book about second chances. This is the "me" that I hate. The "get some good dick and start fantasizing about the future" me. Hadn't she led me astray several times before?

But this is so much more. This is my second chance. I said I was ready and God listened. I have to be smart enough to recognize it.

I hop out of the shower and race over to my phone. I wanna check to see if he texted me already. I turn it on and then set it down as I lotion up.

As soon as it powered up, I could hear my notifications going off like crazy. There are three voicemails and the rest are texts.I count at least ten before I decide to check them. I pull my sports bra over my head and dance into my panties.

I pick up the phone, and I can see the banner. I've missed messages from my mom, Nesh, Gray, Tyree, and Carter. Holding my breath, I open the one from my mom.

Mom: **Lieas, where are you? Your phone keeps going right to voicemail.**

Carter: **Just know you locked down now. Enjoy your day, beautiful. Til later.**

Nesha: **So, were you dessert?**

Tiff: **And you know she was. Enjoy Boo, xoxo.**

Gray: **Lieas your phone keep going to vmail. Pick up.**

Another one came in five minutes later:

Yo. Lieas pick up.

Tyree: **Alieas, call me as soon as you get this text. We been trying to reach you all morning.**

I frown at the message. It came in at eight- forty this morning. My heart drops into my feet as my once-happy thoughts plummet into uncertainty. I can't explain the clashing emotions screaming that something has to be wrong versus more optimistic ones rationalizing that it's nothing.

I shake my head as I contemplate who to call first and fate intervened and said, *we don't have time for that.* As I was about to make the call, it rang in my hand instead.

Tyree's name and picture collages of him, Bri, and the kids pop up. I clear my throat and slide my finger across the screen to accept. "Hey. I was just about to call you back," I let out. My heart had formed its way up to a lump in my throat. It hurts. That dry ache when you know that it's something bad.

"Aunt Nic on her way to your hotel so y'all can meet me and Gray at the hospital."

I nod my head. The lump dissipates into that unexplainable hurting fog. "Is he okay?" I struggle to get the words out.

There is a deafening silence as I listen for the words my heart already knows. "No. He's not," his voice breaks a little. "He's gone. This morning."

Then I break. "Nooooo!" I grumble. "No... No. No." I double over, barely able to keep the phone against my ear. "He was fine when I left," I add in an unintelligible mumble. I shake my head and slip to the floor. Only eighteen hours ago, he had a weak smile as he asked me to stay a little while longer. As I left, I assured him that I would be back. That we'd have enough time.

"If you want to see him before they take him down, you gotta come up. Let me call Aunt Nic. Hold on."

He places me on hold to call my mom as I attempt to make sense of the fact that my dad is dead. I drop the phone onto the floor, and I just sit here crying. The tears stream like an endless waterfall down my cheeks. The pain throbbing in my chest feels like a bullet wound, radiating, expanding as the tears absolve into racking sobs. Then I'm numb.

I can't be sure how many seconds or minutes pass before my phone rings again. I don't answer. At this point, what else is there to say?

As I cry my eyes out, the phone rings again. This time, it is accompanied by a hard rapt on the door.

"Alieas. Alieas, open the door, baby!" my mom's voice booms from the other side.

I open the door, and I can see that she has been crying from the tear streaks that marked her cheeks. "You knew he was sick? And you didn't tell me." I accuse, letting her into the room.

Strong, slender arms gather me up and pull me into a hug. "Get your clothes on so you can see him."

CHAPTER

twenty-nine

Alices

THE RIDE TO THE HOSPITAL is silent except for the humdrum antics of the mid-morning disc jockey on WDAS. My mom keeps reaching over to squeeze my hand. The closer we drove to Center City, the more it hurts. As we approach Tenth St., I close my eyes and pray that this is some horrible nightmare and I'm gonna wake up any minute, ten years in the past.

I open my eyes as we pull up at the valet. My mom jumps out the car but not me. I stay seated. I need a moment or sixty-thousand more moments before I am willing to admit that this is real.

"Miss? Miss?" the valet speaks.

My mom has her phone against her ear when she opens my door. "We're at the front on the Tenth St. side. Come get your sister, Gray. She won't get out of the car."

Everything gets foggy and my mind distances itself from the rest of my body. Maybe I'm dead too, still laying crouched down on the floor of my hotel room passed out from a heart attack after hearing the news.

"Alieas." I can hear Gray calling me. His voice sounds like a distant murmur as my mind wanders incoherently. I feel his hand grab my arm and tug me until I'm out of the car. Then I'm walking aimlessly behind my mother as she leads us through the bright corridors of the hospital.

I lag further behind, feet shuffling, dragging, and sniffling my way into the elevator. My brother hugs me and pulls me into him. He's crying too. I haven't seen Gray cry in years. I think the last time was Ayesha's birth when Nesha almost died from childbirth complications.

"I'm glad he saw you," he whispers into my ear. "He missed you, sis."

The elevator stops and we step off. My aunts, uncles, and a cousin on my dad's side are all standing in the hallway near the waiting room as we approach. I see Bri and Nesha, Tiff standing near the doorway talking.

Mournful eyes meet sorrowful ones. The small measure of composure I have left dissolves when they surround me in a chain of love. Somehow strengthened from their hug, I walk closer to the doorway and I pause. Afraid to go in.

The privacy curtain is pulled halfway closed to conceal his body so I can only make out the silhouette. Gray nudges me further into the room. Approaching quietly, I notice Tyree holding my dad's hand, his eyes closed, head bowed in prayer.

My heart beats painfully for him. He was the first of us to forgive my dad. He's hurting and that rips my heart to shreds. My dad was the only father he ever knew, and he'd lost him too.

Reaching for his hand, I cover my father's lifeless body with my own. I shake my head against his unmoving chest, muttering apologizes for turning my back on him. I cry over missed time. I cry over things that haven't happened yet. Things that I'll never experience. Things never said.

Firm hands are messaging my back, and Tyree's hand covers mine and just squeezes. I cough and cry.

Cry and scream…

Cry and think. Holding on. Praying…

"Daddy, what about our second chance?" I sob.

No response. No breath. No heartbeat.

No response. No breath. No heartbeat.

Except for mine.

I lay there until Gray pries me away. I don't know how long I lay here, but it's obviously time to take my dad to wherever it is that dead people go. So that we can plan a funeral, a final goodbye.

I need to walk and get some fresh air. I step out into the hall, at which point my friends come back to me. I shake my head as I push my arms out into the air. I can't speak, but Nesha reads my mind. "You wanna go outside for a minute?"

Nodding, I agree. I look up and see Ms. Shelia, standing off to the side, doing the same thing as everyone else— sobbing. Moaning. Grieving. Closing the distance, I embrace her. She was here when I left yesterday. I'm not sure if she ever even left his side. She holds on to me as she unleashes to her heart's content in heart-wrenching sobs.

"Carter." I hear his name. Turning my attention to the voice, I damn near swallow my tongue. Deidra is standing beside Ms. Shelia, and I watch as she runs to him.

His eyes are on mine, though, as he advances past her and toward me. "Why didn't you call me?" he demands.

Common sense doesn't prevail in times of trauma. My mind is no different. "You fucking came up here for her?" I ask, advancing toward him, "knowing I would be here?"

Nesha steps up to me. "Alieas, calm down!" she exclaims.

"And what the fuck is she doing here anyway?!" I yell accusingly at my relatives.

"She's my sister," Ms. Shelia speaks up.

"Babe," Carter says, gripping my arms. "Calm down. I came as soon as I heard," he finishes.

"Babe?" Deidra repeats. "Carter, what is going on? Can we speak in private, please?"

His eyes are still on mine. It was almost as if he was asking for permission even though I could read the clear frustration in his eyes. I hold my palms up in the air and step back. I circle around them both and run down the corridor.

I could hear Bri and Tiff calling behind me.

CARTER

I RACED HERE WHEN DEIDRA CALLED. I HAD IGNORED THE FIRST three calls because I didn't feel like being bothered. Hurting her had made me feel like shit but not acting on the love I have for Lieas could've landed me lonely and full of regret forever. So, she texted me that there was an emergency with Mr. Stiles. I only came because I knew Alieas would need me, even if she hadn't made the phone call.

I had to talk myself down. My mind racing, I was fucking livid, driving like a madman to make it here. Truthfully, I was angry because I wasn't the person she called but I wanted to be.

I know that ache that came with a loss. And I didn't want her to experience that alone. Pangs of remembrance stab at me as I think of it. My father died from prostate cancer five years ago, and I miss him every day. I miss his easy smile, his patience, his counsel. I just miss his presence.

The familiar weight bearing down, crushing your heart, I know. I didn't want that for her, so I came without giving a moment of thought that she'd question how or why.I want her to feel my presence and know that I was here for her.

Now that I had a moment to process what happened, I can't determine if Deidra had done it to be smart, extra, messy, or just in the damn way.

I shake Gray's hand and give him my condolences then I do the same for Ms. Nicole. Even though they're divorced, the last time I saw Ms. Nicole, she was still married to Mr. Stiles, and ten years apart doesn't erase damn near thirty years of marriage.

Reluctant, I turn to Shelia and take her into my arms. She and Mr. Stiles had been dating for about nine months. She grips me hard as she sheds tears. She gathers her composure and kind of passes me over toward Deidra.

"Exactly why did you call me?" I'm happy that she did, but my Spidey senses were telling me that it wasn't because of some instinctive need to be held or consoled. While Deidra and her sister were close, they were more than twelve years apart. Their relationship, from my point of view, had always been more mother/daughter, but Deidra was not close to Mr. Stiles. "You knew I would come because of her," I surmise.

Deidra begins shaking her head. "Carter, I don't know what happened between y'all, but I love you, babe." Irritated, I scoff then flag what she says. Gray, Nesha, and Dave are all watching us with their hands covering their mouths. Ms. Nicole is standing in the doorway, eyes on us like we were in a fishbowl.

I pull her to a nearby window with me as she says, "You don't feel anything for me?" Her doe eyes were wide with worry. I can tell she is about to cry. The hitch in her voice twists my insides.

Careful not to embrace her, I grasp her shoulders. "I care

about you, and you're a good woman, but we're over and this isn't the time or the place."

Distressed by the well of tears building in her eyes, Deidra shakes her head in denial of what I am saying. Unwilling to leave it at that, she grabs my hand and presses it to her heart. "I love you, Carter. You used to love me a lil' bit," she adds.

As I pull my hands away, my mind goes out to Alieas. There is nothing I can offer her if I can't resolve things with Deidra. Guilt has me thinking that I'd led Deidra on. I'd been uncertain about continuing our relationship when I realized that I still wanted Alieas. It shouldn't have taken for Alieas to show up here for me to have ended this and allowed Deidra a chance at love with someone else. Now, she is standing before me in tears, begging something of me that I can't give her.

My heart belongs to Alieas. Always had. "I'm sorry, D. I should've said something sooner," I apologize.

Her hands fly to her mouth and she starts to hyperventilate. She starts fanning her cheeks and doubles over. "How could you do this to us?"

Quickly, she stands up, wipes her faces, and hurries off in the opposite direction. Ms. Shelia follows her. I look after her for a moment and then over at Tyree when he clears his throat. Rubbing the back of his neck, he extends his hand out to me and I clasp it. "Sorry for your loss, man," I tell him.

Over the years, we've maintained somewhat of a friendship. "Thanks for coming." He stares around. "So, you here for Lieas or the lil sister?" he nods his head toward the direction D had run off to.

"I came for Lieas." I'm low key offended he even asked me.

"She gonna need you, Cart," he confides. "Give her a moment; she has to work through some things in her mind. And her heart. We all gonna go over to Gray's. You're welcome to come."

"Cool. I'm going out to talk to her. Thanks, bruh." Instead of looking for Lieas, I wait until she comes back up. Or attempt to. They must've walked the entire neighborhood because when I finally went down to the lobby, I couldn't find her.

I texted her that I'd see her later. Then, I called my mom. Her voice settles me. "Hey, son," she chirps. "What are you up to?"

"I just called to say, I love you," I admit.

"Now, ain't that nice. Giving your mama some "sonshine" on this cold ass day. I love you, too." I can see her smile even though I'm not there.

"That was it," I tell her, "I don't want nothing else."

"You sure, baby? Did you think about the anesthesiologist?"

She is an incorrigible soul. "Aah. No. Bye, Ma."

I could hear her cackle as the call disconnected. Then, I texted Mira. **Love you, Bug. See you after school.**

I am irritated that Alieas didn't respond to my text, but Bug made my day responding in smiley faces with heart eyes.

CHAPTER
thirty

Alieas

ETWEEN THE TEARS AND THE headache, I ended up falling asleep. Most of what I was conscious for passed in a blur. My third cousin on my dad's side is a funeral director and had come over to discuss the arrangements with us. My father had already handled the planning of his entire funeral service, down to his navy trouser socks. Everything had been finalized without an ounce of input from me or Gray.

Because I'm a fucking asshole.

Because I ignored his phone calls, text messages, and emails at all cost and as often as I could. Because I spent the last ten years trying to hate him because of the "him" that I saw in me.

And that was a part of my loneliness, a part that I'm never really willing to admit.

I had once come to the conclusion that my being promiscuous and Gray, a womanizer, was because we were genetically predisposed to bad relationship practices, thanks to my father. With all my education, I know that just isn't the truth.

Stretching, I yawn and roll over and am treated to the wide-eyed stare of my youngest niece, Sumayyah. Gray and Nesha have been busy in the last ten years on the family front. They've added five girls to their brood. I'm not sure if they're going to stop anytime soon, but they sure do make some beautiful babies. Nesha laughs when I call her ass a baby-making factory. I have no idea how she runs a hair salon, takes classes, prays five times a day, keeps her kids and husband happy, and still manages to be sane. I need tips, and my life isn't half as hectic as hers.

May reaches out with her little stubby hand to touch my face. At sixteen months, she has Gray's hazel eyes and Nesha's entire face. I smile as her touch settles my heart.

She is life, breathing and growing. She's probably trying to figure out who's sleeping on her couch. Her smile spreads as she recognizes me. All those FaceTime chats are paying off. I grab her up and nuzzle her neck, making her giggle.

I want one. I inhale her fresh scent, and she smells like baby powder and dreams come true. I wander into the kitchen to find her mama.

"Look who's awake," Gray teases as he comes over, slinging his arm over my shoulder. He kisses the top of my head. "You cool?"

I nod. "Gray. I talk to you all the time. Why didn't you give me a heads up? You, Mommy, and Ty always giving these cryptic-behind messages."

Content, May plays with my necklace until she catches sight of Nesha then she's reaching for her mom. Nesha came into the kitchen with the three- and five-year-olds following closely on her heels. "Girl, they all over you," I laugh as May damn near climbs over me to get to her. "You got any Motrin?"

Sighing, Gray takes May from my arms and passes her to Nesha. "I was wrong not to say anything. Didn't realize until recently how bad it was. Ty been spending a lot of time with him, helping out with the business. Nesha been working the office on her off days. Mommy even been putting in hours there."

"Cart in the basement with Ty and them," Nesha says. Filled with intrigue, the smirk on her face lets me know she knew just how I'd spent the previous evening.

"Yea. What's up with that?" Gray eyes me.

I shake my head. I have no idea. I haven't even had time to process it or think about it. "I don't know." They told me what happened at the hospital after I'd cooled off a little bit. But he had left before I'd had the opportunity to address it.

"You ain't slick, heffa. It's really crazy that Deidra is related to Ms. Shelia," she adds pulling out a prescription bottle of ibuprofen from the top cabinet.

Crazy? Is that all? So, my ex, who just spent the night screwing my brains out, is with the sister of my estranged but now deceased father's girlfriend. Crazy? Messy is more like it.

"What you gonna do?" Nesha inquires as she fills up a glass of water and passes both to me.

"And that's my queue to exit left," Gray announces as I gulp down both the water and the pill. "Come on, girls. I'll let Cart know you're awake."

Me and Nesha laugh at him as he leaves. My five-year-old niece, Ayesha lingers but Nesha quickly shoos her away with her father and puts May down on the floor to follow if she wanted.

Taking my vibrating phone from my pocket, I see that Justin texted to see if I'm ok. He'd also called twice while I was sleeping. Said he saw on FB that my dad had passed. The two of us had kind of stayed cool with one another after everything went down and had become 'real friends'. He's happily married to an amazing woman named Deja and they have a new baby girl.

Thanks, Jus. I'm good. I'll call you when I get a moment. Give Deja and the baby kisses for me.

Dej' is worried. Call me if you need anything.

There's no time to answer Nesha's question because, by the time I get done texting, Carter enters the kitchen. Rolling my eyes, I stuff my phone back in my pocket.

Nesha also takes her queue and leaves us alone, picking up May on her way out.

Carter leans up against the granite counter island and folds his arms over his chest. "Are you alright?"

Yawning, I cover my mouth as I answer. "Tired. Drained. Feeling empty. Can't cry anymore."

"Your father passed. You're entitled to all those feelings."

Expelling puff of air, I reply snarkily, "It's God's will, though, right?"

"Absolutely. Doesn't stop us from feeling."

It doesn't. "Why didn't you tell me that Deidra is my father's girlfriend sister?"

He shrugs. I can see in his eyes that it isn't important to him. "It just didn't come up. I wasn't interested in talking about her when I was trying to figure out what's up with you; with us."

Annoyed, I shake my head. I'm waiting for the Motrin to kick it. "This makes shit messy."

"Its' only messy if you allow it to be. I was once with Deidra; now, I'm not."

I almost laugh. It sounds so simple when it is so far from that.

Unable to control myself, I grunt in frustration, "Three days ago, Carter. You were with her three fucking days ago," I emphatically add.

Nerves churning, I begin pacing the length of the kitchen.

I'm so hot that I could walk a burning hole into this beautiful hardwood floor. Maybe instead of screwing, I should've been asking questions, analyzing, and investigating.

I'm too old for this shit.

"Alieas." The hands that grip my arms are forceful. "Babe, you gotta calm down."

Those words add to the hype. Saying "calm down" to me has the opposite effect. It's like having my own personal cheer squad chanting, *Go… Go… Go…* "Carter, did you fucking break up with her or not?" I demand, trying to break free of his grasp.

"Are you going to yell and scream or are we going to have a civilized conversation?" he asks with a scratch of his beard.

We haven't butted heads in ten years, and this could potentially get of control if I'm ramming and not thinking straight or being rational. I have to reign in the aggression if I want to make this work. And I hate it when he tries to check me by being the calm and civilized one.

Rolling my eyes, I inhale deeply, his scent, his strength and then exhale the toxic thoughts and raging emotions. I can be calm and civilized too. *Deep breath. Take a deep breath. And let go.*

Even as I let go, the hands that gripped my arms now hold me close and band around my waist.

I look up directly into his eyes and I drown in them. "You're right. And I guess we really haven't had the opportunity to discuss any of the important things because we were too busy getting busy."

He laughs and kisses my forehead to soothe what's going on inside of me rather than to arouse me. "For the record, you did not specifically say that you ended things with her," I clarify.

"Shit seems complicated but it's not," he reassures with another kiss. "I'm not a young boah."

Those lion eyes lend empathy, give warmth and comfort. They see through me. "Carter."

"I already told you what it is. I let her know that night that you're the one. Time is precious. I don't want to waste any more of it. I play no games when it comes to this." He steps back and covers my hand over his heart. "It's taken me years to shield, guard, and protect it."

"Carter. I— I'm sorry."

He kissed my hands. "It's not about that. I strive to be the type of man I want my daughter to end up with." He shrugs a nonchalant shoulder. "I did fuck Deidra; we kicked it, had fun. Our being together was mutual. I found out that her older sister was dating your pops. That confirmed it more for me that she was my way back to you the tool that the Creator used to show me my destiny."

He chuckles at the look I am giving him. My face must be saying, *Whatever, nucca*, but my heart is doing flips. "Alright, ma. Maybe we can take a step back, figure one another out. Clearly, you need a crash course in relationships with Carter 202." he advises. "Is there anybody I gotta choke out in DC, Maryland, or any of the surrounding areas?"

I'm still stuck on his romantic theory even though I'm frowning on the outside. Speechless, I shake my head. He pulls me back to him.

"Hmmm, mmm." Bri saunters into the kitchen. "Look at y'all. Cart, I see you," Bri snickers. "Make sure my girl good. She's had a very long day. And night from what I understand."

Embarrassed, I bury my face into his chest. "Briannah."

Carter pats my back. "She cool, babe. You still tryna go to my crib or you want me to take you back to the hotel?"

Tucking two, 2-liter sodas under her arms, Bri smiles brightly. "You gon tuck her in too?" she jokes, making smooching sounds while puckering her lips.

"I'm sure your husband is already looking for you. It's been about two minutes," I let her know. They've been in each other's pockets for about fifteen years.

She flags the thought off. "He'll survive.". Then, her face and eyes turn sincere. "How about you?"

"I'm okay. If I have to say those words again, I won't be. I wasted so much time being mad at him and now, it's too late."

CHAPTER
thirty-one

CARTER

I WAS TAKING A HUGE leap of faith just thinking we could just settle back into our love a decade later.

It's absolutely crazy to think that, right?It's hard to believe that she doesn't have a man. Last night, when I was inside of her, a tear slipped out of her eye and I kissed it. Felt like I soothed away all the hurt of our separation. All the hurt and anxiety over the death of her father. My heart felt as if it were at peace.

And— And I can't expect anything from her. Her father just died for God's sakes. And here I am already trying to lock her down forever. I need to think clearly and be rational. I'm damn near forty, too old to have my fucking head in the clouds.

And yet, that's where it is. Hovering above reasonable doubt and rational thinking.

It has only been a couple of days, and all I can think of is all the days that follow and how I want her here with me and Bug.

"Dad?" Mira's curious voice intrudes on my thoughts.

Smiling over at her I absently reply, "Huh?"

There's something on her mind; I can see it in her posture. Bug tilts her head, squints her eyes, and clasps her hands together. "My mom said that she's gonna have another baby," she informs me.

Figures. This makes four since she moved back up north. Peety keeps her pregnant. It ain't any of my business, though, so I only nod. "That's great, Bug. Another brother or sister for you."

She laughs sarcastically and narrows her eyes at me. "So, I'm trying to figure out if you and D are gonna get married and have any babies?"

Whoa, flag on the play. Her inquiry is a true testament that she is maturing and will be a woman soon. I want to hide my head in some sand.But I figure I might as well tell her that D and I are over. Even if it doesn't go any further with Alieas, what was between us is done.

Considering that we have at least fifteen minutes before we get to her school, I decide to fill her in.

I scratch my beard, look over at her, and start by saying, "About that. Me and D…"

Mira rolls her brown eyes and releases an exasperated sigh when she realizes what I'm about to say, "Aww, Dad."

"We broke up, Bug," I tell her in my most sincere and solemn voice.

"But why? She really loves you, Dad."

There is that.

Knowing that I have to approach this subject delicately, I weigh just how in-depth I want to go on this now seemingly long drive. When she began getting her menstrual cycle last year, we discussed boys, boundaries, self-respect, and self-worth. It was a joint effort between Toya and me. The entire experience was nerve-wracking. I was apprehensive as shit, but Toya — she was ready to tackle that and did so like a champ. I ultimately was just there for moral support because I didn't have shit to say but, "Keep your legs closed and your eyes in them books. I will end up killing one of these little muthafuckas." I got eye rolls from both of them, but what else was I supposed to say?

In my head, pregnancy isn't the worst thing that could happen to a young lady. Heartbreak and her attitude toward it had the possibility to irrevocably shape the next twenty years of her life. She had to be ready for all the foolish, broken knuckleheads out in the world. And that was my job— to prepare her.

If I'm the stick she is using to measure all men by, my shit better be straight.

Getting back to the question at hand, I think about it. The why? The reason was simple but at the same time not. It's more intricate than that. This is about love, the feeling of it, reciprocation, and all of the things in between. My parents never really had to discuss how to love another person with me. They were evidence of what love is, how it is expressed, felt, and shown. Growing up, I had the firsthand opportunity to discover exactly how love was supposed to feel.

It may not be that way with everyone. Lieas grew up convinced that she'd get the same love her parents had, and that ended up being a mess.

Love is… complicated, complex, direct, head on.

"Ok. You're right. She is wonderful, but I don't feel the same way about her."

Love is… easy. Sometimes— it just… is. We feel first and rationalize later.

"It is unfair for me to not love her the way she deserves," I confess.

Mira settles back into the cushion of the seat as her mind

works, mulling things over, dissecting the possibilities. "Well, why don't you love her?"

The question pops up again, and I want to be honest with her. At fourteen, she would start seeing stars if some boy hasn't already come sniffing around her. In all honesty, when these niggas do, I need her to be prepared.

"She's not for me. I can feel that in here," I let her know, touching a hand to my heart. "I was trying to figure out if it was gonna grow. It didn't. More importantly, I knew that it wasn't."

Traffic was slow, so I took the time to stare at her. "So, I had to be adult and not be selfish." Admittedly, I had been selfish. But I wasn't going to tell her that. "We had to let go if either one of us is going to find the one who makes us feel it here."

Pursed lips realigned into a comforting smile. "She is nice. But if you don't love her, you have to let her go." She shrugs her shoulders and pulls out her cell phone.

I guess I won't have to go into as much detail as I had hyped myself up for. Then she asks, "Is there somebody that you do love like that? I overheard Granma talking about it."

Clearing my throat, I nod. "Yeah. There is. Still working that out, so that's to be continued. Do you like anybody?" I shoot back.

As expected, she frowns and shakes her head. "Ewww. Dad. I'll talk to Mom about it."

I exit off the expressway and drive a mile to the expensive private school she attends.

Mira waves back at me after she catches up with one of her friends. And I just sit here daydreaming.

Ninth grade.

Fuck me. My bug is going to be a tenth-grader in a couple of months. That means sophomore prom and homecoming dances.

By ten thirty, all the sites were working smoothly. All the

men that were scheduled have shown up and are at all their worksites. The office manager has the office under control, and I had some free time.

All I want to do was spend it with Alieas. So, I dialed her number to see if I could scoop her. Alieas let me know that she was driving home to Maryland for a few days and I all but invited myself to tag along. I was lowkey excited as shit when she was like, 'sure', but then I had to make some last minute arrangements.

I called Toya and let her know that I had a last minute trip and that she could pick bug up directly from school instead if my dropping her off at her house. She kind of laughed it off when I congratulated her on her upcoming addition to her family and said that it was unexpected. I congratulated her the same. I'm gonna call Bug during her lunch to let her know about the change in plans.

CHAPTER
thirty-two

Alicia

I WOKE UP WITH THE annoying feeling that something is off, aside from my father's death. I can't explain what it is, but I can't shake it. My mom suggests that I make the drive home to pack some clothes and whatnot so I wouldn't have to spend unnecessary money to buy new shit. Today is Wednesday; I figure I could stay in my own bed until Friday and be back for the funeral on Saturday.

"Just go," she insists. "The drive will give you something to do and take your mind off of things. See if one of the girls will go with you."

I can't imagine asking any of them to skip work, abandon their husbands, children, and other duties to make an impromptu road trip with me, so I don't even bother. Instead, I pack up my stuff and prepare for the journey figuring I can probably be home by three, strategically missing all the traffic on I-95 if I left early enough.

Carter happened to call me and when I told him my plans to drive home, he offered to come along. It's Latoya's day to pick Mira up from school, so he is free of dad duties until Sunday. I discovered that they now shared custody of the child. Her reappearance into their lives had grown into what I've learned has become a productive co-parenting relationship.

And now, we're here, together in the spacious yet intimate confines of his Mercedes ML350, making our way into suburban Germantown, MD right as the afternoon rush starts. The heated leather seats got me all relaxed and cozy. Carter had slipped some orange cream flavored Cognac in my hot tea to help me unwind, so I'm not sure how long I was asleep. All I know is that I needed it. Silently, I watch him from under my sleepy, hooded gaze. He's come out of his coat and sweater and is stripped down to a v-neck white tee. I swallow to tamp down my immediate lust as the muscles of his arms contract as he steers and the black ink of his tattoos threaten to send me into overdrive. Even though it's taking me a moment to gather my wits, homegirl below is wide awake and ready. I squeeze my thighs to calm her down. His brows knit together as he listens intently to his phone as Google advises him to make the next right. With a swift motion, he looks over at the side view mirror and catches me staring.

Wet... I am soaking fucking wet as his golden eyes widen and that sexy ass smile spreads knowingly across his face, melting me into a puddle of uncontrollable desire .

"I see you peeking," he teases, his husky voice filling the space between us.

Yawning, I stretch my arms and my legs as much as I'm able to. My voice is a little husky from sleep. "You trying to get me drunk on the good stuff so you can have your way with me."

The arching brow and a firm slap to my thigh do me all the way in. "Ha! I don't need to get you drunk to have my way with you." He squeezes my thigh and winks mischievously.

Dripping... saturated... ready...

I close my eyes and they instinctively roll to the back of my head. Desire ripples, stimulating every nerve, vibrating in my bloodstream, emitting waves of "fuck me nooooow". Instead, I offer a meager, "Thank you so much for driving. I didn't realize how tired I was. I owe you."

The wide hand that had squeezed my thigh moments ago now caresses my cheek. "Oh, I know. A brotha definitely cashing that in." Seemingly amused, he throws his head back with a cocky laugh.

"We should be at my house in a couple of minutes. You look all serious. Music all extra low like you driving Ms. Daisy or something."

"You got a brotha actin like Uber in this jawn. You can turn the music station if you want."

Rolling my eyes, I tune in to one of my favorite channels and Kate Nash is asking for the Nicest Thing. And I sing with her.

Carter lets out a sigh and shakes his head. "I see you still be on your white girl vibe."

Laughing, I sit up to stare him directly in his eyes. My heart is pumping with want, and I'm full of desire, so I sing louder.

I wish that you needed me...
I wish that you knew when I said two sugars,
Actually, I meant three... I hold up three fingers at him.
I wish that without me your heart would break
... without me you'd be spending the rest of your nights awake
I wish that without me you couldn't eat
... thing on your mind before you went to sleep
Look, all I know is that you're the nicest thing I've ever seen...

That smile, smug and knowing, says we could be something.

Then his words affirm it. "I'm gonna show you all the things that we can be."

Carter pulls the car onto the shoulder of the road and put his hazards on. And just like he had on our very first date, Carter leans over and kisses me senseless. Tongues tangling, juices swapping, mouths slurping and savoring, all at the same time. My fingers play in his beard. He ends the kiss and then drives the car back onto the highway.

"We have the rest of the day for fun and games; what are you trying to do tonight?" I ask. I would love to show him my town. It's not much nightlife going on here, but we could drive into DC and check out the scene. We can walk the trail at Black Hill Regional Park.

"You."

With that one word, the last thing I want to do is walk some trail. I'm all for screwing the day and evening away. I purr appreciatively at his suggestion.

Carter's face lights up. "*Your fuck game is craaaaazy,*" he playfully mocks, repeating a phrase I've said several times and in a tone I assume to be mine.

I bust out laughing. "You're a damn fool."

"Oh, you frontin'," he jokes, squeezing my thigh again. "I hope you live in a single. Cause the neighbor gon' know my name before this lil' trip is over."

I think of Mr. and Mrs. Brinkman, the elderly couple, who lives in the condo next door to mine and them hearing me scream in the throes of passion, yet I don't care. Nodding, I lick my lips seductively, accepting his offer. Bouncing in my seat, I sing, "I got that cake… cake… cake."

"Oooh ba-by, I like it. I'ma make you my chick, cream all over this dick," he warns. His eyes darken and cloud with lust.

With the challenge issued, I playfully cock my head to the side. "You know what it is."

"Woman, you keep it up, and I'ma have to do you right here," he rasps, tightening his grip on the steering wheel.

Sassily, I call his bluff. "Do me, baby."

Make a left at stop sign and continue around Whitechurch Circle. Your destination is on your right in 1000ft. Google Maps interrupts our play.

Pulling up to my door, Carter beams with pride as he looks over at me. "Damn, shawty," he jokes. "This your driveway with the car in it?" he asks, motioning to my Audi.

"Yup. This is all me," I boast. I work hard for my success.

He parks behind my car and we get out. Our playful banter and laughter must have brought Mrs. Brinkman to her door because she waves for me to come over. I hand the keys to Carter so he could take our stuff in while I chat with her.

At sixty-seven years old, she's still a spring chicken, as her husband refers to her. Tall and slender, her beautiful cocoa brown skin is smooth and unblemished. Her once hazel eyes are now turning to a bluish green. Her gray hair is styled in a sleek and full-bodied bob. She's dressed in her church nursing uniform, so she must've just come from ministering to the sick and shut-in belonging to her church.

"We are sorry to hear about your daddy, sweetheart," she calls out so that her voice reaches me as I cross the yard.

"Thanks, Mrs. B. And thanks for looking after my house while I was gone."

She smiles as she kisses my cheek in greeting. She pulls her sweater closer together as the wind whips past her face and almost breaks her neck looking past me to get a good look at Carter. She waves at him sweetly.

This old heffa is so damn nosey.

"No problem, honey. Your young man stopped by every day that you were gone. Finally, yesterday, Jordy told him that your father died and that we weren't expecting you back until some-time next week. Is that your brother? Or your cousin?"

Clearly, she knew the man with me isn't Jermaine's no-good ass. I shake my head "no" and add, "Let me get back to my company. I'm driving back Friday, so I'll call you later." I drop a kiss to her cheek and was stepping off her front until she reaches out, catching my arm. "One more thing. He said he had something to give you, so Jordy used the key you gave us to let him in so he could put it inside."

What the fuck? Rolling my eyes and huff, "Mrs. Brinkman." I want to tell her old ass if he ain't important enough to know my father passed away, he shouldn't be granted access to my house, but I hold my tongue. In this life, I respect my elders.

Shaking her head, she squeezed my arm. "I know. And I'm sorry. I told Jordy that you wouldn't appreciate us doing that, but it was already too late. And Jordy said that you're such a good girl you can use a good man surprising you when you're sad."

While I can't argue with her logic, their key privileges are getting revoked. Annoyed, I walk off toward my place. No telling what this nucca done left in my house.

Fuuuuuck! I fume, realizing that Carter went in ahead of me.

CHAPTER
thirty-three

Alicia

W HEN I WALK IN, I see Carter standing all the way back in the kitchen, near the island with his back to me.

I'm midway through the dining room with some pep in my step when he turns at the sound of my footsteps. "So much for not having anyone to choke out." His voice is tinged with suspicion as he extends the purple gift bag, stuffed with a bear and balloon, to me.

The eyes that assess me are the same ones from the past—cool, distant, hard, angry.

I halfway shrug. "Soooo, my elderly neighbors let my ex leave that here. They have a key and didn't know that we had stopped messing with each other," I explain, walking by him without taking the bag.

I pull the knitted scarf from around my neck, come out of my coat, and sling it over the back of one of the dinette chairs. Quietly, I stand beside him. Don't know what else I'm supposed to say. Everything inside of me is hoping that he has absolutely no intention of drawing this out.

I never get what I want.

"Open it. I wanna see what boah got you."

It's an order wrapped in a request. He holds the handles of the bag out to me as laughing eyes meet mine. The lump lodged in my throat makes it hard to swallow or speak while my heart beats erratically.

Ba-Bump… Ba-bump… Ba-Bump…

Unrelenting eyes stalk me as I take the bag out of his hands. My heart rate leaves me barely able to breathe. I put the bag on the island in front of me, and I don't dare smile at the polar bear wearing a sparkling tutu from Build-A-Bear. I purse my lips, and Carter takes it from my hand. He presses the soft red heart, and it speaks, "I love you", in Jermaine's lazy, southern drawl.

Ba-Bump… Ba-bump… Ba-Bump…

"He loves you," he mocks dryly, his eyes never leaving mine.

I don't give a damn about him. "He's a fuckin' lie."

"There's more," he continues, completely ignoring my statement. My nerves, alive with indescribable anxiety, tingle all over. Taking it upon himself, Carter reaches inside the bag and pulls out a long, navy leather jewelry box.

Quietly, he places the slim box on the granite island top. "Open it."

Nervously, I decline. "No, that's okay. I'ma send it back to him."

"Alieas," he all but grunts, "open it." He pushes the box in front of me.

Under the heat of his stare, I flip the lid. Lying on the pillowy cushion of the box is the diamond chocker I had admired from Bailey, Banks, and Biddle one lazy Sunday as we shopped.

Carter lets out a whistle. "Niiiice. Now, put it on," he orders. His fingers trail over the diamonds then quickly circles my neck.

My eyes widen, meeting his again. He's serious and the huskiness of the demand intrigues me as my nerves dance into full-fledged fevered animalistic lust.

"Carter," I whisper, ready to succumb to all his demands, whatever they may be.

"You over this nigga?"

Bump… Bump… Bump…

The sound of his voice rings bells in the depths of my soul, awakening her. The look in his eyes lets me know that I better fuckin be over that nigga and every other one ever to have crossed my path. Swallowing hard, I nod. His fingers tighten around my throat, exerting just enough pressure to emanate a pleasurable moan. His searching thumb leisurely strokes the long column of my neck.

Up and down… Up and down… as my pulse beats beneath it. He gently presses and every coherent thought in my brain scatters as I cream in my panties.

Heavy eyes, glazed with desire and still recovering, I let out a sultry laugh. Feeling decadent and delicious, I want him to taste it.

Swiftly cupping the back of my neck, Carter brings my body into direct contact with his. Impatient hands dig into my hips as our mouths mate. His lips devour mine as his teeth nip at my bottom lip and our tongues clash. Traveling hands journey up my sides and across my collarbone to cup both sides of my neck. He takes the kiss to depths I've only explored with him.

Yessss. Kiss me like I'm all you'll ever know… Hold on tight… Never let me go… Let's make love all night… let's do this right… I need you to be mine for life…

I can't tell if I say what I'm thinking aloud or not. I stay making shit up when I'm in the moment.

Carter grunts as his patience snaps and he rips my plaid button-up flannel shirt. Buttons pop, flying everywhere, a few onto the floor as he pulls the fabric from my shoulders and down my arms. Ravaging lips course a trail that dips in between the valley of my breasts as quick fingers unclasp my bra. Leaning back on both hands, I allow him the freedom to roam and graze from my ample bosom, a caramel delight with chocolate peak nipples.

Firm hands pull my tights and panties off. Carter picks me up off my feet and places me on the island countertop.

"Cold," I groan. But then the heat takes over, causing me to forget where I even am.

The urgency to have him inside of me immediately overshadows one of those lazy lovemaking sessions.

I want to get fucked. Hair pulling and ass slapping. And from where I'm sitting, Carter is ready to oblige. The belt loses the fight with my hands as I make quick work of unbuckling it and then his pants. He tugs all that muscle from the v neck and slips his hand in his pocket to retrieve a gold wrapper. As I admire the rippling muscles, he quickly sheaths himself and forcefully pulls me to him.

Grabbing my hair, he yanks it tightly and tips my head to the side. His mouth ravages the exposed area of my neck in huge bites. I gyrate my hips as his hands, full with my ass, bring me into direct contact with the dick I've been waiting to get a hold of since he pulled out of the hotel's driveway.

One swift stroke has me breaking into pieces, only to have him gather them up and put me back together for the next tortured stroke after another. Leaning back until my shoulder touches the counter, I forget everything except the feel of him. Of how he makes me feel when he's inside of me. Moaning and moving in fluid unison, I'm taking everything he delivers, the quick and short, the deep and slow.

I've always loved the sounds of a man who is putting in that work. I know it's over when he lifts my right leg up over his shoulder and leans further in so he can go deeper. I try to rise up, but he forces me back down and continues to pound.

"You are mine," he declares. "No distance, no amount of years apart ever gonna change that," he professes, drilling into my channel."Caaaaarter!"

The sound of our bodies slapping against each other is erotic music to my ears. I become completely undone when his left hand leaves my breast to squeeze my neck. There's a rhythm to his ministrations: long stroke, squeeze, pressure, short stroke, long stroke... again and again. My thighs tighten as his strokes create the winning combo to my pleasure. My mind grows foggy, and I get lost, bursting into flames as the familiar tingle of fire dances through me and manifest in an earth-shattering nut accompanied by the familiar giggle that none of my orgasms are complete without.

"Damn," he huffs, still stroking that long dick and me into compliance. "You gon' come one more time for me, ma?"

Quaking into a million pieces, I just chuckle. I'm not entirely sure that I can handle another one after that.

Carter lifts me from the counter and settles us on one of the pub chairs. "What you say earlier about that cake... cake... cake?" he asks, palming both of my cheeks, jiggling them until I giggle. He bites my bottom lip and pulls me into a deep kiss.

"Me and my big ole mouth," I mumble into his as I proceed to put it on him. I ride his dick like champion jockey until he comes, his toes curls, and he forgets his muthafuckin' name.

CHAPTER

thirty-four

Alieas

I'VE NEVER LEARNED PROPER TEXT *etiquette. Sue me. I'm an '80s baby, and we're still navigating the how, the why, and the when.*

Tiff: **It would have been fun to see the city. But we ain't get the memo or an invite with your shady ass self.**

Nesha: **SMH... Carter probably waxing that ass all over her condo.**

Rolling, my eyes I type, **Resting up for round five. The Brinkmans let Jermaine in and he left some shit there. Carter looked like he was about to trip and then dicked me down. Choking was involved.**

Tiff: **Last time Tim choked me, I blacked out. You can keep that kinky, unconscious shit.**

Nesha: **LMBO. Every time Gray touches me, I end up pregnant. I'm still fighting to get the last baby out of the bed. So y'all go ahead and get choked and waxed for me.**

Tiff: **Tell that old nigga to learn how to pull out.**

Nesha: **Whoa. Pump it, heffa. CTFU. But you need to get that Jermaine shit straight. ASAP. And I like Cart for you.**

I text quickly, catching Carter's eyes. There's the how, when, and the who. **Yes, ma'am. Well, we out on the town. Double date with Lon and her boo. It's rude to be texting you hoes, sooooo.**

Tiff: **Nite then. Tell Cart, I said wassup!**

Nesha: **Holla. I'm bout to hunt Gray down and do him in the basement while the kids sleep.**

Alright now.

Putting the phone in my purse, Carter offers me a sip of his drink and asks, "Who was that?"

Sticking my tongue out, I say, "Jermaine."

He raises his brows. "Yea, aight."

Lon laughs into her cup, sipping on her virgin pina colada, "You better stop playing with Carter, Lieas," she warns.

Carter's facial expression says the same thing. "Babe, I'm only playing. He been blocked before this. Lon, let's go get a drink."

Lon looks over at boyfriend Jason. "You want something?"

"Nawl." He squeezes her hands as she gets up.

The lingering look that passes between them is intimate. Years of observation tell me it's something more. "Look at y'all, all lovey-dovey," I tease as we walk over to the bar.

The music is pumping, and I feel good, so the hips are swaying. "Us? Look at you. I told you. Didn't I tell you second chances are possible?" She was beaming. Her smile could brighten the entire darkened club.

Over the sound of Lorde's voice, I narrow my eyes and I give her the once-over. "You're extra happy and optimistic, even for you."

"Please. Your mean ass seems happy, given the circumstances."

Shaking my head, I glance back over at Carter. "That definitely made me happy. When I come home alone next week, I'll wallow. But for now, he has made me extremely happy." Nudging her shoulder, I add. "You're glowing, though."

I order Carter a Corona, and I get a sex on the beach. When she orders another virgin drink, everything falls into place. I caught her throwing up last week before I left. "Are you pregnant?"

The smile widens and she nods. "Yes," she nervously laughs. "Yes we are, and he asked me to marry him."

Squealing in delight, I lunge myself at her and gather her up into a bone-squeezing hug. "See? I told you he was gonna ask. When? And why didn't you tell me?"

"It just happened yesterday. And my period was due last

week. When I told him about the baby, he already had the ring. He had been carrying it around for days. I didn't want to tell you my exciting news because you were upset about your dad."

"Girl, where's the damn ring?" I demand. It touches me that she'd consider my feelings. But I would've showed up with my ring on like, BOOM, diamonds just stepped in the room.

"I didn't wear it. I'll send you a picture later. I'm really excited," she says and starts to fan her eyes. "I didn't think this was what I wanted. Now I can't imagine my life without it."

My friend could win an academy award for best actress. She is a very emotional person. "Aylonah James, you are crying happy tears in the middle of the club." The music was pumping.

She sniffles back tears and fans some more. "Shut up. I'm just so happy. But I'm sad for you too."

I pull her tightly and let her know, "It's okay to be both."

I was so engrossed in having Carter with me that I wasn't even remotely concerned with the things I no longer have.

My father… A family of my own…

And just because she tried to suppress her joy to spare my feelings, I smile through my own momentary pain to keep that million dollar smile on her face.

First comes love…

Then comes marriage…

Lon is coming with a baby carriage…

Grabbing my drinks, we head back to our table.

Hands grip my waist from behind. "Whoa dere," a familiar voice whispers in my ear. Frozen in place, frown lines appear as I turn around to greet Jermaine in person.

"What?"

"Waddup witchu?" he asks. His eyebrows draw close together, and he takes a swig of from his bottle.

Lon sizes him up and sucks her teeth. "This clown. Come on, Lieas," she says.

In the span of a few short seconds, Jermaine's mouth twists into a sneer. "Whatever, Lon. Take your bougie-ass ova there withcho nigga while I talk to my girl."

Lon returns the facial gesture, displaying pure disdain for the man. And before I can even utter a word, she steps to him. "What, nucca? I'ma send *her man* over here to check you."

"Get your girl," Jermaine warns as she walks in the direction of our table. I can see Carter stand up, eyes directly on us.

"You need to chill," I let him know.

"Nawl, you need to chill. Who's this nigga you in here wit'?" He nods over to my table. It's obvious now that Jermaine had been watching us and had to see me grinding all over Carter. It must have taken all of his restraint not to come over to our table and not make a scene.

It's uncharacteristic of him to be patient. I guess he was waiting for the opportune moment to get me alone, which is completely cool. Jermaine wanted a face-to-face, so here we go. "We're over since that bitch called me all fly and crazy, saying she wasn't your cousin and that y'all fucking. I already told you; I'm not doing this shit. So, you can go back wherever you was at and enjoy your night.".

I flag him and turn around, bumping right into Carter's chest.

Ooooh shit.

"Is there a problem, my man?" he demands of Jermaine.

Jermaine quickly sizes Carter up and realizes things won't end in his favor. Carter has a good two inches and about twenty pounds of muscle on Jermaine, but his rambunctious personality makes up for the deficit in stature.

"Nawl, not at all, my nig. Was rapping to my girl for a moment."

Fierce brown eyes dissect Jermaine. Carter takes the beer from my hand and laces our fingers together. "Must be a problem, cuz this woman right here. This me, homey," Carter informs him. "So, she cool on whatever you tryna offer."

My heart is beating so fast and my adrenaline is pumping. I know Carter is pissed. His face and body testify that he wants to ball Jermaine up and bounce his ass out the club.

"Is that so? She must not know it, then, my nigga," Jermaine challenges and pokes his chest out so he can appear larger.

Carter laughs, a deep-throated, cocky rumble. He raises our joined hands and kisses mine. "Oh, she knows it. Come on, babe."

He pulls me into his body, tucks me under his arm, and we start to walk away when Jermaine adds, "Bitch was just bouncing on my dick last week."

I gasp, and I'm appalled that he'd try to trash me even though I definitely was fucking him about three weeks ago. Carter, already enraged, spins around and punches him square in the face. Blood, red and thick, gushes from his nose as Carter grabs him up by the front of his shirt. "Watch your muthafuckin' mouth and go ahead about your business."

Disgusted, Carter pushes Jermaine and then shakes his hands out. Jermaine stumbles backward.

Suddenly aware that a circle has formed around us, I frown. "Let's go, babe." In the dark, I can see the lights of cellphone cameras recording. I can't afford to be on nobody's website participating in reckless behavior.

Angrily, Carter pulls me from the dance floor, barreling through the crowd of people in our way, Lon and Jay included. I can barely keep up with his strides as he pulls me past the coat check toward an isolated corner.

"Who the fuck was that dude?!" Carter explodes. His face is flushed red, those beautiful amber eyes dark and dangerous.

Take a deep breath and be sure to think before you speak. "Carter, calm down," I attempt to soothe. I put my hands on his chest and look into his eyes. In my heels, we're almost eye level. "That was Jermaine."

"THAT NUTASS NIGGA IN SKINNY JEANS?!"

"Can we just go?" I beg.

Lon and Jay came out right after us. "You cool, Lieas? Carter?" Jason questions, uncertain if he had to step in between Carter and me.

"We're good. Lon, can you grab my coat from the coat check? We're going to go." Jermaine probably already calling his felony ass family so some shit can jump off.

"I'm sorry. Nigga straight disrespectful. The last time I wanted to rip a nigga head off was when I saw you with dude at your crib."

Justin. Shit. Now is not the time to tell him that Justin and I are still friends even if it's in the purest sense of the word.

"We can wait for Lon to bring the coat out in the car. It might not be safe to stay here," I say instead.

CHAPTER
thirty-five

Alicia

WE MADE IT BACK TO the Philly without any more run-ins with Jermaine. Carter was decidedly confused at my attraction to Jermaine or the reasons I was even dating him, to begin with. I was embarrassed because Carter's impression of Jermaine reflected negatively on me. And to be honest and fair besides being a cheater, Jermaine is essentially harmless. As much as he spoke of his drug dealing family members running shit, he himself did not have a criminal record. He has a regular nine-to-five. I refrained from explaining any if that because Carter was not interested in hearing any of it.

I eased it over by saying, we all make bad choices.

"Girl, y'all lucky. Baltimore and D.C straight dudes be reckless. God protects babies and fools," Bri says after I give them the rundown on what happened on last night at the club.

"So, now I'm a fool?".

"You damn sure ain't a baby," Nesha adds with a chuckle

then shrugs. "Aside from that, did Gray let you know that he was letting Ms. Shelia come over a grab some items?"

I haven't seen or heard from Ms. Shelia since the first day at Gray's.She'd come by to offer her input with the funeral arrangements. The rational part of me wants to respect what she'd been to my father, but the crazy part of me is... well, crazy. She has no control over Deidra any more than I do.

I narrow my eyes at my friends. "You think it would be petty to ask her not to bring her lil' sister to the funeral?"

Bri frowns. "Yes, heffa, it's rude. Carter obviously wants to be with you, is with you, so what's the big deal?" She uncovers a photo of my father and Tyree from a stack of pictures in a book. "Look at Ty," she laughs, flashing up with it.

"Awww. Yo, my dad and mom would dress him and Gray up in matching outfits. My mom said Gray used to hate that shit."

"Guuuurl. Females are the only ones who like that boppsie crap," Bri jokes.

"Please, we have matching patterns every Eid. Gray loves it," Nesha adds.

"Girl, he loves that ass so, if you say matching anything, he giving it to you."

Nesha blushes. The fact that Gray does her bidding just to please her and bring joy to her face is all I need to be inspired. My heart flutters with hope.

It's the same with Bri. And Tiff, Trina, and Case.

I'll have to field all my aunts' and uncles' questions regarding my prospects for marriage, if my ovaries work, and if I plan on moving back to Philly any time in the future.

"Y'all better be around to save me from the aunts and the uncles tomorrow.And Janelle's stank ass. If I have to see how happy she and the rich husband are, I'll be sick."

Bri looks up from rifling through the box of pictures. "She's not that bad. I think she just gives you a hard time because she's jealous, even more so now that you're kind of a big-time publisher with a distribution deal."

Enter the eye rolls from Nesha. "Please. Gray had to remind me that I was covered the last time we were in the same room. She so damn shady. I told you, Lieas, if she would've caught me a year before Ayesha's birth. Ooooh wooh, she would've got it."

Bri narrows her eyes at Nesha and considers what she said and laughs, recalling the moment in question. "Yeah, Nesh was 'bout to be on that ass that day. She mentally took her overgarments off."

"These hands," Nesha laughs, holding up her henna printed fists for display. "All over her ass. You hear me?" she finishes then balls up her fist and depicts the old time beat-beat to both eyes and the mouth.

I start cracking up. "Maybe we can all throw shade her way," I offer.

"Why be shady? If just being you is enough to irritate the fuck out of her, just continue to do what you do best, boo," Bri reasons.

That doesn't sound half bad. I guess I can be the bigger person for the sake of the funeral. I can't make any promises, though. "If you insist. We all used to be rowdy as shit, though," I remind them.

"Used to be? Heffa, yooooou still outta pocket. But you have sooooo many people who love and try to keep you under control."

Rolling my neck, I say, "Whateva."

"Yo, bighead." Tyree peeks inside the den. "Come here," he commands.

Both Nesha and Bri glance at me. "You the only one he call bighead. Take ya butt out there," Bri instructs.

It doesn't matter that I'm in my thirties, this negro will

always be busting. "What?" I ask when I go out into the living room.

Gray is lounging on the couch, his long legs stretched out. Tyree settles against the wall with an elbow resting on the mantle. Eyeing both of them cautiously, I shrug. "Wassup?"

"Pops left these," Gray starts to explain holding out three envelopes, "with instructions not to open until after the funeral."

"Okay. So, are we listening to the instructions or are we about to open them now?" I inquire with a speculative glance from Gray to Ty.

Gray holds them out for both me and Ty to take. Ty grabs his and stuffs it in his back pocket. His eyes are dark and brooding. I can almost feel the wheels turning in his brain. Gray has always been much harder to read, but even his hazel eyes are unsure.

"This is dramatic as hell. Even for Unc," Ty chuckles, rubbing his hands over his dark head of waves. "He thought of everything. I'ma miss the shit of that man. We had our differences, but he taught me everything I know about being a man. Being responsible, having good credit..." Tyree lists, tracing under his eyelid as his eyes pool with tears that threaten to spill over.

"Good credit, though?" I remark, taking mine, testing its weight in my hand.

"Personal and business credit? Yes. Fuck yea."

Gray clears his throat. "He made mistakes, but he was an alright dude. He bought out 2nd and Cambria for my twenty-fifth. And I had just got out of jail. That night was crazy."

"Remember he took all of us fishing? And he was gon' fuck Tommy up because he was straight wildin?" Ty asks with a reminiscent smile. "Shit. I could've been Tommy if wasn't for Unc."

"Sure could've, youngin'," Gray agrees with Tyree. "He was a good dad to us. Strict as shit. I used to hate it. And Lieas was spoiled like a mutha. She never had to do nothing at the crib. Straight spoiled. Pop's princess."

"Right?" Ty agrees.

"Okay. That's not how I recall it. After you moved out," I point at Gray and then turn to Ty, "and you stopped coming around. He was always on my back."

"About keeping you focused, and you still got whatever you wanted. Even after you stopped speaking. Pops made sure your car note was paid and your account was right."

Guilt penetrates. "I let him. His prerogative. I really did love him. If I try to cut either of you from my life for any absurd reasons, please don't let me." Feeling sorry for myself, I slide down on the couch beside Gray. He feels sorry, too, and gathers me close.

"He said to make sure she knows I love her. No matter what," Gray reveals. "When he didn't know if he'd see you, he said, 'Tell my Moo I love her."

I only shrug. "I don't know. I thought there would be more time. The last thing he asked of me was to stay for a while longer." I hate hospitals and I was convinced that he'd be okay. "It was like I couldn't breathe. I had to get out of there."

"We both did a lot of apologizing. I've been preparing for it a while." Gray clears his throat. "I don't think you're ever ready for death, but he damn sure lived. Pops was that man."

"We were making small talk for a moment," Ty says. "I was in my feelings, so I thanked him for raising me when he didn't have to. Treating me the same way he did Gray. He was like, you're my son."

His chest puffs up a little as he sucks in a breath. "Not 'like a son'. But, you're my son. Like, it didn't matter that we aren't blood-related. Y'all wouldn't understand 'cause he's actually y'all dad. To have him say that broke me a lil' bit. He put his hand over mine and said, '*I'm proud of you. Of the man you've become.*' I was balling by the time he got done talking about responsibility, forgiveness, family, and love. About living with decisions you've made and in the end realize that it may not have been the right course of action. About the importance of truth and trust. You know his shit, *your word is your bond,* and he apologized for not always living up to that but expecting us to. I remember thinking, Damn, Unc. Death is real." He pushes at what I suspect is the same ache in his heart as mine.

CHAPTER

thirty-six

Alieus

I'M DREAMING. IT MUST BE a dream. I'm at a poetry reading.
On the stage reciting a piece that I wrote.
The lights are bright... Correction, the spotlight is...
Bright. Shining. Blinding. Radiating.
Hot!!!
Maybe I'm not being selective enough in my choice of words.
This shit is Exposing. Illuminating. Magnifying
Things better left hidden in the dark.
The Truth.
Oooh, how we claim we want it. Ready for it. Built for it.
Bound by it. Enslaved to it. That is... Until truth
Shows up and shows the fuck out
Demanding more, not accepting less
Taking the option to readily dismiss away
Forcing you to address what's what, today...

I open my eyes to look out at the crowd, and the only people there are my dad, Tyree, and my Aunt Layla.

Startled awake, I gasp and clutch my chest. Wide-eyed and thoroughly confused, I stare up at the ceiling.

What in the entire fuck?

Strong arms surround me, pulling me to him. "Babe," Carter comforts. "It's okay. It was just a dream," he soothes, kissing my forehead.

It feels so real. I felt the heat of the spotlight just as much as I feel Cart stroking my back.

I shake my head, still unable to make sense of it. "It wasn't a nightmare." Mental flashes of my dad and Ty together play out. Tears easily slip from my eyes. My throat hurts. "It was weird. I was performing at a poetry reading. My dad was there. He was holding hands with my aunt Layla. And Ty was sitting beside them," I explain.

No way is what I'm automatically thinking but I'm imagining shit.

The dream. It was so vivid, so clear in my mind. It can't fucking be the start of a déjà vu moment as both my father and aunt are dead, so it ain't no way either of them showing up anywhere other than my dreams. Incensed, I get up from the bed, send a wary look over my shoulder to Carter, and begin pacing the floor.

I even nibble on my freshly painted fingernail a lil' bit as I analyze the complexity of what my dream insinuates. Impulsively, I grab my phone but put it back down. Then I just stare off into space.

I hadn't seen him move or hear any sounds, but Carter comes to me, held me still. "Lieas, you could just be nervous about today," he offers.

That's not it. Of course, I'm nervous about seeing my dad in a casket, but there's more to it.

There's a clawing fear in the pit of my stomach, threatening to make me sick. The moment I say the words, I fear speaking it into existence.

Truth.

"My dad. He… He always made sure that Ty was right. That he had never gone without. He raised him alongside us. "

Carter shakes me. "Lieas, what are you saying? You're rambling."

Images collide, mesh. Tyree's face. My father's. The likeliness that I've never noticed. Tyree looks like a darker version of my father.

"I think— I think my dad is my Tyree's dad."

I can see in his reaction that this makes absolutely no sense to him. He can't even fathom where this idea originated from. "Alieas, that doesn't make any sense."

"Before my mom." I start revealing even as my mind stitches the story together. "My dad used to date my Aunt Layla."

He shrugged. "Ooh k."

I step back. I'm frustrated. He's not understanding what I'm saying. "That's Ty's mom."

"Well, what do you think that means?"

Irked at his condescending tone and his usage of the word "think", I frown and narrow my eyes at him. He sighs and throws his head back and then stares blankly waiting for me to spell it out for him.

"He dated my aunt. My mom said he was in love with her."

"Hold… hold up. Your dad dated your aunt and he married ya moms? Damn, Mr. Stiles was pimping," he chuckles as he put it together. "Sisters, though?"

I push his arm and send a seething glare, but he shrugs again and shakes his head. "That still don't mean anything," he concludes. "Gray is like two years older than Ty."

Arms folded, I witness him mentally unpacking what I'm

saying. His mouth opens in a little "O", and he mouths the word "shit."

"Exactly."

There was a silent pause. "If it's true, do you think your mom knows? Ty?"

There is no way this side of hell that Nicole would have kept this from me. From Tyree. "I don't know. I doubt it. Maybe none of them knew."

"Don't get mad. But maybe there's nothing to know."

I bite my bottom lip. "Carter, weren't you just listening to me?"

"I was listening. And," he coughs in his hand and clears his throat, "umm, for the sake letting everything go over smoothly today, I think you should just wait until after your dad's funeral to start with changes to the family tree."

"I'm serious," I insist.

"Look," he takes hold of my chin and tilts my face up so that we're looking into each other's eyes, "I know that you loved your dad. I know that you also feel some type of way about the years you two were estranged. Today is the day to celebrate his life. Mourn his passing. And honestly, they can do it without you dropping any bombs." Then, he kisses my cheek. "I'll make you some breakfast," he solemnly adds and leaves me alone with my thoughts.

My father wasn't overly religious in life, so having the funeral at a church was not at all him. We held the service at the funeral home instead. And because he wasn't a complete atheist, void of all thoughts of a monotheistic power, he did have scripture and surah readings.

I sat in a daze, too afraid to look at the body of my father resting eternally in his handpicked deluxe silver-lined casket. At the urging of my uncle, they'd closed the casket during Gray and my Uncle Melvin's eulogies. I kept imagining him sitting up and stepping over the edge to get out.

And me hightailing my ass up outta here.

I hate funerals. I hate death…

My mom would periodically squeeze my shoulder in support. She is sitting in the row behind me. I had begged her to sit beside me, but out of respect for their ten years of divorce, her husband, and Ms. Shelia, she elected to settle for background support.

A huge picture of him stood prominently at the head of the casket. It was fairly recent, showing his graying hair and wrinkles at the eyes. His dazzling smile was still ever present. As a girl, that smile had melted my heart. I remember him emailing me one day asking if I'd approved if it. Of course, I had never even responded. I had looked and admired how handsome he was, and then it dawned on me that was the reason for his unfaithfulness. So, he wouldn't get any passes or approvals from me. Now, I wish I'd indulged at least once. The picture was an exact portrait of how he looked resting. During the entire service, my eyes stayed fixed on the podium or the picture, too afraid to even glance at him once they opened the casket for the final viewing.

Tears mix with anxiety as they lower him into the ground, into the small space where he'd spend forever waiting…

For the trumpets and horns to blow with the return of the King.

For whatever is after death…

"Babe?" Carter leans close to my ear. "You ready?" he hesitatingly inquires.

"You can go ahead to the car. I need a minute," I tell him.

Suppressing the urge to jump into the ground, I back away.

I stay here well after everyone starts to depart for their cars.

I had missed out on spending time with my father, not willing to accept all his faults. Now, I would mourn him for all the days that I had left. I would be horrified if the people who were supposed to love me the most turned and hightailed it if I'd shown them the real me.

How perfect had I been in life? Nowhere near perfection.

How many mistakes had I made? Too many to count.

Once in the car, I put on my seatbelt, and Carter lifts my hand to his lips. He kisses it, then leans in to kiss my cheek. "You did good, babe."

I guess. Knowing my brother and cousin, they had me on, jump-in-after-the-casket watch with Carter on, *Save her*, duty.

I fall asleep and am counting sheep by the time we reach the highway. I slept the entire ride from the cemetery to the banquet hall and I wake up to Carter's deep voice telling me it is time to go in. He squeezes my hand in support.

Yawning, I pull down the passenger side visor and flip open the lid to show the mirror. My face looks how it feels, swollen, tired, tear-streaked, weather-battered, and sad. Smoothing out the puffs beneath my eyes, I yawn again. "I look horrible," I let out.

Carter was about to refute it but stopped in his tracks when I gave him the, '*I dare you*' look.

I quickly look through my purse to find my sunglasses. I put them on and slap Carter's thigh. "I'm liable to cuss one of my relatives out," I mumble. "They'll all be talking shit."

"Behave. We can leave whenever you're ready," he assures me.

Behave? I'm not a damn pet. But for him, I say, "Yes, sir," playfully puckering my lips in air kisses.

So, I had survived Act one: The Service, Act two: The Cemetery and was heading into Act Three: The Repast.

CHAPTER
thirty-seven

Alicia

T HE STILES KNOW HOW TO throw a party. My father was definitely a partier. Not like the dainty dinner parties my mom gave while they were together. He enjoyed gritty, lights down low, disco ball turning, smoke-tinged, music-filled dance floors. The more the merrier. His specific instructions indicated that he wanted it to be a celebration of his life, not some stuffy memorial service with tears everywhere. My uncle Melvin joked that my dad wanted a stripper to jump out of a cake.

I BET. They both two nasty old niggas.

We walk into the hall hand-in-hand. It is decorated in black and gold; I'm guessing that he is paying homage to the bruhs. There are balloons and streamers and pictures. There is even music. I shake my head, unsure if I feel comfortable in the "party" that my father had put together.

I spot Lon and Bri talking, smiling, and huddled close. I suspect they're talking about her splendid news.My mom and Mitchell are seated at the same table. My mom has the same look on her face as me, and I imagine we share the same sentiments regarding the "party". All of my loves are seated at these two tables, I observe, taking in the sight of my girls, their husbands, and children.

That's me. I take them all in. All of my family. And Carter is here with me. I'm still adjusting to the belief that I deserve this smidgen of hope that I feel budding in my heart. That I deserve a second chance with him even though I'm mourning that I didn't get one with my dad.

"Go ahead and sit down," I murmur to Carter. "I have to go to the bathroom." Overwhelmed and emotional, I excuse myself and escape.

After five minutes in the last stall, I feel that I can deal with people and just as I touch the latch, I hear voices.

"She crying now, but she damn sure wasn't when she wouldn't talk to him," a voice that I can't place says.

"Yea, and poor Uncle Darien. He loved her," Janelle seconds.

"She's probably just back looking for money. I heard he split it between the three of them."

"Three? You mean he had a baby on Aunt Nic?"

I have no idea who the other voice belongs to and as I open the door, the voice huffs and says, "The nerve of her. I mean really. Aliie-as," the rest of my name ended in a stutter as I opened the door and came out.

"I should be what?" I inquire of my older cousin's wife, Ebony. I've only met this woman like three times at family events when she and my cousin Jerimiah were dating back in the late nineties. "Janelle," I greet.

Her mouth drops wide open. "I didn't say anything," she quickly defends.

I'm just as quick with my response. "And you shouldn't. You should mind your business," I scold Janelle and then turn my attention to the light-skinned hussy standing beside her. "And I don't even fucking know you like that. So, you definitely should keep my name and business from between them lips."

She rolls a set of slanted brown eyes and her neck. "Everyone in the family knows you weren't speaking to your daddy and now here you go acting like you all hurt," Ebony attempts to read me.

I yawn. I'm tired but not tired enough for pettiness. Stepping up to the sink to wash my hands, I glance back their way. "You better get your sister-in-law," I warn Janelle, "before I show her something else everyone knows about me."

"Alieas," Janelle touches my arm. "I'm so sorry about your daddy." She squeezes it before turning to leave.

There are no words between them, but Janelle shoots Ebony the evil eye on the way out. Ebony follows her out, leaving me thinking that other funeral attendees were basically thinking the same thing.

That I only came for the money.

It couldn't be further from the truth. Money is the last thing I'm worried about. I had kind of already convinced myself that he'd cut me out of the will about five years ago.

Shaking my head and yawning again, I dry my hands and leave the bathroom. I can feel several pairs of eyes staring at me as mine instantly scan the room for Carter.

Distracted, they stumble over Tyree and my uncle James in what seems to be a deep discussion. My uncle looks a little intoxicated. Tyree's brows are drawn close together, accompanied by a speculative scowl as he listens. With the intention to save him, I walk over in his direction only to be pulled into a hug by Justin.

"Hey, Lieas. I ain't think I was gonna make it. Dej was gonna meet me, but Aubrey has a fever so she sends her regards," he explains. He and his wife of four years just had a baby this year.

Smiling, I hug him close. Over the years, he has become something like a brother to me but also a good friend, a male friend I cherish and whom I've technically never had intercourse with. His wife and I have spent several hours in one another's company. "I'm happy that you made it. And I guess I'll see Dej and Aub next time I come up."

"Yea, that's cool. How you feeling?"

I let out a long breath and hold my arms up to my sides. "Shitty. But you know me."

"It'll be alright," he says. "I saw your moms and step—"

His words a cut off by the sound of hell freezing over.

"What did you just say?!" Tyree exploded as he stood towering over my uncle.

My uncle James blinked and shook his head. Then he negligently flagged Tyree, "Don't worry about it, boy," he fumbled the words out. "I'm just talking out my head. I need to go sit down."

Frustrated, Tyree grabs him by the arm. "Nawl, come again. Repeat what you just said."

"What's wrong?" I jump in, nervous at what might happen next.

Uncle James is the one drunken family member who always ends up getting put out of parties and family events because he can't hold his liquor.

When I reach out to touch his shoulder, Tyree whirls his attention to me. "Did you hear him?!" he yells.

As confusion settles into chaos in my mind, I shake my head. "What did he say? I... I didn't hear him."

Tyree's face twists in anger. "He a fuckin' lie. That's what he said."

I can see it in my uncle's eyes that he realized that he'd made a mistake. And it's too late to take it back. But he tried it.

"I said I'm talking out my head. Now, go on, boy," he warns Tyree.

Shaking my head, I pull at his arm unsuccessfully and make direct eye contact with him. "Ty, he drunk. Don't worry about it."

"Lieas, get the fuck out the way," he warns, kind of flinging me off him. There's fire in his eyes, so I know that there is anguish in his heart. "What did you say, old man?" He grabs my uncle by the lapels of his suit.

My uncle looks at Tyree then back over at me. "I told your daddy not to die with that shit on his heart."

Uncle Melvin steps in, but my uncle James just keeps talking. "He was a hardheaded, stubborn son-of-a-bitch. But he should've done right by you. Told you the truth. He loved your mother. He loved you. You made him proud, but I told him to tell you that he was your father."

Oooh shit. And just like that, a thirty-six-year-old secret tumbles from the lips of a drunk.

CHAPTER
thirty-eight

Alieas

MY DREAM. IS IT CRAZY to say that I can't decipher if my heart is pounding or if it has stopped beating completely? They're two vastly different occurrences yet, at this moment, I can't be sure. They both have the same effect.

"James, come on now," Uncle Melvin huffs. "You need to stop that drinking shit."

"So, you knew too?" Tyree demands of Uncle Melvin as Briannah comes to his side as the commotion escalates to other areas of the room.

My mom and Mitchell come over, and Tyree's eyes pop of his head. "Did you know, Aunt Nic?!" Tyree loudly exclaims, finally letting my uncle go with a disgusted shove.

"Know what? Baby, what's going on?" my mom inquires. Reading the distress on her face, I can tell she's upset just because he's upset.

"Did you know that he was supposed to be my dad?" he asks, flat out.

"I— Of course, I didn't know. Who told you that?" she denies.

"Babe, calm down," Bri coaxes him. My heart is pounding in my chest. I'm as unsettled as he is. "Let's go outside," she suggests .

I'm on their heels as they start to walk out of the hall, but Carter catches my hand and tugs me to him. "So, all your exes come to family members' funeral services?"

Fuck me. I sigh. "Carter, one moment. Let me go check on Tyree, and I'll come right back."

The rigid back and hard eyes already inform me that he is not about to be dismissed and that Justin's presence requires an explanation, regardless of the fact that my family is in despair. But I try anyway. "Just a couple of minutes to make sure he's okay," I try to persuade him.

He raises his brows and shakes his head, not budging an inch in favor of me sidelining or tabling this discussion.

Okay… okay… Whew. And here we go. "Carter, I'm sorry. I neglected to tell you that Justin and I are still friends. We have never slept together. He is married with a brand new baby. His wife is one of my good friends, and he came here today to emotionally support me and the family. I— I fucking forgot with everything going on."

The frown that he is sporting starts to deepen as my words set in. "So, let me get this straight. You're still friends with the side nigga that I caught you with ten years ago?"

Deeper breath, more patience. "Yes. But it isn't like that. Let me introduce you," I offer.

Prematurely, I assume that Carter would understand. It made sense in my mind. In some convoluted way, I even justified it and am willing to brush aside his concerns for the larger picture. Justin's presence here has absolutely nothing to do with us, what we have, whatever we're building.

Here I am praying for patience while he is losing what he has left of his. "Nawl, I'm good." And without another word, Carter turns abruptly and walks away, leaving me standing there.

Heart beating painfully, I watch him walk out of the double doors of the hall and possibly my life, for good.

I take a deep breath and close my eyes. My mind is racing. My concern for Ty is overshadowed by my own issues. He isn't going to walk out on me again, not after everything we've gone through to reconcile.

Just give him a moment, the calmer side of me advises when I want to stalk after him and demand that he listen. "What just happened?" Justin inquires, interrupting my inner turmoil.

At the sound of his voice, my eyes open and I lean my head back to stretch my neck and back. "The shit with your cousin sounds a lil fucked up, but I'm definitely talking about your boy," Justin says. "That was *HIM*, right?"

He remembers him. "Yes."

Carter is the only person who isn't aware of exactly how important he has been to me. How devastated I had been when it was all over, said, and done. How heartbroken I had been.

"Well, he damn sure ain't happy to see me here. I'm sorry, Lieas. I didn't realize that you and the boah had reconnected."

Nerves tangle. I'm counting seconds in my head to give him the appropriate amount of time before I go after him. "It just happened this week," I laugh stupidly, matching how I feel inside.

"Look. That man is mad, and I can kinda understand it. If one of Dej's old niggas show up somewhere important, it's the fuck on. Give him a minute."

"Why are y'all so stubborn, though?" The rising heat won't allow me to reason.

"Jealousy is distributed pretty evenly among sexes. I'll go

have a word with him for you to clear up any misunderstandings. And I'm out." Justin kisses my forehead.

"Thank you, Jus. But that won't be necessary," I reply. "It'll be okay."

Justin squeezes my arms and shakes his head. "I'ma go talk to him. I would hate for him to miss out on you over a misunderstanding."

My entire life has been a result of misunderstandings, manifested and played out in separations.

Love got me fuuuuucked up. My follow-up and execution freaking sucks. Maybe it's not meant to be. Maybe none of it is and maybe there is no happy ending for me.

I'm tired. No quips or witty thoughts come to mind as I allow the fatigue of this entire week settle over me and saddle its heavy weight on my heart.

I give him a half smile. "I'll call you" And thanks again for coming." I embrace him.

I look around for my family, realizing that they all must have went outside to calm Tyree down. I peep an empty corner and go over to sit so I can wallow in self-pity for a moment. And the second I close my eyes, someone starts talking.

"I'm not the arguing type. I'm not loud or rowdy, and I don't want to fight," Deidra starts. "I love Carter."

In all honesty, I had checked for her ass one time during the service. She was the shoulder Ms. Sheila had leaned on all day.

And now, here she is, standing before me, dressed in an all-black curve-hugging pantsuit that and heels. I realize that she is pretty enough, her body is built thick; all the extra was in the right places, just the way I remember him liking his women.

I nod my head. I even understand. But... "I love him more," I declare.

I watch intently as she digests my statement. There is no

mistaking that she believes me and expresses it on her face as her smile dims and lips tighten in response.

"There's been this part of him that has always been off limits. When I first met him, he was open and ready for love. Then he shut down. I didn't catch the signs. I was too busy dreaming of forever with him and all the while he... he was dreaming of you."

I'm not in the mood for speeches or other people's feelings or opinions when it comes to the man I love or my involvement in why something isn't happening for them.

"Deidra, I don't know you. But I love Carter and have loved him for a very, very long time. Hell, I thought I would never see him again," I confess.

"You broke his heart," she accuses.

Defiantly, I lift my chin. I'll own that even as I wonder just how much information he divulged about our relationship.

"Carter told me that he told you I was the one. You should respect that."

She shifted her body weight and placed both hands on her hips. "No, honey, you should respect that."

"Excuse me?"

"I heard what happened just now. I was listening and let me give you some words from the wise..."

CHAPTER
thirty-nine

CARTER

EIGHT DAYS. *EIGHT SHORT DAYS*, my mind chants as I walk to the door, hoping to remind myself to calm down. It's only eight days. *Eight mind—changing, life-altering days, Alieas—filled days.*

My love for her makes me crazy. I actually feel out of my damn mind. I hate to walk away. She invited her ex— not just any ex, but the dude I caught her with— to her father's funeral. To a place she knew I would be. Maybe she figured I wouldn't remember boah. Or maybe, just maybe, it's exactly what she said, and it was a slip of the memory. I flag the reasoning notion.

I can still remember walking into her apartment and finding them there hugged up on the couch like it was yesterday.

I was rushing, damn near sweating, even though it was the dead of winter. I had a set of keys to her spot and the downstairs door. I had tried calling her to let her know what was up, but she wasn't answering her cell phone. It kept going to voicemail. I imagine Lieas being thoroughly pissed enough that she'd blocked me. I had tried the house phone as well to no avail.

I was rushing— I was out of sorts. Bug had an asthma attack at the end of Toya's visit to my parents', so we had ended up rushing her to the hospital. They were able to control her breathing and had administered a treatment with the nebulizer. And while I was talking to the doctors, Toya was holding my phone and shit.

When I called Lieas, I saw that she had called me and that the call had been answered. And it hadn't been answered by me. I was fuming and quickly put Toya in her place about answering my telephone. There was no telling what Lieas was thinking, so I knew I had to get to her that night. Once Bug was stabilized, they released her, and I finished with Toya's hateful ass and then took Bug home. My mom said she would stay at my house so she could keep an eye out for her while I ran out to get Lieas, to bring her home with me and Bug where she belonged.

Apologies and explanations were ripe on my lips as I ran everything over in my mind as I rode the elevator up to her fifth-floor apartment. I already assumed that Alieas would be tripping over Toya answering my phone and shit. I was praying that she'd calmed down by the time I arrived because we needed to resolve our issues, put everything out there.

She's everything I ever wanted. We had to put this drawn-out disagreement over her parents out of our relationship and just focus on us.

I let myself in with the set of keys she'd given to me and stepped inside. Looking down, I notice a pair of shoes, their presence immediately had me scanning the room. My eyes must have been playing tricks 'cause all I could make out in the door was two figures on the couch, hugged up. Frowning, I step completely into the living room. I halt in my tracks. Frozen.

My heart tightens in my chest and rolls over with hurt as I make out Alieas in the arms of some guy.

Anger is building to full outrage as I stand still, silently taking in the situation. Neither one of them moves as I close in on them to inspect the sight before me.

She got on my fuckin' ball shorts, anger adds. Killer instinct start to suggest that I rip them apart, fuck something up. The calm, rational me takes control for a brief moment to advise me to, "just leave".

Flagging the display in front of me, I turn to do just that. "I don't have time for this shit." I had to get as far away from her as possible because I knew this shit could spiral out of control.

The sight of her in this nigga's arms has me going ballistic, though. "Calm down," I tell myself as I drop the keys right onto the mail table. I step out the apartment and make it to the elevator to punch the down button before I lose all my senses.

The hell with that; I charge back down the few doors and into the apartment, busting in the door, making it crack up against the wall behind it.

The loud bang has them both snapping out if their sleep and springing to attention.

Wide, frightened eyes find mine. "Carter!" Lieas jumps up. Immediately, she's trying to close the distance between us, but I hold her off as I put my arm out. "Babe," she starts. "This is not what you're thinking."

"That you fucking this dude right here? That's exactly what I'm fucking thinking!" I shout.

"Yo, homey. Calm down, man," the guy speaks as he gets up. "This ain't what you think," he says.

Whirling around to focus on him, I realize that this the same dude I saw her talking to at Tyree's wedding. "Muthafucka, was I talking to you?!" I yell, getting in his face.

"Look, man, ain't nothing happen," he defends, standing his ground.

"Babe, listen to me. Nothing happened," Alieas protests. She places her hand on my arm and attempts to hold it firm. I shake her off of me and step back.

"What the fuck is he doing here, then?" I demand of them both.

She anxiously glances at him then back at me. "Justin, can you go, please? I need to talk to Carter."

"Nawl, this boah can stay, and I'll leave," I throw back.

Alieas pulls on my arm to get me to look at her. "You gon' be cool, Lieas?" the nigga has the nerve to ask her.

I'm in his face and personal space in an instant. "What, nigga? You better get the fuck outta here, homey," I threaten through clenched teeth.

Alieas tries to step between us.

"Y'all got some shit to work out. I understand that, but you're not about to put your hands on her or none of that other shit in here. You cool, Lieas?" he questions again.

He is out of his fucking mind, I think. More anger escapes, threatening to wreck shit as I grip him up by the shirt, ignoring his struggle to break free.

"You betta get your fuckin' hands off me, man," he advises me, attempting to break out of the tight hold I have on him.

"I'm cool. I'm so sorry, Justin," she chokes out through her tears. I let him go when the sound of Alieas' sobs break in.

Sorry? Did she just apologize to this man? She checking for this dude? Worrying about his feelings?

He walks around me to put on his shoes.

It's over. Fuck her is all I can think as I watch the boah leave. He's probably happy he ain't die in this apartment.

"Carter," she says stepping closer to stand beside me. "He's just a friend." Her eyes are pleading as she looks up into my eyes.

It's over and I don't give a fuck. But I had to know. Had to know how she could do this. That sounds like some nut shit but I have to know.

"Friends?" I repeat. I blow out a long breath. "Friends? That's what we going with?" Frustrated, I curse. My heart is pounding in my chest drumming out her pleas. "Explain to me what this nigga doing in your house. That's the nigga from Ty's wedding, right?" I watch her eyes widen and glass over. "The nigga you ain't know, right?"

"Nothing happened—"

I talk over her protest, "Explain to me how a man you didn't know last month ended up in your fucking apartment today."

Shaking, she goes behind me to close the door to her apartment. She lucky I didn't kick that shit off the hinges.

"I should've told you that day that I knew him but he jumped in and answered before I had an opportunity to. Then it just wasn't important because I didn't think I'd really ever see him again."

"So what the fuck was he doing here tonight? Here in your house?" I feel crazy wanting to wait for her to explain. "What the fuuuuuck, Lieas?!" I fume. Distraught, I drag my hands down over my face. Then in anger, I knock all the items from her mail table onto the floor.

"Carter, I'm sorry," she whined.

I can put one and two together to make three. Nigga in her crib; she gave him her number and thought that was un-fuckin'-acceptable.

"I don't even wanna look at your lying ass face right now!" I turn to leave but Alieas grabs my arms to hold me there. "I told you I'm not dealing with no male friends shit. I told you. You wanna do that shit, you can do it single. See as many niggas as you want," I inform, her shaking her ass off my arm.

She doesn't let my arms go but tightens her grip causing me to look down at my arm then at her face. "I called your phone when you didn't show up, Carter. Some bitch answered. Toya. What the hell?"

"Don't worry about who answered my shit. You had a dude up in your spot. You forgot you had a man when you gave him your number right? I wasn't up your ass that day and you thought you could sneak that shit by. Get the fuck outta my way," I order.

She cries out and then places her hands on my chest. She searches my face for understanding. "I was mad, babe. He called me and I let him come over, but that was it. I love you— I swear; nothing happened."

I shake my head. "You think I'm fucking stupid?" I demand, flinging her hands off me. *The thought of those same arms caressing dude that just left plays in my head.* "I would never let another bitch answer my phone because there are no other bitches. Bug was in the hospital tonight. That's why I didn't come. Toya nut ass answered my phone 'cause she was holding it. I thought what we had was real. I came here to get you to take you home

*where you belong with us, but you in here laid up with some nigga. So.
Fuck. That. Do you, Alieas."* I wanted her to understand the pain she's
caused and the trust she's severed.

*This is why I wasn't getting into anything with anyone. I was off rela-
tionships until she showed up and made me need her. She became a part of
our lives. You have to care entirely too much. You have to have trust. And you
have to be ready for the unexpected: for someone you care about to come
along and break that trust.*

"I don't want to do me. I want to do us," Alieas breathes.

"I'm out. This shit is over," I let her know with finality.

Because she blocked my exit, I pick her up to move her out of the way.

*"It was two weeks of not talking and I thought you had... had found
somebody else," she tries to explain.*

*Unable to restrain myself, I grip her face so I could see her eyes. "The
way you found someone else, right? I'm not that type of man you're gonna
dog out and mess around with otha dudes on. Fuck outta here, Lieas."*

*I let her face go and then opened the door to walk out of it and out of
her life. I ignored all her calls and avoided her when showed up at my house
and my job. After a month, she'd stopped all attempts at communication
with me and that had been it.*

*I heard she had moved to D.C., and I was doing a pretty good job at
not caring. Until...*

Until I read that she still loved me.

Until I saw her.

Until eight days ago.

Eight days... I don't care if it's only been one day. Slick
thoughts torment me as I imagine the multiple dudes she's
involved with. I literally see my brain jumping in a car and just
driving off a cliff. That's how fucking gone I am over her. And
to think that she still friends with this nigga but had managed to
cut me out of her life forever. I'm straight thinking, what the
fuck! She's the one who fucked us up.

"Carter?" a male voice cuts through what's going on in my

head. Whirling back towards the hall, I see Justin approaching me. "Can you hold up?" he requests.

This man has the nerve to want to bust it up. He'll be lucky if his ass don't get busted out here. "Why the hell would I do that?"

"We got off on the wrong foot," he explains. "There's nothing between Alieas and me," he confesses.

"Y'all friends, right? You was tryna fuck her ten years ago, right?" I wanted to know the deal with what this "relationship" was.

Blowing a breath into his fist to heat his hands, he nods. "That's right. But that was a long time ago. Now, she like a nagging ass sister, busting it up on the phone with my wife, gushing and cooing all over my daughter."

"You knew about me. That she was with someone. You saw us at the wedding."

Even though I'd read the book, I still wanted to know the truth from the lips of the people involved.

The wheels are turning over in his brain. He takes a moment, possibly uncertain with how much information I'm privy to.

He holds up his hands in surrender. "In her defense, Alieas was surprised to see me at the wedding, but we were over by then. I was still drawling trying to get her to be with me."

I understand; I wanted to draw.

He continues, "In a moment of weakness, she made a mistake."

"Mistake?" Is that how he categorized being caught in her apartment.

He nods. "A mistake that cost her more than she wanted to pay. That night at her crib, ain't nothing happen 'cause she couldn't stop thinking about you. I asked her if she loved you and she said yes. That was it. I was high, but she wanted you. I can only imagine how you feel. I'd be bouncing off the walls, too, if my wife's ex popped up."

"Your wife cool with you being here?" I inquire, wondering if she knew their entire history and how comfortable they were with one another.

"My wife loves Alieas. She knows what happened between us and is secure with it." He talks and I listen, intent on catching all the details.

A crackhead comes up to us asking for a loosie. Justin gives him a smoke from the pack in his pocket, and you'd swear he just gave him a couple of rocks for free. After he shuffles off, Justin continues, "She loved you and has spent the last ten and a half years kicking her own ass because she lost you." He throws his head back and laughs. "Lieas would be mad as hell if she knew I was telling you this. She wants to be happy. I hate not seeing her happy. She deserves to be. Shit, she writes happy fucking endings for a living. On that note, are you ready to put all this behind you to give it to her?"

He extends his hand for me to shake it. I eye it suspiciously then consider what it took for him to come out and have a talk with me. I grasp it and shake.

We both smile then he walks ahead of me to leave me alone with my thoughts.

CHAPTER

forty

Alieas

I
F I HAVE TO LISTEN to the self-appointed "wise" give me any more well-intentioned advice, I'm going to scream.

"Why would I listen to you?"

Rolling eyes was the nonverbal response accompanied by a shrug. "Obviously, you need to listen to someone. And no disrespect, but you're in here and he's out there." She made a gesture towards the door, the bangles on her wrist jangling rhythmically as they clash together.

I don't get it, can't fathom ever giving any advice to my competition except *Bring It.* And for the life of me, I don't even have the mental strength to determine if this is one of those times when the other person is being the bigger one by stepping aside and allowing their adversary to be the victor.

What in the self-sacrificing-ass-bullshit type of crap is this?

"I don't get it. I thought you said you love him," I remind her.

"I also said I'm not fighting, going to be loud, and that I know he loves you. Carter is a great man, but I'm nobody's back up, replacement, stand-in, or anything like that." I can see the regret in her eyes but she continues with what she was saying. "I'm just trying to see where your head is. You said he *chose* you. From where I'm standing, he's waiting for you to choose him."

Everything else was blurry, but that makes sense. That penetrated my hard head. I'm up and running to the door where my Uncle James is arguing with my Uncle Melvin. When my Uncle James spots me, he drunk strolls over and blocks me from leaving out.

"Lieas, tell Tyree I said I'm sorry. Your mama and Gray out dere calming him down. I was wrong. I shouldn't have said anything," he slurs over some of the words.

"Uncle Jay, Just go ahead," I let out. "You've done enough."

"Jay, listen to the damn girl and get from in front of the damn door," his brother tells him.

I kindly place my hands on his slumped shoulders and boldly push him aside. I press the door and step out into the foyer. Gray, Tyree, and my mom are seated on the steps of a wide staircase. I can make out the glistening of tears on my mom's cheeks. Briannah walks over to me.

"Is he going to be okay?" I ask.

"No, he's not. But we're gonna go," she replies. The smile that usually graces her beautiful face is marred with sorrow. "He needs to clear his head," she explains.

No explanation required. I pull her close and hug her. "If he needs me, I'm here."

"Of course," she chokes out with a quick reassuring squeeze to my arms

I don't think there are any words to say, so, speechless, I go over to him and hug him. He has tears in his chocolate gaze. His eyes are red from crying, and his heart is crushed. And I can't imagine what it feels like to be him at this moment.

Another bad decision made that has the potential to destroy lives at the hands of my father, at the expense of everyone else.

"No matter what, I love you," I murmur in his ear. The only thing a person can do is be there for their loved ones in their time of need. As much as it ached, I knew I couldn't carry any of the weight that this put on his heart.

"Thanks, Moo,".

I glance over at my mom and she is a wreck. Tears are streaming down her face. Mitchell hugs her, but I can't imagine her pain. She no longer loved my dad, but the results of his betrayal were definitely coming to the surface. For a moment, I wonder if she knew. All these years. I hate to think that she'd cover it up to keep my dad. I hate to think her capable of that at all. Don't know if it even worth trying to explore. I know damn well Tyree will want to know.

I glance over at Gray and Nesha, who are both beside one another now. Hugging. Giving one another comfort. Bri was attending to her husband by gathering their stuff inside so she could take them home.

And I am alone, on the outside, looking at them while my heart is in the pit of my stomach. Split wide open. Gaping and leaking. And my support is outside those doors.

Carter, I whisper. I should be with Carter.

I rush out the doors, barely feeling any of the cold air and I look for him. Hoping to spot his car, I walk briskly down the street to the small parking lot, and there is not one sign of him.

He left me. I breathe deeply. He left me. Shoulders slouched in defeat, I walk slowly back to the banquet hall. Aimlessly, I look at the ground and realize that I'm alone.

Alone. My best cousin is really my brother; the only people who know for sure are deceased, and the man I love just left me here to deal with it alone.

Fuck all of this.

"Alieas? Where you going without your coat?" Tiff asks, rushing over to me with it in her hands. "Are you alright and where's Carter?"

I bite the inside of my cheek and look around. "Pretty sure he left." I take my coat and mumble, "Thank you," punching my arms into the sleeves.

"He left? Why?"

Filled with regret, I answer, "It doesn't matter. Can I catch a ride with y'all?"

"What happened?" she presses. "Why would he leave you here?" she demands to know.

"Justin came," I confess. "Then the stuff with Ty explodes, and I kind of couldn't focus. And he was basically pissed because Justin came," I continue to explain. "I honestly just forgot to tell him that we were still cool. And he left. He didn't want to listen. Pretty much a replay of what happened last time."

Her eyes soften. "Oh, no," she whispers with her hand to her mouth. "Call him right now."

"I came out here to talk to him. But he— he's gone." Taking in a deep breath, I shake my head. "Whew." I blow out my hurt.

This man left me.

Tiff nods and gives me the "I'm about to go in" face. It's a cross between a frown and a sneer, mingled and sprinkled with good intentions displayed in the eyes. "Do you love him?

"I don't feel like it, Tiff," I warn her.

Tiff shrugs an uncaring shoulder. "Love is the best feeling to have, Alieas. And it's not easy all the time. Not like in your romance novels," she states, gripping my hands.

Offended, I retreat into myself and pull my hands from her. "Love is exactly like in my romance novels. It's forgiving and understanding. It's not boastful or arrogant. It never dies," I counter.

Rolling her eyes, she laughs. "Please don't quote scripture unless you're applying it. Love is understanding. Understand that seeing you with the guy he caught you in a compromising position with pissed him off. Love is getting over yourself so you can see through the eyes of the other person. He's handled himself pretty good. Look what happened with Jermaine. I love you, best friend, and I want you to be happy but you've got to get your shit together. "

I love him and I want to be happy too but ..."He left me," I whisper as I take in her words. I know she's right, but I'm stubborn.

"You were acting all freaking crazy 'cause he was dating a complete stranger that he kicked to the fucking curb for you. And he had to divulge every single detail of the past ten years, but the same doesn't apply to you? Get the fuck outta here, Lieas," she flags her hand and then holds it up when I fold my arms over my chest. "I'm not blaming you; it's only been a couple of days since y'all reconnected and stuff is still new. You have to adjust to being a couple. Tell the truth and be open. Just call him."

Of course, I'm calling him. I'm almost *over* myself as she suggested.

"No misunderstanding big enough coming between Tim and me."

"I am going to call him. I'm just saying that he wouldn't listen to me."

"Maybe he needed a moment. Maybe he is giving you a moment. There's a lot going on today. Don't let losing Carter be another thing."

Tiff kisses my cheek and goes back inside.

All alone again with my thoughts, I pull out my cell to and I call him. I curse as it goes to voicemail, but I call him again.

And again. Same response except for this time, the voicemail came after three rings instead of six.

Sucking my teeth, I start walking over to the door. It's freaking freezing out here and this negro clearing my calls. At the door, I try one more time and now, it goes straight to voicemail. Even as I cuss and hiss, *What the fuck?*, the sound of a horn beeps.

I turn to see his car.

The tinted window slides down, and his face becomes visible. Those pearly white teeth and beard entice me. "Hey, ma," Carter calls.

A huge weight lifts from my chest, frees my heart, and rumbles in my chest as I run in my stilettos, right to him. He's out of the car and catching me in his arms. Carter stumbles but lands against the car door. I stare in his eyes and then rain kisses all over his face.

"I'm so glad you came back," I mumble, placing kisses to his lips. He stills my hands and captures my face in his hands. I close my eyes as his forehead drops to mine. "I was mad as shit that you left and were ignoring my calls," I admit.

Carter lifts his forehead and kisses mine. "I saw us repeating our mistakes from ten years ago and figured I should listen this time. I'm getting old, and I don't want to waste another minute."

CHAPTER

forty-one

Alieas

WE RIDE BACK TO CARTER'S house in virtual silence. *Bad* by Wale comes on, and I start singing. It is one of those songs that have grown on me. The bedsprings squeaking in the background had me instantly turning my nose up, but after hearing it at my office more times than I can count, it wore me down. It was so catchy that I swore I was Tiara Thomas singing.

Is it bad that I never made love?
No, I never did.
But I sure know how to fuck
I'll be your bad girl, I'll prove it to ya
I can't promise that I'll be good to ya
'Cause I had some issues
I won't commit, No, not havin' it

Carter quickly adds, "You will," in response. And being petty, he changes to a different song. A long list of R&B songs entertains us on our drive to his East Falls home. Kem's *Share My Life* comes on as Carter turns onto his street. I smile, recalling the look on his face when he told me that that this was his favorite song. He was inside of me signing it.

...You're still my Queen
Your loves like a river, girl
It's running through meeee.
Share my life... Share my life.

That is not the look he's sporting now. Carter is upset, even though he came back for me. He manages to maintain his composure the entire ride, and he listens to me explain to him how Justin and I ended up being friends.

He grunted that dude is not invited to the wedding.

Carter leaves me to my own devices after leading me upstairs to his bedroom. He strips down and tells me that he is going to take a shower. I quickly dismiss the thought of just stripping out of my own clothes and joining him. Sex wouldn't solve the issues we have between us. Especially since sex is not one of them. I step out my heels and just stretch out on top of the brown comforter and wait for him to finish.

My mind races with thoughts of everything. Then it focuses on Carter.

Shit, I can only deal with one issue at a time. And he is the one I need to concentrate on. What is between us. What our future is going to be. If we are even going to have a future.

Carter was damn sure brooding when he went into the adjoining bathroom to take his shower. But when he came back out, he was focused and seemed to have scraped it off like dirt in the shower.

"Lieas?" he calls over to me. I guess he isn't sure if I caught a quick nap while he washed his worries down the drain. I sit up and stare over at him. It isn't anger that I am reading in his eyes but determination.

He'd wrapped the towel around his waist and is leaned against the dresser. The muscles of his chest flex involuntarily as he brushes his hair. Misguided lust has me cursing myself. With everything that is going on, my fried brain cells still have time to imagine this ending in the best sex ever and declarations of undying love.

It better.

With everything going on, I realize that undying love is exactly what I need. He's momentarily quiet, coating his golden body with Vaseline and shea butter and considering what he wants to say.

"I know you love your family, and I know y'all got a lot of things to work out. We have some things to work out, too, if you truly want this to be more than a quick fuck."

This is more than a quick fuck. "Carter, I'm here."

His face softens and he smiles. "The first time I met you, I thought, 'Damn, that's her'. After realizing that you were a *"hot commodity"*, I told myself that you weren't ready for all the things you were asking for," he recalls, rubbing the moisture into his hands. "You were young, had more things to experience."

From where I was seated on the bed, I nod in agreement. My mouth is dry; my mind is hazy. "Maybe that's true. I made you hate me." The thought of him hating me still hurt. The last couple days of unspoken love had put a bandage on it. "I hated me afterward, which resulted in more unfruitful relationships."

He rubs his hands over his head and then through his beard. "I'm possessive as a mafucker when it comes to mine. I generally have crazy restraint, except when it comes to you. I wanted to break boah up. Seeing him there with you today brought everything back to the surface. I was back in your apartment, wanting to choke a nigga. Same shit the other night. It was like a punch to the gut. And on some real shit, I did hate you," he nodded as the truth of it was out in the open. "But I fucking loved you. I hated how you made me feel. Open. Exposed. Vulnerable. And it didn't work out."

I knew the feeling.

I nod and stare helplessly over at him. My stomach in knots. I imagine him throwing my line, *I'm too old for this*, back at me.

He continues, dips his fingers into the shea butter, and rubs his hands together. "I'on know. I stopped believing in love a little bit. Couldn't trust my own heart. Afraid that it would betray me."

I had put that fear there.

"Let's try something," he suggests, folding his arms over his bare chest. "What are you afraid of?"

I let out a long, thin breath in a whistle. "Everything," I admit solemnly, tapping the mattress. "Of being open. Exposed. Vulnerable. Not finding and feeling love before I leave this earth. That I've wasted my life running from things that could have been good for me."

"What do you want?"

"Everything."

"Then try being open, exposed, and vulnerable with me. Take your clothes off," he tells me.

Carter chuckles when he reads my face as I try to figure out the angle. "I'm not going to touch you. Do you trust me?"

As if Carter cast some spell, I'm standing up. "Yes," I say, peeling my clothes from my body. When the last article drops to the floor, Carter steps away from the dresser but doesn't come over to where I am.

I'm naked as a jaybird. His eyes roam over me, and it's as if his hands are trailing across my body, exploring the same path of his sight.

"I tasted her... There was a sweetness... I couldn't quite explain...

Tempting me to overindulge… And yes, I wanted more… So I binged on her for days … And became forever sick…"

His voice is a husky whisper as he recites the poem from, My First Love… "Intimacy is about being open, exposed, and vulnerable. Being in love is the same."

"My poem," I utter. This man remembers a poem I dedicated to him without his knowledge, but it found its way to him anyway.

He drops the towel from his body and now, he's naked too. "I binged on her for days and became forever sick," he repeats. "Tell me what you need to make us work," Carter pleads. His voice is strong and deep.

The lighting in his bedroom makes me feel exposed like I'm beneath the spotlight. Exposed to him exactly the way he wants. I'd give any and everything to make us work but instead, I give him doubt.

"We live in different states," I lay down the biggest barrier. "And what if Mira doesn't like me?"

"It's a two-and-a-half hour drive. We both own businesses, so our schedules are more flexible than most. And you're fly as fuck, so Mira is going to love you if I do."

Solutions to obstacles one and two provided.

He gives me the cocky look that reads, *You tried it. Now… Next.*

"Trust, truth, respect, love and affection," I decare, looking over at him. I smile despite my nakedness and need to be covered. "I want babies. I want to get married. I want good dick all the time. I need to be calmed down, talked off the ledge, and occasionally checked. I need someone who's rational because I'm irrational. I wish I had the secret to time travel because there are two things I would change. I would have made amends with my father so when his time came, we would've had a lifetime of memories. And I would've shown up at your house and never have allowed Justin to come over to mine." That's just the beginning. "I want to be loved forever."

I rush to him but he holds me off. "And if I could give you all those things, would you take it or be afraid?"

Ba-Bump... ba-bump... Ba-bump... "I would take it," I chuckle. My heart is racing but it's not fear; it's love. "Carter, if you're offering, I will take it."

"Good," he kisses my nose after he finally closes the distance between us. "Whatever happened in the past is the past. No old niggas for you; no new hoes for me. Agreed?"

Slowly, I nod my head. "Agreed," I lean up for a kiss to seal the deal.

He doesn't give me one but grips my hips and pulls me closer to him. "Now, tell me you love me," he orders in a husky whisper close to my ear. "I said it first last time." His breath tickles my neck and sends inviting waves to my girl.

"You said it first but I felt it first."

His lips form a quick frown. "Negative. I was gone over you the night we all went to that poetry slam, and you recited, I Wrote a Good Omelet. You was flirting extra heavy, but you weren't ready. I definitely wanted to be all up in you, but I settled for loving you from afar."

The crazy thing about that, I remember that night and I was ready. I wasn't talking to Justin anymore, and all I wanted to do was have Carter make me feel like Nikki was feeling when she wrote that. It's the night I realized I was in love with him. "Just for the record, I was all the way into you. In love with you by then."

"You all the way into me now?" he murmurs, one of his hands traveling down my hip, the other sliding up and down my spine.

Biting my lip, I nod in response. I'm restrained because I

want him to be all the way in me right now. "All the way. I love you, Carter."

"Yeah, Princess" He kisses my earlobe, slaps my butt cheek. "You're mine forever. What you say that day at your house? *Kiss me like I'm all you'll ever know... Hold on tight... Never let me go... I need you to be mine for life...*"

I step back, somehow amazed at his ability to recall things I've only said in passing. "I just said I love you. I'm still waiting for you to say it back."

"You think I did all this 'cause I like you? I love you, Alieas. I was about to be on some stalking shit to get your contact info from Ty or Dave. I had thought about emailing you or inboxing you on some nut stuff, but I was patient, and you came back to me. I hate that we wasted ten years."

Relieved, I laugh. "I hate that we wasted ten years." I want to tell him about all the mornings I awakened, wishing that I was untangling myself from him. "Carter, I have never stopped loving you."

Carter pulls me into his arms and just embraces me. I lean into him and wind my arms around his waist, laying my head on his chest. He holds on to me for what seems like forever. After a couple moments, I glance up at him when his penis reminds me something that I'd forgotten.

"You know we're still naked, right?" I inquire, hoping to show Carter just how much love I have inside for him.

His stomach rumbles as he laughs and lifts me from my feet. "About that," Carter murmurs, wrapping my legs around his waist. Closing my eyes, I drop significantly lower, swallowing hard as he enters me. In a couple strides, we're by the bed, dropping our wanting and willing bodies onto it. My back to it, his body covering mine.

Breathlessly, I move beneath him, needing every stroke like I need air. "I prayed for you to come back to me," I moan, digging my fingers into his back. All but purring, I scream, "Aaah! Yessss! Yesssss!"

"I love you, Alieas," Carter rasps, his hands gripping my behind, holding me in place as he increases his pace.

"I wished for a second chance," I breathe, lifting my lips to his. His kisses me, devouring my mouth, capturing my cries of pleasure.

"He listened, Babe. I promise to make all your dreams come true."

And just like that, I believed him.

And just like that, my heart feels free.

EIGHT MONTHS HAVE GONE BY in a flash. It's like I blinked my eyes and time literally flew. I guess it does when you're having fun. Standing at the breakfast counter, I lick strawberry shortcake ice cream from the back of a spoon.

I could sing. I'm in heaven, enjoying the deliciousness of eating ice cream right from the carton at six a.m. and no one giving me sideways ass glances. I thought about making breakfast and got distracted by my fat ass cravings.

Barefoot, I sway my hips to Queen Bey as she sings her heart out about being Drunk in Love with Jay-Z. I hold my spoon in the air as I sing along. My headphones lock in the sound of Beyoncé as I pretend to match her vocals.

We woke up in the kitchen,
Saying how the hell did this shit happen
Oh baaaby.
Drunk in loooove

I dip the spoon back into the ice cream for a small scoop and just gush as I savor my love for Carter and ice cream as it melts in my mouth because I finally have everything I've ever wanted: me, Carter, and Bug in the same city, under one roof.

It only took us a couple months to figure out that what we

have is forever and that we didn't want to live apart. He showed up at a radio interview I gave three months ago and got down on one knee and asked me to be his.

Of course, I agreed. I moved back to Philly last month because it made more sense. I can write anywhere, and I could do everything I needed to do for J and S through email, Skype, and biweekly visits to D.C. The café/ bookstore will open soon. We decided a move for Carter's construction company would have been far more difficult and taken an infinite amount of planning; plus, he has Bug.

And I'm—

"Drunk in love, huh?" Carter slides up behind me, taking one of the buds out of my ears. I was so busy indulging in this strawberry shortcake that I didn't even sense him come into the kitchen. "Ice cream and Beyoncé at six a.m.?" He leans closer to kiss my neck. I let out a helplessly in love giggle at the playful kiss and the feel of his hands covering my bulging belly.

Yup, we're pregnant.

Five months and counting. "Your son wanted pancakes and then he changed his mind when I saw the ice cream. It was calling my name. I felt fat and helpless, and I was trying to avoid the judgmental side-eye you be giving me," I tell him.

We have eighteen more weeks to go before baby boy, Carter Reed II, will make his long-awaited appearance, and I— shit, I'm definitely in love with him already. I can't wait to meet this baby who has been growing inside of me.

"Babe, don't nobody be giving you the side-eye. You're carrying our future right there," he declares.

The force of love that Carter has within him for our son radiates into me through his words. It is fierce and unquestionable.

Placing my hands over his, I nod in agreement.

This love I have is fierce, and I never would have known it with him if it were it not for second chances.

Every day, I think of my father and what he gave up with Tyree. They never had a chance and that breaks my heart. We can assign the blame directly to my father. He was a weak man. He couldn't make the decision to come clean, man up, and be a father to Tyree.

Even after the fact.

Like, dude, it never crossed your mind to just tell the fuckin' truth? As close as he and Tyree were, he couldn't just give him that small piece of himself that Tyree had been searching for his entire life. It's hard to be a witness to the fallout.My brother — my Tyree— is the best man I know, aside from Carter, that is. And now, he is a little broken and none of us know how to fix that for him. Not even Bri, who has been his rock forever, can right this. She feels helpless.

And I'm a little bit ashamed. 'Cause while the outraged woman in me was shouting, I wish he had manned up. I'm torn because in all actuality, had he confessed to my mother, it's possible that I wouldn't even have been born.

So, yeah. Riddle me that.

The complexity of this entire situation drives me crazy, and it's only the love that I have inside for my growing baby and my family that helps keep me sane.

It took me a couple months to read my father's letter, and I had to agree with Tyree; it was dramatic as hell. All he wanted to do was basically apologize for being a liar and a cheater and for failing the ones he claimed to love the most.

He did tell me one thing that rings true.

Hold on to love with both hands and never let go.

Even if Darrien Stiles had never done it with a commitment to any familial, agape, or eros type of love, his ass was correct in that one statement.

Turning around, I lift my face so I can gaze into Carter's eyes. Embracing him, I make my favorite confession, "I love you, Carter," the testament of our love resting comfortably between us.

"Love you too, babe."

Turning my lips up to his for a kiss, I am overjoyed when he obliges, and I fall farther in love, wrapping my arms a little bit tighter 'cause there is no way in hell I'm ever letting this go.

"Really, y'all? Get a room," Mira cuts in on us.

"I think she just wants some love too," Carter teases.

She doesn't deny it and comes over to rub my stomach.

Smiling, I close my eyes and just think, "Here's to second chances that lead to happy endings."

BOOKCLUB
questions

Overall thoughts.

Thoughts on characters.

Is honesty always the best policy?

Do you think Alieas was wrong?

Should Carter have allowed Alieas to explain?

If you walked in on your significant other in the same compromising situation, what is your initial response?

When dating several people, how do you handle cutting the loose threads once you want to become exclusive?

Do you believe in platonic friends with the opposite sex with people you have dated?

Do you believe in second chances at love?

What was your worst date ever?

ADDITIONAL NOTES:

acknowledgments

SOMETIMES I REMEMBER THE ME I was before life started happening. It's like fifteen years happened in a blink if an eye and I'm convinced I didn't make all the right choices. But I am also a firm believer in the perfection of His timing. Through it, I've learned to have patience and plenty of it. I believe in love and all the in-betweens. I believe in do-overs and second chances and want them for everyone wishing for one.

Sometimes, love comes back around, right at the moment you're ready.

Special thanks to my 1st round BETA readers: Latifa Scott, Kina DeShazor. I was hungry for feedback and y'all gave it to me… And my editor, Patrice Harrison for her dedication to her craft.

To my supporting cast, *My Golden Girls*, I love y'all forever

And And My Nyah and My Mir, words cannot express all this love I have for you.

To my readers, I want to say, *THANK YOU* for taking the time out to allow me to entertain you with words.

OTHER BOOKS BY

elaine l. allen

No Ordinary Love

Hurricane

Coming Soon—

Check out the fallout in

Briannah and Tyree's story:

Love is

I am overly excited that you chose to witness Alieas' and Carter's *second chance.*

I Hope you enjoyed it.

- Elaine

ABOUT THE

Elaine L. Allen is currently working on her next project. She resides in Philadelphia with her family.

YOU CAN REACH HER THROUGH SOCIAL MEDIA AT:

www.perfectperceptions.wixsite.com/elainelallen
perfectperceptionspublishing@gmail.com
Wattpad: @MsSheWrites
Instagram: Ms_imgonnabweighless

 facebook.com/ElaineAllen

twitter.com/MsSheWrites

 instagram.com/MsSheWrites